Praise

"Kait Ballenger delivers a seductive masterpiece in this fiery romance. Lucifer is as irresistible as he is sinful. With blazing-hot chemistry, this book will leave you begging for more. Wickedly and utterly unputdownable!"

—*USA Today* bestselling author Sara Cate for *Original Sinner*

"*Original Sinner* is a sizzling hot, irreverent, and seductively enthralling read. Lucifer is guaranteed to become your new morally gray book-boyfriend addiction."

—Abigail Owen, #1 *New York Times* and *USA Today* bestselling author of *The Games Gods Play*

"Kait Ballenger is a treasure you don't want to miss!"

—*New York Times* and *USA Today* bestseller Gena Showalter

"An extremely promising high-voltage start . . . Readers will savor strong characterization, steamy animalistic sex scenes with Dom/sub subtext, and an interesting series arc."

—*Publishers Weekly* starred review for *Rogue Wolf Hunter*

"This story has it all . . . The chemistry is electric, and the spicy banter is terrific."

—Fresh Fiction for *Cowboy Wolf Trouble*

"Hits all the sweet spots of paranormal romance. Recommend to readers of Nalini Singh and Maria Vale."

—*Booklist* for *Cowboy in Wolf's Clothing*

"Adventure, intrigue, and a super sexy premise!"
—Terry Spear, *USA Today* bestselling author, for *Cowboy in Wolf's Clothing*

"The romance is sexy, and a fast-paced, rollicking plot will keep readers engaged."
—*Kirkus Reviews* for *Wicked Cowboy Wolf*

WICKED BELIEVER

OTHER TITLES BY KAIT BALLENGER

The Original Sinners

Original Sinner

Seven Range Shifters

Cowboy Wolf Trouble
Cowboy in Wolf's Clothing
Wicked Cowboy Wolf
Fierce Cowboy Wolf
Wild Cowboy Wolf
Cowboy Wolf Outlaw
Cowboy Wolf Christmas

Rogue Brotherhood

Shadow Hunter
Rogue Wolf Hunter
The Vampire's Hunter

WICKED BELIEVER

KAIT BALLENGER

Montlake

This is a work of fiction. Names, characters, organizations, places, events, and incidents are either products of the author's imagination or are used fictitiously. Otherwise, any resemblance to actual persons, living or dead, is purely coincidental.

Text copyright © 2025 by Kaitlyn Ballenger
All rights reserved.

No part of this book may be reproduced, or stored in a retrieval system, or transmitted in any form or by any means, electronic, mechanical, photocopying, recording, or otherwise, without express written permission of the publisher.

Published by Montlake, Seattle

www.apub.com

Amazon, the Amazon logo, and Montlake are trademarks of Amazon.com, Inc., or its affiliates.

EU product safety contact:
Amazon Media EU S. à r.l.
38, avenue John F. Kennedy, L-1855 Luxembourg
amazonpublishing-gpsr@amazon.com

ISBN-13: 9781662528880 (paperback)
ISBN-13: 9781662528897 (digital)

Cover design by Christian Bentulan
Cover image: © New Africa, © Jamorn22, © Oksana Stasenko / Shutterstock

Printed in the United States of America

To the women who know Eve was framed . . .

Clever girl.

AUTHOR'S NOTE

Dear reader,
Thank you for picking up a copy of *Wicked Believer*. I'm so thrilled you enjoyed Lucifer and Charlotte's story in *Original Sinner* enough to take a chance on this dark and devilish sequel.

Original Sinner is the book of my heart, a passion project that doubled as an exorcism of my own demons, and I poured just as much of myself and my creative joy into *Wicked Believer*.

Wicked Believer is exactly the kind of sequel I love, a book that revisits all the sinful and delicious things that made us all fall in love with Lucifer and the other Originals, while also leaving room for Charlotte and Lucifer's world and, more importantly, their relationship to mature and grow even as it takes darker turns. As such, *Wicked Believer*'s content might not be suitable for all readers.

Wicked Believer is a dark, sexy paranormal fantasy romance and features a villainous, morally gray billionaire who previously blackmailed his former employee into dating him. While Lucifer may have been irrevocably changed by Charlotte's love in *Original Sinner*, at his core, he's just as seductive and horrible as he's always been, and while his newfound fiancée, Charlotte, may have escaped the trauma of her fundamentalist religious past, the challenges she'll now face as a new immortal are far from over.

Wicked Believer contains heavy themes of religious trauma, with frequent references to shame, sex, virginity, self-worth, body image, body shaming, purity culture, the concept of sin, and the role those assigned female at birth are expected to play in the fundamentalist Christian church, as well as one on-page reference to religiously motivated hate speech. It discusses emotional, physical, and sexual abuse that is parental, religious, and spousal in nature, which occurs mostly off page but is recreated in several brief on-page memories. It shows consensual nonconsent during primal roleplay in a BDSM scene, consensual partner sharing, and breeding kinks, along with stalking, on-page drinking, and drug use. It mentions forced marriage and forced pregnancy; shows vivid depictions of catastrophic, apocalyptic devastation; contains graphic violence, religious genocide, and mass murder; and, as always, has a healthy dose of swearing.

Readers who are sensitive to this content, take heed, and prepare to fall even deeper in love with mythology's ultimate bad boy . . .

THE ORIGINALS

Lucifer—Pride

Azmodeus—Lust

Mammon—Greed

Belphegor—Sloth

Satan—Wrath

Leviathan—Envy

Beelzebub—Gluttony

OTHER CELESTIALS

Charlotte

Hell is empty, and all the devils are here . . .
—*The Tempest*, William Shakespeare

CHAPTER ONE

Charlotte

People love to make heroes and villains out of ordinary men.

I stare down at my father's coffin, the black lacquered casket gleaming. His supporters shout in the distance, which in the middle of a dusky Kansas cornfield means it's impossible to tell who the protesters are and who are paparazzi, but still, I refuse to look at them, pretending to listen to my father's eulogy. The autumn air outside is cold. Frigid and wet. Cold enough my high-heeled toes are nearly as numb as I feel. But I don't need to hear the minister's prayers to know exactly where my father's heading.

Lucifer will make sure of that, even if I ask him not to.

I don't ask.

I feel his smooth hand in mine, his tall frame looming at my side. Lucifer's dark gaze levels on the minister in an expression that's supposed to appear solemn, or so it seems. Ever since I went to work as an intern for his company several months ago, I've belonged to him, and he to me. Or so I thought, until recently.

Now I'm starting to think Lucifer might belong to no one. Least of all me.

He feels my gaze on him then, his dark eyes flicking toward me as the corner of his mouth curls. "Eyes forward, Charlotte."

Like a good girl, I do as I'm told, turning back to the minister as I whisper, "Yes, sir."

Lucifer's grip on my hand tightens, his thumb caressing my skin in approval. He may not be my boss anymore, but he's never had to give me a paycheck for me to call him *sir*. I've been his submissive since long before I understood what that word truly means. But being his completely, irrevocably, suits me.

Though these days, I'd be lying if I said I didn't have my doubts.

"Would you like to say a few words?"

I blink, suddenly realizing that the minister's speaking to me. I'm the only surviving member of my father's family, after all, not to mention the closest thing to a mortal here, aside from the so-called minister, at least. Whoever he is, I'm pretty sure he's no more a preacher than I am a virgin, but with the obscene amount of money Lucifer's paying him, he'll be whatever we need him to be.

Reluctantly, I step forward, shuffling past the gathered line of mourners, which consists of a few paid pallbearers, and the Original sinners. Lucifer, Azmodeus, Leviathan, Satan, Belphegor, Beelzebub, and Mammon. Or "Mimi," as she insists I call her. Pride, Lust, Envy, Wrath, Sloth, Gluttony, and Greed, respectively.

It's a rare sight, all seven of them together like this. These days they prefer to live topside. In New York City. Though currently we're a far cry from home.

I hurry past them, trying hard not to make eye contact, though I can feel their gazes on me. The hairs on the back of my neck stand on end.

I'm fairly certain if it weren't for Lucifer, I'd be dead before morning.

But for all the cruel games they play, Lucifer's siblings fall in line easily, each of them keeping their distance as I head toward the podium. They know better than to risk Lucifer's fury, for today at least. Things are different now that Lucifer gifted their Father's redemption to me. I'm no longer their brother's harmless mortal plaything.

Now I'm something else entirely.

Not that we've figured out what, exactly.

I step onto the makeshift pulpit beside my father's grave. A few extravagant bouquets of narcissus flowers wait for me alongside several large photographs of me and my father. The pictures make me look like the ever-dutiful daughter I once tried to be. The daughter I *was* for the first twenty-three years of my life. Before I decided I no longer wanted to be Daddy's broken little girl.

Now I serve a different kind of villain.

I glance toward Lucifer, my stomach fluttering the moment our eyes meet in a way that's all too familiar. The nod he gives me is meant to be supportive, encouraging, but still, it makes my knees go weak. I can't help but imagine what wicked things he's thinking—maybe how I'd taste on his honeyed tongue. Like he hasn't already claimed me in every way imaginable. Though with him, I'm always eager for more. We're insatiable, really.

Sex has never been our problem.

I swallow down the longing that thought sparks in my chest before my gaze flits from him out toward the waiting crowd. It's a motley crew from three distinct sources. My father's congregants—members of the Righteous, the far-right fundamentalist hate group my oh-so-loving preacher for a dad founded to spite me. Then there are Lucifer's fans and mine, our supporters. And finally, the true bottom-feeders, the paparazzi who stalk us endlessly.

From here, it's hard at first to tell any of them apart. In the twilight, the flashes of their cameras nearly blind me. But despite the fact that I'm here at the funeral of the one man who *should* have protected me, several of their signs are clearly meant to hurt me.

Little whore.

That's one of the Righteous's favorites.

Followed by **Bride of Satan**.

I roll my eyes at that one. Lucifer and I aren't actually married, and though I'm still wearing his ring on my finger, our initial engagement was fake. The media's not exactly aware of that little detail. Not to mention, Satan is technically Lucifer's brother, Wrath. People often get that wrong. To the Righteous, the Originals are all the same. Seven devils cut from the same cloth.

But my personal favorite is a sign that simply reads **YOU'RE GOING TO HELL**.

I scoff.

Like I'm not already its willing queen.

I shake my head, turning back toward the funeral. It's only fair, I suppose. My father, their precious martyr, wouldn't be dead if it weren't for me . . .

My attention slides back toward Lucifer. We haven't spoken about it directly, but he doesn't need to say it out loud for me to know. He doesn't regret a thing.

Killing my father. Lying. Manipulating me.

The last one, most especially.

I keep silent, tamping down the resentment that stirs in me despite my desire.

My father's place in Hell will be particularly punishing.

Though I can't help but wonder if Lucifer killed him for me or his own twisted ends . . .

I glance down at the lectern. A prepared speech is there, something Imani or someone in Lucifer's PR team wrote for me. In the mix of the media chaos over the last few weeks, I didn't even think to prepare my own father's eulogy, and honestly, I'm not certain I would have if I'd been given the chance.

My gaze finds Lucifer's again, this time staying there.

Like there's no one there except for him and me.

His intensity sears through me, his expression downright devilish. With dark hair and even darker eyes that I swear sometimes hold a hint of hellfire when he looks at me, he's painfully beautiful. So beautiful that it makes my chest ache.

His is the face of God's once-most-cherished angel.

A stark contrast to the villain I know he can be.

"My father used to beat me," I say into the sudden quiet, surprising myself as the unscripted words drop from my lips. Several cameras flash distantly.

I ignore them, focused on my memories. Lucifer knows this, but it's the first time I've admitted it publicly, and though it was supposed to be just me, his siblings, and the pallbearers present, this will no doubt be plastered across every newspaper stand and media outlet around the world come morning. "And his followers, his congregants, turned a blind eye."

The words come out barely above a whisper, but I'm certain everyone hears me.

I look toward the nearby crowd, their silence as cold as the frozen ground beneath our feet. "He wasn't a good man. He didn't even try to be." I stare down at my hands then, unable to stop the tears that gather, though I'm not sure whether they're meant for my father or for me. "And I'm not sorry he's dead."

"Murderess! Jezebel!"

I suck in a harsh breath, gripping the lectern as someone from the crowd interrupts me before they're quickly silenced and hauled away by the attending police.

Lucifer and I don't go anywhere without a police escort these days. Not after the anthrax that was delivered to his penthouse—meant for me and sent by someone who didn't know I'm immortal. I'm guessing they know now.

Privacy is a distant dream.

"But I wish . . . I wish I could be . . ." I mutter, struggling to collect my thoughts. "Sorry, that is." I blink, surprised when a tear falls onto my hand where I clutch the lectern, the first and only I've shed for him, but I refuse to look up from where I speak into the microphone. "I wish he could have been the father I needed him to be. Wish he could have been so many things . . ." I glance toward Lucifer again, and I don't need to see how his throat writhes as he swallows to understand he feels my words keenly.

They're as much for him as they are for me.

I suck in another ragged breath, knowing this next part is likely to start a riot among the already-violent crowd, the people who are so eager to have a piece of Lucifer, of me. To tear me limb from limb for what they think I represent. But I don't say it for them.

I say it for me.

And for Him.

The God I still pray to every night, when Lucifer isn't listening.

"May God have mercy on his soul." I barely manage to choke the words out before I'm stumbling off the platform.

The crowd turns mutinous in an instant, the mixture of my father's congregants, the Righteous, and the paparazzi pushing past the SWAT team's barriers and shields with ease. They're overwhelmed by the sheer numbers. I don't look toward them or the other Originals to gauge their reactions as I rush into Lucifer's arms. All I know is that he catches me, pulling me into his chest and allowing me to bury my face in the smooth Italian wool of his Armani suit.

My eyes sting with tears as he ushers me away. The crowd surges forward, and before I fully know what's happening, Lucifer's shoving me into the safety of a waiting Lincoln Town Car. The door slams behind us, locking instantly as the vehicle starts to pull away.

"Vultures. All of them," he growls.

Harsh faces plaster against the Town Car's tinted windows, surrounding us as they scream their hatred at me. Somehow Dagon, Lucifer's demon chauffer—freshly topside in a new human-skin suit that's taken some getting used to—manages to inch the vehicle forward without running anyone over as I bury my face in my hands. I clamp a cold fist over my mouth, stifling my scream. I can't look at them. I can't.

We pull free from the crowd, and finally I lift my head to look out the window, watching at the last second as my father's casket is hurriedly lowered into his grave and the riot police fruitlessly attempt to regain control.

But it's the sight of what's beneath that chills me.

My face presses against the cool glass as I struggle to breathe.

From the hole in the ground, dozens of pale, shadowed hands reach up toward my father's casket as if to pull him down into the bowels of Hell beneath, and as I glance toward Lucifer, uncertain whether it's the gravediggers' doing or the fallen angel beside me, my stomach drops, and I know that, not for the first time, my prayers have fallen on deaf ears.

CHAPTER TWO

Lucifer

Killing Charlotte's father felt . . . different than I anticipated.

The Town Car pulls to a stop outside Charlotte's childhood home—the dark, tinted windows blocking what little view I have of the uninspired two-story building. There's not much to be seen out here in the dark—no neon lights or flashing cameras, which now stalk our every move—but I don't need to glimpse inside my fiancée's head to know what she's thinking.

I haven't changed. Not one bloody bit.

I'm still the villain in this story.

Only now she doesn't resist me.

Charlotte's stuttered breath tears through the cab, the shocked noise instantly reminding me of why I brought her here this evening. I'm not entirely certain what she anticipated following her father's funeral, but clearly it wasn't arriving here, with me.

All the more reason to tempt her.

"Shall we?" I offer my hand along with my most charming smile, and she takes it, the beat of her pulse fluttering against my palm like a wounded bird as she allows me to lead her from the cab out into the night. She braces against the wind before she presses into me, seeking my warmth. My Father's redemption may have changed her, made her immortal and mine, but it hasn't made her any less breakable.

Not to me and my siblings.

"Search the grounds. Again," I order Dagon. "Thoroughly."

He nods, turning to direct the security team that now lives within our shadow.

The police's poor handling of the funeral has left me particularly on edge this evening.

When we reach the front door, it's unlocked and waiting, the premises and its surrounding acreage having been searched by my team prior to our arrival. Inside, the interior is painfully drabber than I anticipated, with sponge-painted walls, mismatched architecture, and beige, well, everything, which speaks to the poor taste of the nouveau riche and a bygone human era.

Charlotte doesn't say anything as Dagon shuts the door behind us. Instead, she creeps further inside, her footfalls so quiet in the silence that they're deferential. I watch as her gaze darts about the empty room. Like if she moves too suddenly, she might disturb the ghosts and memories which haunt her here.

Though that's exactly why I brought her here this evening.

To lower her guard. Make her vulnerable to me.

Even more so than usual.

She stops at a narrow console table, her fingers falling to a photograph of a gangly, long-limbed child beside a woman who, based on the uncanny similarity, must no doubt be her mother. Her fingertips hover near the frame momentarily before her hand slowly falls to her side.

"Why did you bring me here, Lucifer?" She looks toward me then, an uncertainty in her expression that I've seen more times than I care for as of late.

If I were less confident, it'd almost cause me to think she regrets the choice she made. To stay with me. For eternity.

Though she can't possibly begin to understand what giving her my Father's prize cost me.

I place my hands in my pockets, not bothering to leave the foyer. This empty human home is no place for me, even if it was once a part of her life, before she belonged to me. "I thought you might want to retrieve some of your things."

She swallows. "Before the vultures descend?"

I give a curt nod.

It's the truth, though not entirely.

Paltry though many of these items may be, the bulk of them will go to auction within a matter of days and fetch a small fortune, thanks to Charlotte's newfound celebrity. The house and most of its contents belong to her father's church. The pathetic congregation he loved so dearly. But if I thought for even a moment that she wanted any of it, I'd make it hers in a heartbeat.

I may not be a gentle lover, but I am trying to be gentle with her heart, it seems.

When it suits me.

She turns back to the photo, a sad sort of smile pulling at her lips as I struggle not to tug uncomfortably at the collar of my suit. There are tears in her eyes, and these days I find I can hardly stand the way she softens me.

It makes me keen to destroy anything and anyone who's ever hurt her.

Slowly.

"Is that your mother?" I incline my head toward the photo.

She nods, smiling affectionately at the woman pictured as she finally allows herself to pick the photo up. "She died when I was nine. Crohn's disease." She sighs, and the weight in the sound says everything. "When the doctors didn't believe her about how bad it was, my father and our congregation told her to pray instead, but by the time she was sick enough someone was willing to listen, it'd . . . become cancerous."

"I'm sorry," I mutter, and it surprises me to find that I mean it.

Human life is insignificant really, but somehow, this matters to me. Because it matters to her.

I frown. On occasion, I find I resent the way she makes me feel. The subtle ways she's changed me.

She releases another long sigh, placing the photo back upon the table. "In their eyes, she became more of a good Christian woman after she got sick, because of her suffering. Like . . . like she was a martyr or something."

I give a curt nod, already anticipating where this is heading. My fiancée knows more than a thing or two about martyrs as of late, thanks to her upbringing and the zealous, self-righteous legacy her bloody excuse of a father left in his wake.

"Did you kill him, Lucifer?" she whispers softly.

I straighten. We've danced around this topic several times over the last few weeks, but this is the first occasion where she's deigned to actually ask me.

She glances away from the photo to a section of the floor near my feet. Like she does when she kneels in submission for me. As if she can't possibly bring herself to look at me.

For fear of what she'll no doubt find there.

These days she's better at reading me than I ever intended her to be.

"Don't ask questions you're not prepared to hear the answer to, darling."

She sucks in a harsh breath, closing her eyes, and one of the tears escapes, sliding down her cheek. "Please be honest with me. Just this once."

This time, I don't hesitate.

"Yes," I admit, my voice turning cold. "Yes, and I'd do it again in a heartbeat."

She inhales another slow, pained breath, though we both know it's only confirmation of what she already believed.

She knows who I am, *what* I am, explicitly, and somehow, she's still chosen to love me.

It astonishes even me.

She opens her eyes, swiping away the errant tears and smearing a bit of her mascara as her gaze sparks with fury. "I didn't ask you to do that. I wouldn't have wanted that."

I scoff. "Don't lie to yourself."

She looks away from me then, biting down on the inside of her cheek as a flicker of doubt passes over her features. "Did he . . . did he suffer?"

"Not nearly long enough, if you ask me."

She winces, then nods, like she takes some form of comfort in this, though the reason is beyond me. She could read any number of the coroner's reports on file with my legal team, but I've spared her the details—shown her mercy—and we both know she's not fully prepared for the true answer.

The one where her father's continued torture falls to me.

For now, and the rest of eternity.

She straightens, brushing herself off. "How long do I have?" she asks, glancing around in clear recognition that this is yet another gift I have given her.

Bribery isn't beyond me, even if the money I paid to bring her here will no doubt go to her father's so-called ilk. The Righteous. Or so they call themselves.

Despite their increasing threats, they're nothing more than a bloody thorn in my side. I will handle them. Personally. Given time.

"Take as long as you need, little dove."

With my permission, she spends the next hour flitting about the quaint space, placing items in and out of a box that Dagon retrieved for me. Somewhere halfway through, I note that it's all the photos she's taken as I finally lower myself enough to sit upon the meager excuse of a sofa, waiting.

I could watch her until the ends of time and never tire of it.

By the time the box is nearly full, according to my Patek Philippe, a few hours have passed, but it feels no more than a blink. The price of immortality is steep. My fiancée has yet to learn that particular lesson.

Though she will. Shortly.

Suddenly, Charlotte clears her throat, and I glance up to find her standing barefoot at the top of the stairs, her black mourning dress replaced by a tight all-white gown that's two sizes too small. Her delicious breasts strain against the sweetheart neckline.

I growl, my cock instantly thickening. "Whatever game you're playing at, I like it."

She blushes, smoothing her hands over her generous hips. "It's my purity gown. I just . . . wanted to see if it still fit."

"Purity gown?" I lift a brow as my gaze rakes over her.

There is nothing pure about the thoughts I'm thinking.

From the coy grin on her lips, that was exactly her intention.

"It's this sort of father-daughter dance, where you pledge to your dad that you'll stay a virgin until marriage." She shrugs.

"How incestuous." A devious grin twists my lips. "Well, we both know how that turned out, don't we?"

I move toward her, prowling across the open living room to where she meets me at the foot of the stairs. I capture a lock of her hair in my fist so quickly her eyes widen. I twist the smooth strands around my fingers, gripping them in my palm, and roughly use it to tug her toward me. "Are you feeling particularly pure right now?"

"With you?" She bites her lower lip, shaking her head. "Never."

She barely manages to get the word out before I have her pinned against the banister beneath me. My mouth is on hers in an instant as I bite and lick my way past her lips, forcing her open for me. She moans sweetly, wrapping her arms around my back so that her nails scrape into me. She tastes like Heaven. Like milk and honey, and the warmth of the sun on my face for the first time in months, though I don't remotely know how that's possible.

I pull on her hair a little, breaking the kiss only enough to allow her to speak. "Do you care if this dress survives the evening, little dove?"

"Yes, sir," she breathes.

I trace my knuckles over the curve of her cheek. "Pity. A shame, really." A devilish smirk twists my lips. "Because when I give you the word, I want you to run."

Her eyes widen in a mixture of excitement and fear that's now familiar to me.

"And for the sake of your dress, you best not let me catch you."

I release her, her eyes already darting about the room as she plans her escape.

"Now," I hiss.

CHAPTER THREE

Charlotte

I tear from the house, not pausing to consider the unusually cold autumn temperature or even my painfully bare feet. If I hesitate, Lucifer will catch me, and while I want every delicious, painful thing I know will follow, I like this game we're playing.

Cat and mouse. Him hunting me.

Though Lucifer is far more dangerous than any animal could ever be.

Behind me, the screen door slams in its frame from where I've just barreled through it, the cold hitting me in the face like a sudden shock. It feels like I've plunged myself beneath the surface of a freezing lake and I'm drowning, but I recover quickly.

The numbness in my toes and the chill searing my lungs is nothing compared to the pain I've endured over the past few months.

My father's betrayal. Mark's abuse.

Dying.

And the worst by far . . .

Lucifer. Remaking me from the ashes.

I blink, and for a moment I'm back there. That dark, cold place where it felt as if my soul had been ripped from my body. Only for him to fill the empty void in me with a fire so hot I didn't know where it began and I ended.

Until the pain *became* me.

I shove the memory aside, leaving it for the nightmares that now haunt me whenever I close my eyes. Instead, I try to hold on to the thrill of pursuit and run for the trees. I feel Lucifer standing in the open doorway behind me now, his cruel laugh trailing me as I smile to myself. We've been here before. Or I have, at least.

Running alone through the woods. Lucifer's shadows chasing me.

Like I was destined to be his before he even knew me.

That possibility slams into me, the stark truth in it causing my steps to temporarily falter.

If I thought I could sense Lucifer's presence before I became what I am—whatever that is—it's nothing compared to how aware of him I am now. I *feel* him. Always. Even when we're apart. Like I'm an instrument, and he doesn't even need to touch me in order to play me.

Though he will. Touch me, that is.

As soon as he catches me.

The moment he sees where I'm headed, I hear his dark laugh like a taunting caress against my ear. He's giving me a solid start. Moving at a normal, leisurely pace.

Though we both know if he wanted, I could be his instantly.

"You think you can hide among the shadows?" His voice wraps around me like a disembodied hiss. The darkness reaches out, and a tendril of it brushes my cheek, causing me to shiver. "That's where you're wrong."

Suddenly, I feel him behind me, his power radiating through me. I turn, stumbling through the underbrush just in time to see the shadows bend and curl in the moonlight until Lucifer stands fully formed in front of me. I freeze. He leans against a nearby tree, his suit coat artfully slung over his shoulder like he doesn't have a care in the world. He casts it aside before he makes a show of unbuttoning his cuff links and rolling up his sleeves, his muscled forearms flexing. I swallow thickly, recognizing the move for the delicious threat that it is.

This is what he does before he punishes me.

Before he claims me. Body and soul.

I feel myself slicken, my ragged breath swirling around my face like smoke.

"Did you really think you could outrun me?" He tsks like he's disappointed in me, though we both know this is all a part of the game we're playing.

He steps forward.

And I take a step back.

A twig snaps beneath my foot.

My pulse races with a deep, primal need that's so sharp, so heady, it warms me from the inside out, making me brave. Reckless even.

More reckless than I should be.

Finally, I give a coy shrug. "I thought I might be able to now, considering . . ."

Lucifer goes still.

Considering I hold some of his power inside me.

My mouth goes dry at the admission, but I don't need to say it out loud for him to know.

This strange connection that's formed between us. Ever since he remade me.

I . . . think it might have cost him more than it did me.

A spark of hellfire lights in Lucifer's eyes, his gaze searing into me. A cruel, familiar smirk twists his lips, and I know in an instant that my taunting has only made him more feral, more dangerous. Even as a . . . whatever I am now, he's still a threat to me. And for that subtle blow to his pride, I'm sure he has a particularly damning punishment in store for me.

"Playing the brat tonight, are we?"

He comes up off the tree, and I take another step back, the sound of a frozen branch cracking like a whip at my feet.

"Don't worry." He grins wickedly. "I'll make a good girl of you yet."

Without warning he lunges for me, and I turn, trying to bolt into the darkness, but Lucifer's on me in an instant, predator to prey.

Even at mortal speed, he's ridiculously fast. Faster than I'll ever be.

We slam into the ground together, his shadows managing to soften the blow slightly, even as he uses his weight to pin me. Mud and leaves and dirt coat us both from head to toe as I struggle to break free, but I can't bring myself to care. The moment he captures both my wrists, roughly pinning them above my head, I go still. Frozen like the willing prey I was taught to be.

But for once, Lucifer isn't having it.

"Fight me, Charlotte," he growls.

I bite my lip. "Sir?"

"I said, fight me."

"Lucifer, I—"

"Are you safe-wording or are you going to obey?"

I drop my gaze. This isn't what we agreed on, and a sudden feeling of cold chills me, but I . . . have my safe word and I . . . don't use it.

Lucifer grips my face in one mud-covered hand, forcing me to look at him.

His suit is ruined, just like my dress, but somehow, with his hair tousled and covered in grime like this, he looks even more stunning.

"Don't hold back now. I killed your father, after all." He smiles viciously. "Aren't you angry with me?"

His expression is like a kick to the gut for how it knocks the wind out of me. The way he says it is so cold, so remorseless, that even though I *know* he's trying to provoke me, I can't help the sudden rage that sparks inside me. Rage that's been building.

Even as my eyes fall to his lips.

A gnarled tangle of emotions twists inside my chest. Every awful, terrible thought I've been holding inside myself. Though what I can't begin to understand is why.

Why is he coaxing them out of me?

"No," I lie, shaking my head and trying to force the feeling back down.

Like the good girl I'm supposed to be.

Good Christian girls do not get angry. Good Christian girls smile through the pain.

Like my mother.

Even when we're dying...

"No." I shake my head, denying it. "No, I'm not."

"Don't lie to me," Lucifer hisses, using his shadows to shackle me in place. "You're furious with me. You have been for weeks."

It's the truth, and we both know it, but I refuse to admit it.

To him, most especially.

His eyes narrow. "But what I want to know is why."

I turn my face away from him, unwilling to meet his gaze, but Lucifer only chuckles before he forces my chin toward him and kisses me, stealing my breath and my focus. The feeling of his mouth on mine undoes me, his kiss knocking me off guard. He breaks his lips away from mine only moments later, leaving me breathless and panting with pleasure, before he whispers, "Or perhaps it's your lost humanity that has you furious with me."

"I haven't lost my humanity," I mumble against him without thinking.

A spark of hellfire lights in his gaze. Like a shark that's scented blood.

And that's when I know he has me.

"Haven't you?" he purrs, gripping my chin even tighter, his fingers smearing a mixture of mud and dirt all over my face. "Or perhaps what truly infuriates you is that you wish it was you who'd killed him, instead of me?"

My breath rushes out of me like a force.

And whatever denial was poised on my lips dies instantly as his other hand, wiped clean on the inside of his suit coat, finds that delicious spot between my legs and parts me. I arch into him, a fresh round of anger sending my pulse racing at how thoroughly he's able to play me, almost as if he's called my desire forth to taunt me. His grip on me tightens, his thumb circling my clit as his fingers thrust into me. But I won't let him win that easily.

Not without a fight, at least.

Without warning, I thrash violently, attempting to wriggle and writhe my way out of his hold as he continues to finger me, but my resistance only seems to fuel his enjoyment.

"That's it." Lucifer's fang-laden smirk widens as I fruitlessly attempt to escape him. But I don't use my safe word, and to my surprise, he lets me nearly manage to get away before one of his hands clamps around my ankle like a vise and pulls, and before I can stop him, he's dragging me back toward him, crawling up the length of my body.

I kick out my other foot, unexpectedly catching him hard in the mouth. Harder than I would've ever thought possible.

I gasp as Lucifer goes still.

Oh God. He's going to kill me.

The sound of my heartbeat thrashes in my ears, and a cold sweat breaks out over my skin.

But Lucifer moves first. He probes the wound gingerly, his eyes widening at the sight of the blood on his fingers, before he throws back his head and laughs wickedly, the forked tip of his tongue darting out to lick some of the blood from his lip.

"Now we're getting somewhere." He smirks down at me. "Fight me."

His tone is so patronizing, so cocksure, that my pulse races, my own embarrassment at how much I'm still enjoying this slamming me into overdrive, and before I fully understand what I'm doing, I'm clawing at him, and the ground beneath us is shaking, vibrating, the anger buried deep inside me barely leashed. Like he's coaxing all my darkest desires out of me. And suddenly, I can't stop myself from wanting to release it.

My desire. My anger.

At him. At this fucked-up existence he created for me.

I may have chosen to be with him, but I never would have been forced to if Lucifer hadn't first chosen for me, manipulated me for his own twisted means.

The way he's still doing. Right now.

The ground continues to shake, the subtle vibrations growing more violent and intense by the second. Like my rage can destroy the earth beneath me.

"That's right. I killed him," Lucifer hisses, his voice rising. "Doesn't that anger you?" His pupils narrow until they're serpentine slits, even as the hardened length of his cock presses against me. Even as I seek it out. "I *enjoyed* the taste of his blood as the last of his pathetic heart pulsed in my hand."

I'm shaking nearly as much as the ground now as I struggle to hold my anger in, my pussy soaking the thin layer of my thong, which he quickly rips from me, but as he undoes his belt buckle, my skin tightening, I can't bring myself to fight it anymore. To resist him.

So, I give in. To my desire. To the fury.

I hit him again, letting out a strangled cry. I fight and kick with every ounce of rage he's released in me. It doesn't take long for him to pin me again, yet still I'm pulsing with need. He clutches me by the throat, the swollen lips of my pussy already anticipating him.

The earth continues to shake.

"That's it," he snarls. His deranged chuckle is a dark, twisted thing. "Fuck me. Destroy me. I stole your humanity from you, after all."

Roughly, he holds me down, choking me with one hand as I claw at him uselessly. With the other, he lifts my dress and exposes himself before crudely shoving his cock into me. The fullness of him stretches me, his shadows wrapping around us like a shield as he thrusts until darkness dances at the edge of my vision, and with each delicious stroke, I feel my world shatter. Like he's tearing me apart. Even as it feels like he's putting me back together again.

I can't make sense of all the feelings at war in me.

I love him.

But I . . . might also hate him a little.

For everything he's done to me.

And yet, I hadn't even allowed myself to think it until now, to unleash this feeling. That's how much I want him, how much he's damaged me.

This ache he creates in me, the invisible force that binds us.

It's life altering. Universe creating.

So catastrophic I can't begin to wrap my mind around the scope of it.

Lucifer and I are infinity. Infinity made flesh.

Lucifer thrusts into me, his cock finding a rough and perfect rhythm, hitting that exact spot he knows makes me come undone as his other hand fingers my clit feverishly. "Let it out now, dove. Let it out."

"It . . . should have been me," I rasp, barely managing the words he's coaxed from me through the fog of my own pleasure and the grip of his hand at my throat. I glare up at him, a furious tear sliding down my cheek as I hiss, "It should have been me who killed him."

A satisfied smile crosses his lips.

Two of his fingers lightly pinch my clit, rolling it in a way that makes me arch up off the ground until I gag.

Lucifer smirks. "Forgive me."

The pleasure inside me heightens, the force of it nearly reaching an apex, but Lucifer senses the exact moment when I start to let go, the exact moment I'm unleashed.

My body begins to pulse, an abundance of light bubbling inside my chest before it tears through me. My mouth opens on a silent scream, but Lucifer's there to catch me, his shadows smothering it out before it escapes the clearing.

He releases my throat, my breath rushing back to me, and I see stars.

In his eyes. In the open sky above me.

From the feeling of his rock-hard cock pumping inside me.

"That's it," he coaxes. "Come apart for me." He strokes me in a way I would never dare pleasure myself, rough and terrifying, his cock splitting me in two, but somehow in his hands, it works for me. I shudder beneath him, my pleasure and whatever else is inside me far from over as he lays a gentle kiss on my neck. "Don't hold back. I want all of you, even the darkest parts of you," he whispers. "Let it out now."

And I do.

At his command, I come apart completely.

Another pulse of light and pleasure bursts through me, my release so intense it breaks past Lucifer's shadows, shattering the barrier he's created and nearly blinding us both. He thrusts into me, emptying himself inside me on a guttural curse as I orgasm so hard, I swear I feel not only the earth shake, but the heavens too.

And maybe I do.

Maybe whatever this is between him and me really is life altering.

I shudder and shake beneath him, a strange sort of relief filling me, and for a moment, for the first time, I fear what eternity means. The depth he's created in me.

Once the earth has crumbled and humanity has fallen, Lucifer and I will still be here.

Love everlasting.

Lucifer's own orgasm finishes shortly, the final grunt of his pleasure settling me into a familiar, sated kind of subspace as I stare dazedly up at the stars.

I don't know what just happened, or what the hell he unleashed in me, but it feels like it's more than my dress that's ruined. Though he'll find a way to replace it for me. He always does. And as I lie there, panting and trembling beneath him, the cold, hard ground suddenly feels less solid in the face of our infinity. Less stable.

Like he cut whatever gravity tethered me to the earth.

What the fuck did he just do to me?

Lucifer's hand comes to my belly, his touch now so gentle it's reverent, as he uses a mixture of dirt and some of his cum, which leaks from me like paint over my bare skin.

Some kind of angelic symbol.

"What does this mean?" I rasp, my voice uncharacteristically hoarse from where he choked me. I'm not certain whether I mean the symbol or the shock of power he just fucked from me, though I'm not sure it matters.

"It means forever, little dove," he whispers to me.

I let out a contented sigh, despite the shakiness in my limbs, the uncertainty and fear that coils in me. I know better now than to believe everything he tells me. This and most of the things that leave his lips are a lie.

A beautiful, terrible lie.

And yet, for one sweet, blissful moment, I lean into him and allow myself to believe it, completely.

CHAPTER FOUR

Lucifer

It's sometime later as Charlotte and I lie beneath the stars, and she finally begins to emerge from the haze of subspace, that she whispers, "What the hell did you just do to me, Lucifer?"

I don't deign to answer her.

Instead, I roll to my side, coming to stand beside where she lies on the cold forest floor. I've barely managed to put my sullied clothes to rights and tuck my semihard cock back into my suit pants when suddenly I feel another celestial presence behind me.

The attention Charlotte's little light show drew no doubt caused a stir.

I freeze time with a snap of my fingers, turning my attention toward our unexpected visitor. "Hello, Mother."

I pivot soon enough to see her step forth from the shadows, her shock of dark hair trailing behind her as it slips through the ether. "Sweetheart," she croons, smiling up at me with a motherly love that's unbefitting of such a youthful face. "It's been too long."

She draws closer, opening her arms as if she means to beckon me, for me to kiss her on the cheek like I would have over the last several centuries, but instead I step to the side, shielding a still half-naked and vulnerable Charlotte, who lies frozen upon the ground beside me.

My fiancée has yet to learn how to defend herself from such trivial things as celestials trifling with time and space, but she will. And soon.

Now that I've unleashed what she's stolen from me.

Mother smiles wickedly.

I nod over my shoulder, indicating Charlotte's state of undress. "You never were one for privacy."

Mother drops her arms, resigned, and shrugs. "And why should I be?" She sticks her lip into a pout that reminds me a little too keenly of Mammon. "I created you, after all."

"And her?" I arch a brow, nodding toward Charlotte.

"Lucifer," Mother says, lowering her chin as she looks at me. "You can't possibly be angry with me."

My expression darkens. "I think you'll find my frustration with our family knows no bounds, Mother."

She sighs, trailing her hand along a nearby tree, watching idly as the bark rots and crumbles away. My Mother can give or take life with as little as a touch.

Such is the burden of a goddess. A true deity.

"You never did like me or your Father meddling," she says wistfully before she glances my way again. "Even when it was for your own good."

"And that's what this is?" I sneer. "You meddling?"

She waves a dismissive hand. "Now, Lucifer, you've said yourself you shouldn't ask questions you don't want the answer to." She smirks, turning my own words against me.

I always did have my Mother's smile.

And clearly, she's been keeping tabs on Charlotte and me for far longer than I'm comfortable with, frankly.

A warning snarl tears from my lips, my more demonic features flashing.

But my Mother isn't deterred by the terrible sight of my angelic form.

Nor the way time and Hell have changed me.

Mother bats her lashes innocently. "I simply gave her a little push in your direction, that's all. The rest was all you, sweetheart."

I don't believe that for a second.

"And Father?"

She scoffs. "As if He'd ever involve Himself in something this thrilling."

I lift a brow.

She cocks her head to the side, examining me. "Why, ending the world. That's why He let you and my other babies out of Hell, after all. Your Father grows tired of humanity."

The moment the words leave her lips, I feel no surprise that she's said it.

Simply anger that I failed to trust in my own judgment sooner.

Naturally, I was right, of course. My Father tires of humanity. No doubt that's why He disappeared after freeing us.

To leave Earth's destruction in our capable hands. Me and my angelic siblings.

He never was one to admit when He was wrong.

But what does that mean for the once-human woman beside me?

"Don't worry, dear. You've been distracted," Mother says, clearly clocking the frustration on my face as she draws closer before she reaches out to pat my cheek, as if to reassure me I'm not losing my touch. She looks toward Charlotte. "She is a beautiful, tempting little thing, isn't she? Now that you've polished up your Father's work a bit."

"She's mine," I snarl, unable to stop myself. "Never His. Not any longer."

"As she should be." She gingerly steps away from me. "Keep working on giving me grandchildren, won't you? I'd love to be a Mimi in our next universe, though I do suppose your sister might be a bit put out if I steal her nickname, wouldn't she?"

"And what's your role in all this?" My eyes flick toward Charlotte, my expression hardening. "Why her?"

"Mammon?" She lifts a curious brow as she turns to look at me.

"No, Charlotte. Why create her for me?"

It's the one question that still doesn't make any sense. Even to me.

She shakes her head like I'm being naive. "I already told you. I simply nudged her in the right direc—"

"Oh, come off it, Mum," I growl. "Michael already told me."

She sighs, her coy demeanor deflating. "Michael never was one to keep a secret. My own fault for creating him that way, I suppose."

"Mother." My eyes flash in warning.

She huffs. "Really, Lucifer? Don't you trust me?"

I don't answer her.

I trust no one.

Least of all Father. And now, her too, by proxy.

"I see," she says, her expression an odd mixture of yearning and regret. "Of course you don't. Not now that you have something to lose." Her eyes fall toward Charlotte, who starts to stir, but to my surprise, there's no hint of malice there, only a wistful maternal longing. "I always thought it rather clever how your Father created Eve from Adam's rib, so when He severed your wings, well, what's the harm in holding on to one of your most cherished son's bones?"

My expression goes cold. "You didn't."

Mother forces a laugh. "It was just the initial creation spark, that's all, darling. The rest was all you, I swear. Her mother prayed for conception. What kind of monster would I have been to ignore her like your Father would?" Her lips pinch with thinly veiled resentment.

"But to what end?" I snarl.

Mother sighs again. "I would have thought you'd learned this lesson from your Father's mistakes long ago." She places her hand on my cheek once more, her russet skin like a shadow against me. "Every king needs a queen. Every god, a goddess. Even you." She pats my chin. "Do try hard not to break her."

She snaps her fingers.

And in a blink, she's gone.

Vanished from the clearing. Too fast even for me.

I swear loudly, not bothering to unfreeze time considering she already undermined me. Seconds later Charlotte finally rises onto her elbows, looking around dazedly. She places her hand on her head as she glances toward me, and from the frown on her lips, my Mother is not the only woman I'm going to disappoint this evening.

"A few seconds ago, you were standing beside me, but then I . . . could've sworn I heard you talking to someone, and now you're . . ." Her voice trails off. "What's going on?"

In this, I won't lie to her.

I clear my throat. "My Mother just paid us a visit, unfortunately."

"Y-your Mother? Lilith?" she stutters. "Did she . . ."

She moves to cover herself, but I stay her movements with a lift of my hand. "Don't bother. It's nothing she didn't help create."

"Create?"

I pull a pack of cigarettes and my lighter from my suit-coat pocket. "My Mother is a goddess. Who do you think inspired my Father to . . ." I light my cigarette before I gesture at the woods around us.

"Birth humanity?"

"I suppose you could put it that way." My cigarette flares, the flame a spark in the darkness as the scent of tobacco fills the clearing.

Charlotte blows out a short breath. "There's no such thing as an original idea, I guess."

"She expects grandchildren." The corner of my mouth lifts. "And soon."

That gets her attention quickly.

Charlotte sputters. "She what?"

I chuckle at the shock in her voice, at the sudden realization that children are still a possibility for her, even with her newfound immortality. Though the thought sobers me quickly.

And for once, I make the decision to be honest with her.

I only hope that whatever humanity is left in her doesn't make me regret it just as swiftly.

"There's . . . something else you ought to know, little dove."

CHAPTER FIVE
Charlotte

The moment the words fall from Lucifer's lips, I . . . don't know what to make of them.

"Fated," I repeat, the word suddenly feeling foreign. Too otherworldly, too . . . supernatural to be real. Made from one of his bones. Like Adam and Eve. "As in . . . as in I never had any free will?"

Lucifer shrugs, the cigarette between his fingers burning as he flicks some of the ashes onto the forest floor. "I fail to see how that's relevant."

I blink, nearly at a loss for words.

"How is it *not* relevant?"

We're standing in the middle of the barren forest, my bare feet so numb I can no longer feel my toes. My dirt-covered dress is torn from where he fucked me so hard I saw stars. Not to mention how he made me cause a freaking mini-earthquake and unleash whatever the hell else that pulse of light mid-orgasm was, but somehow, it's *this* that undoes me.

Makes me feel like the ground beneath my feet is moving.

Like there's nothing left to tether me.

I swallow hard. The choice he gave me to stay with him was never really a choice at all. The same as working for him. The same as becoming his fake fiancée. The same as my father's death. Only worse than all those, and the knowledge of that steals the last little bit of my sanity.

"Fated," I exhale.

"Or something close to it, really," he mutters before blowing out another cloud of smoke.

The end of his cigarette pulses, the vapor disappearing. There and gone instantly.

Like I would've been. If he hadn't remade me.

My stomach reels, the thought nearly making me sick.

"Fated," I breathe.

I had my suspicions that God may have played a role in bringing us together, of course, and when Mark killed me, when Lucifer stood beside me in limbo in Grand Central Station, he'd warned me that his Mother might have had something to do with it. But that'd been *before* he'd used his Father's redemption to reshape me, to bring me back to life, and the confirmation is another matter entirely.

Made from one of his bones. Like when God made Eve.

To be subservient to Adam.

My stomach twists.

"How long?" I whisper. "How long have you known we were . . . destined? Or that I was made from you? Or suspected it, at least?" I can hardly bring myself to say it, the words nearly choking me.

Lucifer makes a circular motion with the hand holding his cigarette before he casually brings it to his lips. "Since I realized I couldn't see your sins, I suppose."

My breath stops, his words gutting me. "So, from the very beginning?"

"Naturally." He shrugs as he takes another long drag. "Though I fail to see how that's relevant, Charlotte."

"Of course it's relevant," I snap, cutting him off in a way that's uncharacteristically bitchy of me. In a way I'll no doubt be punished for later.

For the first time, that doesn't excite me.

Lucifer arches a brow at me as he quirks his head. "Careful now," he says, flashing a slow, crooked grin at me. "You don't want me to put you on the rack tonight, do you?"

I blanch before I lower my gaze. Submitting to him. Exactly like I was taught to do. Another thing I have my late father to thank for.

Or was I made this way from the start? All by Lilith's design? To please Lucifer?

No. No, I cannot go down that line of thinking right now.

"I'm sorry," I whisper, my pulse racing with my own shame, even as I purposefully keep my eyes low. "But it . . . matters to me, sir." I glance up at him apologetically, silently pleading with my best doe eyes.

Please listen. Please understand me.

But Lucifer simply shakes his head, chuckling like he isn't certain what he's supposed to do with me. He crosses the clearing and tucks a bit of my hair behind my ear, gently brushing his knuckles over my cheek. "You humans have always been so bloody preoccupied with the concept of free will."

"Of course we are," I say, more than a little shocked at how dismissive he's being. "Why wouldn't we be?"

Lucifer huffs like I'm being naive. Humiliation wasn't on the BDSM consent menu this evening, but still, my face flushes with heat.

"Because I fail to see what difference it makes. He always gets His way in the end, don't you see?" He flips his middle finger irreverently toward the night sky as if to indicate his Father.

God. The Almighty.

And it's only then that I realize I'm shivering. "I would have thought you'd understand this more than anyone."

My choice being taken from me.

Just like his was taken away.

When God chose to make him the villain of every story . . .

Lucifer flicks the ashes of his cigarette impatiently, balancing it between his fingers as he steps closer. Close enough to trail both his hands down my arms affectionately. "I fancy the idea of free will as much as you do, but free will, fate, these are *human* concepts, and human is the one thing I will never be."

"And what does that make you?"

"Divine," he says, tipping my chin so that I'm forced to look at him. Gently he kisses my forehead, baptizing me. "As are you."

Now that he's gifted me God's redemption and unleashed whatever this . . . darkness is within me. The bit of his powers he unwillingly transferred to me.

I shake my head. "Could have fooled me."

I pull away, trying to escape the nearly irresistible influence he seems to have over me as I move toward the edge of the clearing, but he quickly captures my wrist.

"Charlotte—"

"Inferno," I snap, using my safe word before he can go any further.

Lucifer stares down at me incredulously, but he releases my wrist instantly.

I open and close my mouth several times, failing to find the words until I close my eyes. I inhale a slow, steadying breath, just like my therapist taught me. "The Lucifer I know would *never* be okay with the idea that someone had manipulated him. Made him a pawn in their game." I open my eyes again.

And even through the shadows, I can see his gaze darken.

The anger in his eyes as he looks at me.

At how I've damaged his pride.

But the . . . resentment I see there is new to me.

"Perhaps you're right. I've changed," he sneers, staring down the bridge of his nose as he begins to circle me, a predator once more. Suddenly, I'm backed up against a rotting tree, his shadows clutching me at the base of my throat. "But it's you who did this to me," he hisses against my ear. "Would you have me undo it?"

My knees quiver, and his lips part as he steps closer, breathing me in. He trails his nose along the length of my jaw, his tongue flicking. Like he can taste the salt on my skin.

"Now," he purrs, "let's head back to that blasted thing you once called a home before either of us says something we do not mean."

Abruptly, his shadows release me, and he stalks toward the edge of the clearing.

But I'm not finished yet.

"I don't know what I would have chosen, you know," I call after him, my words stopping him in his tracks.

His shoulders go rigid.

"I don't know what I would have chosen had I known everything."

Lucifer turns to face me, his eyes so full of hellfire, they glow. Like two burning amber jewels in the dark. "If you value our life together, I beg you not to speak another word."

"Or what?" I gape at him. "You'll hurt me?"

"Never," he snarls, like the mere suggestion that he would do so without my consent is an insult to him. As if I don't know *exactly* how beastly he can be.

"Then why? Even if I wanted to, you wouldn't allow me to leave."

I've been held captive to Lucifer's will before, though I . . . thought things had changed recently.

The flames in his eyes flash, burning bright. "Because I cannot be held responsible for what I would do to keep you with me."

I let out a shuddered breath.

In another life, another moment, one where he hadn't killed my father without my permission, one where he hadn't remade me from the ashes of God's redemption, where his crazy Mother hadn't stolen all my free will from me, those words might have meant something, made me melt.

Now, as I stand here, the last grasp I felt I had on my human life slipping through my fingers like sand through an hourglass, the full reality of all that he's planned, of how thoroughly I've been manipulated, chills me.

He destroyed the last human part that was left of me.

And not by my choice like I thought, but by fate.

And I think that, not for the first time, I might truly hate him for it.

"Is that all I am to you? Still?" I breathe. "A toy? A pretty little dove for you to keep in a cage?"

For a moment, Lucifer's mask falters, and I think I see a deep flash of hurt in his eyes before it's gone instantly, his expression darkening. "If you think for even a second that's the way I see you, then you truly don't know me at all."

"Maybe I don't," I say defiantly, old hurts bubbling up inside my chest. *In for a penny, in for a pound, I guess.* "After all, you've been lying to me from the start, haven't you?" I close the distance between us as I whisper, "You used me. Manipulated me. And I let you."

"Because you love me." He reaches out to cup my cheek.

But I shake my head as I take a small step back.

His hand falls to his side reluctantly.

"Because I fear you."

This time, Lucifer's pain is obvious, his tongue darting out to wet his lips as he shakes his head at me. "You don't mean that. You don't even know what you're saying. You're hurting, still reeling from the power I had to unleash in you, all because you refused to release it yourself, to embrace your immortality. I know you're scared, but there's no turning back now, and you can't—"

"Don't you dare try to tell me how I feel," I snap, my tone sharp enough that in the quiet of the cold forest, I may as well be shouting.

The words settle in the ether between us, and for a long moment, Lucifer doesn't say anything. He simply stares at me, amber gaze blazing until finally his eyes narrow. "I think that's quite enough for tonight." He turns to leave.

But I grab his shoulder. "No. *I* decide when I've had enough."

Lucifer rounds on me. "For fuck's sake, Charlotte. You—"

"Hit me," I say, gesturing to his now clenched hands. "Show me I have just as much say in all of this chaos as you do."

Lucifer shakes his head. "Not now that you've used your safe word," he growls, tossing the butt of his cigarette onto the ground and grinding it beneath his Armani shoe. "I'll do no such thing."

"You want to destroy the last of my humanity? For me to embrace immortality? Fine. Then hit me," I say again, my voice lifting in anger. "Rip the power out of me. Fuck me until I can't see straight. Whatever you have to do." I square my shoulders, drawing nearly nose to nose with him, or as close as I can, considering he's nearly a foot taller than me. "But if you can ask that of me, why can't I ask it of you?" My breath becomes heavy, swirling like smoke in the space between us, the butt of his cigarette still smoldering beside our feet. "We're equals, aren't we?"

Lucifer doesn't answer. Instead, he simply stares at me.

"Aren't we?"

I reach for him, and for the first time ever, he recoils from me.

Until I have no choice but to allow my outstretched hand to fall.

Something dark flashes in Lucifer's eyes then. Something pained. "If I've told you once, I've told you a thousand times. Don't try to top from the bottom. Not with me."

He turns and disappears into the shadows, leaving me breathless and alone in his wake.

I suck in a sharp breath, clutching at my chest, overwhelmed by the feeling. As if my own heart has just been ripped out of me.

I stumble forward, standing there frozen in the dark for what feels like hours, until reluctantly I begin to make my way toward the house.

Unhinged by everything I now realize he's stolen from me, and the knowledge that the monstrous immortal I've chosen to give my life to can think so little of me.

CHAPTER SIX

Charlotte

The idea of fate is far more romantic than the reality.

I float naked in one of the penthouse's larger tubs, the water having long since gone cold. My hair and ears are fully submerged, the sound around me muffled save for the echo of my own heartbeat. Thump, thump. Thump, thump.

But my mind is blessedly empty, my thoughts almost blissful—they're so peacefully silent for once. So silent I don't recognize I'm no longer alone until I feel the sudden vibration of the water, someone pounding on the bathroom door.

"Miss Charlotte? Miss Charlotte?"

I close my eyes, not wanting to emerge from the feeling of numbness that's now come over me, the feeling of weightlessness.

As if the whole world isn't on fire all around me.

I'm still not exactly certain if everything I thought I overheard in the clearing is true. Lucifer didn't mention the world ending, but I . . . can't seem to stop thinking about it.

The distant voice echoes again. This time, the pounding against the door grows more urgent, extreme enough that I can feel the ripples in the water with ease.

I sigh, jackknifing upright so that the sounds of the penthouse come back to me in a sudden rush. The quiet hum of the bathroom lights. The water dripping from my body.

And the now-incessant pounding on the door.

"Miss Charlotte?"

"What?" I finally snap, my tone uncharacteristically bitchy.

I try hard to be extra patient with the staff, to treat every one of them kindly. It wasn't that long ago that I could have been one of them, after all.

Was one of them. Lucifer's employees.

Even if I'm technically still on the company payroll.

"Yes?" I call again. This time softer, to mask my annoyance.

It takes a long time for me to escape my own mind these days. The dark thoughts and memories that haunt me each time I close my eyes. So, it's moments like this I cherish the most.

The moments where I feel nothing.

Ramesh or another one of the staff—though I'm fairly certain it's Ramesh from the sound of his voice—clears his throat from the other side of the door. "Apologies, Miss Charlotte, but the car is waiting."

The car?

I wade to the other side of the bath, careful not to splash any of the water onto the edge where my iPhone waits. Drying off my hand on a nearby towel, I press the side button, lighting up the home screen.

8:30 p.m.

My stomach flips as I glance down at my severely pruned fingers.

I've been in the bath for over four hours.

Time has felt . . . different these last few days.

I shake my head, my sopping wet hair flopping about my shoulders so that a few drops of water sprinkle across the screen. I don't bother to dry it off before I tear out of the bath, more water sloshing onto the marble floor behind me as I wrap a towel around myself and hurry to the bathroom mirror.

I'm still not particularly comfortable with my own nudity.

With the woman who stares back at me.

I scramble in search of my makeup bag, realizing I must have left it upstairs, but somehow amid my mindless rushing, I end up accidentally turning the faucet on, even though I don't need it. I'm supposed to meet Lucifer for dinner at nine o'clock.

And I've never once been late.

"Would serve him right," I mutter to myself.

Things have been . . . tense between us. Ever since the funeral. That night in the forest.

Another knock at the door interrupts me.

Ramesh's voice is softer, though still concerned as he calls out, "Is there anything I can get for you, Miss Charlotte?"

"No," I call back, my shaking hand lashing out to rush and turn the faucet off as I glance toward the door. I hear a subtle crack, followed by a loud crunch, and I turn to find the faucet's now-broken handle clutched in my palm, the porcelain crushed completely. Several of its shards poke out of my skin as my blood begins to pool.

I stare at it, fear and shock leaving me unable to move.

But I . . . feel nothing.

"Miss Charlotte?" Ramesh's voice sounds uncertain. Clearly, he heard the porcelain breaking.

"I'm coming," I shout, adrenaline getting the better of me.

Even as I'm too numb to feel.

I use my other hand to cradle my injured palm as blood begins to drip into the marble sink. The crimson splotches speckle amid the rock's natural pattern. Shaking from head to toe, I grab hold of a nearby hand towel, shoving the fluffy white linen against the cut in a futile attempt to stop the bleeding, but that only seems to push the shards deeper.

I let out a pained hiss. So much for numb.

"Miss Charlotte, are you all right?" Ramesh mumbles, his voice strained with concern.

"Yes. Yes, I'm fine," I lie, forcing my grip to remain steady as I begin to pull the first shard from the fleshy mound near my thumb. I swallow down a panicked whimper.

But my tone betrays me.

"If you need any assistance, I would be happy to send one of the maids in."

Silence answers. I mouth another string of curses, pulling yet another shard from my skin. The pain cuts through me.

"Or perhaps you would prefer I call Mr. Apollyon?"

"No," I say quickly. Too quick. I want to shut that idea down fast.

The thought of facing Lucifer, of him seeing me vulnerable like this, especially after we fought . . . well, it . . . it no longer feels safe to me.

"No. No, that won't be necessary," I say, shaking my head, though I know Ramesh can't see me. If he could, Lucifer would be on the phone and then here before I could blink. "Tell Dagon I'll be down when I'm ready."

Ramesh lingers, and even through the door, I can practically feel his hesitation before finally he mutters, "Yes, of course, Miss Bellefleur."

A moment later, I hear his steps slowly retreat down the hall.

Leaving me alone.

I sink to my knees, collapsing onto the tiled bathroom floor just as a pained, strangled whimper escapes me. I wince, a sharp searing sensation racing up my arm as I slowly pull yet another shard from my palm. My blood coats the floor and sink as I sit there, painstakingly removing every piece, and I can't help but think that no matter how well meaning, Ramesh can no longer help me. No mortal can.

And that thought chills me to my marrow.

As the last of my humanity slips away from me . . .

CHAPTER SEVEN

Lucifer

"She's late."

"I'm sure she has a good reason." Imani casts me a knowing smile from overtop the glass of cabernet she's nursing, her dark features cutting straight through me.

She's a stunning middle-aged Black woman, whose marketing acumen nearly matches her refined look, but though Imani may have known me longer than any other human, my now-immortal fiancée included, it wouldn't take a genius, or someone with even half her image expertise, to see right through me.

I haven't been myself ever since Charlotte and I exchanged words the other evening.

And as the head of my PR team, Imani knows it.

She sits across the table from me, her slender frame perfectly poised. Being a former model isn't exactly why I hired her, but the graceful image she projects suits Apollyon Incorporated handsomely. Though my luxury conglomerate and its many holdings are the furthest thing from my mind as of late.

"Are you going to tell me what's happening between you and Charlotte, or do I have to ask again?"

I scowl. If any other employee ever dared to be so familiar, they'd find themselves disemboweled and floating in the East River shortly before morning, but Imani has made herself invaluable to me. In a way only one other employee ever has before.

My lip curls as my thoughts turn to Astaroth. My former demonic head of security. Before he betrayed me. Perhaps I'll pop downstairs this evening and pay him a little visit.

Blow off some fucking steam.

"So?" Imani prompts me again as she signals to the waiter to bring me another whisky. "Clearly you haven't had enough alcohol for this."

"There's not enough alcohol in this whole bloody city." I lash out my hand, nearly knocking over the crystal water glass in front of me as I snatch my refilled drink from the terrified waiter.

Imani mutters a soft apology, and he scuttles off. "That bad, is it?"

I grunt as I take another long sip, which only causes her to smile. But I refuse to be a source of human entertainment. Even Imani's.

I spear her with a vicious look that would make a lesser human piss themselves.

Charlotte's father certainly did.

His is a death I will relish for all eternity.

Imani shakes her head then, fiddling idly with her napkin. As my most senior employee, she's wise enough to know when to push me, and insightful enough to understand when it's in her best interest to tread lightly. "Look, Lucifer. You know me, and I'm about to tell you something that you don't want to hear, but I need you to hear it anyway."

My eyes narrow. "I'm listening."

Imani sighs. "This is love, you fool. This is exactly what you signed up for."

I snarl, the sound so sudden and animal in the otherwise empty restaurant that the waiter heading toward our table reroutes immediately.

"What in the bloody fuck are you on about?" My voice lowers to a serpentine hiss as I feel the heat of my hellfire burn in my gaze.

Unfortunately, discussion of my personal life is no longer off limits. Not now that I'm in bed with a former employee.

And Imani's intern turned assistant, no less.

Imani simply leans across the table, as if she means to place her hand on my arm, before she hesitates and thinks better of it. "It means that when you love someone, you also give that person the power to hurt you."

I frown, sniffing derisively. "I don't remotely know what you're talking about."

"Don't you?" Imani lifts a brow. "You and Charlotte had your first real fight, obviously." Her gaze sweeps over me, taking in my disheveled appearance.

To the undiscerning eye, I look as impeccable as ever, my Attolini suit pressed and tailored specifically for me. But upon closer inspection, one of my cuff links is missing from where I failed to put it on this morning, too distracted as I watched Charlotte tear out of our bedroom like she couldn't wait to be rid of me, and as the clock hand ticks by, my fiancée growing ever more late by the minute, my tie has slowly begun to loosen from where I've been tugging at it uncomfortably. And that says nothing for how many times I've raked my hand through my own hair.

What the fuck has she done to me?

"You look like shit," Imani says savagely. "Gorgeous, expensive, luxury shit, but for you? Still shit."

"You don't pull any punches, do you, Imani?" I take another long sip of my whisky, the refilled glass already near empty.

It'll take far more than a glass or two to drown whatever this . . . feeling is Charlotte's created in me. There's only one other's approval who ever mattered more.

And I haven't laid eyes on Him since He severed my wings.

"You know I don't," Imani answers. "It's why you hired me."

"Among other things." A mischievous smile plays on my lips.

Mine and Imani's relationship is strictly professional.

Deals with me typically are.

But Imani and I have a *unique* history.

She sighs, backing off at the mention of our agreement as she swirls her Bordeaux. "Look, all I'm saying is that maybe you should apologize."

"Apologize?" I sneer.

The assumption that *I* am the problem here is enough that I feel the glass in my hand crack slightly.

"Lucifer," Imani says, her eyes darting in warning from the buckling tumbler to the otherwise empty restaurant.

The Rainbow Room at Rockefeller Center. I would never take Charlotte anywhere I considered beneath me.

We're in public, Imani's expression seems to say.

Meaning that humanity, and, by proxy, the press is watching. Always.

I scowl, my throat writhing, even as I loosen my grip. Considering all the offerings the public's pride and vanity bestows on me, I can't say I miss the days of my relative anonymity before mine and Charlotte's debut, but I do miss the quiet.

The *illusion* of privacy.

No matter how much it cost me.

"I'm the devil," I say, snapping my fingers at the waiter, who hops to and quickly retrieves another glass. "I do not apologize."

Imani's eyes narrow. "You will if you want to keep that poor human girl you plucked from obscurity."

"She's not human." I swirl my new glass. "Not any longer."

Imani's eyes widen.

"Lucifer," she breathes slowly, "what did you do?"

But any chance for her to probe further is bolloxed as a pair of familiar, gold-flecked eyes shift toward me. My gaze locks on to my fiancée's the moment she enters the room.

I feel her presence keenly. As if she is another limb.

One not even my Father can sever from me.

It's been several days since she and I last exchanged more than a handful of words, our combined appearance schedules following the funeral keeping us both busy, but tonight she looks as beautiful and fragile as ever.

No, not fragile. Not for long.

Not now that I've released the powers she's stolen from me.

I'll make an immortal of her yet.

At her approach, I stand, my gaze never leaving hers, and despite whatever bad blood lies between us, whatever Imani says next is lost to me.

I have eyes only for Charlotte.

I pull out her chair, ever the gentleman. "You're late."

Those innocent doe-like eyes flick toward me. Like she expected something different. "I . . . got caught up with something."

My gaze tracks the less-than-subtle movement of her hand as she slips it behind her to smooth out her skirt. A pathetic attempt to hide it from me.

But already I've seen and sensed the damage. The flash of a freshly healed wound on her palm that, had she still been human, would have scarred deeply.

My jaw tightens.

What *exactly* is my fiancée keeping from me?

I return to my seat. "Don't let it happen again."

At the reprimand, she goes rigid in her chair.

And that's the exact moment I hear it. Her voice inside my head. Her thoughts suddenly open to me.

Or what?

My eyes widen, and I cough, sputtering on my sip of whisky.

Imani's brow furrows in confusion. "Lucifer, are you . . . okay?"

And no wonder. In all the years she's known me, I've never once been this uncollected, this unhinged.

"Fine," I mutter, swiftly shifting my attention back to where my fiancée sits before me.

Unaware that her bratty thoughts are now an open book.

And *I* am her most eager reader.

Charlotte glances between us, her expression a little hurt as she says, "I thought it was going to be just the two of us tonight, considering I think we have some..." She casts a sidelong glance at Imani, hesitating, like she's uncertain how much she's allowed to say. "Urgent *family* matters to discuss. Something I think you might have forgotten to mention to me."

My Father's apocalypse, she means.

No doubt she overheard my Mother the other evening.

My Father's apocalypse waits for no one, even me.

But I refuse for our lives to be interrupted by something as bloody trivial as His divine will.

To Imani's credit, she doesn't miss a beat. "I'm happy to do this later, if you'd rather—"

"No. Stay," I order. "We'll dine after."

"Lucifer," Imani says, questioning me.

But the look I give silences her. Even Imani knows when not to push me.

A trait my fiancée has yet to learn. Though she will.

Now that I've realized how thoroughly she can hurt me.

"Right," Imani says, clearing her throat. "I'll make it quick then."

She reaches to the small stool one of the staff placed beside the table for her, where one of her Hermes purses and her portfolio wait. She retrieves the portfolio, a standard leather company issue, which naturally showcases Apollyon's logo—a coiled serpent, prepared to strike—then flips it open, the hard angle of her jaw practically giving me the cut direct.

"Media coverage is looking surprisingly good after the Met Gala debacle. Our numbers recovered quickly. The riot at the funeral did us a favor. Bought sympathy. And the impressions on your socials are still holding steady, though Charlotte's account growth outpaces yours by a mile, Lucifer."

"He never posts." Charlotte glances at me from beneath her long lashes like she means to defend me. "I've tried." She smiles like the expression is meant to tease me.

But I don't need her to come to my defense.

Not when I'm still struggling with what she said to me the other evening.

I know more than a thing or two about words said in anger, about giving voice to things one does not mean. Hell is full of the pleading cries of those who will say and do anything for an ounce of mercy, who, even in their pain, feel no true remorse.

Not until I get a hold of them, you see.

But the idea that all I have given her, all I have done might not be enough . . .

It guts me.

In a way not even my Father's rejection ever could.

I frown and bring my glass to my lips as I give a subtle push against our connection.

Charlotte's eyes widen like she feels me, but then she shuts me out just as quickly.

Though if she's aware of the exchange, she doesn't appear to be.

"Well, whatever you're doing to engage your followers, Charlotte, keep doing it. It reflects well on the company. You're making my job easy."

Charlotte beams, though there's a reluctance in her expression that wasn't there previously.

The pleasure she takes at her efforts being recognized is no surprise to me. Praise is a tool I use frequently when she submits to me, but what *does* surprise me is the pride I find there. A subtle offering to me. A white flag of surrender, if you will.

Though she's still uncertain after our fight. I can feel it.

As I am with her, of course.

More than ever before.

"With the CFDA Awards only a few weeks away and you two hosting, we need to start planning. The Council of Fashion Designers won't be happy if we throw another Met Gala–size wrench into their fashion calendar," Imani says, glancing hesitantly between Charlotte and me again. Like she can sense the silent volley of communication but doesn't dare mention it. "Though both your respective teams seem to have it well in hand."

Charlotte nods but then lifts a brow toward me. "Are we really going to go through with all that, considering . . . ?"

I give her a meaningful look, and she nods, understanding instantly.

Even in the face of my Father's apocalypse, the show must go on.

The less humanity knows, the better.

"Right." Charlotte nods. "I'm supposed to meet Xzander for another fitting in the morning. His schedule's just been so busy with IMPACT's Black Advisory Board, but Olivia's headed there tonight."

The undiscovered human actress we hired as Charlotte's decoy.

A body double meant to deter the paparazzi.

A more than necessary expense, considering theirs and the Righteous's ever-increasing threats to her safety.

My Father's impending apocalypse isn't the only peril that's been leveled at us recently.

"Good. You could use a break," Imani says. "The press has been circling like sharks."

"And?" I prompt, urging Imani to get to the next part of the dossier that made me ask her to join us this evening.

"*And* Lucifer had two other points he wanted to discuss," she says, swiftly closing her portfolio. "Didn't you, Lucifer?" She gives me an incisive look, one that seems to imply *tread lightly*, though I can't begin to fathom why.

I get what I want. Always.

In this, and all things.

"The PR firm," I say tersely.

The little idea Charlotte had to expand her role recently. Make a name for herself. Independent from my company.

"What about it?" she asks.

I abandon my glass on the table, leaning back in my chair as I steeple my fingers. "Imani and I believe it may not be the best path for you."

"You and Imani?" Her eyes dart between us.

As if we've been privately conspiring against her, rather than planning an alternative future. One of which she's far more deserving.

And one that better insulates her from my family.

Charlotte needs to become equally as powerful and influential in her own right.

Imani sighs, shaking her head at me as she gently places her hand over Charlotte's. "Considering the increasing safety concerns, it may not be the best idea for you to start taking on a list of outside clients right now. Clients that are unknown to us, and Lucifer seems to think that—"

"You can do better."

Charlotte blinks. "I'm sorry?"

Quiet fury barrels down our connection, though Charlotte's voice remains soft, breathy.

Hesitating, Imani glances between us before, finally, she sighs again. "Lucifer seems to think it'd be better if we focus on building your individual brand. Clothing lines, skin care, fragrances. You name it. You'll be a style icon."

I nod in approval. "Why bother opening a PR firm when you're destined for something so much greater?"

Charlotte's eyes go wide. "Destined?"

And even *I* recognize that I have chosen the wrong wording.

I spear her with a reprimanding look. "Charlotte, be reasonable. You're better than this. You could do so much more with my funding."

"With *your* funding?" She unfolds her napkin, tossing it onto her lap as if it's personally offended her. "What if I don't want your funding, Lucifer?"

"Why the hell wouldn't you?" I reach across the table for her hand, but she quickly snatches it away from me. I frown. "I have more money than God. I'm happy to give it to you. The amount means little to me."

"Oh, the amount means *little* to you?" Her voice rises in pitch. "Just like the fact that this was *my* idea? *My* choice? The one thing in my life that was still in *my* control?"

"Charlotte," Imani says, glancing at the nearby waitstaff, who are now casting concerned glances in our direction.

But my fiancée simply lifts her hand, silencing Imani as if she's her employer rather than her mentee.

I smirk. Finally, she's beginning to see.

Even if she hasn't fully recognized her true power yet.

"Why dismiss me so quickly?" she asks. "My ideas have been worthwhile before."

"Don't put words in my mouth, little dove. You're too valuable to be running some paltry PR firm like—"

"Like Imani?"

Imani's expression goes cold. "Whatever this is, don't you dare drag me into it."

Charlotte blushes, looking temporarily embarrassed before she mumbles a quiet, "I'm sorry."

Imani gives a curt nod, but I'm . . . taken aback to find I wish the apology was directed to me. And it's that thought alone that makes my next words even more vicious, even more brutal.

"You want my blessing? Then earn it," I challenge. "We both know you've always been desperate for my approval."

"Lucifer," Imani gasps, prepared to come to my fiancée's defense.

But Charlotte merely shakes her head, her lower lip trembling as the whole restaurant seems to still.

For a moment, I question if perhaps I've made a mistake challenging her to be the immortal I know she can be. The immortal I know she soon will be.

Like her heart was forged in hellfire and wrapped in steel.

"Fine," she whispers, her eyes suddenly misty. The waitstaff soon return to their duties. "Fine. You want me to earn your approval, I'll do it. Imani and I will put a proposal together." With a shaking hand, she lifts her water glass off the table, a distraction, so she doesn't have to look at me. "What was the second thing?" she asks meekly.

Imani purses her lips. "I don't think it's wise if we—"

"The wedding," I say, cutting her off.

Charlotte freezes mid-movement. "I'm sorry?"

"I think I better leave you two to discuss this *alone*."

Imani retrieves her purse, casting me a scathing look, but Charlotte quickly stays her with little more than a hand.

"Will you wait for me downstairs please?" she mutters. "I'd like to speak with you alone."

Imani nods before leaving.

The moment she's gone, Charlotte turns her attention to me, and the glare she levels at me is so reflective of my own, it cuts whatever words I might have deigned to say short.

"What do you mean 'the wedding'?"

I lift my whisky glass, swirling its amber contents. "Our impending nuptials, of course. It'll be the event of this millennium, naturally. A good distraction for humanity."

She blinks at me, gaping. "We're . . . not even engaged. Not for real."

I frown, taking another sip. "Last time I checked, that's my ring you're wearing, is it not? My cock you're begging for each evening?"

She flushes, placing her ring finger out of view beneath the table. "You know better than anyone that sleeping together doesn't mean we have to get married. Not unless we're suddenly taking your Father's words to heart." Reluctantly she glances down at her hands, then back to me, worrying her lower lip between her teeth. "He . . . doesn't actually care about that, does He?"

My Father couldn't care less about sex out of wedlock, but the bastardized lessons of His "blessed" human Bible still haunt her regularly.

I press my lips into a hard line, tracing the rim of my glass with my finger. I nod to where her ring hand rests in her lap. "I forged that diamond myself in the fires of Hell, you know."

The admission seems to catch her off guard.

She sighs, fiddling with her crucifix necklace, one of the few personal items she retrieved after her father's funeral. For a moment, she gazes out the window past me, eyes unfocused, the whole of the city beneath her feet. Finally she reaches across the table for my hand, her voice softening.

"Lucifer, it's not that I . . ." Her other hand toys absently with her necklace as she swallows. "It's not that I don't want to marry you," she whispers, hesitating in a way that would make me doubt the truth in her words if her lies didn't have such a distinct taste.

If I couldn't feel *exactly* what she's feeling.

"I *do* want to marry you," she admits, looking up from our joined hands as she meets my gaze in earnest. "Desperately. But you . . . you haven't even asked me. Not for real, I mean."

An unamused smile pulls at my lips. "Ah, you want a proper proposal, I see."

She nods vehemently.

I lean back in my seat once more, releasing her hand as my voice goes flat. "Is this hesitation about the other night? Your newfound powers? Your immortality?"

"What? No." She shakes her head. "I was unfair to you then. I was just . . . shocked by what you told me your Mother said, and I took my anger out on you when I shouldn't have. I know you didn't have any more say in her toying with our lives than I did, and what I'm really angry at is this whole . . ."—she gestures around us—"this whole situation."

I lift a brow.

"Being made from one of your bones like I'm not even my own person. Like my only purpose is to be your wife and make babies. You know, a Quiverfull theology. Like I had no real choice in the matter.

Just like with Mark. Not to mention the *apocalypse*." Her eyes go intentionally wide to emphasize the word. "I wasn't imagining what I overheard your Mother say. That really is the reason your Father let you out. Just like you said it was, isn't it?"

I give a reluctant nod. "I'm afraid so."

She blanches slightly. "We have to do something to stop it. We have to—"

"No."

She falls silent immediately.

The tone I use brooks no room for discussion.

"But—"

"I am handling this. For your own safety, you will stay out of this."

"You can't be serious. You can't possibly expect me to sit by and not—"

My expression turns cold. "Do you truly think it wise, considering the other night? How you reacted to my Mother's news of us being fated? Your powers?"

Charlotte tenses, her lower lip quivering before she glances down at her hands. "Maybe you're right. Maybe I don't have what it takes."

With my free hand, I lift my whisky, taking a slow sip. "The apocalypse does not happen overnight. For now, you will leave this and my family to me."

I stroke my thumb over her palm soothingly, where her hand continues to rest in mine. A small attempt to remind her of all I have given, of all she is to me, until finally she whispers, "Sometimes it feels like I . . . like I traded my old life for almost the same thing. Like I didn't spend enough time on my own after escaping Mark and my father to know what I truly wanted before . . ."

I stiffen.

Her voice trails off as she forces a watery smile, but it fades quickly. "I escaped that life for a reason, Lucifer." She lifts her gaze to mine, her expression almost pleading. "Please don't make me do it again."

My resolve softens. "Is this where your hesitation about our wedding lies?"

"No. No, this is about you and me doing it on *our* terms. The right way. For real this time."

For real. As if she still believes this is all a game to me.

After everything I sacrificed for her.

"And was it real enough when I gave up my Father's redemption for you?" I ask, my amusement fading. "When I killed your father so that when we fuck and you call me Daddy, you can no longer feel guilty? Tell me."

She blushes furiously, but the frustration I feel barreling through our connection undercuts any pleasure I might have felt at the sight of it.

"That's not fair," she whispers.

I scowl. "I'll tell you what isn't fair." I lean across the table, the hellfire I feel in my eyes blazing. "Fair isn't you bringing me to heel every time you bat your pretty little lashes. Fair isn't me sacrificing the *one* thing I've ever truly wanted, all for the love of you, only for you to tell me that you fear me."

Her breath stops short, her mouth parted slightly as she stares at me. As if she's just now realizing how thoroughly she's hurt me.

I do fear you.

Her thoughts scream down the line between us, even as the gentleness in her eyes continues to lie to me.

Fear how much you mean—

But I slam the door shut between us, unwilling to hear anything further.

"I was hurt," she says softly, shaking her head. "I just need time to adjust to all these changes, that's all. I . . . I didn't mean—"

"And what else didn't you mean?" I sneer. "What other empty human promises are lost now that you've decided to make me your Judas?"

"I don't blame you. I—"

My fist connects with the table, the glassware shaking as my voice turns cold. "Don't lie to me."

The restaurant falls silent again.

Charlotte's eyes go wide, and for a moment she says nothing. She simply stares at me, her chin barely quivering before finally she whispers, "Fine. I won't." Abruptly she stands, tossing her napkin onto the table. "I can't do this with you right now. I can't." She stalks away, heading toward the elevator.

But I don't make a habit of giving my employees the last word.

"Don't bother to wait up for me this evening," I say coolly, throwing back the rest of my whisky.

The screams from Hell tonight will be particularly damning.

Charlotte watches me for a beat, for once the hurt and longing in her eyes making me uncertain, making me question if I have done the right thing.

In a way I never would have asked myself before.

Resentment coils like a poisonous viper inside me.

"I wouldn't have anyway," she whispers before she turns and leaves.

Leaving me alone with nothing but an empty table, an empty drink, and a heart nearly as hollow as it used to be.

CHAPTER EIGHT

Charlotte

I find Imani waiting for me on the ground floor. Olivia, my hired body double, is beside her, dressed in a replica of the custom Dior dress I'm wearing.

"Olivia, could you give us a moment please?"

Olivia smiles before she wanders to the other side of the empty lobby. Lucifer makes a habit of renting out the whole place wherever we go. A small attempt to give us a passing chance at privacy. My face heats at the thought of the concerned waitstaff gawking at us a few minutes ago.

So much for that.

Once Olivia is out of earshot, Imani nods toward the elevator to indicate where Lucifer waits on the sixty-fifth floor. "What the hell was that?"

"Never mind," I say, another embarrassed flush filling my cheeks. "I'll explain later."

"And you no longer being human? You'll explain that too?"

My eyes go wide, a sudden feeling of heaviness settling inside me. "He told you, apparently?"

"Charlotte." She drops her head, closing her eyes and exhaling through her nose like she's trying to find patience. "Please tell me it isn't true. Please tell me you didn't agree to that."

I swallow. "It's . . . complicated."

Imani knows the big picture of what happened following the Met Gala, of course. Mark's attack, Astaroth's betrayal, and then the unexpected death threat against me. Everyone on Lucifer's immediate team does. Not to mention there's been loads of speculation about it all in the media. But Lucifer and I thought it best we keep the more . . . celestial details between him and me. No one knows the true nature of the threat, that it was anthrax, except for us.

And whoever sent it, of course.

Another decision I'm suddenly doubting.

"Another time," I say, placing a reassuring hand on her arm as I swallow the lump that's formed in my throat. I hate to see her disappointed in me. "But can you meet me for coffee on Thursday? I want to discuss this whole PR-proposal thing."

"You really think pushing him on this is a good idea?" She quirks a brow at me.

But the question doesn't faze me.

I know she values my opinion. She always has.

It's one of the many things I admire about Imani. Even when I was nothing more than a fresh-faced intern with no idea what was in store for me, she still considered me and my opinions, treated me like I was a valuable member of the team.

Though we both knew I didn't deserve to be there.

It's the most grace anyone has ever given me.

I look down, dropping my hands to my sides as I realize I've been wringing them together repeatedly. The whole thing feels a little pathetic in the face of an impending apocalypse. Futile, if Lucifer doesn't put a stop to everything his family's doing. But I can't help but think this is the one thing I know how to do, the one thing I know I can control.

"I've had to prove myself to him before. What's one time more?"

Imani's face softens. "I think you've forgotten how that first time went."

No doubt she means my very first executive meeting, the one where, following my presentation, Lucifer embarrassed me like never before. But in retrospect, it was *him* who was truly embarrassed.

By his own private admissions, since he wanted me even then.

I blush slightly at the memory.

"Hindsight is twenty-twenty." I shrug. "My idea worked out in the end."

"But at what cost?" Imani lifts another brow.

She means the leaked press release. The one that sealed my fate.

The one that eventually led to my lost humanity.

"Worse things have happened to me than having to fake date Lucifer." I offer a small smile, but it fades quickly.

How I feel about him has never been anything close to fake.

Would he say the same?

I glance down at my hands, suddenly ashamed of the doubt that fills me.

"You say that now that you're sitting on the throne he's given you." Imani shakes her head, but then she takes my hand, giving it a reassuring squeeze. "He's trying to protect you, you know. With this branding thing. In his own twisted way."

His "own way," meaning Lucifer calling the shots on my future career.

Without consulting me.

Another choice that should have been mine to make.

Fate be damned.

I shouldn't be surprised, I guess. Our Dom-sub dynamic is now a twenty-four seven thing, bleeding into all parts of our lives, our careers included. But I took for granted the idea that he would have consulted me on something as significant to my future as this.

Communication in our lifestyle is key.

I bite down on the inside of my cheek, struggling to fend off tears.

At least he's giving me the chance to say my piece. Convince him my ideas are worth the investment. It *is* his money, after all. Even if I've more than earned every penny he's given me.

"Just bring those investor proposals we talked about on Thursday," I say to Imani, giving her a tight smile. "Please?"

"You're asking for trouble trying to go behind his back on this, Charlotte. He's already given his answer, and you know he doesn't want outside investors."

My mouth goes dry, my ribs tightening.

Am I?

For a moment, I doubt myself . . .

But then blood rushes to my ears at the thought of how long he suspected we were fated and didn't tell me. Where was his protection then?

My chest expands on a full breath, strengthening me. "It's no different than what he'd do to me."

Imani gives me a side-eyed look. "If you insist. But I won't keep your secret. Not if he asks."

"I understand."

As a mentor, she's already done more for me than I could ever reasonably expect her to.

"See you, Thursday." Imani's nod is decisive as she watches me from the corner of her eye—like she's seeing a whole new side of me—before finally she shakes her head and exits out onto Sixth Avenue.

Olivia is at my side a second later, like a reflection.

"Ready to leave?" she asks, her smile cheery.

She slips down the Miu Miu sunglasses on top of her head, a copy of my favorite pair, though it's dark outside—their only purpose is to hide her identity. I glance toward the exit. Rockefeller Center's lights shine overhead, illuminating where the paparazzi wait, but even this close, it's uncanny how much she looks like me. The golden highlights in her hair. The red undertones of her cheeks.

She could easily be me.

We found her off a private casting call that some of Jax's Broadway friends helped organize to place some distance between her connection to Lucifer and me.

It didn't even take a week.

Olivia smiles, waiting for my response, her expression genuine and sweet.

Maybe in another lifetime she and I could have been friends. She clearly wants to be. We're the same age, the same height, the same body type, and now with Sophie and Xzander's assistance, the same everything.

Down to the tiniest details.

Except for the whole her being human, and me being, well . . .

Divine—the memory of Lucifer's voice echoes inside my head.

Or whatever it is that I'm becoming.

I offer her a return smile, but it fades quickly.

How easy would it be for Lucifer to replace me?

For his Mother to make someone *else* for him?

I clutch my purse closer to my chest. "Yeah," I mumble, too quiet. "Yeah, I'm ready."

Her grin fades. She seems disappointed at my clipped response, at the distance it places between her and me, but it's better this way. Safer. For us both.

But then she's back to smiling again. Ever the ray of sunshine.

Just like she was hired to be.

Her job is to smile for the press, after all. Be the perfect me. Something that's starting to feel like an impossible task these days.

"All right then. Your call." She gives me a bubbly wave. "See you tomorrow?"

I nod weakly.

I stand out of sight as she heads through the exit door, unsurprised at the flashes that light up outside the center. The sounds of clicking camera shutters and the paparazzi shouting my name follow. But I stand in the background, watching until the door seals shut.

She really could be me.

A short time after Olivia leaves, I exit through the second entrance on the concourse level of 30 Rockefeller Plaza along with several members of the security team, the silence in the mostly empty city center a welcome reprieve.

It isn't until I ask Dagon to drive me toward mine and Jax's old apartment in Chinatown that I start to truly question if I'm doing the right thing.

Or if taking control of my own future is just as underhanded as Imani believes it to be.

CHAPTER NINE

Lucifer

I'm out on the roof at the Top of the Rock, smoking a cigarette as I overlook Fifth Avenue when Wrath and Azmodeus finally decide to join me. "Took you long enough."

Azmodeus rocks on his heels. "We like to leave you guessing when you summon us, of course. Remind you you're only in charge because we want you to be."

The side of Wrath's mouth quirks in agreement, and my attention cuts toward him.

My youngest brother isn't a man of many words. Simply because he chooses not to be. He far prefers his actions speak for him, and the trail of violence, bloodshed, and war left in his wake speaks volumes. The American military and CIA wouldn't be nearly as volatile, nor as overreaching, if it weren't for the quiet influence of Wrath and his many oil and aerospace holdings. Though to the public, arms, defense, and information security are what he deals in, technically. Not that anyone ever bothers to follow the money.

Humans will sell their souls to line their own pockets.

They're every bit as utilitarian as I told Father they would be.

"So, who are we going to be fucking tonight?" Azmodeus says, plucking my cigarette pack from my inside pocket and bumming one before he extends both it and my lighter to me. "Or don't tell me you and Mammon are both on the rag again. What a fucking bore."

"The Righteous, unfortunately." I take a long drag, exhaling, considering all that those bloody bastards and my fiancée's pitiful excuse for an ex-husband did to her.

He never deserved the title of ex *anything*, didn't deserve to lick the ground beneath her feet, while meanwhile, *I* would do or give anything. And for what?

"We're not even engaged. Not for real."

My jaw tightens. "Charlotte needs to know that I will protect her. Always."

Azmodeus nods. "Took you long enough."

I cast him an unamused look as I snatch my lighter from his outstretched hand, pocketing it coolly. "Mother paid me a visit recently." I inhale another drag from my cigarette.

"Did she?" Wrath grumbles, the deep timbre of his voice matching the Black human form he's chosen for this century. A statement about exactly which humans are most likely to be unfairly punished for his sin, I suppose.

A little too on the nose, if you ask me.

I toss down the last of my cigarette, stomping it out beneath my shoe. "She seems to believe Father tires of humanity."

"And?" Azmodeus shrugs as if this whole thing is painfully obvious. But it's Wrath who nods appreciatively. "Do you believe her?"

Azmodeus places a mocking hand over his heart, his eyebrows raised in feigned shock. "Brother, you aren't actually suggesting that *our* loving Mother of all goddesses would choose to sow discord between us for her own means?" He blusters, looking temporarily affronted, before his mouth fades into a wicked smile.

Wrath snorts loudly. "And to think you're one of the ones she favors."

I give them both a warning look. "I care less about whether it's true and more about *who* believes it to be."

"You mean our angelic siblings?" Az lifts a brow.

Wrath stands silent for a moment, watching me with his arms crossed. "You don't truly think Michael would lead them to—"

"That's exactly what I think." I flick the ashes of my second cigarette.

"Well, that'd certainly make things more interesting, wouldn't it?" Wrath scratches at his stubbled jaw. "Except for when it comes to your pet."

"His little *human*, you mean?" This from Az.

The shadows across the rooftop twist and curl, nipping at Azmodeus's heels. "Call her human one more time, brother." The burn of hellfire flashes in my eyes.

"She *was* human." Azmodeus grins. "Until recently."

"Not any longer," I growl.

"Touchy, touchy," Azmodeus taunts.

"And what *exactly* is she now, Lucy?" Wrath takes a purposeful stride toward me, crowding my space as only he would dare as he makes a show of straightening my tie for me. "We all grow impatient waiting for the answer, you see."

My siblings are more than eager to bear witness to Charlotte's budding abilities, and if any one of them ever dared to believe they could reclaim the bit of my Father's power I gifted her, well . . .

An image of what could be flashes through my mind, my jaw tightening.

All the more reason I need to get out in front of this.

Already Death nearly stole her from me once.

I won't allow it to happen again.

"And you'll have it," I say, smiling coolly as I take Wrath by the shoulders. "All in due time."

Wrath steps back to his rightful place, capitulating.

For now, at least.

Azmodeus brushes something from my shoulder. "Don't forget, big brother, you still owe *me* another favor, you know."

A yet unnamed favor.

I don't need Azmodeus's little reminder to know that particular debt will cost me. I incline my head toward him. "And you'll receive your payment in full when the time comes."

"And Michael? The others?" Wrath mutters beside me.

Our angelic siblings, he means.

"Deal with the Righteous and Mother. Find out what she's up to." I turn, grinding out the last of my cigarette as I step into the ether. "Leave Michael and the others to me."

CHAPTER TEN

Charlotte

A short while later, we pull up outside The Happy Dumpling, the Chinese restaurant housed below mine and Jax's apartment, and to my surprise Dagon manages to snag a spot directly outside the storefront. I exit the vehicle, a member of the security team in tow, only to be met by an elderly Asian woman, who leans out the restaurant door, shouting at me in Chinese. She gestures wildly toward the car.

"Sorry, Mrs. Huang," I call to her, wincing at how furious she looks before I signal for Dagon to circle the block or park somewhere else while he waits for me.

Miller and Garcia, who I'm pretty sure are both ex-military, if they're even human, exit the second detail car that blocks the street. They come up onto the sidewalk to flank me.

Clearly, I'm not even allowed to go into my own apartment alone anymore.

With a surreptitious glance, I approach the door that leads to mine and Jax's second-story flat. Mrs. Huang watches me warily, her arms crossed over her chest.

"Fo' customers," she says in heavily accented English, pointing to the now-empty street parking.

I make an apologetic expression. "Sorry, Mrs. Huang. It won't happen again."

She makes a little harrumph noise like she doesn't exactly believe me, but then she smiles as soon as I flash the black company Mastercard Lucifer gave me.

Twenty minutes later I'm loaded up with enough Chinese food to feed the whole security team and then some, as well as Jax and me.

I pass some of the food to Miller for the other members of the team—who I'm not entirely certain *need* to eat, but I figure it's polite to offer anyway—before I heft the remaining food bag onto one hip and make my way up the narrow, drooping stairs. Mine and Jax's apartment used to be an old tenement building, and despite that it and the storefront below have been refurbished plenty of times since, it shows.

When I reach the top, it takes me a moment to find my keys buried at the bottom of my Louboutin purse with Garcia watching me like a hawk from only two steps below. He lifts a waxy paper bag stuffed with egg rolls in thanks, the little red dragon on the outside crinkling. I manage to find my keys a few seconds later, and I shove the right one into the lock and twist.

The door opens, and a loud burst of music greets me.

"Charlotte, what are you doing here?" Jax smiles from ear to ear before tapping off whatever Spotify playlist she was playing. She hurries across the room to help me with the bags.

I open my mouth, almost ready to say, *Why wouldn't I be here?*

After all, it's my apartment too.

Though honestly, I haven't been around much in a few weeks. I'm still paying rent, and all my old stuff is here, but even in my head, saying so sounds bitchy, and the other two faces on the sofa stop me.

Ian and Evie.

"Charlotte!" Evie comes up off the sofa to quickly kiss both my cheeks. A habit I think she picked up from her late Moroccan model of a mom, who, based on the photos I've seen, could've pretty much been her twin.

I finish greeting her, closing the door before I'm forced to face Ian.

"Hi," I say, lifting my hand awkwardly.

"Hi," he says, like he isn't exactly pleased to see me.

We both stand there for a strained beat.

The last time we were together, Ian made it pretty clear he had feelings for me.

Feelings that I . . . don't reciprocate.

And no matter how kind he's been or how unfounded, I still can't squash my sneaking suspicions that he may have been more involved when Jax was drugged at Azmodeus's club than he seemed to be.

We never did find out who did it and why.

I force a weird smile, not knowing whether to hug him and try to play it friendly or leave our cringy greeting at that. Finally he turns to say something to Evie that I don't really register. I nearly sigh in relief.

Good. Now that we've gotten that out of the way.

I turn my attention back toward Jax, who makes an exaggerated yikes face and mouths the word *awkward* now that Ian's not looking before she pulls me in for a squeezy hug.

"So, what are you doing here?" she says. "Don't tell me you were just in the neighborhood."

I glance toward our other two friends, unsure how much I want to share in front of them. "I just thought I'd come home for the night, that's all."

The words settle over the room like a wet blanket.

Jax and Evie look toward one another uncertainly.

"Oh," Jax says, her voice a bit more high pitched than usual. "Oh sure, it's just . . . Evie needed a place to crash, and since you haven't been here in a few weeks, we figured—"

"That I could stay on your side of the room," Evie finishes. "No biggie."

"Of course," I say, a little too fast to be convincing. "Of course. You're more than welcome to it, Evie."

I glance between them, meaning to say something more, but I must take a second too long, because Jax gives a tense clear of her throat before she says, "I sent you a text earlier. To ask if it was okay, I mean, but you didn't get back to me."

"It's totally okay." I nod. "My notifications have been crazy. Don't worry about it." I wave a hand, trying to look like I don't mind, but even to myself, I sound unconvincing.

My throat tightens painfully.

It's not as if there aren't plenty of spare beds I could use in the penthouse, even if I don't want to sleep alone in Lucifer's bedroom tonight.

I just . . . wanted space, that's all.

Somewhere I could call my own.

My chest grows heavy, the pressure there that never seems to go away lately making it harder to breathe.

Don't bother to wait up. Lucifer's words echo through me.

Which means he'll likely be in Hell all night. Or wherever else it is that he disappears to these days. I'm not entirely certain where he's been running off to, actually.

"You're more than welcome to it, Evie," I add, trying my best to sound reassuring, though as I glance toward her, suddenly I realize why she didn't ask me if she could take one of the rooms at the penthouse in the first place. "Oh my God, you did it, didn't you?"

She nods, pressing her lips together before she slowly grins. She launches herself into my arms then, both of us squealing.

Evie finally made her move to temporarily disappear, to get off the media's radar and out from beneath her older brother's thumb. As New York City's former "it" girl and a professional model turned influencer, to the unknowing eye, Evie appears to have everything, but it didn't take long knowing her for me to recognize that her fame came at a price. A price demanded by the Russian bratva down in Brighton Beach, their off-the-books operations run by her father and her ultra-controlling older brother, Dmitry.

"I wouldn't have been brave enough without your encouragement, you know," she whispers to me, sounding uncharacteristically grateful.

I grip her tighter, a sense of pride filling me.

Escaping that kind of toxic, insular life isn't easy. I know that firsthand.

Though what exactly did it cost her?

I don't ask as I pull back from our hug, her eyes momentarily settling on me as a haunted kind of knowing passes between us.

It's the look of survivors, of those who've had the courage to escape.

I only hope that Evie doesn't land herself with yet another villain like I did.

A lump forms in my throat, and I swallow past it, turning away quickly. The memory of my father, of Mark, and of all the members of their congregation who hurt me still haunts me.

Only for me to find myself in Lucifer's waiting arms in the end.

I guess I really am as wicked as they said I'd be.

I frown, pushing the errant thought aside.

"Good for you, Evie," I say as I turn my attention back toward helping Jax unload our takeout.

I'm happy they've connected. I am, truly. I introduced the two of them a few weeks ago when Evie needed entertainment for an A-list celebrity party. Jax was more than willing to do a few readings for Evie and her famous friends, especially at the astronomically generous rate Evie was offering. As an aspiring Broadway actress and a psychic by trade, these days Jax knows how to entertain even the most glamorous crowds. She's a far cry from her days busking for tourists in Times Square, which is how we met actually.

I catch her eye, and she smiles knowingly. Sometimes I wonder if she realizes how much her kindness then still means to me. I'd had barely any money when I first showed up in the city, and at NYC prices, only enough to float me for maybe a month or two, at most.

I'd been standing in the middle of the street, half awestruck, half overwhelmed by the enormity of it all—by the skyscrapers, the savory smell of the food carts on the corner serving Nathan's hot dogs, the hundreds of people, the massive flashing billboards—uncertain where to go or what to do next now that I'd made it to safety.

Or what I thought was safe, at least.

All I knew back then was that Times Square was somewhere I could get a hotel, even if it would cost me.

I stare up at the flashing neon signs, at the vast living thing that is New York City, my mouth going dry at the sights before me.

I can be literally anybody now. Anybody I choose to be.

I take a step back and bump into something hard, nearly knocking it over. A card table. And a girl, the contents of her table now scattered.

Oh crap.

"I'm sorry. I'm so sorry." *I scramble to help the girl sitting there pick up her cards. A Tarot deck. A pile of them have fluttered across the table and down near her feet.*

But she simply smiles at me. "The Wheel of Fortune reversed," *she says, pointing to one of the few that fell face up on the table near me.*

I'd been instantly transfixed by her "witchery." By what I'd been taught my whole life is the work of the devil. After all . . .

Thou shalt have no other gods before me.

Though these days, those words hit a little different.

"Followed by the Chariot." *She points to a detailed image of a pharaoh flanked by a black and white sphinx.* "And lastly . . ." *She points to the final card, though another still sits unrevealed, in her hand.* "The Devil."

A slow smile builds on her lips as she watches me curiously. "We're going to be very good friends, I think."

Several hours later she was letting me into her apartment, renting me a place to stay, at least temporarily, though temporary turned into permanent quickly.

That's just the kind of person Jax is.

She makes fast friends wherever she goes, trusts fiercely, jumps first and asks questions later. She's more courageous than I'll ever be.

She smiles at me, almost like she knows what I'm thinking.

We're ride or die now. True besties.

A knot forms in my stomach.

Even if I . . . haven't been a very good friend to her lately.

Ian joins us at the counter a second later, oblivious to my reminiscing. "Mind if I take one of these to go?" he asks, snagging a small, unclaimed container and giving it a little shake. He's looked a bit put out ever since I arrived.

"You're leaving?" Jax makes an exaggerated pouty face. "But you just got here."

I glance between them reluctantly.

She's denied it at every turn, but I think if he were interested, Jax would date Ian in a heartbeat.

He looks down at his phone, clearly too distracted to notice her disappointment. "I need to swing by my place to get changed before my shift starts."

His shift at The Body Shoppe. One of Azmodeus's clubs.

I flush at the memory.

"I'll leave you ladies to it." Ian makes a few quick goodbyes, giving me a stiff nod with a muttered, "Mrs. Lucifer," before he ducks out of the apartment.

The moment the door swings shuts behind him, a pang of guilt runs through me.

"Sorry to make it awkward," I mumble to Jax and Evie.

Jax waves a hand. "It's fine. It's *his* problem." She shrugs, but the way her hands flutter over the food anxiously like she's now completely lost track of what she's doing says it's anything but.

"You don't owe any man your attention, Charlotte." Evie frowns at Jax, seemingly annoyed by her disappointment. "Not even the nice ones."

Evie is model-level gorgeous—not that Jax isn't also ridiculously pretty—but Evie comes from money and has the looks to prove it. She likely knows a thing or two about thwarting unwanted attention, male or otherwise. She wouldn't understand the kind of swipe-left dating scene Jax is facing.

I nod, searching for a change in subject.

Anything that'll make this visit feel more normal.

But as I dish up my plate, I can't help but feel that Jax is just . . . yet another person I've disappointed lately.

CHAPTER ELEVEN

Charlotte

The three of us settle into an easy conversation after that, the warmth of the Chinese food and Jax and Evie's laughter making me feel truly at home for the first time in weeks. It isn't until Jax and I are boxing up the last of the leftover containers and trying to make space for them in the too-tiny fridge that the conversation finally turns to Lucifer and me.

"So, what's going on between you two?" Jax asks. "These days you're only ever here when something's wrong."

"That's not true," I mumble, shoving a bit of half-eaten wonton into my mouth, but the yeah-right look Jax gives me coupled with Evie's sly grin in agreement let me know in no uncertain terms that I've been a shitty friend lately.

A familiar pang of guilt races through me.

I haven't found the right moment to confess everything that happened between Lucifer and me after the Met Gala just yet. Sure, Jax knows some of the details, the sort of things anyone on social media knows, but how do you explain to your bestie that you died, but it's okay, because your literal devil of a boyfriend remade you with God's redemption and you're immortal now? No biggie.

Yeah, not the easiest of conversation openers.

And that doesn't even cover the whole "we're barreling toward apocalyptic doom" part.

Jax takes one of the containers from my hand, her fingers accidentally brushing my palm as I start to apologize, but at my touch, her whole body goes rigid.

She drops the container, the lo mein noodles splattering all over the floor.

"Jax? Jax?" I rush around the counter toward her as her eyes go distant and hazy, almost like she's about to pass out, or . . . like she's in some kind of trance.

I grip her shoulders, giving her a little shake to try and snap her out of it and get her to look at me, but she isn't budging. Beside us, Evie freezes, like she isn't certain what to do, but a violent shudder runs through Jax from head to toe and then she blinks, coming back to herself only a moment later.

Evie and I exchange confused glances.

"Are . . . you okay?" I ask her, concern furrowing my brow.

But Evie is already staring at Jax as if she's her latest party novelty. Her eyes flash with interest. "Oh my God! Was that like a vision or something?" She claps her hands together excitedly.

Like she truly believes this whole psychic thing.

Who knows, maybe she does? Celebrity influencers have believed stranger things.

Honestly, I've never really given Jax's psychic work much thought. She's a performer, whether onstage or at a card table, or so I figured.

Until now, actually.

And who am *I* to judge, considering who I'm dating?

"What did you see?" Evie squeals as I mutter a low, "You okay?"

"It's nothing," Jax says, waving us off. "It was nothing."

But I don't miss the wary glance she casts toward me.

A few minutes later, after several reassurances from Jax that she's all right and her brain just sort of glitched or something, the rest of the takeout is put away, and once the spilled lo mein noodles are up off the floor, the conversation returns to Lucifer and me.

"So, what *is* going on with you two anyway?" Evie says dreamily. "Give us the real version. None of the nonsense all over my socials."

The "nonsense" being that things between Lucifer and I are better than ever. Even if I'm currently mourning the loss of my father. There's been a lot of speculation about what I shared at the funeral. About how my father's congregation and their "alleged" abuse might have helped push me into Lucifer's arms.

Imani's worked to make sure most of the articles paint us in a positive way. With Lucifer as my valiant savior, and me playing, well . . . the role of the disadvantaged victim.

I force a cough, trying to hide my disgust at the thought.

Is that what I've been doing lately? By refusing to embrace my immortality? Letting my public image bleed into my private life?

How the press sees me is so far from the truth that it doesn't even deserve the few moments' consideration I'm forced to give it each day, though that says nothing for the several kill notices Imani's had to send to keep some of the nastier conspiracy theories and conjecture at bay.

Every employee on Apollyon's legal team has been working overtime.

"There's not much to it, really." I launch into a shortened explanation about our disagreement over the PR firm, though I keep the finer details to a minimum, considering Evie has access to her *own* private PR team, not that she's currently in contact with them. She's off the grid totally.

While her brother's still searching for her, at least.

When I finish, she nods. "I think Lucifer's right," she says in her usual breathy tone. "Why run a PR firm when you could be launching your own brands? Building your own empire?"

Jax rolls her eyes. "Maybe because Charlotte doesn't *want* an empire. Not everyone loves being in the limelight that way you do, Evie. Isn't that right, Charlotte?" She says it with such conviction—like she knows me better than anyone—that I have to fight hard not to wince when she looks at me.

Her eyes widen, darting between me and Evie like she's truly seeing the similarities between us for the very first time, and Evie and I may have more in common than she thinks.

"That's not entirely true, actually?" I mumble, more than a little ashamed to admit it.

My father worked hard to instill the exact opposite in me.

Women in our congregation were meant to be seen, not heard. One of his lessons that never really stuck, I guess. No matter how many times he punished me.

Jax's mouth opens and closes a few times. "You're telling me you *enjoy* this whole circus? The death threats? The unwanted attention it's getting you?"

"Death threats aside, who wouldn't?" Evie shrugs as if being in the limelight is the most natural thing in the world.

To her, it no doubt feels that way.

For Evie, the temporary loss of fame she'll endure for cutting ties with her brother will be only a minor blow. She'll likely come roaring back into the spotlight stronger and better than ever. Women like her always do. She was meant for this.

But maybe, thanks to Lilith, I'm more like Evie than I thought?

"Yes, and no?" I shrug, answering Jax's question. I think of the anthrax, of how we still don't know who sent it, yet here I am, still living and breathing. "It's . . . complicated."

Everything in my life is lately. Sometimes, I miss the simplicity of when I wasn't anything more than Lucifer's intern.

Goddamn fate.

"There's nothing complicated about all the death threats you've been receiving," Jax says, her lips pursed in frustration, but I know that underneath it, she's just concerned for me.

She has my back. She always does.

"That's easy to say when you've never received that level of attention," Evie says.

But I hear the unspoken words underneath.

When what little self-esteem you have has been built on the back of the praise you receive, of how you can be of service to others . . .

The limelight is addicting.

Another part of my life shaped by my father's design.

Or Lilith's? I'm not sure which anymore.

I'm not sure about anything.

I glance toward Jax, gauging her reaction, and from the I-can't-believe-you're-siding-with-her look she gives me, suddenly I feel a chasm open up between her and me.

One where celebrities like Lucifer's siblings and Evie are on one side, and mere mortals like Jax and Ramesh are on the other.

The fault line that was drawn when Lucifer chose me.

A sinking feeling pulls at me.

Maybe Lucifer didn't need to make me immortal in order to change my life forever.

Maybe he'd already done it the moment he fell for me . . .

"That's enough," I say, trying to shut this conversation down, but the thought still twists my stomach into knots. "I don't want to talk about this anymore."

"Look, all I'm saying is you came here because you need our help, obviously. That's what you wanted, right? Advice?" Evie's fearless diva attitude cuts through the tension, almost as if she's blissfully unaware of it. Or maybe it's that she thrives on it. The drama. The gossip.

That's the thing about Evie.

She may appear to be all innocent and dreamy, but when push comes to shove, she's more devious than I'll ever be.

A product of the violent, glamorous world she was raised in.

A world I'm now a part of. Like it or not.

I nod reluctantly, trying to brush off her comment but failing. "Yeah, I guess so."

But it's Jax's advice that I truly want. The comforting embrace of my bestie.

Not this collision between my two worlds that Evie being here brings.

Unaware of my internal war, Evie gives me a stern look that I think is meant to be encouraging but ends up being somewhere closer to *Oh, girl, please.*

"It's simple, really," she says, shrugging off my concerns as if multimillion-dollar investments and billionaire boyfriends are no major thing. "If you want to survive in our world, Charlotte, to prove your worth to Lucifer"—she spears me with an unscrupulous look that, paired with Jax shaking her head in the background, feels strangely foreboding—"all you have to do is show him how vicious you can be."

CHAPTER TWELVE

Lucifer

The sound of my footsteps echoes inside the abandoned diner car, the decaying countertop barely keeping me upright where I lean against it. I light a cigarette, inhaling deeply, before I slump down onto the checkered floor. Somewhere amidst all the chaos this evening, my shirt was torn, and the sheen of sweat that drips from my hair and torso likely make it look as if I've been swimming in one of Hell's more fiery lakes.

Torture is a physical thing.

Astaroth lies underneath the table of a dilapidated booth nearby, his bloodied, mangled form and the chains that bind him strewn across the bottom of the booth's empty wooden child's seat. The chains are for show, really.

This is my realm. My domain.

And here, I am more than a king.

I am a god of my own making.

The end of my cigarette flares, and I flick some of the ashes onto the grease-coated floor, watching as they char a hole into a bit of spilled sugar that's escaped from a cracked glass dispenser. All the New Jersey diner's original contents are still here, replicated for my own amusement. A nice touch of detail, if you ask me.

"She's going to regret it, you know," Astaroth rasps, his voice a garbled, disparate thing.

From where I poured boiling fry oil down his throat, only for him to heal so I could do it all again several times over. The methods of humanity's medieval period still inspire me.

Even if they *did* blame me for their disgusting little plagues.

I wrinkle my nose.

"*Hmph?*" I grunt, barely acknowledging him as I take another long drag, only half listening.

My pulse is still settling from how I've exerted myself tonight, but I'll be ready for round two shortly.

Astaroth was simply a warm-up.

Even if the information he's harboring is integral to my plan.

He turns his head toward me, the movement a disturbing and uncanny loll thanks to all the ways I've broken him. And will continue to do so for centuries. Longer even.

However long it takes to appease me, considering the bloody bastard went and betrayed me, sold Charlotte to the Righteous for dead.

And for what?

The pressure in my jaw tightens.

It's one of the few questions that continues to plague me.

"You," Astaroth rasps, coughing up yet another bit of blood. The kitchen floor is practically soaked in it. "She'll regret you eventually. Give it time."

Charlotte, he means.

I stiffen, my cigarette suddenly crushed in two.

The truth in those words coils in me.

"Perhaps." I feign a calm I do not feel as I stare past him, my expression distant.

I relight what's left of my cigarette, inhaling one last pull and rising to my feet, before I casually make my way toward him. The broken glass on the diner floor crunches beneath my Armanis. At my approach, he recoils, attempting to wriggle away, but in Hell there is nowhere beyond my reach, nowhere to escape me.

I seize him by the hair, stubbing the last of my cigarette out on the whites of his eyes as he screams. His aren't the only cries that will chorus through Hell tonight.

"You'll lose her!" he shrieks, his voice growing louder. "She'll regret you, trust me!"

I cast him onto the floor beneath me.

"You think she won't turn to His side?" he rasps. "After everything?"

Once she learns what I've done, he means.

All that I've planned. The truth of her power.

I abandon my stubbed-out cigarette in one of the diner's ashtrays as I drive the hard part of my shoe into the bloody mass where his balls should be, causing him to black out.

"She already has," I muse into the quiet, mulling over the idea as I perch on one of the old, rusted barstools. "But I suppose by then, it'll be too late, really."

CHAPTER THIRTEEN

Charlotte

I head back to the penthouse a short while later, Evie's words still ringing in my ears, but it isn't until I'm halfway to the glass staircase, my heels stripped off and my dress partially unzipped, that I realize I'm not alone.

I turn and face the woman before me. "Who the hell are you?"

She's wearing a tailored Ralph Lauren blazer dress that's unbuttoned low enough to show off a generous amount of braless cleavage. She glances up from the tablet she's holding. "Oh, I'm Mia. Lucifer's house manager." She shrugs dismissively.

"House manager?"

I've been practically living here for over a month, and I've never once laid eyes on this woman.

Ramesh passes through and gives me a courteous nod in greeting, utterly nonplussed by her presence. Which I guess means that she *is* supposed to be here. She wouldn't have made it past the security team otherwise. After the anthrax situation, everyone and everything that comes in or out of the penthouse is thoroughly screened.

"Oh," I mumble, trying my best not to look as embarrassed as I feel as I extend a now friendly hand toward her. I can't be too careful lately. "I'm—"

"I know who you are," she says curtly, giving me all of a two-second glance before she turns back to her tablet. "It's part of my job, obviously."

I frown. Amid the marble floors and custom-art furniture, she's statuesque. Like a sculpture in a gallery, more poised than I am currently.

A knot forms in my belly, my jaw set.

"And why haven't I seen you before?" I ask, my pitch going a bit high at the end.

"It's a big penthouse." She doesn't bother to glance up from her tablet.

Like that's all the explanation I need.

I tilt my head, studying her as I mentally weigh her response. "Lucifer's never mentioned you." A detail that now seems suspect on several levels. Especially when he's not here.

Finally, she sighs, giving me a glassy, blank-eyed stare. "It's my job to be discreet." Her eyes flick over me. "Unlike some people."

I jerk back, my mouth falling open. "Excuse me?"

But Evie's warning pulses through me.

Be vicious, Charlotte.

Abruptly, my body language changes from shock to brutal indifference. Like she's nothing to me. She *is* nothing to me.

That dark thing Lucifer unleashed inside me writhes.

I stare down the bridge of my nose. "And what *exactly* is it that you do here?"

My tone sounds like Lucifer's. Like she couldn't be further beneath me.

"I manage all Lucifer's household *affairs*." The fake, cheeky smile she gives me radiates superiority as she eyes me up and down. "Long before you got here."

I don't miss the way her cruel, red-lipped smile seems to linger on the word *affairs* a little too long. Like she's trying to sow a seed of doubt in me.

A seed of doubt I'd never even bothered to entertain until now.

Lucifer is loyal to me.

Isn't he?

I cock my head to the side and force a smile. "Of course. It makes so much sense that he wouldn't mention you then." I climb all of two steps before she takes my bait.

"What do you mean?"

I allow myself a triumphant grin before I toss my hair over my shoulder, the cruel glance I give her reminiscent of Greed. "It means that the only *affairs* that are going on here are between Lucifer and me, when we're alone in his playroom." I sneer. "But I suppose you'd know that since it's your job to get on your hands and knees and clean up after us." I turn on my heel and stalk out of the room, not pausing to let her get another word in edgewise.

As soon as I'm a safe distance away, I let out a sharp breath I didn't realize I was holding, swiping a rough hand through my hair. I'm legitimately used to other women falling all over Lucifer. His fans and the media can be especially pushy at times, but I never expected to be confronted by it in my own living room. The reality that I know next to nothing about what Lucifer's sex life was like before me makes me suddenly feel naive.

It never occurred to me that I should care until now. The past is the past.

Until it isn't, I guess?

Until I'm being confronted by what could possibly be one of his exes in our living room.

His living room, that familiar voice of doubt whispers to me.

I squash that thought like the pesky bug it is, not stopping until I close the door to one of the guest bedrooms behind me. I sink against it.

I have half a mind to crash in mine and Lucifer's master suite, thanks to Mia and her perfect, stupid face, but I won't let the deluded fantasies of one of his employees get to me, potential ex or not.

You *used to be one of his employees,* that awful thing inside me hisses.

The thing that's been prowling around inside my chest since that night in the forest.

My anger, my powers unleashed.

I let out a frustrated growl, my hands suddenly clenching.

Without warning, I strip off my heels and toss one of them across the room, its spike hitting the wall with a loud thud and taking an unexpected chunk out of the drywall. My eyes go wide.

Oh shit.

I blink, staring at the hole I created in disbelief, before I start to pace back and forth, my chest heaving in and out as I remember the porcelain sink handle and how I crushed it in my hand so easily.

What in God's name is happening to me?

I continue to pace, my fists clenching and unclenching as the lights at the edges of the room start to flicker, until I stop and let out a fierce shriek.

The electricity inside the penthouse surges, and the sound of shattering glass follows, dying alongside my scream.

Immediately, I go still.

The lights come back on a moment later, a few shouts from the staff downstairs alerting me to the fact that it wasn't just me. It was *real*.

It wasn't inside my head.

None of it has been.

Slowly, I lift my hand to my mouth, my fingers shaking as I cover my lips and stumble toward the en suite. I grip the doorframe, needing its support as I flick on the bathroom light.

A large, newly formed crack runs down the bathroom mirror, distorting my reflection.

And the haunted woman staring back at me.

Oh God.

I reach out my shaking fingers and touch her, horrified by what I see.

Not because of the damage I've caused, but because I . . . did it because I wanted to hurt another human being.

CHAPTER FOURTEEN

Lucifer

I leave Astaroth's unresponsive form lying in the diner for one of my other demons to retrieve. He'll suffer until I return and restore him shortly, only for us to begin this whole bloody process over again.

It's tedious, really.

I snap my fingers, finding myself amid the grime-ridden meat locker I reserved specifically for Charlotte's father. My Mother quickly grew tired of torturing him. His head hangs limp upon one of his shoulders, where he's tied to a rusted metal chair above a steel drain. The too-cool fluorescent light overhead casts the dark circles under his eyes in stark relief, making the dried blood that's crusted into the grout of the green tile beneath him appear almost black.

It's one of my better arrangements, truly.

The scent of rotting flesh hangs in the air.

I step toward him, the sound of my footsteps immediately causing his bloodshot, jaundiced eyes to land on me. "The thief comes only to kill and destroy," he rasps.

I approach slowly, watching as a puddle of urine pours over the edges of his chair as I draw closer, the steam from it rising in the locker's frozen, frigid air.

"John 10:10." A devilish smile twists my lips. "Lovely. But I came to play a different game, actually. Make a bet, if you will." I crouch down so that we are nearly eye level as he attempts to buck and strain away from me. "How many of your followers do you think will drink from your church offering cup this evening? Help me kick off this whole apocalypse charade?"

His nostrils flare.

But he doesn't answer me.

He lifts his eyes skyward. Like my Father can still hear him. His commitment to his own zealotry is impressive, I must say. "Beware, for it is written, 'The way of the wicked is like darkness; they do not know over what they stumble.'"

"Proverbs 4:19." I begin to circle him. "Funny, I can do that little trick too, you know. Want to see?" I cast him a devious grin, placing my hands on the sides of his chair so that he's forced to look at me as my eyes turn serpentine. "'For they, too, will drink the wine of God's fury, which has been poured full strength into the cup of his wrath. They will be tormented with burning sulfur in the presence of the holy angels and of the Lamb. And the smoke of their torment will rise for ever and ever.'" I make a dramatic gesture, mimicking smoke dissipating. "Revelation, chapter fourteen, lines ten through eleven." I grip his wobbling chin. "Care for another?"

"My lord."

I freeze, my concentration immediately broken. "Kalimor." My voice is low and steady, spoken through gritted teeth. "You *know* I don't like to be interrupted."

"Apologies, my lord, but I . . . thought you might want to see . . ." His voice trails off.

I turn toward him, and he passes a human newspaper to me, one he clearly retrieved somewhere topside. The blue headline is written in Taiwanese.

永和陷入神秘狂熱：居民被附身連續狂歡

I translate it instantly. I mastered every language known to man some eons ago.

> Yonghe Erupts in Mysterious Frenzy: Residents Possessed with Nonstop Revelry.

"Revelry?" I lift a brow.

Kalimor lowers his gaze. "They . . . won't stop fucking, my lord."

I scowl. Apparently, my family's apocalypse and the Righteous aren't the only problems on my hands. I expected as much.

As a former lord among my legions, Astaroth's rebellious betrayal was just the tip of a very large demonic iceberg, and I must secure my own house before I deal with my family.

I release a slow exhale through my nose, rolling the newspaper into my hand, before I turn and use it to tip up my victim's chin.

Charlotte's father blanches.

"I will deal with you later."

I stalk from the meat locker, tossing the paper aside as I snap myself topside.

When I step out of the ether and reform, I'm standing in the middle of an abandoned street outside a 7-Eleven in Yonghe, the nighttime lights of New Taipei City gleaming down at me.

The sound of a motor scooter whirrs somewhere in the distance, and a stray dog barks loudly. I search the block, not finding what I'm looking for until my eyes settle upon the pink exterior of the convenience store beside me.

The hair on the back of my neck rises on end.

I prowl toward the 7-Eleven, barely clocking the obnoxious, over-the-top theme. Inside, the fluorescent lights are obscured by the shape of puffy white kawaii clouds over a rainbow-themed ceiling. The word "HELLO" is spelled in all caps with caricature creatures beside the outline of a white cat with a little red bow overtop its head.

I approach the counter, where the clerk sits, her naked back facing me. Her head is thrown back in a silent, orgasmic throe from where her coworker, another woman, kneels behind the countertop eating her pussy.

I snap my fingers in front of the woman on the counter's face a few times, but she doesn't acknowledge me. A warm, fiery glow from beneath the swinging double doors that lead back to the stock room catches my eye.

"Astaroth, you fool," I grumble in my fury.

I make my way toward it, my jaw clenching.

When I push through to the other side, I'm unsurprised by the sight that greets me.

A cavernous hole in the floor teems with lava, leading down into the pits where my hellfire flickers and gleams. My realm brought topside. And not on *my* orders.

Several of my demons' heads turn toward me, the expressions of the human bodies they've claimed as their own paling at the sight of me, despite their blackened eyes.

"My lord . . ." One of them steps forward.

I slowly strip off my suit coat, making a show of rolling up my shirt sleeves to prepare for their punishment as I snarl, "It appears that you all have been busy."

CHAPTER FIFTEEN
Charlotte

I'm barely conscious, barely clinging to life, by the time Mark finally unties me.

The chair has splintered into dozens of pieces beneath me, and I let out a weak moan, trying and failing to use my elbows to crawl toward the door. I'm inside the old Brooklyn Navy Yard again, and already, Mark's broken me. But this time, it isn't Mark or even Lucifer who stands over me.

It's Death.

His skeletal face stares back at me.

"Lucifer?" I rasp, searching for him, hoping he'll save me.

But he isn't there. "Forgive me," Death whispers.

Abruptly, he shoves his hand inside my chest, burying it deep. I gasp and choke on what he's just shoved inside me, but it's not light that I see.

It's darkness...

I jerk upright, my heart pounding and a cold sweat drenching me, only to find I'm still in the guest room. Lucifer didn't carry me to our bed like he usually would, which means...

He didn't return home all evening.

My eyes fall to the closed bathroom door, to what I don't want him to see, because he isn't safe anymore.

Though was he ever, really?

The thought pains me, the feeling of Death's cold embrace still gripping me.

I glance toward the window to where the curtains peek open, allowing some of the early morning light to flood in. So different from the darkness that tried to consume me.

Another night. Another nightmare. More hellfire.

It was just a dream.

A dream laced with memory. A memory that hasn't stopped haunting me.

Along with the feeling of someone's arms that I . . . can't quite place.

Death's cold embrace.

I slip from the bed, stripping off the sheets, hoping that the maids take them to the wash quickly so that when Lucifer *does* come home, he doesn't discover I've sweat through them again. My nightmares worry him.

Or they did. Before we fought, at least.

Now I'm not sure what he feels for me.

Now that I know he was just as trapped by fate as I was.

I shake my head, casting aside those insecurities before they can go any further.

Lucifer loves me. Of course, he does.

In his own twisted way.

I take a fast shower and head upstairs to dress, trying hard not to look toward the cracked glass of the bathroom mirror as I leave. I'll have to ask Ramesh to call someone to replace it as soon as possible so that Lucifer doesn't notice.

I glance at the date and time on my phone. The CFDA Awards, the Oscars of fashion, are less than a month away, and with Lucifer and me hosting the awards show, I'm supposed to meet Xzander at his studio in an hour for the first of several fittings.

If the apocalypse holds off long enough for us to see the end of the year, our next big event after that won't be until February. When we head across the pond to Paris. Thank God.

I smile, a bit of lightness filling me. I've never been abroad before, other than a few misguided mission trips on this side of the Atlantic, and the idea thrills me, even if the thought of walking the red carpet honestly seems insurmountable. A few months ago I could barely manage a regular pair of heels, though these days, they've basically become my standard footwear, thanks to Xzander and Imani.

Once I'm dressed, I head down to breakfast like I usually do, Ramesh and the other members of the staff greeting me. I like to take my breakfast on the first floor near the head of the room-length dining table on the off chance Lucifer decides to join me.

The dim light from the nearly three-hundred-and-sixty-degree view—overlooking Midtown and Madison Square Park—and the accompanying fireplace warm me. Even on a chilly autumn morning like this, condensation from the penthouse's heaters fogging the glass, the sight is breathtaking.

I sit in my usual spot by the window, this morning's paper and breakfast already waiting for me. Normally, I read the headlines on my phone first, considering that even in PR, everyone knows print is practically dead, but this morning the bold type of the *New York Times* catches me.

> This Generation's Jonestown: 1666 Dead in Mass Church Suicide.

I snatch the paper up from the table, scouring the article and the horrific picture accompanying it. Dozens upon dozens of bodies slumped over the megachurch's pews.

Not New Life Nexus, my Father's congregation, but one of its sister churches.

Mark's church. Hope Alive. Another Righteous stronghold.

I scan through the article, the contents of my stomach souring with each additional word. *No children.* My breath shudders out of me. *No children, at least.*

My hands are shaking so violently that by the time I put the article down, I can't bring myself to look at any of the other coverage.

Over a thousand dead. Another Jonestown.

This can't be what he meant when he said he would handle—

No.

No, this is . . .

This is because of me. What they did to me.

It has to be.

My stomach roils, and I run for the nearest bathroom, not caring that I knock over my chair along the way. As soon as I reach the porcelain bowl, I vomit up the few bites of breakfast I've eaten along with what remains of last night's Chinese food.

When I'm finished, I can hardly bring myself to stand, the sight and smell inside the bowl causing me to dry-heave all over again. But this isn't the kind of mess I would ever leave for the maids to clean, no matter how generously Lucifer pays them, so I flush several times.

Still shaking, I clean myself up, washing my mouth out and stumbling back to the dining room table a few minutes later.

I stare down at the headline again.

It's not a surprise to see the Righteous on the front page these days. Ever since the bombing at the Met Gala, speculation about them and the role they played has been all over the media, though so far no official arrests have been made.

America doesn't tolerate religious terrorists.

Except for the homegrown ones, it seems.

I try to swallow the lump inside my throat. I'd hoped, prayed even, for justice against the people who'd conspired to hurt me, but . . .

Not like this.

I sit back down at the breakfast table, my stomach still protesting before I glance at a nearby scone. I should eat. Lucifer would order me to, considering my schedule today extends late into the evening, but the thought of anything even close to food right now repulses me.

All those people. All those people . . .

Suddenly, the shadows at the edge of the room bend meaningfully as Lucifer steps forth from the ether, or . . . whatever it is he calls it, not far from the table.

With a deafening scrape, he pulls out the chair at the table's head before abruptly dropping down into it, swaying slightly. Like he might be drunk.

Something about the movement reminds me oddly of a pirate, or Azmodeus actually . . .

I haven't seen him this relaxed in weeks.

He blows out a long breath before he looks at me, grinning.

His hair is an artful mess, similar to how it looks just after we've fucked, and his tie is undone and hanging from his neck like he's at the end of a particularly long day. The scent of smoke, of whisky and brimstone, clings to him along with the sulfur-like smell that lingers on his clothes whenever he returns from Hell. If I didn't know any better, I would have said he hasn't rested in several days.

Time works differently down in Hell, moves slower, or so he tells me.

He exhales, stretching like a languid jungle cat as he casts a fang-laden grin at me. "Ah, I love the fresh smell of torture in the morning, don't you?" He grabs the glass pitcher of orange juice on the table, pouring himself a full glass as if it's the most natural thing in the world before he takes a slow sip. His eyes widen, his brow lifting toward one of the nearby waitstaff in appreciation as he says, "Is this freshly squeezed?"

I blink, slow and deliberate.

I don't know what comes over me, but the next thing I know, the paper is in my hand and I'm standing.

I slam it down in front of him so hard that the table legs shake and some of the orange juice sloshes onto the glass tabletop.

"Charlotte?" Lucifer lifts a chastising brow, like he isn't certain what's gotten into me.

"Tell me this wasn't you," I demand, pointing down at the headline. "Tell me this wasn't you. *Please*."

He glances down at the headline, his face expressionless, before he quirks his head at me. He waves off the waitstaff, his voice dropping low. "Would you feel better if I told you it was Azmodeus and Wrath, actually?"

My blood runs cold, my knees feeling weak.

"On your orders?"

His lips press together, his eyes going cold. He doesn't answer me. But his silence is answer enough.

I turn, prepared to storm out of the room, but Lucifer catches my hand. "Charlotte," he says, his voice low in warning.

"I can't, Lucifer. I can't—"

"If you *must* know, I'm far more subtle than that." He sneers down at the paper as if what he sees is beneath him, his voice shifting to the familiar tone he uses when he dominates me. Like *I'm* the one being unreasonable. "Though, naturally, I can't say I didn't enjoy the sudden influx of souls it's given me."

Which isn't a no.

He's not denying it then.

I collapse into his lap, suddenly unable to support my own weight.

"Have you eaten?" he asks after he's allowed me to curl into the fetal position, my head resting defeatedly between his neck and shoulder.

"No." I give a small shake of my chin.

Which only causes him to grumble. He doesn't like when I don't take good care of myself. I'm *his*, after all.

"No, sir, you mean."

I close my eyes, a tear escaping. "No, sir," I whisper, correcting myself, though I'm . . . not sure I can handle the thought of him punishing me this evening.

Not after this.

All those people. All those people . . .

"Charlotte, please look at me," he says, sensing my unease.

Reluctantly I tip my chin toward him, and the full force of his beauty hits me. Even now, after everything I've been through, being pinned beneath Lucifer's gaze, it . . . still makes me forget myself. Like nothing else in the world matters.

Nothing except him and me.

He cups my cheek. "What would you have me do? Turn the other cheek to the people who would hurt you? Who would've stood by and reveled while they watched you bleed?" His eyes light with fury. He shakes his head, wrinkling his nose as if that isn't even an option to him.

Nearly as unconscionable as this whole situation is to me.

"No. No, I think not. I haven't enjoyed torturing a fresh batch of souls this much in ages." His eyes darken. "I may not have been the one to make them drink the proverbial Kool-Aid *this time*," he emphasizes, "but they deserved everything they got and then some. He certainly seems to agree." His eyes dart toward the ceiling, and I know that it's God he's referring to.

He once told me that it isn't him who decides where we go in the end.

It's God, and God only.

"What do you mean?" I ask, sensing there's something deeper to what he's saying, but he doesn't answer me. Not directly, at least.

He sighs, staring past me for a long moment, before finally he says, "Someone needs to send them a message. Punish them for what they did to you."

For Mark's role in hurting me. A blatant warning . . .

And a declaration of war to whoever else it was who sent the anthrax. That goes without saying. Not that we've figured out who that is yet.

I take a shaky, resigned breath, crumpling in on myself. All I can feel is a desperate longing to go back to before, to erase all this from my memory.

"I . . . don't think this is the kind of message they need," I whisper softly.

A heavy weight presses down on me.

And the . . . sympathy, the mercy I feel for the people who hurt me surprises me. Innocent people who . . .

I shake my head.

No, not innocent. But people all the same.

People whose lives mattered. People who should have been forgiven, shown mercy, despite all they did to me, despite what they'd continue to do if given the chance.

Lucifer lifts a brow. "Then what *do* they need?"

I fumble over my words, instantly exhausted. Suddenly, I'm tired, so, so tired. "They need . . . less arrogance," I whisper. "Less entitlement. Less animosity to those who are different."

"And?" he prompts.

"More humility. More generosity. More compassion and understanding."

My eyes dart to his, and I think we both understand it isn't only the Righteous I'm talking about anymore.

"Now you sound like my Father." Lucifer huffs, though there's less amusement in it than there used to be. He nods slowly. "All right, Charlotte. In the future, I shall take your opinion into advisement. Happy?"

I nod. That's all the capitulation I'm going to get.

For now, at least.

If I can change his heart, his mind, even a little . . .

Well, maybe that's the true reason why he's destined for me.

My breath bottles up inside me, the memory of the hope I felt the night he cast the aurora borealis over the city coming to mind. I thought I could change him then, too, but even then he was . . .

I can't bring myself to think it.

I bite down on my lip.

I have to hope, have to believe, to hold on to that feeling, because the alternative . . .

Well, the alternative isn't particularly flattering to me.

I sag against him.

Lucifer grins, mistaking my defeat for closeness, before he tips my chin up toward him, kissing me so that all I can do is melt into him. Like he's reveling in the flavor of me.

"If you could have only seen their faces the moment they realized they weren't in Heaven. That they were mine," he whispers against my lips. "They belong to me, Charlotte. They *all* belong to me." His eyes darken like he's trying to impart some deeper meaning to me, but I . . . can't begin to understand what it is. "As do you." He presses his forehead against mine.

"Yes, sir," I whisper.

He traces his finger down the exposed skin between my breasts, curling it slightly.

All at once, I sit forward, my fatigue gone from the rush of lust he's coaxed from me, but he's not Azmodeus. He can't create what isn't already there, buried deep inside me.

He can only call it forth.

The darkest desires of my heart.

He sits back in his seat, smiling appreciatively at how flushed and ready I am. "Like what you see?"

My gaze rakes over him. My body says yes, but . . .

For once, I can't bring myself to answer.

Even though my pussy is practically whimpering *Yes, please*.

This is what Lucifer does. Makes me wild and wicked.

Until the darkness inside me is unleashed.

"Stand before me," he orders.

"Yes, sir," I mutter, my cheeks reddening at how eagerly I obey his command. All it took was the single crook of his finger, and I'm more than ready for him, craving him.

Unable to resist.

I rise from his lap, coming to stand in front of him exactly like he ordered.

Slowly, he takes my hand, and I let out a startled eep as I'm hauled back down into his lap, this time with my hips positioned so

I'm straddling the thick length of his cock where it strains against his suit pants.

"I would burn this world for you, little dove," he whispers to me, bringing his lips only a hair's breadth from my own as he gently tucks a strand of my hair behind my ear, his other hand kneading one of my nipples. "Do you understand?"

I nod, leaning into his touch, unable to resist closing the gap between us.

He's told me this before, but I . . . think today is the first time I fully understand what that means.

He feasts on me for a moment, his tongue laying siege against my mouth and his hands at my breasts, until a few seconds later I'm rocking and moaning against him, practically begging.

"Please, sir?" I whimper.

I want him inside me.

"Is it playtime, Daddy?"

"First on your knees," he orders, gripping me by the hair and lifting me from his lap, only to force me down onto the floor before him. A devilish smirk crosses his lips as I take out his cock, running my tongue along the thick vein that pulses near the head. "I'm feeling particularly indulgent this morning."

CHAPTER SIXTEEN
Charlotte

I can still taste the salt of Lucifer's cum on my lips when I stumble out of the penthouse nearly a half hour later. I'm running late, the car already waiting, and my ass is redder than it's ever been from where he bent me over the dining room table, and . . .

"Nothing like a fresh fuck to start the day, *hmm*?" An audible sip follows, but it's the too-handsome face that accompanies it that stops me.

Azmodeus leans against the outside of the building, smiling appreciatively at me as he drinks from a disposable coffee cup. Though he looks more like Lucifer than any of their other siblings, the resemblance stops at the fact that he's so painfully beautiful, it's almost obscene. And there's something surprisingly relaxed about him these days that seems distinctly different from Lucifer.

Like he doesn't carry the weight of the world on his shoulders like his older brother does.

I pause on my path to the Town Car and turn to him. With both of us out on the street, the paparazzi who are constantly positioned outside 172 Madison Avenue are more desperate than ever.

They shout both our names. "Azmodeus! Charlotte! Give us a smile, will ya?"

A few members of the security team are the only thing that stands between us and them.

Az glances toward them, nodding with a cheeky grin. "Care to throw them a bone?" His gaze rakes over me. Exactly how he can make the dress he's wearing look masculine and sexy is beyond me. "Or have you already been boned enough by my brother this morning?"

"Do you *have* to make a sex pun with every other breath?" I let out an annoyed huff.

"Of course." He wrinkles his nose, feigning offense. "It's in my nature." He smirks, and I scoff.

I don't have time for this. Not today. I have to be at Xzander's studio in a handful of minutes, and Manhattan traffic is its own kind of hell. Plus, we'll need to circle the block a few times to throw the paparazzi off our tail. Speaking of which . . .

Where the hell is Olivia this morning?

I sigh, rolling my eyes as I wrap my vintage Alexander McQueen coat tighter around myself. "Lucifer is upstairs," I say coolly, my voice low and private as I move to step away, but Az's hand is on my arm, stopping me.

"You two have become my favorite power couple, you know?" He drops his voice as he leans down and whispers into my ear. "What are we up to now—twice, sometimes three times a day?" He eases back. "My skin has never looked this goddamn radiant."

I pause, glancing toward him. And he's right.

His skin *does* look really fucking great.

Not that Azmodeus would ever be caught dead looking like anything less than perfection. He's the city's favorite pansexual playboy. Lusty polyamorous love life and all.

I sigh again. "Is it really necessary for you to comment on mine and Lucifer's sex life every time we meet?"

"No." He shrugs, smiling deviously. "But I appreciate the offerings all the same, lovey."

According to Lucifer, that's how it works. Commit the sin, and more power is funneled to the corresponding Original. Like an offering. Or some kind of strange divine currency.

Though I doubt that great skin is the only power our sex life has afforded Azmodeus lately.

My thoughts turn to Lucifer, remembering what he said before he ordered me to blow him, and a shiver runs through me.

Would you feel better if I told you it was Azmodeus and Wrath?"

Suddenly, I'm more eager to get to the car than ever before.

"I told you, Lucifer's upstairs, and I'm already running late." I shoulder my way out of Az's grip.

"Actually, it's *you* I came to see."

I stop, turning to face him, and he nods toward the waiting car, where one of the security team holds the door for me.

"Ride with me?" He quirks a brow.

I give him an incredulous look. "It's *my* car."

"Is it?" He cocks his head to the side as if to say *Girl, please,* his expression stating the obvious.

Everything I have is because of Lucifer.

And I'm not yet a part of their celestial family. Not officially.

Not until Lucifer and I tie the knot.

Lucifer's urgency on that seems wiser than I'd previously thought.

I glance between Azmodeus and the waiting paparazzi, their cameras flashing. Their boom mics are lifted in hope of catching a snippet of what Az and I are saying, so even if I wanted to tell Azmodeus to fuck off, I couldn't, not without making headlines.

And from the smug look on Az's face, he knows it.

Of course he does. I have to fight not to roll my eyes.

Lucifer isn't the only devious one among his siblings.

"Fine." I gesture for Az to slip inside the Town Car ahead of me.

At the sight of the two of us leaving together, the cameras go wild, the paparazzi's shouting reaching an apex that vibrates my insides, but despite my anxiety about what Azmodeus wants from me this morning,

I have the strength of mind to pause, whispering to Dagon, "Tell Lucifer that Azmodeus is joining us." I duck inside the car.

Dagon nods. "Of course, Mrs. Apollyon."

He closes the door behind me, speaking into the com that connects him to the rest of the security team. It's not exactly a foolproof plan, but it's the best I have right now, and with Lucifer aware of exactly who my company is, I doubt that Azmodeus will try anything stupid.

Or so I hope.

Az grins at me as I sit beside him on the bench seat like he knows what I'm thinking. "Of all our siblings, I'm the least likely to be a threat to you, you know."

Clearly, he overheard me.

Supernatural hearing can be a real pain in the ass sometimes.

"Oh yeah, why's that?" I ask as the car begins to move. I quickly direct Dagon to do whatever he needs to do to throw the paparazzi off before we head to Xzander's studio.

Another round of cameras with Az in tow is the last thing I need.

Especially considering this morning's headlines.

I'll be expected to comment about the debacle at Mark's church for sure. Imani probably already has something worked up for me.

When Azmodeus doesn't immediately answer, I push further. "Because as long as Lucifer and I are making offerings to you, you plan to keep me around? Is that it?"

He scoffs. "Please. I don't love you two fucking *that* much." He's watching me carefully. Like whatever it is he sees is far more interesting than he expected it to be. "It's because I don't want it," he says flatly, dropping back into his seat.

I lift a brow.

"You know, the whole leadership role." He wiggles his fingers dismissively. "Lucifer and his place at the head of our family. That's more Envy's thing. And Greed's."

"And what's *your* thing?"

A flicker of amusement crosses his face, and something about it reminds me of Lucifer. "Well, it wouldn't be very fun if I told you, would it, lovey?"

"I suppose not. But if you *did* want it? His position?"

"Well . . ." Az's smile turns wicked. "Well, then it'd be mine in a heartbeat."

His gaze rakes over me.

Clearly, it's not just Lucifer's role in their family he's insinuating.

I give an uncomfortable clear of my throat, squirming in my seat.

I'm uncertain if it's the truth or simply divine bravado, but he doesn't allow me to consider it long before he adds, "But that's not what brought me here."

"And what *did* bring you here?"

That's the question that has me stumped.

I can think of a few reasons why Mammon would pull something like this. Or even Bel—a.k.a. Sloth. He *always* seems to want something from Lucifer.

But Azmodeus is a wild card to me.

A dangerous, flamboyant wild card.

The window partition is now rolled up, and we're alone in the backseat, but Az lowers his voice all the same, his smirk widening. It's the signature look that makes the media lap up everything he feeds them, exactly like the rabid dogs they can be. Though when we're alone like this, there's something about it that's less lusty and more . . . devastating.

My skin grows hot.

"Rumor has it you and my brother are having a bit of a snafu over some PR firm you're planning to launch."

My eyes go wide. "How would you know about that?"

Lucifer and I are both careful to keep all Apollyon's business moves private until it's the right time to go public. Not to mention the NDAs all the employees are required to sign are nearly a hundred pages long.

I know that firsthand. It was one of the very first lessons working for Lucifer ever taught me.

Always read the fine print.

"Waitstaff talk." Azmodeus shrugs. "And fuck just as nicely. My brother's kept you more in the dark than we thought, I suppose."

We. Meaning he and the other Originals have been curious.

About how much I know.

About the power Lucifer unleashed in me.

And I'm positive that kind of curiosity can be dangerous, even to a . . . whatever I am. It's not that I was ever naive enough to assume they wouldn't find out, especially after the whole anthrax situation. But the how and why, the scope of my—I swallow, struggling to think the words—*my abilities . . .*

Well, that's unknown even to me.

And I plan to keep it that way.

For as long as humanly possible.

"Pillow talk is an intimate art, Charlotte," Azmodeus says, changing the subject as he mindlessly toys with one of his coat buttons. "I deal in secrets. And *you* have secrets aplenty, don't you, Miss Davis?" He grins at me.

The use of my former name, the one I was forced to take when I married Mark, catches me off guard, and I look away quickly. Now I understand how Lucifer knew I was already married. Though he helped ensure I was divorced in a matter of hours.

One thing I'll always be grateful to him for.

My mouth goes dry. "I don't know what you mean."

"I mean that you and I could have a bit of fun together, if you're up for spreading your proverbial wings a bit. Or your legs, if you want. Your call." He glances toward my back, his brows lowering like something interesting just occurred to him. "You don't *actually* have wings, do you?"

I shake my head, pretty sure I know where this is heading. "I'm not even remotely interested in fucking you, Azmodeus."

At that, he throws back his head and laughs at me, the sound so relaxed I'm temporarily dumbstruck by it.

He's acting like we're old friends.

Or future siblings-in-law, at least.

"Oh, Charlotte." He chuckles, his voice deepening. "If I wanted to steal you from my brother, I could do so, easily."

As if to prove his point, he brushes my cheek in the same way Lucifer does, like he knows *exactly* how Lucifer touches me, and the moment his skin meets mine, my whole body is an inferno. On fire with need.

Suddenly what I said about not being interested in fucking him is a bold-faced lie, even as my mind tries to rebel against it furiously. I know this isn't from me. It feels so wrong, it's like knives under the pleasure. And I would *never* betray Lucifer that way, never, but the . . . lust Az's touch ignites is so powerful that I'm . . . not sure I'd be able to control myself.

Az drops his hand, the feeling gone instantly.

All I'm left with are wet panties and a nearly irresistible urge to have Dagon circle the car back around to the penthouse where Lucifer's waiting.

I clench my legs together.

What in the lust-filled fuck?

Azmodeus shrugs, ignoring my obvious distress. "I much prefer my lovers be enthusiastic and consenting of course, and I've been on a bit of kick of enjoying cock lately, as I'm sure you've seen in the tabloids, though pussy and everything in between is always equally appealing if you and Lucifer ever want to—"

"Get to your point, Azmodeus." My molars clench.

Normal people do *not* have to deal with their future brother-in-law propositioning them for threesomes this early in the morning.

"Does there need to be a point?" Azmodeus asks like he enjoys needling me, but then he lowers the partition window and snaps his fingers at Dagon, pointing to the nearest street corner as though he plans for us to stop there. "You're soon going to be my beloved sister-in-law, after all. Mimi says that makes us family."

Mimi? I roll my eyes. *Of course she does.*

I can't even bring myself to think of Greed and what she's up to. I have enough problems as it is.

"And?" I ask.

"And I think that you and I could have a bit of fun together. That's all."

For now, anyway.

I know better than to trust in whatever Azmodeus's idea of sibling bonding is.

"Luce might even let you off your leash, if we all play nice, of course."

My eyes narrow as the car pulls to a stop at the curb. "I'm *not* on a leash."

"Who are you trying to fool, Charlotte?" he says, giving me some major side-eye. "Yourself? Or me?" Az opens the door as he grins. Once he's out of the car, he reaches inside his coat pocket—a Charles Jeffrey from the looks of it—and holds out an all-black business card with embossed gold lettering to me. "If you ever want to have some real fun, call me." He smirks. "I'm more than happy to pop your celestial cherry."

When I don't take the card, he straightens, tucking it back into his pocket with a shrug like it's my loss. "Suit yourself."

He moves to step away.

But a sudden idea sparks in me.

What if there is *a way for me to do more to stop the apocalypse?*

I may not stand a chance on my own, but what if . . . what if a huge chunk of economic and celestial power, more than enough to help humanity, has been sitting right in front of me this whole time?

In the form of six other Originals.

You know he doesn't want outside investors. Imani's warning echoes back to me.

But what about insider trading?

"And what if I did?" I ask, unable to stop myself.

Azmodeus pauses, propping himself between the roof and the car door.

I let out an audible breath. "What if I *did* want . . . want to know more about . . . ?"

"Being divine? Immortal?" he asks, his smirk widening.

I give a reluctant nod.

He pulls out his card once more, this time pressing the glittering cardstock into my open palm. "Meet me at The Velvet Fold next Friday, Charlotte." Az grins wickedly. "And I'll show you what being divine really means."

CHAPTER SEVENTEEN

Charlotte

I arrive at Xzander's studio nearly twenty minutes after we're scheduled, but fortunately, Xzander has his own excuses for running late this morning.

"Your doppelganger forgot to drop the key back off to Tameka last night, so I had to double back to find the spare." He pulls the key in question from his pocket, though he doesn't seem very annoyed that Olivia ducked out of her shift early. This close to the CFDAs, with Xzander serving on IMPACT's board to uplift Black and brown talent in fashion, plus designing my outfits for the awards show, he likely doesn't expect a moment's peace.

I make an apologetic face. "I'm sorry. I'll talk to her."

Like most of the Garment District, Xzander's studio is near Midtown South, on Seventh Avenue somewhere southeast of Bryant Park and north of Penn Station. Despite all the tourists that frequent this part of the city, with Broadway and Times Square so close by, I've always enjoyed this neighborhood, especially this early—when the streets are clear and the new morning light makes it feel like the day is full of endless possibilities.

There's something a little sexy about the city that never sleeps, and I think sometimes the people who've lived here all their lives take that for granted.

Kansas could never compare.

"Coffee?" Xzander asks, nodding to where his assistant Isabela's waiting.

Clearly, she's going to be the one to fetch it for us, though if she's anything like Siobhan, Xzander's other assistant, she likely knows our orders by heart now. Xzander's been designing for me almost exclusively ever since I debuted to the press beside Lucifer.

I'm one of his top clients these days.

I recite my order anyway—a Venti latte with white mocha, sweet cream, and caramel drizzle with an extra shot of espresso, hot, exactly the kind of warm, sugary pick-me-up I need—before Xzander pushes the key into the studio lock and we step inside.

The inside is dark before he flicks on the lights—none of his other staff have arrived. The first floor functions as a showroom while the second floor is where the true magic happens, the home to all his textiles and sewing machinery.

I glance around, my eyes adjusting to the lighting, and my brow furrows at the sight of my purse from yesterday on the floor. Or a replica of it anyway. "Olivia must have left her bag here." I move to pick it up.

Xzander drops a limp wrist at me, shaking his head. "You need to get better help if your doppel-girl is this sloppy."

But Olivia *isn't* this sloppy. Not usually, anyway.

She's been a real dream. The perfect me. On time and eager to follow directions on every occasion we've needed her. Honestly, sometimes it feels like she's better at being me than I am.

Not a hard job these days.

I push the thought aside, ignoring the feeling of unease I get as I glance at Olivia's bag in my hand. I'm sure she just forgot it. She was probably eager to get home for the evening.

Completely unbothered, Xzander leads me toward the elevator with an old-school metal grate. "I think you're going to love what I have in store for you, diva," he says when we reach the second floor, spreading his arms in the shape of an invisible rainbow as he reopens it. "Picture this. Dark brocade. All handmade. And—"

And that's when I see myself lying there.

On the second-floor tile. In a puddle of blood.

Or what *looks* like me, anyway.

Xzander freezes. "Ah, hell naw," he swears quietly, his voice way more Harlem than usual. "This is *not* the kind of rich-white-people bullshit I signed up for."

I step off the elevator, feeling like I'm looking down at myself from above, though I'm suddenly trembling from head to toe. I stare down at the body of the woman who was *supposed* to be me. At the blood that formed around her hair like a macabre halo. Hair that was dyed and styled to look exactly like mine.

"Olivia?" I whisper.

I don't know why I say her name. She can't hear me. From the looks of it, she's been dead for . . . several hours? Longer maybe?

Long enough not to return Xzander's key.

Bile burns at the back of my throat as I slowly approach and crouch beside her, desperately trying to make sense of all this, but I . . . feel nothing.

I'm more numb than I've ever been.

"What . . . what do we do?" I reach out a hand to brush her eyes closed, put her at peace.

"Charlotte," Xzander says, his voice several octaves lower as he grips me by the shoulders, bringing me back to myself before I can touch her. Gently, he urges me back. "Charlotte, you've got to get outta here *now*, diva." He swallows, his features turning ashy as he nods toward the window.

Several nondescript cars pull to a stop outside the studio.

My legs go weak.

The paparazzi.

They found me, of course.

With Olivia dead, there's no one left to deter them.

And with last night's hit on the Righteous in today's papers...

A sour taste coats my mouth as I back toward the exit.

"What about you?" I ask, my eyes darting toward Xzander.

"Don't worry about me. I can handle myself. Now, go. Round the back," Xzander mutters, more grave and focused than I've ever seen him. He grabs a nearby hat and several scarves off a mannequin, shoving them toward me like they're supposed to be some makeshift disguise as he ushers me inside the elevator.

"Xzander, what if they—"

"*Go*, Charlotte," he snaps, causing me to jump.

Adrenaline kicks in suddenly, the awful numbness inside me melting and paving the way for something far more debilitating. Everything I've been holding back. All my fears, my anxieties, all of it unravels inside me. I jam my finger into the elevator button, struggling to control my breath. There's not enough oxygen in the room, and I'm more than grateful for the security standing guard outside the front door.

I make my way to the first floor, several members of my security detail running up the stairs, having just heard Xzander's calls for help. They don't even notice me.

Slowly, I back against a nearby wall, dropping all the items Xzander shoved into my arms...

It would have been me.

Should have been me.

The room spins, and I try hard to think clearly, but my vision blurs, my eyes watery.

Olivia.

All those people. All those people.

All because of me...

The temperature in my body drops, a cold sweat coating me, and before I fully recognize what I'm doing, I'm running toward the back door.

Fight-or-flight takes over, and apparently, I choose flight, my thoughts stuck on repeat.

All those people. All those people.

This can't be happening. It can't. But I know from the anthrax that was sent to the penthouse before that it is. It *is* happening. And this time, people have died.

People have died because of me.

I slam through the back entrance to the studio, the door nearly coming off the hinges from my newfound strength. I don't have time to register the flash of panic that sparks in me as I stumble into the back alley just as I hear the first paparazzo reach the front door.

My chest starts to tighten to the point of pain, but I don't stop, don't hesitate.

I run down the back alleyway, wherever my feet will take me. I don't care where I'm headed. I just . . . need to escape, need to keep moving. When I come out onto another street, losing one of my heels as I go, I push past the sea of morning commuters, colliding with several of them, unaware of my surroundings.

My breath comes in ragged pants as I struggle to breathe, my vision blurring.

All those people. All those people.

And now . . .

My fault, that ugly thing inside me starts to hiss, rearing its monstrous head.

My fault, my fault, my fault.

I clutch at my chest, trying to slow my heart rate, but the sounds of the city, the glow of the traffic lights, the morning sun—all the sights, all the smells and sounds, are too loud, too much. I don't stop. I don't stop running for several blocks until I feel myself stumble; until suddenly my lungs give out, my vision turning black at the edges.

Until the monster inside me wins.

And I collapse to the ground, feeling nothing.

CHAPTER EIGHTEEN

Lucifer

I'm out on the platform of the New York Stock Exchange, overlooking the trading floor, a poorly mixed Harvey Wallbanger in my hand, as I pretend to hobnob with the other executives before the opening-bell ceremony. The press is out in full force, and the sea of too many white men clapping one another on the shoulder and shaking one another's hands congratulatorily bores me, but the celebration of the initial public offering of one of our latest subsidiaries is exactly the kind of distraction the media needs this morning.

I take another sip of my drink, frowning slightly at the weak, watered-down taste.

"Lucifer." One of the subsidiary's human executives approaches, his hand extended to me, but before I can even deign to consider if I want to debase myself enough to take it, my attention is quickly interrupted by an unexpected touch upon my shoulder.

"Sir." Dagon stands before me, looking winded and a bit red in the face. Like he jogged all the way up here from the street.

I wave a dismissive hand. "Not now, Dagon."

Whatever it is, it can wait.

"Sir." Dagon steps closer, undeterred as he lowers his voice and speaks directly into my ear. "Sir, there's been a breach."

My spine runs cold.

"Charlotte, she's . . . she's gone, sir."

I don't ask what exactly the word *gone* means. My mind is already too busy reeling, remembering.

The feel of her lying limp in my arms.

The sight of her no longer breathing.

The way my stomach felt as if it'd been dropped down into my feet, like I'd been disemboweled, at the sight of her standing there in limbo.

So close to Azrael's arms, so close to being beyond my reach.

The glass in my hand shatters, the juices spilling over my skin.

The room goes instantly dark, all the light inside it being pulled and sucked inside me until nothing but a pitch-black void remains. Someone screams, a woman it seems, as the trading floor erupts in chaos, but I don't stay long enough to gauge their reactions or to excuse myself from the room. I'm gone in a blink. The tail end of the crowd's gasps as the lights and electronics come back on barely registers as I become shadow and step through the ether.

The next thing I know, I'm standing inside Xzander's studio, time frozen around me.

From the second that anthrax was first delivered, I began memorizing Charlotte's daily schedule down to the minute. But the sight of the body lying upon the floor stills me.

"No."

A sound I don't recognize tears from my throat. Something tortured, something garbled and tormented with pain.

But my light, my power, must recognize that it isn't her before my mind fully comprehends what I'm seeing, because instead of lifting her into my arms, I remain frozen.

I would *know* if she were dead. I would feel it.

Our connection is still intact. Which means . . .

She's mine. Still.

Now and always.

The nausea that plagued me subsides, and it takes only a matter of seconds for me to regain control, the terror that gripped me giving way to momentary relief before it turns into something far more insidious, far more unhinged.

Fury.

Violent and barely controlled.

I step toward the actress's corpse, hardly noticing where Xzander, the security team, and the accompanying police remain frozen in time around me. I crouch next to her, examining the bloodied spot in the middle of her spine where the assassin's blade made entry.

Carefully, I use the edge of my suit coat to lift the custom Dior dress she was wearing—a replica of the one Charlotte wore yesterday—as I take stock of the wound that killed her.

Black spider veins shoot out from the point of entry, squirming and writhing.

Exactly as I feared.

"Fuck," I snarl.

The confirmation settles in, though no one within the studio can hear me.

I stand swiftly, following the vague scent of Charlotte's perfume. I can taste it with a simple flick of my forked tongue. I chase the scent and taste down the stairs and into a back alley, the whole city still frozen in time around me.

I come to a stop on Seventh Avenue where, at the mouth of the alley, the trail ends, muddied by the medley of other scents of the city.

I find one of her scuffed Louboutins.

My jaw clenches tight enough to spark pain as I take the abandoned shoe into my hand.

If anyone has so much as laid a hand on her, I will burn down this whole bloody city without a second thought.

With a furious roar, I slam my free fist down onto the pavement, the full weight of my strength opening a massive fissure in the earth. From the hole in the concrete, dozens of large black serpents begin to escape, my lowest demons, summoned to serve me.

"Find her," I hiss to them, watching as they scatter about the city. "Find your queen."

CHAPTER NINETEEN

Charlotte

I wake with a start sometime later, something damp and cold across my forehead.

"It's all right. Breathe," a calm voice says to me.

I inhale a sharp, sudden breath, jerking upright, but that only causes my vision to swim. I weave unsteadily.

"Easy now."

I clutch something hard to steady myself.

There's a . . . tingling sensation at the back of my skull, and my lips are chapped and cracking.

"Here, drink this."

Someone pushes what feels like a Dixie cup full of water into my hand.

I take it, the waxy paper wobbling as I bring it to my mouth. Once the cool liquid hits my throat, I down it, my vision starting to level out as I take in my surroundings.

A church. I'm inside a cathedral that, based on the high-vaulted ceilings, the stained glass windows, and the nearby altar full of votive candles beneath a small statue of the Virgin Mary, must be a Catholic sanctuary. I reposition myself from where I was lying, half propped on a pillow on top of a wooden pew, so I can lean against its side.

My eyes fall to the Black man positioned beside me, who's wearing a staunch white priest's collar. "Maria here and one of my parishioners saw you collapse," he says. "So, they brought you inside."

"Here. Have another drink," a second, newer voice says, and I look up to see a young Latina woman, a nun in her habit, who appears to be around my age, passing me another cup of water. Maria apparently.

"Thank you," I rasp, sipping it.

My stomach feels as if I've swallowed a whole mound of rocks, and my forehead is clammy. She smiles warmly at me, muttering something in Spanish to the priest, before leaving the two of us alone.

Olivia, my mind hisses, the thought causing me to jerk upright.

"I have to—"

"We said a prayer for her, for your friend." The priest nods. "It's already on the news."

My friend?

Which means it's likely been at least an hour since I went missing, maybe longer.

I nod uselessly, my pulse slowing. There's no point in correcting him, I guess.

Olivia wasn't my friend, but only because I . . .

I swallow.

Because I didn't allow her to be.

So if something like this happened, I wouldn't feel so . . .

Grief tightens my throat.

That line of thinking seems foolish, cruel even.

"Name's Father Brown." The priest extends a hand toward me like he's unaware of my distress. Or just polite enough to ignore it.

"I'm—"

"I know who you are, Charlotte." He smiles softly.

My insides turn cold. Of course he does. My face is constantly plastered across every kind of screen these days.

Which means I'm . . . not welcome here.

Why would I be?

Gingerly, I set the empty Dixie cup down onto the pew beside me, my gaze shifting toward the exit. "I suppose I should—"

"You're welcome to stay here as long as you like," Father Brown says, reading my expression easily. "*All* God's children are welcome here, you included. In fact, I'd wager a guess this'll be the most interesting conversation I have all day, though let's keep that last bit strictly between you and me." He chuckles, watching me for a long beat, like he's trying to gauge my reaction. "But if you really want to leave." He gently nods toward the door to show he won't try to stop me.

My eyes dart toward it. To where the rest of the world waits.

It won't take long for the paparazzi to find me.

If Lucifer doesn't first . . .

Honestly, I'm not sure which of those possibilities terrifies me more.

I swallow. "I'd . . . like to sit here for a moment actually, if you don't mind."

"Of course. Take all the time you need." He nods like somehow he gets it, though he couldn't possibly begin to understand.

No mortal can anymore.

A thick feeling constricts my throat.

I half expect him to leave then, or for this conversation to take a turn for the worst as he tries to convert me, make me repent and see the error of my ways for being "the devil's whore," like my father or Mark would have done, but instead he just turns toward the front of the church and sits with me, both of us together in a companionable silence.

I stare up at the stained glass window overhead, watching how the colors stream in from the early morning light, and after a while, the feeling in my chest grows tighter until I find my eyes stinging. A sharp twinge of grief settles in as I realize the sight, the smells, the sounds of this place make me . . .

Incredibly homesick.

Though how can I feel homesick for somewhere I've never even been?

I gaze up toward Heaven.

"I still pray to Him, you know," I whisper, unable to stop myself.

Father Brown casts a proud sidelong glance at me, smiling a little. "Do you?"

I lower my head. "But I . . . don't think He's listening."

"How can you be so certain?" he asks.

I open my mouth to answer, but something stops me. "I suppose I'm not," I mumble, "certain, I mean. But if He is listening, I . . . wouldn't know it."

"Mmph." He gives a meaningful hum. "That's the thing about faith." He casts a conspiratorial grin at me. "Sometimes He's listening when we least expect it."

Out of the corner of my eye, something slithers between the pew aisles beside us, drawing my attention, and a moment later, the church's heavy double doors fly open as if they weigh nothing at all, their deafening bang against the walls echoing through the sanctuary.

Lucifer stands in the doorway, his silhouette backlit so that he looks like an avenging angel made of shadow. Darkness embodied.

"Charlotte," he grumbles, curling a single finger toward me.

Beckoning me. Like I'm his to command.

I can tell by the tone of his voice and the connection between us that he's furious with me, though whether it's because I slipped my security detail and ran, or out of concern for how careless I was with my own safety, I can't be certain.

Nodding, I immediately stand, knowing better than to disobey him right now, only to find that Father Brown does the same beside me.

He turns and looks toward Lucifer, and if he feels any hint of judgment or disgust at the fallen angel that stands before him, it isn't visible.

"Sammael." He nods in greeting.

I stiffen, my gaze volleying between the two men, Lucifer's head quirked to the side as he looks at the priest curiously.

"No one has called me that for a very long time," he says slowly.

"Allow me to be the first this century, then." Father Brown smiles. Surprisingly, he turns toward me, giving Lucifer his back as if he's unafraid. "You're welcome here any time, Charlotte."

I nod. "Thank you," I manage, my eyes darting to Lucifer before I step away from the pew. "For everything."

Hastily, I hurry to Lucifer's side.

Lucifer wraps his arm around my waist, tucking me into him easily. "Father." He inclines his head, smirking irreverently at the priest's title, but it's the amused look in the priest's eye as he says it that—

Without warning, a sharp tugging sensation pulls at my navel like I'm clay being bent and molded, collapsed and reformed, and the next thing I know I'm standing inside the penthouse, completely whole again, Lucifer beside me.

Holy shit.

"What in the bloody hell were you thinking?" Lucifer growls, releasing me only to tear his already loosened tie off as he starts to pace. "Running off like that? You could have been killed. You could have been—"

The sight of my quivering chin stops him, like he's momentarily at a loss for words.

"Charlotte," he mutters.

I nearly collapse onto the floor, Lucifer catching me as silent tremors begin to shake my whole body.

"They killed her," I whisper, my voice so strained with emotion I can hardly speak. *All those people. All those people.* "They killed her because of me."

"You are *not* responsible for their sins," Lucifer whispers feverishly into my hair, holding me together. "Trust me. I speak from experience."

He pulls me closer. Like if he holds me tight enough, he might be able to keep me from breaking. But my heart is already cracked open, flayed down the middle.

I'm not sure what it is about his reassurance that sends another fresh wave of grief rolling through me, but the pained whimper that escapes me seems to soften him all the same.

Lucifer folds me into his arms, cradling me up and onto his chest, so he can carry me to our room. He gently deposits me onto our bed a few moments later, sitting on the edge of the mattress beside me as he combs his fingers through my hair.

"I will do whatever it takes to be worthy of you, little dove. This I swear to you."

I don't know what it is about the way he says it, but the idea that he still thinks he's unworthy of me, of my love, after everything we've been through, only manages to make my shoulders shake even harder.

"Shh. Shh." He hushes me. "Rest now," he whispers, comforting me until the last of my tears have been wrung from my body. "Leave their punishment to me."

And I do.

My lids grow heavy as they droop shut, trusting that no matter the fallout, in his own cruel way, he'll always take care of me.

And that maybe, for him, that's what his love truly means.

CHAPTER TWENTY

Lucifer

The moment I'm certain Charlotte is asleep and will likely stay that way for some time, thanks to a fresh glass of wine and a few painkillers I ordered Ramesh to leave at her bedside, I pop down to Hell.

To summon my ruddy siblings.

They appear among the black obsidian walls of my throne room seconds later. Az is naked from the waist down; Mimi's in a lush, pima cotton bathrobe, the accompanying silk eye mask askew on her face, making her look particularly perturbed that I interrupted her beauty sleep; and Bel's in a skintight wetsuit, his damp hair still dripping. The rest are, thankfully, fully clothed, but simply have the gall to look annoyed with me.

"What the fuck, Luce?" This from Envy. Leviathan. Or Levi, as we call him.

The middle child among us. And always the most eager to thwart me.

He's wearing a thin gray hoodie, loose jeans, and a VR headset that, unfortunately, makes him look like the quintessential tech bro.

But I don't have time for any of his bullshit this morning.

There is no universe where all this isn't connected—my Father's apocalypse, my Mother's meddling, Michael and the Righteous, Astaroth's and my legions' rebellion, and now this.

"Which one of you did it, humph?" I snarl, my eyes turning serpentine. My forked tongue flicks across my lips in fury as I glance at each of the faces about the room.

Mammon's mouth pinches into a thin white slash as she snaps her eye mask onto her forehead, sighing annoyedly. "Well, it would help if you bothered to tell us what you—"

The sight of my true angelic features silences her.

Or what Hell has no longer decayed away . . .

Eyes all around. Wheels upon wheels of horror.

"Well, which one of you? Which one of you useless, pathetic, parasitic cretins intended to kill her?"

"Hey now, I resent that." This from Az. He glances down at his chipped nail polish like he's particularly bored with this whole thing. "I've always considered myself smarter than you, actually. Though Mammon's right, if you bothered to give us a hint, maybe we—"

I clench my fist, his voice cutting off from where I've used some of my power to choke him.

This is my realm. My domain.

And here they *will* bow to me.

Like it or not.

Az stumbles slightly, his face turning red before I abruptly release him, sending him sputtering and sprawling onto the floor. When he regains his composure, he glares up at me, his eyes shooting daggers.

But he doesn't dare speak over me again.

Bel shakes his head like a wet dog, drops of water flying everywhere. "Some unknown human actress who looks like Charlotte showed up dead at her designer's studio this morning."

All eyes turn toward him.

One of my brows lifts, my irises narrowing to serpentine slits.

"What?" Bel shrugs dismissively. "It was all over the news at the marina."

Mammon steps forward then, stripping off her eye mask, her jaw clenched. "You mean to tell me that you interrupted my beauty sleep and dragged us all down here all over that skinny little bitch you're keeping?" She sneers, her gaze raking over me as if she's disgusted by what she sees. "I won't be able to get the stench off for weeks." She sniffs her robe, wincing, before she lifts her hand as if she means to snap herself topside.

But the movement yields nothing.

She snaps a few times more. "You . . ." Her jaw drops. "You let me out of here, you . . . you puffed-up, prideful peacock!" she shrieks, stomping her foot like the entitled princess she's always been.

"Mimi," Gluttony grumbles in warning.

Her twin is the only one among us who's ever come close to being able to control her.

I shove my hands in my pockets, crossing my legs where I perch on the arm of my throne. "Not *one* of you leaves this room until I have answers."

"Well, might as well settle in for a millennium then." Levi—Envy—casts his headset aside as he drops down onto an empty spot on the floor.

His businesses are more than capable of running without him, considering he works mostly in tech these days, the advent of social media having benefited his sin the most significantly. Though he's never allowed that to stop him from being a petulant child and coveting every other fucking move the rest of us make.

"And what makes you so certain it was one of us, humph?" Mammon says incredulously. She stares down the bridge of her nose at me as she waves a pudgy, annoyed hand at the ceiling. "Especially with all our *other* asinine, angelic siblings out and roaming about."

The others nod in agreement.

I cross my arms over my chest, scowling. "For the sake of us all, Mimi, you best hope it was one of you fools."

Wrath slowly steps forward, eyes narrowed, his curiosity piqued. "Why, brother?"

The hair on my nape stiffens, my expression suddenly grave.

"Because whoever killed Charlotte's double did so with our Father's Holy Spear."

CHAPTER TWENTY-ONE

Charlotte

I come to on the floor of Grand Central Station, my body aching and bruised from all the ways Mark's hurt me, but when I try to sit up, a pair of harsh hands gently hold me in place.

"Don't move."

The rough voice is familiar. One that seems to have haunted my dreams.

But this time when I glance toward him, it's not Death's skeletal face that stares back at me. It's the face of an angel.

The Angel of Death.

"Where am I?" I rasp, gazing up into his handsome features.

He doesn't answer me.

Instead, he strokes a gentle, reverent hand through my hair, his breath hitching as I relax into his touch. "Your soul looks just like his before..."

Somehow, I know without asking that he means Lucifer.

"He hurt me."

I don't know whether I mean Mark or Lucifer—how he lied to me. Maybe both?

My angel's face softens. "Charlotte, we only have a few moments, and there's things you need to know. Things he's been keeping from you that would—"

Abruptly, my angel glances up, his expression hardening.

I scrunch my face in confusion, noting the hint of fury tightening his jaw. "How do you know my—?"

But Lucifer's warning snarl rings out loud and clear. "Azrael."

I wake to the sound of my alarm clock a moment later, quickly realizing, even through my half-awake haze, that I must have slept for nearly twenty-four hours and I'm going to be late to my coffee date with Imani. I roll over, groaning and pulling my pillow over my head like somehow that might hide me.

I don't want to see all the notifications on my phone. To face the outside world.

The media. The paparazzi. Lucifer.

The concerned texts I know I'll have from Jax, Evie, and so many others.

Imani will have drafted a statement for me by now, to address both the tragedy at Mark's church and Olivia's murder. All I'll have to do is read it—look convincing—but I . . . can't seem to bring myself to face it just yet.

I roll onto my side, peeking out from beneath my pillow and trying to push all thoughts of that strange dream from my mind, only to find a fresh bouquet of white tulips waiting for me. I smile. The card beside it, scrawled in a familiar flowing script, only says two words.

Forgive me?

Followed by a few scribbled music notes. The melody of the song Lucifer wrote for me.

Forgive him? He must mean for leaving again.

I sigh, deliberately cutting off the desperation I feel whenever he's away. My limbs grow heavy, and I chew on my chapped lower lip until it starts to bleed. How are we supposed to find our way back to one another when the chaos of our lives keeps getting in the way?

My heart thumps painfully.

Finally, when I can no longer avoid it, I throw on the nearest set of clothes I can find. A pair of leggings and an oversized T-shirt that, thanks to the designer labels, cost several thousand dollars, though to be honest, my old ones that were off the rack are just as comfy. I couldn't care less about what I look like right now.

Not when Olivia will never take another breath.

Not when so many others have lost a part of their family.

I trudge down the stairs, my legs feeling wooden and like I'm barely managing to put one foot in front of the other, until I find Imani waiting on the bottom level for me.

"I thought it best I bring the coffee to you, all things considered." She nods to the floor-to-ceiling window.

My gaze darts toward it, to Madison Avenue below, as all the wind rushes from my lungs like I've taken a punch to the gut. There's a huge crowd outside, large enough they're blocking the road, their protest signs extending for several blocks.

Daughter of Babylon. Satan's whore. The usual. Followed by an even more horrible one that reads: **God hates fags.** I cringe. Another far-right hate campaign.

And the largest by far.

Hell hath no fury like Lucifer's wretched queen.

The Righteous. Among others like them.

As if this situation couldn't get any worse.

"They're not wrong," I whisper, stepping closer toward the glass. "About me, I mean."

I press my hand to the chilled window, trying not to notice how it feels less solid beneath my newfound strength.

Imani doesn't say anything. She joins me at my side and pushes the coffee she brought into my trembling hand.

I stare down at it blankly. Normally I'd suggest drinking on the balcony, or maybe in the sitting room considering how cold it's been getting outside, but all I manage is a weak "I . . . think we might be safer inside this morning."

She nods. "Good call."

We end up sitting alone together inside the empty kitchen. Lucifer's private chef, Farouq, and the other waitstaff have been paid to stay home for their own safety.

The stainless steel industrial-size refrigerators gleam.

"How are you holding up?" Imani says, shutting one of the kitchen doors behind us so that the distant sounds of the crowd are sealed away. Her wig is rumpled, and she looks even more concerned for me than usual. Like she's afraid I might break at the slightest sign of trouble.

I shake my head, my eyes darting toward the closed door that blocks out the city.

Where the Righteous wait for me.

They blame me for Olivia's death. Mark's congregants' deaths, too, apparently.

They're right in any case.

I stare down at the disposable coffee cup in my hands, trying to let some of its warmth soak into me. The more I focus on it, the more the numbness inside me starts to dissipate.

When I was little, my mother and I used to drink tea together like this each morning. As soon as I was big enough to hold a mug, she'd made me my own tiny cup before she woke me—decaf, of course—so I wouldn't sip nearly all of hers with a repeated, "Mama, peease?"

Her tea monster. That's what she called me.

The tightness in my chest constricts.

Sometimes I wonder if she ever suspected what kind of monster I'd truly be.

A feeling of heaviness washes over me.

"It's my fault," I whisper, glancing down as I try and hide my tears.

Imani grabs my hand, squeezing it. "Don't you dare believe that nonsense for a second," she says fiercely. "You didn't do this. You hear me?" Righteous fury fills her eyes.

Like to believe anything less of myself would be an insult to both her and me.

She's lifted me up and helped me build my confidence at every turn, giving me chances to succeed when no one else would. Not even Lucifer.

I curl in on myself.

"Olivia's family?" I ask weakly.

She swallows. "They've been notified. We're paying for the funeral, and they'll be compensated with—"

"Double it," I say, without hesitating. "Whatever it is. Double it. Triple it, if you want. I never want them to have to worry about anything ever again. It's . . . it's the least we can do."

Imani's eyes soften. "She knew the risks when she took the job, Charlotte."

But did she really?

I definitely didn't when I agreed to all this.

I look upward, shaking my head, a hard edge suddenly in my voice. "Yeah, but at what point does it become extortion when we offered her more money than she could ever reasonably expect to earn in her lifetime?" I stare directly at Imani, no warmth in my eyes as my mouth pinches into a sour expression.

Imani looks away, sighing dejectedly, though she doesn't offer any excuses. For either of us. We both know who we chose to work for. "The media coverage is less than favorable right now. This doesn't look good. For you or for Lucifer. There'll be a lot more attention on the CFDA Awards, on both of you, after all this. The NYPD is involved now. There'll be an official investigation, but we both know that the legal team will make sure that they don't . . ." Her voice trails off, the unspoken words hanging in the air between us.

That they don't find anything.

Whoever did this is likely the same person or celestial who left that envelope full of anthrax for me. That much is obvious. They got past the penthouse and building security without a trace, but if they've been watching us that closely and they know I'm immortal now, then surely they would have known about Olivia, which means...

This was meant as a warning to me.

My heart stops.

Somehow that makes it all so much worse.

My thoughts take a dark turn, to the ashy, terrified look on Xzander's face as he pushed me out of his studio. *Oh no.*

Xzander. The studio. The police.

Oh God.

I hadn't even been in the right frame of mind to stop and consider that I should have never left him alone to—

"What about Xzander?" I ask, panic rising as I grab hold of Imani's wrist. "The police. They didn't—?"

"No, he's fine," Imani says, knowing exactly what I mean. "They took him in for questioning, and he's shaken, but he'll be all right. Our lawyers took good care of him."

"He shouldn't have had to risk himself like that. Not for me."

Police brutality didn't end when the Originals came topside. If anything, all the division lately has made everything so much worse.

"None of this is your fault, Charlotte."

I nod. Logically, I know she's right, but...

I can't stop the pain it brings me.

All those people. All those people.

My heart constricts.

Imani seems to recognize where my thoughts are heading. "He said to tell you he'll be back shortly."

My "fiancé" she means. I sigh, my heart aching.

A real proposal feels like it's a long time coming. Even though it's only been a few days since we last spoke about it. Does wanting it make me . . . complicit in all this? Like the Righteous say?

"Where is he off to this time?" I don't try to hide my disappointment. These days it feels like Lucifer's gone more than he's here.

"To Hell. Handling things. The other Originals are there, too, I think."

I lift an unconvinced brow.

"Look, I don't ask, and he doesn't tell. It keeps things easy." Her gaze flits over me.

But shouldn't he be here? With me?

I don't say it out loud, but still, I think it. He promised he'd do whatever it takes to be worthy of me, and yet . . .

All those people.

I nod, staring down at my coffee.

It's times like these, when I'm at my loneliest, that I miss my mother the most, and the grief sneaks up on me. I suppose grief is cyclical like that. Fate can never allow you to grieve only once. It has to circle around. Make you ache twice as hard.

Though maybe Lucifer's feeling just as many doubts as I am lately. My lip trembles.

"Oh, girl, don't start the waterworks on me now. My mascara can't handle it, baby." Imani pulls me into her then, giving me a fierce, tight hug before she quickly smooths the sides of my hair for me. If I had a crooked crown, Imani would be the kind of woman who would straighten it. She's a girl's girl through and through.

When she pulls back, she smiles at me. "Have I ever told you about how I met that monstrous man of yours?"

Monstrous? I nearly snort.

The word seems too light, too mythical to hold the full truth.

Lucifer is both devil and angel.

To me especially.

My shoulders sink, my posture slumping. If only Imani knew how some of Lucifer's power lives inside me now. But even after what he did to the Righteous, he . . .

He's not monstrous. Not truly. At least, not like they claim.

My mind turns to when I first fell in love with him, the night he cast the aurora borealis over the city.

I have to hold on to that feeling. Believe in him, in the goodness I know he's capable of, in us now more than ever.

Because if I don't . . .

Well, then the immortal abilities I've been hiding—the way Lilith or fate or God or whoever the hell oversees the universe when He's gone has made me complicit—is . . . terrifying.

Monstrous.

Without question.

I shake my head, my thoughts turning back to Imani's question. We both know she hasn't told me anything about when *our boss*—I frown—first started Apollyon Incorporated, but the way she says it gives me the chance to opt out, if I want to . . .

To avoid thinking about what all this means for Lucifer and me.

But the fact it's taken her this long to tell me, coupled with her you-sure-you-wanna-know look makes me think that it's more than a little juicy, and honestly, I could use a gossip-fueled distraction right about now.

I can't believe I've spent all this time with her as my mentor without actually asking.

"Spill the tea," I whisper, leaning in.

She launches into a tale that's nearly two decades old. One that starts with a young aspiring model and ends with her plucked from obscurity into a life of total glitz and glamour . . .

Never to worry about anything ever again.

A modern-day fairy tale.

Until the devil comes calling for his due, of course . . .

"Is that true?" I scrunch my nose in a you've-got-to-be-kidding-me face, though she can't see my expression from where my head is perched on her shoulder.

"Girl, don't be naive." She laughs. "I ain't you, though I could be." She shrugs. "But it made you stop crying, didn't it?"

Together we both chuckle as I lift my head, swiping at my swollen eyes.

"Promise to tell me the real story eventually?"

She snorts. "Maybe if you get enough drinks in me." With that, she whips out her portfolio. Today the fabulous purse she's carrying is an Yves Saint Laurent, the gold YSL emblem gleaming at me. "You still wanna go through with this whole proposal thing? I wouldn't blame you if you'd changed your mind after all this." She waves toward the closed door to indicate the protesters down on the street.

I nod, settling onto the stool beside her and pulling some of the papers toward me, thinking of my revelation with Azmodeus yesterday. "Actually, I have a new idea, a change in direction, and I'd love to know what you think."

She nods, prepared to listen, as I settle in for a long explanation.

This will take some convincing.

But even as it feels as if my whole world is spinning out of control, I can't help but think this is the right move, the one thing I know without a doubt belongs to me.

The choice to pave my own path forward.

Fate can suck it.

CHAPTER TWENTY-TWO

Lucifer

It takes a little more than twenty-four hours to extract every relevant detail from my siblings about how all the events of late are connected and another several for me to finally wheedle an answer about the rebellion in my realm out of Astaroth, but the satisfaction I feel at his inevitable admission is worth it.

"For fuck's sake would you turn that ruddy song off?" he screams, writhing as he covers his now-bleeding ears.

Toto's "Africa" plays on a never-ending repeat throughout the empty shopping mall, the ghastly, terrible noise echoing off the faded pink ceramic tile. A fake potted palm tree sits nearby, its gauche and faded fronds feeble and wilting, and he makes the unfortunate mistake of reaching for it, though he no longer has the strength nor the will to truly use it against me.

I step onto his outstretched hand, using the vintage remote control in my grasp to increase the volume as he moans.

"Fine. You win!" he shrieks. "I did it for you, you miserable, sodding jackass! Once Michael and the Righteous had her, I thought . . . the spell she has over you would be broken."

I press my foot down harder, his bones crunching. "And?"

When he doesn't immediately answer, I bend back his outreached arm, the audible pop as it's removed from its socket and twisted oddly satisfying.

He snarls, bending and arching beneath me. "I knew Lilith had created her for you from the start, but I . . . I thought you wouldn't want to be undermined. You were about to abandon the plan all for the love of her. Everything we'd worked for."

I twist harder. "You misread me."

"I . . . didn't know you'd still see it through."

"And Mother? What's her play in all this?"

He keens, writhing at the continued pressure. "There are . . . whispers among the demons, among the Nephilim. We . . . hear things," he pants. "She wants you to open the seals. Play Michael's apocalypse game. She means for you to challenge God. Take His place."

"Does she now?" I drop his now-useless arm before I move to his leg. I'll tear him limb from limb for my own bloody amusement, if that's what it takes. "Too bad you staked your life on those claims."

"I meant to *protect* you," he howls. "She changed you. I don't know anything about the spear. But Abaddon and the legions . . . they grow restless. If you don't appease them, they—"

"And do you think I need protecting *now*?" I force him to roll over, kicking him hard enough that he groans. He coughs up a bit of blood onto the tile nearest me. "Your true death will come swiftly. Consider it a mercy for your *loyalty*," I sneer, licking my thumb and using the bit of my spit like Christ's ashes as I begin to make my mark on his head.

"No. No, Lucifer. I—"

Hellfire crackles beneath his skin, scorching him from the inside out as he crumbles into dust on the empty Florida mall floor. Nothing more than the matter that I used to make him. A subtle rush of wind billows through the corridor, causing his ashes to blow away quickly. The leaves on the fake palm tree shake. I'm no longer alone.

I sense the other presence behind me before I see him.

"You summoned me?"

The graveled voice that speaks is one of cold Death, the sudden chill of his primordial powers making him one of the few beings still capable of affecting me.

And one of the few celestials who *isn't* one of my siblings.

I turn to find his all-too-familiar face. One I know intimately.

"Yes, actually." I straighten, brushing myself off.

Azrael's expression is one of masked indifference as he looks at me. "I need a favor."

At first, Azrael doesn't respond. He simply glares at me, his dark, narrowed gaze filled with a cruel and infinite knowing.

"You attempted to steal her from me. I can't allow that now, can I?"

Azrael appears unmoved. "It wasn't personal, Lucifer."

I scowl. "Why do I find that difficult to believe?"

We stare at one another, both refusing to blink. A whole lifetime of communication seems to pass silently between us. Every hurt. Every doubt. Every wicked deed.

The doubt is more than I bargained for, quite frankly.

"Well, in any case, should something like that happen again"—I level Azrael with a hardened stare, my lip curling—"whatever we were would fail to matter."

Azrael's jaw clenches. "I don't respond kindly to threats."

Another chill blows through the abandoned mall, and an unpleasant tingling sensation crosses the back of my neck, but I refuse to look away.

I would rip apart the world for her.

Make any threat. Sign any deal. Kill *anyone*. Do or say anything.

No matter how barking mad and disturbed it may be.

I am exactly what my Father made me, after all.

"Azrael," I whisper, my jaw clenched and my voice humiliatingly . . . vulnerable. "I will ask you this only once." I cast a furious, pleading look at him. "Please don't take her from me."

Azrael tilts his head to the side. "I've . . . never heard you beg for anything."

"Nor will you ever again." I nod, my gaze hardening as I push a stray hand through my hair. "Should I consider it done then?"

Azrael sighs, long and low. "You know I can't do that. Not even for you, Lightbringer."

My expression turns cold. "Well, I had to try at any rate."

"You love her?" Azrael watches me curiously as if he knows without a doubt that it's true, but he's simply astonished to find that I'm capable of it.

That makes two of us.

Before there was her, there was, well . . .

A thousand lifetimes. Another eternity.

"Yes. Yes, I do," I say, meeting his gaze head-on as my grin turns devious. "Though you know, I've always preferred to share."

Azrael quirks a brow in interest as he nods, like he's taking that knowledge into advisement. "If that's the case"—his cold gaze rakes over me—"I think I may have a better offer that suits you."

CHAPTER TWENTY-THREE

Charlotte

The following days pass by in a blur, an endless parade of media coverage and seemingly nonstop interviews, until I basically collapse in a heap on Imani's desk late one night. The first twenty-four hours after Olivia's death were the worst. Locked away alone in the penthouse, like a princess trapped in a tower, until the last of the protestors finally dispersed and stopped screaming their hatred at me. But honestly, I'm not sure which was more exhausting—all the invasive interviews I had today or the loneliness that's been gripping me.

Lucifer hasn't been home in several days.

I fiddle with a spare paper clip on my desk, trying hard not to look as miserable as I feel. This morning when I arrived at Apollyon headquarters, there was an odd sense of comfort in seeing how full my inbox was, even with all the security staff not allowed to be more than five feet from me, but now that I've gotten my inbox under control, that familiar feeling of emptiness whenever Lucifer's away is back again, needling me.

"Go home, Charlotte," Imani says, sensing I'm well past my limit. "Get some rest."

I don't need to be told twice.

When the security team delivers me safely back to the penthouse, a feeling of thickness tightens my throat. I wrap my arms around myself, unable to stand the sight of the empty halls as I wander aimlessly.

Maybe I should text Jax and see if she's available tonight? Or maybe even strike up a conversation with Ramesh to see how his wife and kids are doing.

Anything to avoid being alone.

I open my text app, reading through all the unanswered messages beneath Jax's name.

Shit. There's too many of them.

What kind of lame friend is so busy they unintentionally ghost their bestie?

But as I wander up to our bedroom, typing out a reply, I find a familiar face waiting for me.

"Lucifer," I exhale. It feels like I can breathe for the first time in days.

"Charlotte." Lucifer grins, his smirk beckoning me.

I want to drop my phone along with the Dior bag I'm carrying and launch myself into his arms without a second thought. Give in to the relief that fills me. Beg him to do whatever it takes to make me feel whole.

I'm an honest-to-God mess whenever he's gone.

I'm addicted to him, truly.

But I . . . can't seem to stop the hurt that holds me in place.

I watch him for a long moment, opening and closing my mouth several times. At first, no words form, until I manage a weak, "Where have you been?"

Lucifer quirks his head. "Everywhere, darling." His eyes narrow as he watches me, the darkness in his gaze intensifying as he clocks all the evidence of how I'm feeling.

My hunched shoulders, the slight press of my lips, the long-pained look I give him before I glance away.

"You're . . . upset?"

He says it like it's a curious observation, his attention combing over me as if he legitimately expects to find me injured but doesn't.

I try not to cast a weak, sad smile at him, at how unsure he seems, but I would never let him know how amusing it is to see him openly confused like this.

To Lucifer's credit, he must be getting better at reading human emotion, or me at least, because he spends a moment longer looking a bit perplexed before his eyebrows shoot up suddenly. "You're upset with *me*?"

"Hurt, actually. There's a difference." I shrink a little. I don't consider for even a second how risky I'm being by correcting him, or what punishment will be in store for me later.

All I want is for him to see me.

To see how badly I needed him here. With me.

"Is this about the other day?" he asks, stepping carefully toward me. Like if he moves too fast, I might break. Too many people have been treating me that way lately. "Your PR idea or perhaps—"

"The death threat I received?" Time seems to stop, my breath hitching as my heart slows to a pause. "How you left me alone in the aftermath? Or maybe how you murdered my father without my permission, haven't given me any more information about what all this fated business means for our relationship, or maybe the over a thousand people you killed? You tell me."

Lucifer goes still. "I did what I had to do for our future. Even if you can't see it yet. Every one of those *people*," he sneers, "had a hand in helping plot against you. The bombs at the Met Gala. Your abduction. You think that was the act of a sole individual, who—"

I wince. "I can't do this with you right now."

The tension in the room expands until I can't even tell where it begins and I end. Heat rises in my face.

"She took my choice from me," I whisper, my voice breaking.

"Charlotte," he breathes, hesitating before he reaches for me. He captures a lock of my hair, stroking it between his fingers as I turn away from him, and that familiar emptiness creeps back in.

I want so badly to close the distance between us—to be honest, open, and transparent with him, give in to the vulnerability I'm feeling, to voice all my desires and concerns—that I almost step toward him, but after what he said following my father's funeral, I'm . . . not certain I can trust it, trust *him*.

Not any longer.

In the aftermath, you weren't there, I want to whisper, thinking of all the days that've passed since Olivia. *You weren't there for me.*

I shake my head. "I don't want to talk about this anymore." I turn away from him.

But Lucifer snarls, fast and punishing. "You will not turn your back on me. Do I make myself clear?"

I freeze, my breath going shallow before I face him. "Crystal."

I don't want to fight with him anymore, but the growing divide between us seems so insurmountable that I can't begin to see how either of us is ever going to cross it.

Lucifer draws closer to me, prowling like a languid jungle cat until he reaches out and slowly brushes my cheek. The movement is soft at first, tentative, but when I try to turn my head away from him again, he grips the back of my neck, his fingers digging into my skin possessively.

The next thing I know his mouth is on mine, forcing me to kiss him, driving all other thoughts from my head. The feel of his lips is almost too much at first, his touch filled with a hunger that matches my own.

And I can't stop the relief that fills me.

I missed you, his kiss seems to say.

Followed by, *Forgive me?*

It's not an apology. I know better than to expect that. I'm not certain an apology is something he could ever truly mean.

But that he would ask for my forgiveness is the harsh reminder I need.

You're mine.

Totally. Completely.

A warm tear slides down my face as I soften for him, the need inside me growing until I'm meeting him tongue for tongue, touch for touch, as desperate for him as he is for me. His mouth on mine hardens, turning into something crueler, more tempting.

The energy between us shifts, growing electric and heavy.

Until neither of us can resist.

It's not his softness I need right now.

I grip his shoulders, my nails digging in.

Suddenly, his hand dips below my skirt. He shoves the crotch of my panties aside as he probes me, my pussy already damp for him. Like the brokenness in him knows exactly how to heal the brokenness in me.

Love made toxic.

"Ah, I see," he purrs, stroking down the center of my folds in a way that makes me whimper. "This is why you've been so poorly behaved lately, hmm? Being late to dinner. Running from your security team. And now? Turning your back on me. You've been begging for it."

I can hardly think through the haze of desire that grips me, all logic and resistance driven from my head as he strokes me, slow and deliberate. "I . . . don't know what you mean. I—"

But Lucifer simply smirks at me, curling his fingers inside me in a close mimic of that beckoning come-hither gesture that seems to summon all my desire.

I melt into his arms instantly, allowing him to hold me upright as he supports my weight.

"When you cannot ask for what you want, why not misbehave? Right, little dove?" He lays a kiss on my neck, one of his fangs nicking me. "A brat-fueled temper tantrum gets my attention all the same, doesn't it?"

I shake my head, the admonishment clearing the haze. I want to be a good girl for him. I always do, except when I . . .

Deliberately try to drive him mad.

"No, sir. I—"

But the dark look he spears me with silences me, making it clear that he's read me for filth.

And he knows it.

"How many times did you wish for my cock while I was away?" His voice wraps around me, making my pussy practically purr with anticipation. His gaze rakes over me as he wets his lips, drinking me in appreciatively. "How many nights have you touched yourself when I ordered you to be patient for me?"

I freeze, my face and neck growing impossibly hot.

I open my mouth, trying to find some excuse, but I . . . don't answer.

I wish I could be as bold as he expects me to be. To ask for what I want.

But no matter what I do, I can't seem to make this . . . this feeling go away. The constant shame that my father created in me. So, I do the only thing I know how to do. The one thing I've done every night since he first claimed me, broke me in two even as he put me back together again, until he made me forever and irrevocably his, even as he destroyed me completely.

I look up at him, willing the softness in my eyes to say it for me.

Conquer me. Claim me, I plead. *Remind me I'm yours.*

"Please, sir?" I whisper, my neck and face on fire with shame.

Lucifer smirks wickedly. "In the future, you *will* ask for what you want, or you will not receive it at all, do I make myself clear?"

"Yes, sir," I practically keen, my breath hitching as he strokes that spot deep inside me again, the one he knows makes me come undone.

Seconds later, I'm openly panting for him, sliding up and down on his slick, coated fingers until my pussy is a wet, dripping mess.

The dirty little slut only he can make me be.

Lucifer's responding grin is heavenly, sin and desire all rolled into one.

Already he's won this round, and we're only just beginning.

"Go to the playroom and wait in position for me," he orders, removing his hand from my pussy only to lick his fingers clean. When I don't immediately move, his eyes darken as he growls, with all the force of an experienced dominant, "*Now*, Charlotte."

CHAPTER TWENTY-FOUR

Charlotte

I kneel on the floor of the playroom, my knees sinking into the soft St Genève pillow that's been placed there for me. A pillow I had to *earn* during the first month we began this ritual. I bite my lower lip, struggling to sit still as my anticipation nearly gets the better of me.

This is how he shows his love for me. How he claims me. Body and soul.

I clasp my hands together, trying hard not to move from where I've been instructed to sit and wait, unable to think of anything else but when he'll finally decide to join me.

My knees will never forget the bruising in those early weeks, the tenderness they felt from all the times he made me sit tight *without* the cushion, but that only makes the comfort of the pillow beneath me all the more luxurious now. All the more delicious even.

A reminder of exactly how good I've been.

I hear his footsteps before he enters, the sound sending an echoing hum through my chest. I settle into my position, placing my hands in my lap and lowering my head like I'm supposed to. Like I'm a good girl.

I *am* a good girl. Only for him, it seems.

But lately I've . . . needed a reminder of why I should behave.

I don't allow myself to look up as he enters, no matter how much I'm tempted to. And I'm *so* tempted that it feels like I can't control myself. I'm obsessed with him.

And, at the moment, I hate it.

I hate him. I hate me.

Hate the version of myself I become when I'm with him, the way he makes me feel.

Like there's this constant ache inside my chest that needs soothing, and he's the only one who can possibly ease it.

I hate how much I crave what he does to me.

But I still want it.

I keep my head low, straining to stop myself from looking up until he tells me to. The first time I made that mistake, he ordered me to sleep on the floor at the foot of his bed for nearly a week, but I'll never take for granted what a privilege it is to sleep beside him now, wrapped up in his arms. I know our protocol backward and forward.

And I'll never break it again.

Not unintentionally, at least.

The sounds of his steps draw closer until, from where my head's lowered, I can see the smooth polish of his Armanis, the shine of his shoes, but still, he doesn't say anything.

"Please, Daddy?" I whisper, defiant, cheeky. Like I used to be.

Like he sometimes likes me to be.

He growls. "You know better than to speak before spoken to."

I lower my head in feigned obedience, and he huffs slightly.

"Sir will do for tonight." He pats my head like I'm his creature, his pet, and I have to force myself not to lean into it because I'm just *that* desperate for him to touch me. "You know what to do, darling."

My cheeks flush as I lower my head and kiss his shoes. On occasion, when I've lost myself in the haze of subspace, I've wanted to curl up and rest my head there, gazing up at him adoringly. But now, the thought of my own need simply fills me with shame.

Shame he's going to work out of me.

Like he's exorcising my demons away.

I try to silence those unfair thoughts, but without him, it feels useless.

I shouldn't like this. I shouldn't *want* this, and yet, I do.

Even when it feels like the whole world's crumbling around us.

I crave this, crave him.

Nearly as much as I know he craves me.

The smell of his shoe polish and the Italian leather of his Armanis fills my nose as I gently lay a second kiss on his other shoe, the scent reminding me of some of the toys he might use on me this evening.

Sometimes, if I've been particularly good, he'll let me choose which tools he uses as a reward, a special treat. Though tonight, I have no intention of being good.

It's his punishment I need.

And we both know it.

He turns away from me then, not offering me the privilege, and despite all the ways I've purposefully misbehaved, somehow the thought that I haven't been good for him guts me.

I want to be good.

I want to be good for him so badly it scares me.

It's my own insecurities that drive me to test boundaries, the limits of his love. Only for his punishment to reassure me that he'll always be there for me in the end. Nothing I could ever do could drive him away, make him abandon me like my father did.

Like his Father did to him.

I can be my most dark and wicked self with him.

And he'll love me despite it.

The same as I do for him.

"You can look up now, Charlotte."

I bite my lip, but I do as I'm told, lifting my gaze to find him standing a few paces away. He's stripped off his suit coat, and his suspenders are cut across his back like some kind of shoulder holster. I watch hungrily as he rolls up the cuffs of his sleeves.

Holy fuck.

How is it possible for me to want someone so badly? For anyone to be so beautiful? For me to feel so greedy for him, even when he's away?

I want him on me, in me, everywhere.

This second.

But I have to wait patiently. Show him how good I can be—when I want to.

My subservience will be worth it in the end.

He finishes rolling up his shirtsleeves and then steps toward me, his movements so deliberate it feels like a delicious dance choreographed just for me. "How many times did you touch yourself while I was away?"

"I . . ."

"Answer me," he growls.

I swallow thickly. "F-four times, sir."

"Every *day*?" he says, his voice going a bit higher at the end like he can't believe how impossibly bratty I've been.

I nod weakly, heat filling my cheeks.

"On the bondage table," he orders, his tone full of reprimand. When I don't immediately start moving from where I'm too busy sulking at how ashamed I am of myself, he snarls, "*Now.*"

I scramble to my feet, eyes lowered as I head toward the bondage table, where he directed me, and kneel on top of it. It's smooth handcrafted wood, the top covered in a layer of lush black padding and the sides lined with gleaming silver hooks. For a piece of furniture, it's incredibly sexy. Custom made. The height of luxury. Just like everything Lucifer owns.

Me included.

I bite down on my lip, trying to suppress the nervous giggle that bubbles up in my throat, but I fail miserably. It's true, after all.

I'm the most expensive whore New York City's ever seen.

"Is something funny?"

"No, sir."

Lucifer appears at my side a moment later, a length of rope in his hands as he tips my chin up, forcing me to look at him. "Next time you won't be laughing if you don't crawl for me. Do you understand?"

"Yes, sir," I whisper, dropping my gaze.

"Good girl," he purrs, though from the derisive way he says it, we both know he's taunting me, daring me to disobey him again. "Now, spread your legs for me."

I do as I'm told, spreading my thighs as he checks how wet I am, drawing a whimper from me. Using the rope, he starts at my wrists, binding me with an intense, methodical precision, the repetition so mesmerizing that I quickly fall into what feels like a trance.

A familiar feeling of lightness settles over me, the natural fibers brushing against my skin as any thought of the outside world, of anything beyond *this*, beyond us, simply fades away. The process is so focused, so deliberate and meditative, even, the unyielding tension of the rope and his movements as he binds my hands and feet together behind my back so soothing that I feel all the stress I've been carrying start to melt off me.

His attention to detail and precision is overwhelming.

This is how I know that he cares for me.

Why he deserves the submission I give him each evening he's home. This is an act of love, an act of dominance. For me.

I stay as silent and still as I'm able, my eyes never leaving his face save for when he needs to step behind me to better secure my binding, until I feel so overwhelmed, so vulnerable with the emotion of it all, that I think I might cry, if he'd let me.

He's making up for his absence with all the attention he's paying me, rope by rope.

I love you, his actions seem to say. Followed by, *I'm sorry.*

Or as close as he could ever get to it, anyway.

I swallow down the lump that forms inside my throat, the part of me that wishes for a time when things were simpler between us, despite how connected I feel to him. If I try to move against where he's tied me, rope burn can set in easily, and while I enjoy a bit of pain, that's not the kind he's aiming for tonight.

Tonight, he wants my submission. Total control of my body.

To remind me of how I disobeyed him this week. Touched what's his.

My sole purpose is to please him.

Take his punishment until I remember I'm *his* completely.

Finally, when he finishes, I can feel that the knots are more decorative than prohibitive compared to others he's done previously, but still, I can't move my hands or feet easily.

He takes in the sight of me bared for him before he leans forward and softly kisses my shoulder. A familiar brush of lips against skin.

Like all our shared sins have melted away.

"Forgive me," he whispers as he pulls back.

The mood shifts abruptly, and even though I know what's coming, I'm still not prepared for the shock of it.

Lucifer shoves me down face-first onto the table, my cheek now roughly jammed flat against the cushion so that my pussy and my ass are lifted and bared to him.

"You've been waiting for this, haven't you?" he growls against my ear. "Begging for it all week?"

"Yes, sir," I whimper, but my cries aren't enough to satisfy him, so he pulls back his hand and uses one of the tools he's just grabbed from a nearby rack to paddle me.

The blow lands on my left butt cheek, the sting and then burn that follows radiating out from the impact. It charges me like a live wire, making my pussy even more impossibly wet to the point that I feel some of it smear across the leather cushion as I slide forward a little on the next blow.

Shame burns through my cheeks.

Oh God.

And to think we're only just getting started.

He paddles me again, and I let out a greedy, uninhibited moan. "Fill me up, Daddy."

The words are out before I can stop them, making me flush so hot that I couldn't manage to say anything else even if I tried.

Lucifer's amused chuckle that follows is a cruel, tempting thing, but I want his cock so badly that I can't bring myself to regret it.

How the fuck does he do this to me?

"There's the nasty little slut I fell in love with," he whispers to me, his tone smug as he trails his hand over the curve of my spine until he cups me, dipping his fingers inside like he's pleased at how ready I am. "Mmm, you're soaked for me. Have you been misbehaving to get my attention, darling?"

You know I have, I almost confess.

But I bite down on my lip, shaking my head to deny it, even though we both know it's true. It's the brat in me.

I've never been able to resist tempting him, goading him. Right from the start.

"Are you lying to me, Charlotte?" he says as if he heard exactly what I was thinking.

I shake my head again, whimpering as his fingers brush against my clit only to disappear back into my folds, edging me further and further.

"Do you know what will happen if you lie to me? If you keep defying me?"

I shake my head, playing coy.

Suddenly, his mouth is on my ear, his fangs nicking me. The serpentine hiss of his voice wraps around me as he pinches my clit, rolling it between his fingers. "I'll fuck you until you're so full of me you'll be begging for my mercy. Do I make myself clear?"

I bite down on my lower lip, trying to stop myself, but this time, I . . . can't.

"Is that supposed to be a punishment, sir?" I ask, lifting my ass in tribute to him.

I can hear his low growl of arousal in response.

But he's not having it.

He grips me by the hair, pulling it back so hard that I let out a sharp cry as several of his fingers are rammed up inside me, pushing so deep they nearly brush against my cervix. A reminder of exactly who's in charge. "I said. Are. We. Clear?"

"Yes, yes, sir," I whimper, scrambling to correct myself. "Yes, sir, we're clear."

"Good." He shoves me back down and onto the table again like I mean nothing to him. I *am* nothing. Not beyond what he's made me. "For your punishment tonight, you will take me bare, Charlotte."

I choke. "Wha—what?"

"Only *after* you've come so many times, you beg for me. You *will* learn to ask for what you want."

He thrusts something up inside me then. A vibrator or some other kind of sex toy from the feel of it. A thin lubed butt plug follows, plunging into my other hole a moment later.

And before I can stop him, the toy is on, vibrating.

Fully within his control.

And I'm powerless to stop it.

I try to writhe against where he's bound me, escape the too-intense sensation of it, but I can't move. Quickly the pressure builds and builds until I'm coming out of my skin from the pleasure of it. It's too much. Too much.

Until, suddenly, it . . . stops abruptly.

"No. No, no, please."

By the time he's built me up and edged me close to oblivion for the fourth time, only to cruelly rip it away from me again, I'm swearing, writhing from a mixture of too-intense need and sweet fucking torture until I'm shaking.

I'll die if this doesn't end soon.

"Please, please, sir," I beg. "I need your cock in me."

That's my only chance at relief.

The pharmacy has been filling my birth control, and I take it religiously, but I'm not sure it's still working, considering I'm immortal now. Human medicine and other substances seem to have less of an effect on divine beings, if the amount of alcohol Lucifer and his siblings are capable of consuming without consequence is any indication, and while this wouldn't be the first time he's taken me raw, filled me up, since he made me immortal, it's the first time since then that I know for a fact I'm ovulating.

And Lucifer knows it too.

My cycles aren't that hard to track.

They're regular. Like clockwork.

And sometimes it feels like he knows what my body needs better than I do.

I'm *his*, after all.

I swallow hard, hesitating. The thrill of the risk, of the fantasy, beckons. The idea of Lucifer cumming inside me, of him breeding me, is so hot, so reckless and insane, a relief from this torture that it's almost . . .

Intoxicating.

And if I'm honest, a part of me *wants* to be reckless with him.

It's one of the few lines we've never crossed. A forbidden fantasy.

And right now, I want it so badly that I can't bring myself to put a stop to this.

This is what he does to me, tempts me into being the most wicked version of myself.

Eve was framed, honestly.

"Please. Please, Lucifer," I whisper, watching as he casts that unholy smirk of his at me.

I want him. I want his cock so much, I can't believe it took me this long to ask for it.

Fuck Lilith and her games.

I chose this.

Chose him.

And everything that goes along with it.

I want this.

It surprises me exactly how much I do, but it's true.

My brain may hardly be able to string a sentence together, but I know what my pussy needs. Without a doubt.

"Please. Please give me your cock, Daddy," I plead, louder this time.

All my life I've been taught this is my one true purpose. To be a wife. To be fruitful and multiply, to build God's kingdom. And the idea that I could fuck that, subvert it and corrupt it with him like the nasty little slut he makes me want to be, feels so delicious and freeing that I want it, despite any unintended consequences it would bring.

I'm Eve with the apple all over again.

Only worse, because I'm pretty sure Eve never fucked him.

But I want the whole world with Lucifer. Every darkness. Every terrible, wicked thing.

Even after everything.

I choose him.

A sudden confidence fills me at my decision, at the reminder of the love that brought me here. That love can't possibly be a mistake.

"Isn't this what you wanted when you chose to misbehave? To be my filthy cum slut?" he growls, refusing to stop this torture, to give me any relief. "To be so full of me that there is never any doubt that you are *mine*?"

I don't answer, but my body answers for me. I rock my hips up and back as much as I'm able, just like I do when I'm eager for him to be inside me.

Like I'm greedy for it.

"Give me a color, Charlotte," he orders.

"Green," I whisper, swallowing hard.

Bright fucking green.

Lucifer chuckles like he knows what I'm thinking.

And that one spoken word changes the tension between us completely, making it even headier, primal even. The fact that I'm so turned on, so feral and horny for him, seems to please him, and I whimper impatiently as he turns off the vibrator, pulling it out of me only so that the fat head of his cock brushes outside my pussy's slick folds.

Oh fuck, what has he done to me?

I rock back eagerly.

It's the ultimate act of submission.

But I . . . I want it.

Want him.

I bite down on my lower lip so hard, I nearly draw blood as he draws out my embarrassment, teasing me. "Ask me for what you want."

"Fuck your cum into me. Please, Lucifer."

Oh God. This is reckless and stupid, and I might regret it later, but right now, I can't bring myself to care about anything beyond what he makes me feel.

And the power in that is seductive.

Intoxicating.

"Beg," he orders, his tip probing the outside of my entrance. Teasing but not yet taking. *Or the vibrator is going to come back, only to stop again.*

Fuck, he's going to make me say it.

Ask for what I need.

It's another lesson. Another punishment.

I have half a mind to try and sink back onto the length of his cock, to brat out and take him into me from where he's positioned right outside my entrance until he's too tempted to do anything but let me ride him greedily.

But I want him inside me so much more than I want him to return that vibrator right now, so I hold my position, obeying. No matter how much I'm straining.

"I . . ."

"Beg for it," he growls. "Like you mean it."

"Please, Daddy," I whisper, my voice high and needy. "Please, I . . . wanna be full of you."

I can hear the smirk on his lips as he chuckles at how filthy and depraved he's made me be. "You will beg and take me like this every night until you are round for me"—he grips one hand over my lower stomach, letting me know exactly what he means—"until you never have any doubt that you are *mine*."

He thrusts into me then, the hard length of his cock filling me to the max in one hot, thick stroke, but I know that's not nearly all of him. Fuck, he's huge. My body seizes, struggling to adjust afterward, until I'm wrapped around him so tight I'm not certain where I end and he begins.

Like he was made for me.

Considering the whole fated thing, maybe he was . . .

Or maybe *I* was made for him.

Made to kneel at his feet. His obedient queen.

The thought shudders through me, and he pulls back and thrusts into me again, the force of it making me gasp as my face slides across the bondage table.

Oh God.

I don't think I can take another inch of him with how tightly wound I am from that vibrator, but then he slams home, topping out, his balls smacking against me as I moan, all thought lost completely.

We both become animals then. Lost in each other.

He fucks me hard, gripping my hips so tight I know without looking there will be bruises from where his fingers dig into me as the table's legs start to buckle and shake, cracking beneath Lucifer's immortal strength.

One of the legs splinters, but I'm still unable to move or do anything but take him, and to my surprise, when he reaches around to finger my clit from behind, lifting my ass up like I'm his perfect little whore, an even more intense orgasm builds inside me.

He pulls out the butt plug roughly. Lubricated with his spit, he shoves one of his fingers into the tight bud of my ass, giving me the extra amount of stimulation I need to nearly send me careening over the edge. He's wringing it out of me, drawing this out. Making it more torturous and intense than before.

"You will *not* come yet, Charlotte," he growls as I almost clench and shatter completely. "Do I make myself clear?"

"Please, sir," I beg, crying and panting, starting to pulse around him as I feel the hot spurts of his cum paint the walls of my pussy.

At this point, I'm no longer above begging.

"Please!"

The feeling of him emptying himself in me, of him throbbing until he's been milked clean where my pussy's been stretched for him, when I'm already so hot, so close, is so delicious and perfect and torturous and nasty it makes me shake from head to toe as I struggle to hold back my own release. An even more powerful orgasm threatens.

But he hasn't given me his permission.

I strain against the ropes painfully.

"Oh fuck . . . I can't . . . Please, Lucifer!" I shout, a string of incoherent babble tearing from my lips.

I can't get enough of him.

I want him on me, in me, everywhere.

Any place that I can take him.

"*Please!*" I sob.

"Show me you've learned your lesson."

"I'm yours. I'm yours, okay? Even when you're away. I won't touch what's yours. Just . . . please let me cum, Daddy?" I cry, unable to control myself any longer.

His dark chuckle rolls through me. "Cum big, little dove."

My orgasm tears through me, furious and out of my control. I pulse and pulse, a sudden gush of hot fluid rushing out from somewhere deep inside me, like his whole point was to show me that I'm *his* and his alone to command. The devastation that reminder wreaks on my heart, on every inch of my body that strains against the ropes, is nearly overwhelming.

I chose this. I chose him.

Horns and all.

Fuck Lilith.

I feel myself continue to throb and throb, the awareness of my own heartbeat and the fluttering in my chest making me lose myself completely.

I'm nothing without this, without him.

Only as good as he makes me.

Finally, when I start to come back down from my haze, the last shudders of my release quivering through me, Lucifer's smooth, lithe hand gently strokes me, brushing me like I'm one of the keys of his piano, until one final drum of pleasure cleaves me in two.

I'm swollen and dripping, I'm so full of him.

Though neither of us is close to calling the scene yet.

Playtime has only just started.

With a few quick movements, he releases me, my bindings falling overtop the table and onto the floor just as one of the legs finally cracks and gives out beneath me.

Lucifer catches me, holding my limp body in place and lifting me into his arms before he seamlessly carries me and drops down into his devil's chair.

I reach for him shortly thereafter, once I've regained strength in my limbs, sliding down his lap and snuggling my head onto his shoe and gazing up at where he sits above me.

"Was I good enough, sir?" I whisper, placing my hands on both of his muscled thighs as I lift myself with shaky limbs to rest my head there.

So close to where I want to be.

"So good, little dove," he purrs.

I stare up at him. "Sir?" I pout, practically begging.

"All right, darling." He chuckles, his head lolling back as I start to remove his unbuckled belt now that I have permission, working to get him hard once more. "Consider this your reward for taking my cock like a fucking dream."

CHAPTER TWENTY-FIVE

Lucifer

Charlotte kneels on the floor beneath me, her playful ministrations quickly working to get me hard again. The thought of what we chased tonight, of her full and round and bred for me, is enough that my cock is soon as stiff as it's ever been. But that's all it is. A dream.

A fantasy.

Nothing more.

"I want to suck you," she whispers from beneath me, nuzzling her head against the side of my thigh. "Please, sir?"

I chuckle, watching how she licks her lips eagerly. "I might die if you don't, love."

She smiles then, but there's a hesitation I feel through our connection that stops me.

She moves to put me inside of her mouth, but I lift my hand. "Give me a color, Charlotte," I order.

She swallows thickly like she's embarrassed that I asked. "Yellow."

Immediately, I ease back. "Explain."

A dark blush fills her cheeks as she kneels before me. "It's just that I . . . love this, but I feel like I'm not very good at it."

"*This* being blowing me?" I quirk a brow, confused by what she could possibly mean.

"You . . . I . . ." The color blossoms down from her cheeks all the way to the curve of her breasts as she exhales. "The first time we ever did this back in your office, you said what I 'lacked in technique' I made up for in 'enthusiasm,' but I"—she lowers her gaze—"guess I want to learn the technique now, sir." She tacks on the address with a hint of panic. Like she fears I might punish her again.

I growl in approval.

Though the reminder that such meaningless, trite words could affect her thusly, that she is still so inexperienced and will continue to be so for some time, humbles me.

And for a moment, I find I can't help but feel . . . remorse for how I've treated her, kept her at arm's length. For her own safety. Her own protection.

I would never push her away for anything less.

Never allow her to think she's anything but my immortal queen.

That's what she'll become. Once she's confident enough to stand by my side.

Once she no longer needs the desperate reassurance of our scenes.

But perhaps I have to help her, guide her.

To be everything I know she can be.

I give a slow nod, tilting my head back and exhaling slowly. "All right, you win." I am agreeable for her and her only. She'll be the ruin of me.

She always has been. Right from the bloody start.

When I meet her eyes, my voice is gentler than I would ever dare use with anyone else, concerned even. I rub a hand over the back of my neck, making a signal to pause the scene. "Why didn't you say something sooner, darling? I would never ask you to do anything that you—"

"I wanted to practice," she says, her eagerness to please me, to show her love for me, only softening me further. "But I feel like I'm not really getting any better at it, so I think I'd like you to"—she bites her lower lip, worrying it between her teeth—"instruct me."

"Instruct you?" I repeat, speaking low to not break the spell.

The charm she's cast over me is a particularly brutal one, vicious and unrelenting.

She nods feverishly.

"And?" I prompt, sensing there's more she isn't readily sharing.

She blushes again, the color bleeding from her face down into her bare nipples. "And I . . . want you to make me cry"—she swallows—"with your cock."

I have to press my lips together to stifle my uninhibited crow of male pleasure.

Bloody fuck, woman.

Her eyes go wide, and she blinks up at me. Like she may now possibly be privy to my thoughts. "Did you . . . did you say something?"

"Quiet," I order, making our signal to resume the scene and shutting that mental door.

"Yes, sir," she whispers, lowering her eyes in submission.

My obedient good girl once again. Thanks to my punishment.

If she recognizes what she just heard, she doesn't mention it as I rise from my throne. A devious smile quirks over my lips at how readily she scurries to make space for me.

Even as I squash the internal sense of panic I feel.

No one has *ever* been privy to my thoughts. Not even my Father, nor His most powerful Seers. But there will be a time and place for that later.

A time to guard myself against the vulnerability she's created in me.

Right now, she needs my steady hand. My guidance.

I look toward her, unable to give voice to all that I'm feeling. *Could you ever possibly know how thoroughly I'm wrapped around your finger, little dove? How I ache for you?* The love, the unhinged obsession I feel for her, is overwhelming.

A small, still-intact part of me wants her to hear it, the things I would never allow myself to speak aloud. I curse under my breath, ever the coward that only she can make me.

I'm the fucking devil, for Christ's sake.

And yet, I can't ever seem to find the right words to truly tell her all that she means to me.

So I must show her.

Get ahold of yourself, Lucifer. She's just a woman, I admonish myself.

But she's *not* just a woman. Not any longer.

Not to me.

Not since the night she first put her faith in me, trusted me as no one else ever has.

She wasn't the only one irrevocably changed when she fell in love with me.

She's simply the only one of us who is still whole enough to admit it.

My tongue darts out to wet my lips, my expression hardening as I try and fail to suppress all the ways she makes me *feel*.

Things I thought I was no longer capable of, quite frankly.

"All right, Charlotte. Your play." I use two fingers to beckon her forward, my expression betraying nothing. "Crawl to me."

She does as she's told, closing the small gap between us with slow, languid movements until she's once again kneeling before me. The sight of her knelt at my feet is one of my favorite things. Her innocence undoes me. The way she submits to me practically makes me come alive. I would do or give anything. Say or be anything.

Anything she needs me to be.

Even my Father's faithful servant . . .

If she asked it of me.

And that kind of power in unexperienced hands?

Well, I can't allow that now, can I?

"Grip my shaft," I order.

"Yes, sir." She places her hand around me, her fingers unable to fully circle me, following my instructions like a good little student.

That's all she's ever wanted to be, ever since we met, of course.

My pet. My creature. My whore.

And soon, my vicious queen.

She was made for this. Made for me.

"Use your hands on any part that your mouth cannot reach," I instruct. "Focus your tongue on the underside of the shaft."

She does as I order, taking me in and out past her lips several times until my head starts to loll back, but she's stopping each time I reach the back of her throat. Like she's too scared to push past her gag reflex for fear of choking.

But I know better than she does what she's capable of.

Charlotte doesn't just need rough. She craves it.

The feeling of being pushed past her current limit.

By me and me only.

"You're not relaxing," I growl. I grip her hair, pulling her up and off my cock so fast that her lips make an audible little *pop* from where she'd managed to get some decent suction on me.

She frowns, her mouth forming a sad pout, like I've deprived her. A greedy brat if there ever was one.

Fuck, she is perfect for me.

I give her a sly grin, my voice dropping low. "I'm going to fuck your face now, show you how to open for me." The fat head of my cock brushes against her cheek. "Slap my thigh as your stop signal."

But I know she won't stop.

Not when I'm giving her what she needs.

Helping her break the shameful shackles her bloody excuse of a father created for her.

I'll spend the rest of our immortal lives undoing the damage humanity's bastardized teachings of my Father's blasted Bible has wrought on *my* pussy.

And that's exactly what she is.

Mine.

Wholly. Completely.

No matter the desperate prayers she still whispers to my Father when she thinks I'm not listening.

She gives a greedy, eager moan.

When I first shove past her gag reflex, she sputters, her eyes watering and her throat attempting to close as she coughs around me, but as I pull out and thrust back in again, my movements fast and punishing, she relaxes for me, submitting to me.

"That's it, darling," I coax. "You're my nasty little slut, aren't you? Open your throat."

She lets out a muffled cry as I push farther in, until she's deep-throating me, my balls slapping against her chin.

Fuck me.

"You take me so well."

I thrust and thrust, my movements becoming more and more feverish as I hold her still by her hair until her eyes are leaking, practically weeping, exactly like she wanted, to the point that she's soaking my thighs, her mascara running down her cheeks, until I can tell from the redness in her face that she's forgotten to breathe.

"Breathe, Charlotte. You deserve this."

She does as I instruct, inhaling through her nose so that her throat tightens around me, sending another delicious pulse up my cock to my spine. But it isn't until she grips my backside unexpectedly, her sharp manicured nails digging into me, that the muffled hum of her cries sends me careening over the edge.

"Fuck, how do you do this to me?" I snarl as I empty myself into her, only her throat at first as she tries to drink me clean, taking every last drop of the perverted Eucharist I offer, before I pull her off just in time to coat her chest and face. As I finish, she beams up at me, a bit of cum and spit on the edge of her lip, which I brush away quickly.

Her lipstick and mascara are ruined, and she looks a right bloody mess, covered in my cum, but she's *my* mess, and she's never been more beautiful to me.

"How did I do, sir?" she whispers, those seemingly innocent doe eyes staring up at me in complete and total adoration.

I smirk, unable to suppress the euphoric high she creates in me. "You were excellent, love. Made for me. You want to be a good girl for me now, don't you?"

She smiles and nods like my praise means the world to her, the pride she offers to me bringing a fresh round of tears, her long lashes gleaming. It's the relief that fills them, the love she gifts me that lets me know what's truly happening. Even if I couldn't recognize it, I feel it through the connection between us, identifying this show of emotion for what it is. This happens occasionally. Subdrop settles into her quickly.

"Hush, little dove. All's forgiven," I whisper, bending down and taking her into my arms.

She wraps herself around me, snuggling her head against my chest as I lift her and begin to carry her toward our bedroom with ease.

"Was I a good girl?" she sniffles, relaxing against my shoulder.

"So good," I purr, eager to indulge her, lavish her with the praise she needs.

"And do you love me?" The desperate look she gives me then, her need for reassurance, makes my pulse race in a way that is . . . uncharacteristic for me.

Until there's nothing left but a feeling of emptiness in the pit of my stomach, a sense that she makes me feel something close to whole in a way no one else ever could.

My throat constricts.

"How could I not, Charlotte?"

I carry her to our bedroom, whispering reassurances to her over and over, long past when she lies beside me asleep, until I find that I'm too in awe of the gift of her submission, by her love, to continue to speak, to worship her in the way she deserves.

I want to give her the promise of a better life, a better future, everything I know she so desperately desires, but it's the one thing that I cannot offer her.

Safety.

From me. From my family.

My chest tightens as I draw her into my arms.

I only hope that she stays with me after she learns all that she is, all that I've kept from her, all that I've done. Now that my Father's redemption has made her the one and only key to reopening the pearly gates, and the only immortal weapon with the power to destroy me.

CHAPTER TWENTY-SIX

Charlotte

Lucifer wakes me and carries me into the shower sometime later, where he takes slow and deliberate care to clean me. This is another favorite. The aftercare. The way he soothes us both. He settles us into our bed after that, once we're both thoroughly dried and clean, his hand brushing over my stomach when he spoons me.

But he's uncharacteristically quiet tonight.

"Do you really want children? With me?" I whisper, breaking the silence.

Lucifer goes still. "Would *you*? Would *you* want that? For me to make you mine in every way?" He's deflecting, evading answering first, but I'd like to think that this would be an area of our life where he could be fully honest with me.

"I would." I nod. "Eventually. You?"

He's quiet for a long moment before finally he says, "Yes, Charlotte, I would. I would wish for that very much."

The confidence in his words warms me, though there's something about the way he says it that sounds almost . . . pained. Like he's keeping something from me.

Like it's yet another thing that he believes he could never possibly deserve.

I arch against him, grinding my ass into his now semihard cock.

He chuckles, playfully palming my breasts. "Shall I carry you back to the playroom for another round?" He trails a line of kisses down my neck until I groan softly.

"Not tonight." I shake my head, clocking his temporary disappointment. "For now, I just want you to hold me."

That's the only thing I've truly wanted all week.

For a moment, he seems a little put off by that, like he can't believe such a simple and vanilla request could be what sates me, but he doesn't say anything as he turns me toward him. We lie in our bed together for a long time, my arms and legs wrapped up with his body until I feel his breathing start to slow from where my head rests lightly against his chest.

He almost never holds me like this.

Except during aftercare. And never when he's asleep.

Lucifer sleeping is a rare and fleeting occurrence. Sleep isn't something he needs, and it doesn't seem to come easily to him. It's an indulgence. A refuge. Which means whatever he has to tell me now that he's back home must be, well, pretty damning for him to be holding on to me.

For now, I try my best not to think of it, to pretend like the world doesn't exist beyond the walls of our bedroom.

I drift off to sleep in his arms and then wake again sometime later, feeling him stir beside me. "You've been gone a lot lately," I whisper into the dark.

"Is that why you were hurt?"

I nod. "After what happened to Olivia, it . . . felt like the whole world was crashing down, and I needed you, but you weren't there."

"I wanted to be," he says, giving me the reassurance I need. "Trust me when I say I hate being apart just as much as you do—perhaps more, if you fully understood what I've been up to—but someone needs to protect you. Who else, if not me?"

"I don't need you to protect me . . ." I mutter, the rest of the thought trailing off.

I just need you to love me.

As if he heard the unspoken words inside my head, he goes still beside me. It's the one thing he's still not fully certain how to do. Not completely.

Love requires vulnerability. Honesty.

A vulnerability that's hard to come by when you're *the* fallen angel.

We both fall quiet then.

"Have you been in Hell?" I ask a few moments later.

"Mostly."

"Will you take me?"

"To Hell?" he asks, his voice holding a bit of confused disbelief at the end, like he can't possibly understand why I'm asking.

I nod vigorously, and he chuckles at me before smoothing a hand over my hair.

"I think I need to see it, your kingdom. If I'm supposed to be its queen," I say.

He lays a soft kiss on my cheek, my shoulder. "Soon, little dove. Soon."

"And your siblings?"

I'm not sure whether it was one of them or someone else who killed Olivia, who sent that anthrax to hurt me, but if they did, I'd imagine he already has an idea which one of them was behind it by now.

"They're curious, you see."

About me. About my newfound powers.

The memory of how Azmodeus cornered me last week is still fresh in my mind.

I frown. "Well, they'll just have to put up with me."

"Charlotte." Lucifer grips my chin, turning me in his arms so he can look at me. We're skin to skin. "You are bone of my bone. Flesh of my flesh. I've been waiting for a more opportune time to present itself, but I think you might prefer something more private these days anyway."

Before I can understand what he's getting at, he's out of bed and down on one knee in front of me, pulling a medium-size jewelry box he must have stashed beneath the bed. Immediately, I sit up, my hands flying up to cover my mouth.

Lucifer kneels for no one.

No one except for me, it seems.

An unexpected tear slides down my cheek, and the desire to throw myself into his arms and tell him "I will" a thousand times over—before he's even officially asked me—is nearly overwhelming. He opens the box, and I can't help the sharp inhalation of breath that escapes me.

A Tiffany diamond collar.

His collar.

Not my training collar or the one I wear in the playroom.

One to wear for all the world to see.

Lucifer takes my left hand in his gently, grinning at the sight of the sixty-carat black diamond that's already there. "Charlotte, my dove, will you be my collared sub? Will you marry me? 'For real,' this time?" He smirks irreverently, teasing me with the words I said to him back at The Rainbow Room. "Will you spend your immortal life with me? For now, and the rest of eternity? The choice is yours this time."

I nod vigorously, suddenly unable to speak as I watch in shock while Lucifer's eyes get a little misty. I launch myself into his arms with such divine force, we're both nearly knocked back onto the bedroom floor. But Lucifer catches me, lifting and spinning me in his arms before he pulls us back down onto the bed together.

I climb on top of him eagerly.

He laughs, the sound uncharacteristically light and unguarded as he holds me. "Darling, eventually you're going to have to—"

"Shhh, I don't want to talk about that." I shake my head, kissing every part of him I can reach.

My newfound powers. My abilities. I *know* that conversation is coming. Lucifer's bound to have noticed the minor damages around the penthouse by now. He notices *everything*. It's one of the many things I admire about him, actually. But I want to hold on to whatever tiny bit of my human self I can salvage a little longer.

"None of that," I mutter as I trail my lips across his chest, down the thin trail of dark hair below his navel to the muscled grooves of his hips.

He chuckles. "All right. Have it your way. For now. Though who *exactly* do you think is in charge here?" He grips my hips, his fingers digging into me in warning.

We both know this conversation is far from over.

He never gives in to me this easily. Not on something as important as this.

I mean to end the discussion there, to not push my luck and ruin the moment, but somehow, I can't stop the next question that escapes as I roll to the side and settle my head onto his chest, where he holds me. "This changes everything, doesn't it?"

He lifts a brow, glancing down at me.

"The apocalypse. Getting married. Olivia's death. All of it."

He nods slowly, his expression turning grim. "The spear that was used to kill your actress belongs to my Father. It can end an immortal life, yours included. Mine and my siblings, too, I'm afraid. It will aid its possessor in winning any battle, even Armageddon."

"Why does that not surprise me?" I sigh, rolling onto my back beside him and staring up at the ceiling. "You weren't kidding when you said you didn't know why He released you and your siblings, were you? Until now I mean?"

Lucifer's grip on me tightens, his voice gravely serious. "Do I look like I would kid about something as important as your safety?"

I turn toward him.

No.

No, he doesn't.

In fact, now that I take stock of him, he looks . . . more tired than I've ever seen him before. Dark circles have formed under his eyes, and there's a haunted, almost gaunt quality to his face that concerns me.

Like the weight of the whole celestial world sits on his shoulders.

"What happens now?" I whisper.

Lucifer glances away as he swallows. "Now, we go to war, darling."

Though he doesn't elaborate on what that means before he rolls over on top of me, unexpectedly pinning me in a way that causes me to squeal and silences all the worries that bubble up inside my head, until I have no choice but to smile and wrap my legs around him as I give in to our own perfect brand of infinity.

CHAPTER TWENTY-SEVEN

Charlotte

By the time we fall asleep again, naked in each other's arms, I'm thoroughly spent, but a nightmare still wakes me—Mark hurting me, until that cold, never-ending embrace from my dreams saves me, Death cradling me protectively—leaving me lying there awake beside Lucifer a few hours later, uncertain what all this means. It isn't until I hear the sudden snick of our bedroom door closing and the overhead light flicks on that Lucifer's warning of war fully settles into me.

War isn't coming. It's already here.

And there's a man in our bedroom I've never seen before.

A man with wings.

"Lucifer," I gasp, unable to scream, but the fear in my voice must wake him.

He sits upright swiftly, effortlessly shoving me behind his back to protect me. "For fuck's sake, what *is* it with you and Mother? Really, Michael?"

Michael shrugs. "Lest you forget, brother, *you* were the one who summoned *me*."

The words pique both my nerves and my interest, but I don't dare move from behind where Lucifer has shielded me.

"*Now* is not a good time," Lucifer growls through clenched teeth.

"Really? I think now is an excellent time," Michael says, leaning to the side to peer around Lucifer and grin at me. "Considering we both know who's at stake." He snaps his fingers, conjuring a chair from out of thin air as Lucifer's shoulders stiffen beneath my palms. Michael twists the chair around, his chest leaning forward against the chairback, to make room for his wings. "After all, it's your soon-to-be father-in-law you killed in order to kick off this whole apocalypse charade."

"Apocalypse," I echo, unable to stop myself.

Lucifer shoots me a warning look over his shoulder, like he's ordering me to remain silent. I don't think I've ever seen him this on edge since, well . . .

Since Mark tried to kill me.

Or did, rather.

My breath stops short, my eyes darting to Michael.

Michael seems to read the question on my face easily. "Keep quiet and out of my way, and I have no plans to hurt you, Charlotte. Even if I do have possession of our Father's blade. Besides, Lucifer was the one to kill 'Daddy.' But naturally, Lucy here only did it to get *our* Father's attention, of course. To kick the hornets' nest and make a martyr to stir Father's followers. That's the only reason he does anything."

I shake my head.

No. No, that isn't true. I may have had my doubts, but Lucifer killed my father to protect me, the same way he killed all those people at Mark's church for trying to hurt me.

Didn't he?

I lean forward, glancing at his side profile from over his shoulder, but Lucifer doesn't look at me.

"Tell him he's wrong. Tell him he's wrong, Lucifer." I desperately search his face for some reassurance. But I . . . don't find any.

"Not *now*, Charlotte."

But the way he says it is enough for me to know.

It's true.

It *is* true.

I sputter, unable to form words as something inside me breaks.

"Same reason why he killed all those churchgoers." Michael smirks at me. "To rabble-rouse the human masses. Piss off all the holy rollers, because it might irk Dad."

"That's where you're wrong, brother." Lucifer sneers. "It was *your* attention I was trying to get, actually."

I stiffen. He didn't kill *them* to protect me. Didn't do it out of some warped and twisted expression of love for me.

At the news, Michael has the audacity to look smitten. Like a cat whose just dropped a dead canary at his master's feet. "Really, Luce? You shouldn't have."

"I know what you're up to. You and your little angelic army. Retrieving the lance. You truly thought you could do it without me?"

Michael makes a get-outta-here expression and shrugs. "Who says I'm planning anything?"

Hellfire sparks in Lucifer's gaze, bright and terrible. "Don't be coy. Opening the seals, freeing the Horsemen, starting the apocalypse. Really, Michael? Are you that desperate for Dad to return?"

"Father *will* return," Michael hisses, his expression suddenly vicious. "My army and I will make sure of it, even if that means we must rid the earth of humanity."

Bile burns at the back of my throat.

What did that asshole just say?

"And you *knew* about this?" I ask, glancing between Michael and Lucifer, until my gaze finally settles upon Lucifer's face. "You knew and yet you did nothing? You told me you were handling this."

Lucifer doesn't answer.

"What did you expect, Charlotte?" Michael scoffs at me. "For my brother to defend humanity all because he fell in love with a human? Now *that* would be a twist no one would see coming."

I look toward Lucifer, my eyes pleading. "Tell me it isn't true. Tell me you weren't going to sit by and do nothing to stop him, or worse, actually help him while—"

"Quiet, Charlotte," Lucifer snaps, reminding me of my place.

My heart stops. My muscles tighten and my jaw sets.

Well, fuck that.

Fuck all his goddamned secrecy.

Either he'll treat me like an equal moving forward, or he won't have me by his side at all.

I throw off the sheets, coming to stand beside where he remains on the bed with only a blanket to cover myself, but he catches my wrist, a silent reminder, as if he means to say, *Choose your battles wisely.*

I can practically hear the words spoken inside my head. Like I imagined them.

And here in front of Michael isn't the time nor the place, so I swallow down my rage. Save it for later. For my own safety.

Lucifer has at least helped improve my self-preservation skills *that* much.

"Well, you called this little meeting, Luce." Michael makes a show of stretching and shaking out his wings. "So, what do you have to offer me?"

"I want in," Lucifer says. "Call off the Righteous. No more attempts on Charlotte's life."

No . . . this . . . he . . .

"And?"

"And in exchange I'll open the seals for you."

"What? No!"

I don't know *exactly* what that means, but considering we're talking about an impending apocalypse, I know enough from all my years of Bible study to gather that it can't be anything good. Lucifer and Michael both ignore me.

"Father may have given you the scrolls, but He gave *me* the power," Lucifer says coolly, holding Michael's gaze. "You need me."

Michael hesitates, glaring at Lucifer like it physically pains him to consider it, but then abruptly he stands, kicking aside his chair so that it scrapes across the floor. "Done."

For a moment, I'm too stunned to say anything. Then my brain comes back online, my thoughts reeling.

"Lucifer, you can't," I try to plead with him, but for the first time in a long time, his eyes are cold. Nearly as empty as when he first met me.

"It's too late for them, darling," he says softly.

Them.

Them meaning . . .

Humanity.

The panicked feeling inside my chest starts to tighten, becoming a very real, very urgent thing, until I can't help but repeat the same word over and over. "No. No, no, no, no, no."

Neither of them pays any attention to me.

"Father would likely agree." Michael shrugs. "Mother, too, of course." He smirks. "Well, in that case, I look forward to having you back on the team, brother. I'll be in touch."

With that, his wings give an almighty flap, and he's gone in a blink.

Nothing but a blown-about pile of Lucifer's stray sheet music and a few large white feathers remain, scattered across the floor. The chair Michael conjured lies on its side, the only other indication he was ever here in the first place.

Michael. The fucking archangel Michael.

The newfound leader of the apocalypse.

The false prophet.

"What the hell was that?" I round on Lucifer.

He tears from our bed like a man on a mission, refusing to look at me as he heads toward our closet. "None of it concerns you, Charlotte. Let me—"

"None of it *concerns* me?" I shout, my heart racing as I follow him into the walk-in, where he's now haphazardly buttoning his dress shirt. "At what point are you going to stop treating me like I'm a child?"

He rounds on me. "Perhaps when you stop behaving that way!"

We both freeze.

It's the first time he's *ever* raised his voice at me outside the playroom. My hands start to tremble.

"You sounded just like him then."

Lucifer lifts a brow. "My Father?"

I shake my head slightly. "No, mine."

Lucifer swears under his breath, muttering to himself before he rakes a rough hand through his hair, then runs it down over his face, exhaling. "There are many things in this universe you know nothing about. Things of which—"

"So, tell me, then. Tell me, goddammit!"

Lucifer's eyes darken with a quiet fury, his fists clenching and unclenching as he draws nearly nose to nose with me. "You barely survived the news of our being fated, and yet *this* is how you want me to treat you? Like an equal? Like my queen?"

"Yes," I snap. "Yes, I do," I say, meeting him toe-to-toe.

Amber hellfire burns in his gaze, harsh and punishing. "I'm asking for you to trust me," he says through gritted teeth, "for you to have faith in me, in us." He reaches for me.

But I shake my head, stepping out of his reach.

"How could I?" I whisper. "How could you ask me that after all the ways you've lied to me?"

Lucifer swallows visibly, lowering his head so that it hangs from his shoulders as he places his hands on his hips. Finally, he looks skyward like he's trying to find patience. Or praying.

If he were anyone else, I'd think that he was.

But I know better.

He presses his lips together, his nostrils flaring as he squares his shoulders, like he's shoring up for the battle ahead. "All right, Charlotte. You win. You want to make me your villain? So be it." His expression hardens, his entire body language shifting as the shadow of where his wings used to be is suddenly cast onto the wall behind him.

The change I see in him then is so immediate it . . . terrifies me.
My blood runs cold.
This is *not* the Lucifer I know.
This is a Lucifer I've never met before.
The vicious king of Hell.
Exactly the monster everyone believes him to be.
I take a step back.

Slowly, Lucifer prowls toward me, until I'm forced to retreat so far I'm backed up against the wall, cornered between his lithe body and the doorframe. He stares down the bridge of his nose at me like I mean nothing to him, that cold, deadened stare tearing me in two.

"You want to be my queen? Fine." The amber hellfire in his eyes flames as he snarls, "Then start acting like it."

He stalks past me, exiting our bedroom, leaving me standing there, alone and breathless, the marble floor where he stood only moments ago blackened and singed. I stay frozen there, breathing hard, unable to make sense of what all this means, as if the whole world isn't crumbling around me and my future husband isn't one of the few leading the charge to scorch the earth beneath me.

CHAPTER TWENTY-EIGHT

Lucifer

I find myself standing alone inside the cathedral Charlotte took refuge in the other morning, the rage coiled inside me a very living, breathing thing. I don't truly understand what it is about this establishment that draws me, but I drop down into the first-row pew, burying my head in my hands. A short while later, I feel an unexpected presence join me.

"I'm not surprised to see you here."

I look up to find the priest who cared for Charlotte watching me. Father Brown, if I recall.

Not that I honestly give a fuck.

He sits down on the other end of the pew, looking up toward the altar, where an array of candles and gold fixtures frame the image of Christ on the crucifix. Behind it, a stained glass window depicts several of the disciples bearing witness to Christ's ascension.

I wasn't the only child my Father chose to sacrifice.

Just the only one whose pain was never allowed to mean anything.

"What brings you here, Lucifer?" the priest asks.

I scowl. I'm not exactly pleased by his sudden appearance, nor the prospect of his company. "You tell me," I challenge, my eyes narrowing at him.

It's petty and foolish, particularly by my usual standards, but I have little respect for those in the clergy. For those responsible for the numerous lies humanity believes of me. Even if there was once a time when I was more like them than I care to admit.

My Father's eager servant.

And for what?

For Him to cast me out at the first sign of doubt in Him?

To my surprise, Father Brown doesn't flinch away, like this is *exactly* the sort of devil-may-care attitude he expects from me, and the fact I've played so readily into his trite, human expectations only infuriates me even more.

"She still prays, you know."

There's only one woman he could possibly mean.

The one and only person who has ever truly mattered to me.

"And why tell me this? For your own amusement?" I sneer, lifting a furious brow. "To remind me that she is unfaithful to me in the only way that matters?"

"Why should she have to choose, Lucifer?" he asks.

Bloody hell.

As if the answer isn't obvious.

When I don't deign to respond, he sighs. "You fear losing her."

"I fear *Him* stealing her from me. Like He's taken *everything* from me. My pride. My purpose. My wings. My ability to create. And now . . ." My jaw tightens, my lip curling in disgust at the unguarded admission that just fell from my lips as I gaze up toward Heaven.

The stained glass image of Christ stares back at me.

My brother. Or my Father, as it were.

According to humanity, they're one in the same.

Whatever the fuck *that's* supposed to mean.

"Already, He nearly stole her from me, thrust her into Azrael's waiting arms, and if I were to tell her everything . . ." I hang my head, no longer able to look at the image. At the reminder that, to her, I am still *exactly* the villain my Father made me to be. "He may be your favorite deity, but He's a piss-poor excuse for a Father, if you ask me."

The priest remains quiet, and I think I might have finally accomplished the minor feat of scaring him off, though that doesn't inspire as much amusement in me these days as it used to.

"The only thing that will push her away is if you force her to choose." He comes to stand at the far end of the pew. "Don't make her choose, Sammael."

With that, he turns and leaves, abandoning me to the early morning quiet as some light begins to seep in, making patterns on the floor through the colored glass. And yet I sit there, unmoving, more confused and at war with myself than I've ever been since the moment I first chose to tempt Eve with that damn apple.

CHAPTER TWENTY-NINE

Charlotte

The following morning I'm still so furious with Lucifer that I don't even want to look and see if he's on the other side of the bed waiting for me. Thankfully, when I do finally sneak a peek, he isn't there, and once I cave and eventually decide to search the penthouse for him after breakfast, I find he isn't anywhere else either. So, I hightail it into my office at Apollyon headquarters as soon as humanly possible, hoping to avoid him completely before he returns from wherever it is he's been going.

Whatever it is he must be up to with Michael. I scowl.

The thought fills me with so much rage, it's hard to breathe.

I seal myself inside my office, and I do the only thing I can do. I throw myself into my work. I make phone calls, answer emails. I review the finalized schedule for the CFDA Awards along with mine and Lucifer's show-host script. I arrange several interviews—*People, Entertainment Weekly, TIME*—update all the corporation's social media accounts, including my own (one billion followers and counting), coordinate with *Vogue* about an upcoming photo shoot I have scheduled, and generally, girlboss my way too close to the sun.

I barrel through my to-do list with such an intense fury that I don't give myself room to think. About Michael's little visit last night. About his deal with Lucifer.

About our engagement.

About what that all means for Lucifer, for humanity, for me.

Fuck that noise.

By the time I finish working, over nine hours later, it's early evening, and I almost forget that I told Azmodeus I'd meet him at his club tonight. I still haven't figured out exactly what his endgame with this sibling-bond thing is.

I have half a mind to find an excuse not to go. Lucifer told me to leave his family to him, and I'm in no mood really, but it's the sight of my investor proposal sitting on top of my desk that stops me.

You want to be queen? Fine. Then start acting like it.

Lucifer's words echo inside my head, taunting me.

"Maybe I will, asshole," I mutter, my plan cementing itself inside my brain.

I call down to Jeanine at the front desk and ask her to get ahold of Dagon for me, then collapse back into my office chair to wait. Dagon arrives nearly thirty minutes later with the Town Car and full security team in tow. Four members of the team come up to my office to escort me down to where the car's waiting.

They're all even more on edge than they were previously.

Apparently, Lucifer laid into them about the whole Olivia thing. He fired several, only to hire several more in their place. Three to every previous one position. Not that it was any of their faults, really. Olivia wasn't even with me then. How could they have known when they were busy protecting the *real* me? Though I suppose I did slip their detail a bit too easily.

Another thing I'll likely be feeling guilty for.

I take accountability for my actions.

Unlike some people.

My lip curls in frustration, the thought of Michael and Lucifer's deal both infuriating and terrifying me.

The apocalypse? The *apocalypse? Are you freaking kidding me?*

I try to silence my thoughts, try to hold myself together. But I'm barely hanging on by a string. I know from all my years of Bible study how this goes.

Or what John the Baptist's prophetic version says in Revelation, anyway.

Though based on what Lucifer's told me about the Bible being full of human error, I can't be certain how much of it will prove true.

"Seven seals. One for each apocalyptic event; each one unlocks a new trial humanity will face," I recite out loud to myself. Like I'm back in Sunday school. "The first four unleash the Horsemen. Pestilence. War. Famine. Death. Each tribulation worse than the last, until . . ." The final battle. Armageddon.

I blanch.

No. Don't go down that road.

I can't allow my emotions to get the better of me right now without risking my newfound powers bursting out of me. The two seem to be inextricably connected, and giving in to the fear won't help anything. I have to keep moving, keep going, in order to remind myself of that. If I have even a small chance of getting Lucifer to change course, then I *need* to show him my strength. The whole world is counting on me.

I groan, glancing up toward Heaven, or the Town Car's cab ceiling, in any case.

"Big Guy, why me?"

By the time Dagon gets me back to the penthouse and I change into a Valentino minidress that's better suited to the club scene, night has already fallen.

The city below glitters at my feet.

I turn, prepared to head toward the car, only to startle when I find Azmodeus already standing in the first-floor foyer, watching me.

"What're you doing here?"

I was supposed to meet him at his club, The Velvet Fold, full security detail in tow.

Azmodeus shoves his hands in his pockets, stepping toward me ruefully. "Change of plans, lovey. A little birdie told me my brother put you on lockdown, so I thought you might need my help escaping, though I also hear congratulations are in order." He glances at my collar.

"On lockdown?"

It's the first I've heard of this, though after what happened to Olivia, and with Michael suddenly appearing in our bedroom before dawn this morning, it wouldn't surprise me.

I march toward the penthouse's front door, opening it to peek outside. Sure enough, two of the security team are now *inside* the building, stationed where they weren't previously, despite the fact that our floor requires a special security key for elevator access.

And they're not positioned like they're trying to block someone from getting in.

It's like they're trying to stop *someone* from getting out.

Namely, me.

I let the door snick shut, turning back toward Azmodeus. "How did you get past them?"

"Let's call it a celestial loophole." He shrugs. "You might want to bring it up with Lucifer in case you're actually—"

"I'm not scared."

It's a bold-faced lie, but I manage to say it confidently.

If I want to be Lucifer's queen, I can't show any sign of weakness.

Not in front of him and his siblings.

And now that I know that Lucifer isn't putting a stop to this apocalypse like I thought, well I'll be damned if I won't go down swinging. I'll be exactly the righteous, obedient servant my father trained me to be.

Number One Leader of Team God. That's me.

I frown a little at the thought.

I *have* to believe He doesn't want this, that He's still out there, that this was always His plan for me, because if it isn't . . .

Azmodeus simply smirks, drawing me back into the moment. "Of course not." Though I have a feeling he's patronizing me. "I'm no monster, you know."

"That's debatable, I think."

His grin widens, my insult not even fazing him, as he holds out his arm to escort me. "If you want a true monster, you might take a good long look at who you fuck each night, Charlotte."

I frown, my hand flitting to the new diamond collar at my neck. It feels incrementally tighter. "Trust me. I'm aware."

He quirks his head at me. "Are you?"

I take his arm, opening my mouth to answer, but then a sharp tug pulls at my navel, like I'm being sucked forward into a gaping black hole, and whatever response was poised on my lips dies instantly.

CHAPTER THIRTY

Lucifer

Time works differently in Hell. Moves at a slower, more torturous pace.

But even the slow crawl of the circular span of time stretched so thin it nears breaking—making the passage of mere minutes feel like hours—doesn't provide enough space to satiate my rage. When one of my demons brings the latest headline to me where I'm now draped across my obsidian throne, it's only early evening topside, though it feels as if a whole age has passed since Michael appeared in mine and Charlotte's bedroom last night.

I snatch the human paper extended from Kalimor's trembling hand. I have little patience left, if any.

I glance down at the bold typeface.

Violence Strikes in Regina! Residents Brawl in Mass-Festival Feud.

I curse under my breath. "I fucking hate Canada."

Astaroth's successor, the new demonic leader of the quaint rebellion my legions are waging, is lucky that I need him. Temporarily, at least.

"The hounds are corralling him toward the subway, my lord. York Street station. He described it as more neutral territory." Kalimor grimaces.

"Small favors, it seems." I sneer, my sour mood reflected in my dour expression.

When I finally stuff down my irritation enough to snap myself topside, I'm standing in the middle of an empty subway station in Brooklyn, near Dumbo, wherever the bloody fuck that is. Manhattan is the only part of the city that interests me.

Beside me, an open subway car waits. Though no passengers have boarded.

Yet.

The car is paused on the track like it's no longer running. The frozen sign overhead labeled F Train reads **ONE MINUTE** along with several large red- and green-lettered exclamations of **YORK TO JAY STREET—METROTECH** and the estimated wait times.

As if that would ever inspire me to hurry.

Behind me, I hear a sudden scuffling sound, and I turn to find one of the city's massive rats scuttering about the place, its bulging hide protruding from behind a nearby trash bin as it searches the otherwise abandoned station for more food.

It hisses at me, unaware of who, or more precisely what, it's threatening.

I roll my eyes, flashing my true features as a sound like a lion's roar tears from my throat.

The creature squeaks in terror before it turns tail and scurries away.

The empty platform is littered with rubbish, spilled food wrappers that were feverishly abandoned during the evening commuters' hurry, billowing past several of the subway's more permanent residents. Two of them lie supine in their own mess across the floor.

An unhoused woman, whose face appears weathered from too much time spent outdoors, lies overtop what I can only assume is her partner, a man who, from the looks of it, seems to have resorted to mindlessly chewing the threads of his own fraying clothing, some of the fabric's gristle caught in his unmoving teeth.

I wrinkle my nose.

These are my Father's creations. His precious children.

If He was going to kick them out of Eden, the *least* He could do would be to ensure they were fed, housed, and clothed properly.

I scowl, taking a spare moment to drop the thick wad of bills that currently resides in my wallet onto the floor beside them.

My thoughts turn to when Charlotte nearly found herself in a similar situation. If not for the unexpected kindness of her Seer friend.

The turn of fate that eventually led her to a job at my company.

My distaste softens.

"Who knew you were such a humanitarian?" The unfamiliar voice comes from behind me, but the cadence and rhythm are the same as they've always been.

I have an ear for that sort of thing.

I scowl. "I've been challenging my Father's choices since before I ever willed you into existence, Abaddon." I turn to find him sitting with his back toward me inside the open subway car, clearly having just glanced over his shoulder at me.

When I join him a moment later in the narrow, confined space, I lean against the silver handrailing across from him, placing my hands inside my pockets. "You call this *neutral* territory?" I sneer. "You're better than this."

Abaddon sighs, midway through a bite of poutine he must have hoarded from whatever insignificant festival it was he was terrorizing in Canada, before he drops his plastic fork into the red-checkered paper basket. "I thought if I stayed aboveground, it'd take longer for you and your hounds to find me."

I shrug. "You forget that these days Earth is practically mine."

He sighs once again, his current form making him look like the fat, aging father of a Canadian lumberjack. He likely *was* before Abaddon possessed him in a pathetic attempt to lead my legions out of Hell. Rebel against me.

"What are you going to do?" he says, his eyes darting from me to the sudden canine snarl that comes from just outside the subway car.

My hellhounds returned to me.

I lean down, patting one of the invisible snarling beasts on its head as some of its spittle pools on the floor where it comes to heel beside me. The demonic black of Abaddon's eyes now blocks out the whites, so that the irises can no longer be seen.

"My lord?" he says, like he intends to plead.

Though nothing he could say would ever satisfy me.

"Consider this your lucky day, Addie." I drop down onto one of the subway's plastic benches across from him, leaning my elbows onto my knees. "I'm going to give you some *new* instructions, so listen carefully."

CHAPTER THIRTY-ONE

Charlotte

When Lust and I blink back into existence only a few milliseconds later, we're standing in the middle of an art gallery, the show floor noticeably empty. My hand falls from his arm, and I step forward. "Where are we?"

"Transmitter. It's a midsize gallery in Brooklyn."

I spin in a slow circle, taking in the stark, open show floor. The all-white walls. The wooden panels. The recessed lighting. The mounted ceiling spotlights directed toward the paintings.

"Your idea of fun is an art gallery?" My forehead pinches in confusion.

Azmodeus tilts his head like I'm being ridiculous. "Yours isn't?"

I can't help but gape at him. "I guess from you I just expected something more—"

"Vacuous?" He quirks a brow.

I blush, the whole exchange reminding me a little too much of those early days with Lucifer. "I didn't mean—"

But Az takes my response in stride, exactly like his older brother would. "Come," he says, holding out a hand toward me.

Reluctantly, I take it, and he leads me from the room where we landed, which showcases a wide array of bright, multicolored pop art, to a different part of the gallery. One that's clearly meant for private exhibitions. He keeps a gentle hold of my hand the whole time, the soft warmth of his palm and the glow of the gallery lights feeling oddly . . . comforting. Familiar even.

Like I'm less alone in the gravity of everything I know I'm about to face.

Even though I still don't know exactly what it is Azmodeus wants from me.

But this is my wheelhouse, my unexpected trade. Appealing to the rich and powerful. Being a subservient little pet to whichever immortal happens to be beside me.

When it comes down to it, Azmodeus is no different than Lucifer.

And if I can change the hearts and minds of even one of the other Originals . . .

I know *exactly* how to play this role, how to get both what I want *and* what humanity needs. That's all PR is anyway. Networking. Making friends. Connections. To help influence and control a narrative. I'm so practiced at it that it feels almost effortless now. My father taught me this game backward and forward, but it was Lucifer who made me a true master at it.

Only this time, I have to do it all *on purpose*.

Convince Lucifer's siblings to help me save humanity.

It isn't until we reach a smooth velvet rope meant to block off the exhibit from the general public that Azmodeus releases me. He unhooks the rope latch and steps to the side, gesturing for me to enter like I'm his soon-to-be queen. Or his brother's, in any case.

I glance over my shoulder. "Shouldn't we . . . ?"

But the gallery is empty. Save for the two of us. There's no one here to stop us.

"It's my private exhibit, Charlotte." Azmodeus lowers the rope, clipping it to the other side of the stand. "I had it curated just for you."

The words still me.

I swallow.

What is it you want from me?

But if I'm going to convince Lucifer's siblings to help me, or at the very least allow me to control a small part of their power by doing their PR—their public personas are a major part of how humanity makes offerings to them—I can't go into it half-heartedly. I better be down for whatever, or whoever, Azmodeus throws at me. Anything he asks.

Can I do that?

I can't afford to make any mistakes.

Humanity's counting on me.

Me and my PR proposal.

Who would have guessed it'd come down to this?

I tuck my arms in at my sides innocently, shuffling my feet as I fully commit to the role. "Don't you think that's a little—"

Azmodeus watches me, waiting for me to finish. Apparently, he's going to make me say it.

He's that much like Lucifer.

I wet my lips. "You know, a little intimate?"

Az smirks deviously, keeping his hands in his pockets as he crowds my space so that I have no choice but to gaze up at him. At how gorgeous and tall he is.

He really *is* just as beautiful as his brother.

He ducks his head toward me.

And my breath hitches.

That part I don't have to fake.

But he reroutes at the last second, his lips landing right next to my ear instead of on mine, like I was anticipating. "My brother may have invented sin, but *I'm* the one who invented foreplay," he whispers against me, the brush of his mouth sending a very real, very sudden jolt of lust through me, enough that I shiver.

He pulls back a moment later, the amused look in his expression clear.

If he meant it that way, I'd know it, but that's not what he wants from me, after all.

He's simply toying with me.

I blush furiously, the thought of how easily he flipped that switch inside me the other day making me curious. Azmodeus is dangerous. Very, very dangerous.

In more ways than I think I can imagine.

But if not that, what does he want from me?

What can I give him that he can't already get from Lucifer?

"Come, Charlotte." He beckons me again.

The innuendo is intentional, I think.

This time, I don't hesitate as I allow him to lead me into the next section of the gallery, but when I step into the other room, my breath stops short, and my whole perception of Azmodeus shifts.

Azmodeus isn't *just* the city's favorite playboy.

"I thought you might want to know a little of our family history, considering you're going to be one of us now," he says, smiling almost ruefully.

But I'm too stunned to speak.

The walls of the gallery are lined with the works of old masters.

Michelangelo, Caravaggio, Rubens, and more.

It's stunning.

I walk to the first frame. A small three-paneled triptych oil painting on loan from the Museo del Prado. **HIERONYMUS BOSCH**, the placard reads.

THE GARDEN OF EARTHLY DELIGHTS.

This is what Azmodeus wants, I realize.

The one thing Lucifer can't give him.

To be taken seriously.

To be seen as something *other* than what a master he is between the bedsheets.

"Az, would you like to plan mine and Lucifer's engagement party?" The question is out and hanging in the gallery like the paintings between us before I can stop it. "The real one, the private one we're going to have now that we're really engaged. You said you deal in secrets. I think you're the only one who could handle a celebrity party of that caliber discreetly."

Az grins from ear to ear like he's feeling smug that I asked him, but also, a little surprised. "I'd be honored, Charlotte." He makes an exaggerated court-jester bow before he pinches his lips together as if he's considering how he could possibly make that statement into an innuendo, but then gives up.

He begins to explain the exhibit, launching into a tale about when he and Lucifer and the other Originals were first made. The paintings on the wall help curate the story.

Apparently, it started with nothingness—the blank infinite canvas before an explosion of chaos created everything, God included—and then there was light, and water, and stardust, then . . .

God's pride at what He had made.

His own emotion bleeding out from His pores while He made love to Lilith—which Azmodeus takes care to narrate in *very* explicit detail—resulting in the birth of God and Lilith's first and eldest son.

Lucifer. Sammael. The Lightbringer.

God's own pride in His creation embodied.

According to Azmodeus, each one of the Originals played a key role in God's own genesis and creation story. The pride He felt at what He'd created. How slothfully He rested when it was all said and done. His envy at man's innocence. The gluttony and greed He felt hoarding the Tree of Life and its knowledge for only Himself, and the wrath that was ignited in Him when Eve betrayed His first and only command.

When Lucifer tempted her into seizing her own freedom, into gaining knowledge of everything.

I hang on Azmodeus's every word, listening in a total rapturous awe that I don't have to fake, the temperature in my body rising at each unexpected turn of the story. Azmodeus's descriptions of the Garden of Eden, in particular, are so *specific*, so detailed and vivid, that all at once I find myself feeling homesick again.

For a place I've never been.

But my heart seems to know it intimately.

Its truths. Its secrets. Its histories.

I glance at my hands like I might be able to see some of God's redemption inside me, or maybe even Eve's apple in my palm, but all I feel there is Lucifer's darkness, the powers he accidentally transferred to me stirring inside me, and yet . . .

I *know* this is the right choice. The right path.

I can feel it thrumming inside me.

Faith.

In God and His plan for me.

When Azmodeus and I have finally made our way through the full exhibit, nearly two hours have passed. It flew by in a blink, but my impression of Azmodeus, of the exhibition, of the story he curated for me, is a lasting one.

Like all the Originals, Azmodeus is more than the sin humanity gives him credit for.

He's God's desire for Lilith embodied.

When we reach the last painting, Azmodeus falls quiet, the painting's narrative taking a dark and menacing turn. A two-paneled diptych. A Van Eyck.

THE LAST JUDGMENT, the placard reads.

How the story ends.

I swallow thickly, the reminder of everything that's at stake rushing back to me. "Do you . . . do you think that's why He let you all out?" I ask. "You and the other Originals?"

Azmodeus seems to get the subtext of what I'm actually asking, and his expression darkens, making him look more serious than I've ever seen him. "I don't know, lovey," he admits. "None of us do."

I turn back to the painting. Death. Destruction.

A dropping sensation churns my stomach, and I feel temporarily nauseated, my palms turning cold. I have to do whatever it takes to make certain that doesn't happen.

No price is too high to pay.

Whatever it is, Lucifer has the kind of cash to pay it tenfold.

But *I* need to have the strength.

For both our sakes.

"There's something else I want to show you." Azmodeus takes my hand again, but this time it feels intimate in a different way.

Like he's . . . treating me more like a friend.

An equal.

Unlike Lucifer.

Maybe he *does* really want some sibling-bonding time with me.

Or maybe he and the other Originals are just as uncertain about all this as I am.

Az leads me out of the exhibit and toward a back door that looks like it might open into an alley. **EMERGENCY EXIT**, the large red letters graffitied across its surface in all caps read. Azmodeus pushes open the door, but instead of an empty alleyway, a dark staircase greets me.

Az nods for me to go ahead, but I . . . hesitate.

"Do you trust me, Charlotte?" he asks.

I feel suddenly dizzy.

When we first arrived here this evening, the answer to that would have been an absolute and complete "hell no!" but now?

Now, I've seen a whole other side to Azmodeus, and I realize that within the past few hours, he's been more open about his family with me than Lucifer ever has.

Something in my stomach sours.

I glance between Az and the darkened staircase, the steps seeming to descend forever, though I don't say anything.

I *have* to do this.

For myself. For humanity.

Whatever consequence it brings.

My apprehension must be painted across my face, because Azmodeus says, "We can end the evening here, if you want."

Those words echo through me.

If you want.

What true celestial choice has ever been given to me?

What decision that wasn't wrapped up in someone else's divine plans for my destiny?

And it's right then and there I decide that I won't *ever* allow anyone else to make my choices for me again. Consequences be damned.

For once, I'm going to put my trust in *me*.

"I trust you," I say, leaning into my instincts and taking Azmodeus's hand as I give it a warm, sisterly squeeze. "I don't know why, but I do."

Azmodeus grins at me. "Then after you, Charlotte."

CHAPTER THIRTY-TWO

Charlotte

We descend into the darkness, the stairs seeming to stretch on forever until I feel a warped sort of force pulling at me. Like I'm being bent and curled at the edges.

"Where are we—"

"Just a few steps farther," Azmodeus says, not allowing me to finish. Though I'm not certain I could have anyway.

The pressure inside my head is reaching an apex. Like what I imagine it would feel like to go diving, if you hadn't been trained in how to do it the right way. Just as I'm about to tell Azmodeus that I want to turn back around, that I might not actually be able to go through with this, a veil is lifted, and the darkness of the staircase ends abruptly.

We're standing in what appears to be an abandoned cellar, blue and green neon lights illuminating where two bouncers stand outside a door they're guarding.

The sound of electronic club music thumps distantly.

"What is this place?" I turn back toward the stairs in search of Azmodeus, who's been trailing behind me the whole time, but I can't find him, yet when I face forward, he's somehow in front of me, smirking.

"Welcome to In-Between, Charlotte."

He nods to the bouncers, who open the doors, a wave of electric energy and sound rushing over us. The open cellar is packed with people, or what *appear* to be people, anyway.

The fast-paced club music plays on a nonstop loop at such a loud decibel, I can hardly hear myself think. I smile.

Perfect.

I squint in awe at the writhing crowd, the lights that paint them and their half-naked bodies. One of their heads snaps toward me, their eyes flashing an otherworldly shade of green. I inhale a sharp breath.

Where the hell am I?

I take a tentative step back, some instinctive, still-human part of me wanting to flee, but Azmodeus catches me by the shoulders, leaning down to me.

He has to practically shout next to my ear for me to hear him over the music playing. "I promised I would pop your celestial cherry," he yells. "You didn't think I'd disappoint, did you?"

I laugh, opening my mouth to say that *this* is more of what I expected from him, but I'm silenced by the sight of a small star-shaped pill balanced on his finger in front of me.

"Do you trust me, Charlotte?" he asks again.

I give a quick nod. I'm not sure it's true, but Azmodeus hasn't done anything to hurt me, and even though I know it's a risk, it's one I choose.

The power in that is heady. Intoxicating even.

Suddenly, the feeling of wanting to let go, of wanting to jump off this cliff into immortality and my God-given purpose until I'm in freefall, is overwhelming.

Azmodeus must read my face, because before I can change my mind, he grips the back of my neck like he means to kiss me.

My heart pumps feverishly.

Drunk on the feeling his touch creates.

"Open your mouth, Charlotte."

I stick out my tongue like I did when I was a child and I'd try to catch a falling snowflake, and Azmodeus drops the little star-shaped tablet onto it. It melts instantly, the taste like an odd mix of pomegranate and freshly bitten apple.

"Stardust," he says. "It's celestial ecstasy."

Ecstasy is the right word.

Already I can feel the pleasure of it coursing through my system. The beat of the music. The feel of Azmodeus's touch. The light shining down on me.

Within only a handful of moments, I come alive.

More electric, more relaxed, more ecstatic, and just . . . *freer* than I've been in weeks.

Every bit of the numbness I've been trying to shield myself with melts away from me.

I drop my head back, eyes closed, total and complete euphoria coming over me. I haven't felt this way since, well . . .

Since Lucifer cast the aurora borealis over the city.

I smile, the memory bringing with it a happy, joyful effervescence that I've been missing for what feels like a lifetime. Like hope in a bottle.

I open my eyes, only to find Azmodeus's wide, devastating grin aimed at me.

"Dance with me," I shout, grabbing him by the hand and pulling him out onto the floor.

The music overtakes us both, the beat of it coming alive inside my skull, each pulse in time with the sway of my hips and the wave of sweat-covered bodies pressed against me.

I lose track of all time, the rhythm and sway of the crowd eclipsing everything. It could be days, weeks even, as Azmodeus moves against me, the heat of the crowd and our collective joy erasing everything.

But I don't care.

Not when I'm realizing how to keep the whole world from burning.

Not when I've finally figured out what my role in all this is supposed to be.

Somewhere during the light show the ceiling opens, and it begins to rain stardust, or glitter—I'm not sure which—until I'm giggling like a schoolgirl, Azmodeus laughing right along with me as we struggle to hold each other upright.

"I'm going to get us more drinks, lovey," he shouts to me. His eyes lock on to the large Black man—*er . . . demon? Maybe?* I'm not sure what some of these beings are—behind the bar as he weaves his way across the sea of dancing bodies.

I fold my arms over my head, closing my eyes as I sway, and try to catch my breath a little. The stardust is starting to wane, finally.

This isn't so bad. This is fun, actually.

I can do this.

I can stay the course. Make Lucifer see how much this means to me.

But it isn't until I open my eyes, my gaze snagging on the edge of the crowd, that the relaxed feeling of freefall into the abyss abandons me.

A large handsome figure looms at the edge of the dance floor, my gaze latching on to him.

He's the only one who *isn't* dancing.

I lift a brow. *Where have I seen you before?*

He stares straight ahead at me, his shadowed face unmoving, until someone walks past like they don't even see him, and I freeze as his features shift.

Instead of a face, a skull leers back at me. Like those freaky masks guys wear on social media, only real.

A chill runs down my spine, an unsettled, familiar feeling. I've seen that face before.

Cold arms wrapped around me. Never-ending and infinite.

Death.

Suddenly, someone grabs my arm, and I jump, knocking into the drink Azmodeus just extended toward me. The glowing pink liquid of the raspberry lemon drop pours down the front of my shirt. "Fuck! I'm so sorry."

I take the now-empty glass from Azmodeus, completely off kilter and feeling like I'm being watched, but when I blink and glance toward the edge of the crowd once more, the figure's already gone. Like I imagined the whole thing.

Leaving me with a feeling of deathly dread.

"I . . . think it's time to go home," I stammer.

Azmodeus and I decide to call it quits shortly after that, and the next thing I know, the cold night air is hitting me in the face as we both stumble, more than a bit drunk, and possibly still rolling, out onto the street.

I don't see the paparazzo until the lens of his camera is practically on top of me.

"Smile, Charlotte."

The flash goes off less than a foot from my face, nearly sending me sprawling onto the pavement, but Az catches me, his expression turning lethal.

He's known for going toe-to-toe with them. According to Gerard, my favorite gossip on Apollyon's legal team, apparently there's a few different charges pending against him.

But Az's expression ignites something inside me, and suddenly it's *me* who's launching myself toward the paparazzo, shoving my hand against his camera lens and shouting, "What the hell is wrong with you? Can't you vultures leave us alone?"

The paparazzo laughs. "If you enjoy this, you're going to love the headline in the morning." The constant shutter of his lens continues. More flashes. "Does Lucifer know you're cheating on him with his brother?"

"Cheating on him?" I nearly shriek.

I blink several times, completely stunned by the accusation.

Rage wells up inside me, practically causing me to choke.

The insinuation that anything—*anything*—that's gone on between me and Azmodeus tonight somehow means I'm not completely and utterly loyal to Lucifer infuriates me.

So much that I can hardly see straight.

My jaw sets, the dark thing inside me writhing.

So I went to a museum and a club with his brother without telling him. So what? He fucks off to Hell or wherever *else* it is he goes all the time without telling me. So Az and I flirted a bit. Who cares? Azmodeus flirts with anything and everything that moves.

Not to mention, he's my future brother-in-law.

There's nothing more to it than that and my pathetic bid to save humanity, except . . .

Except that Az is a surprising new ally. Maybe even a friend?

But that's it. End of story.

And I'm so sick and tired of me and everyone I'm close to being scrutinized for our every move when, meanwhile, the goddamn apocalypse is brewing yet *no one* seems to be noticing, that I . . . I lose it.

The temptation and immediate satisfaction of showing this asshole what's what wins out over reason, clouding my judgment and any consideration I might have once had for the long-term consequences. I take the near-full water bottle I'd been drinking when we exited the club and chuck it him. Not caring who or what I'm aiming at.

To my shock, my aim proves true, and it clocks the paparazzo upside the head, sending him stumbling onto the pavement as I rush at him.

"Charlotte!" Az shouts at me.

But I don't hear him. Or I don't register what he says, at least.

All I hear, all I can feel, is the sound of my pulse thumping in my ears. My rage.

And that harsh, feral thing snarling inside me.

All those people. All those people.

My vision goes red.

My fault.

My fault, my fault, my fault, that thing inside me hisses.

"Get out of here!" I shout, suddenly finding myself standing over the paparazzo, kicking him over and over again with my heel. Anywhere I can reach.

"Charlotte!"

Az's voice is closer now, practically on top of me, and before I can stop him, he's locked his arms around me, hauling me up and off the now-bloodied and groaning paparazzo, like I weigh nothing. "Charlotte, get off him!"

"Let go of me!" I shriek. "That asshole was going to—"

"Any more and you're going to kill him," Az growls.

Sure enough, when I struggle and twist in Azmodeus's fireman's hold to look back to the scene, the paparazzo is lying there unmoving.

A shout comes from somewhere across the street a moment later. "There they are!"

A chill runs through me.

Another paparazzo.

No, not another. A whole group of them.

Someone must have tipped them off that we'd be here this evening.

I glance toward Az's face as he sets me down, trying to gauge whether it was him. It's not like he hasn't pulled that kind of shit with me and Lucifer before.

But he looks just as shocked as me.

And thankfully, in a right enough mind to act on what I'm already thinking.

We need to get the hell out of here.

Now.

"Fuck," Az swears. "Hold on tight, lovey."

Before I know what's happening, Az is shoving us both through the ether, but I don't have time to close my eyes. The breath is ripped from my chest as I watch the whole world fade away and condense until we're stumbling through what looks like a model of the very city we just left, made entirely out of stars. The buildings seem to zoom out until the city's no more than a pinprick, until a model of the world sits before us. A projected map made of dust and glittering sand. Or stardust.

And I realize then that's what we all are in the end.

Stardust.

And now with the apocalypse coming, that's all *any* of us are going to be.

A choked noise tears from my throat, and before I can fully comprehend what's in front of me, I feel myself being sucked back in, that familiar tug at my navel coming at the exact moment Azmodeus touches one of the glittering particles like he's selected our destination off a menu. That singular movement sends us whirling. My feet slam onto the rooftop of the penthouse seconds later, my knees buckling.

It all happened so fast. In no more than a blink.

Without warning, I turn and vomit the contents of my stomach into the rooftop's empty pool, the heat from where it exited my body causing steam to rise into the cold night air.

Azmodeus drops down into one of the lounge chairs beside me, raking a lazy hand through his hair. "Well, fuck me, I haven't had that much fun in ages." He throws back his head and laughs in a way that reminds me all too much of Lucifer. "This makes us besties, now, right? I'm not above playing the gay best friend when it's fun for me."

And it's not until that exact moment I realize the true danger Lust poses to me. It's not the sexual innuendos or the horny feelings Az creates.

It's the impulsive decision-making he inspires.

Shame constricts my throat. I'm unable to answer him as my stomach churns at the thought of the paparazzo, of the human man I nearly killed without consequence this evening, and I turn back toward the pool, vomiting again as Az laughs at me.

CHAPTER THIRTY-THREE

Lucifer

My wretched bitch of a sister makes her home in a refurbished carriage house on the Lower West Side in Greenwich Village, and when she finally returns from her hot yoga class for the evening, I'm there waiting.

"What the fuck are you doing here?" She tosses her purple yoga mat down upon the sofa beside me, flopping into an armchair across from where I'm seated on the other side of her living room. She levels a furious glare at me as she uses a wide plastic straw to stir some of the sediment at the bottom of the green juice she's carrying.

My eyes track toward it, one brow lifting.

"I'm on a cleanse," she grumbles defensively. "Or so my followers think."

She takes a generous sip then frowns, scrunching her nose before she scoffs, depositing the clear cup upon the coffee table. "Haven't you disturbed my peace enough this century?"

"Apparently not." I toss the dossier I brought with me onto the Chippendale table, nearly knocking her juice over with it.

She scowls at me, staring at the dossier like she may refuse. Finally curiosity gets the better of her. She thumbs through it quickly. "What does this have to do with me?"

"I came to make a—"

"No," she says before I can even get the word out.

She stands and heads toward the kitchen, forcing me to follow her.

"Mimi," I growl.

"I said no, Lucifer," she tosses over her shoulder.

Standing in the light of her fridge, looking through a multicolored array of cold-pressed juices her trainer or chef must have prepared for this week's latest trend, she plucks a pink one from the top shelf and takes a sip, sighing contentedly. "Better. Though still not enough." She closes the fridge, her eyes narrowing at the sight of me on the other side. "Why are you still here?"

"Mimi—" I start, but she's halfway across the carriage house.

"No. No, no, no, no. I've told you this, Lucifer. How many times do I have to say it?"

"Until I get my way, it seems."

She rounds on me, clearly prepared to tear me in two, and that's when I reach inside my suit-coat pocket and extend the one thing I know without a doubt will persuade her to listen.

The little gold Scottie dog sits on my palm, the luxury game piece gleaming.

A sharp intake of breath follows before my sister snatches it out of my hand greedily. "Where is it?"

I nod toward the sitting room.

She's there and gone in a flash like an impatient child at Christmas.

When I find her perched on a stool by the sitting room table a few moments later, she's already set up half the Monopoly board. "You know I always want to be the car," she says to me, casting the Scottie dog back into the set's wooden drawer.

I sit down at the table across from her, claiming the battleship for myself.

Mimi levels a warning look at me. "If you take Boardwalk and Park Place from me, I will end you. You know they're my favorites."

But I have every intention of letting her win like she wants.

"The red properties are more strategic," I comment.

My sister ignores me.

She takes the first turn, rolling the dice before she rubs her hands together enthusiastically, and after several fevered rounds of purchasing, she lets out a victorious shriek as she plucks one of the red properties right out from under me.

My sister may have gotten her sinful title for choosing her own selfish desires over strategy, but when it suits her, she can be nearly as cutthroat as me.

"We need to discuss it, you know," I finally mutter once we're halfway through the game.

How she tried to undermine me. Hired Michael to kill Paris Starr.

Thus far, she's bought up Boardwalk and Park Place, all the greens, and half of the bloody reds, but I have every railroad, all the oranges, and now she's eyeing the tax money we place in the middle for if anyone lands on Free Parking.

"Do we?" She rolls again, getting doubles for the third time in a row, causing her to let out a furious scream as I'm forced to move her golden car into jail for her.

"Working with Michael serves my purposes currently, but considering he was working with you first . . ." I flash the orange card from my pile at her that reads Get Out of Jail Free.

"You want to trade?" She lifts a brow.

I nod. "Naturally."

"Technically you're not allowed to trade when you're in jail," she says, her eyes narrowing suspiciously, "but since it's just the two of us." She seizes the orange card from my hand and returns it to the discard pile, before moving her piece to Just Visiting. "Michael wants to start the apocalypse. Thinks it will get Father's attention and make Him come back, you see."

"Tell me something I don't know."

She cradles the dice within her palm, glancing toward my properties. "It'll cost you."

I huff, slipping my one remaining red across the table toward her. Kentucky.

She claps her hands, grinning delightedly as she lines it up in the little row of cards in front of her. "He knows he can't open the seals without you, but the others don't."

I smile. "Interesting."

She rolls the dice and takes her turn, scowling when she doesn't land on Free Parking and instead ends up on St. James Place.

Which currently belongs to me.

Begrudgingly, she shoves the fourteen dollars of fake money toward me.

"And his plan?"

She shrugs.

Clearly, if I expect her to be forthcoming, it's going to cost me. I sigh, leaning back in my chair as I tip my chin toward the small pile of gold hundreds in the middle before I make a show of glancing over my shoulder pointedly. "Did you hear that?"

When I turn back toward the table, the stack of bills is mysteriously missing, and Mammon's own pile of money is incrementally higher.

She makes a meal of thumbing through her five hundreds. "He thinks he can get Mother to open them without you."

"Mother?"

"Or the Horsemen. All of us. Whichever comes easier, it seems."

"Seems a bit—"

"Single-minded," she finishes for me. "You know that was always Michael's weakness."

"Mmph," I grumble in agreement, moving my piece.

This time, I land on Park Place, and I'm forced to pay her the exorbitant rent fee.

"And what does any of this have to do with your skinny little bitch?" she says after several more turns in silence. She nods toward the living room, where my dossier remains. "She's all that's *ever* on your mind these days."

I shrug. "Someone needs to teach her what it means to be divine, to use her power, and who better than my one and only beloved sister?"

Mimi scoffs.

"Don't play coy, sissy. You've wanted another woman on this side of the celestial divide ever since Father chose to cast us out."

"I wanted *attention*, connection." She bristles. "You don't know what it's like being the sole female among so many—"

"Prideful peacocks?" I finish for her, quirking a brow.

She smirks. "I was going to say douchebags, actually."

I lean back in my seat, resting my arm over the adjacent chair. "Be that as it may, I'd be willing to lend her to you if you needed—"

"What? Companionship? A friend? Don't insult me, Lucifer. If I wanted a sister, I could do so much better than your little former-human pocket pussy. That's for certain."

But even *I* recognize that it's simply a matter of her own pride getting the better of her.

I lean forward. "If you took her under your wing, she'd adore you."

Greed grumbles, refusing to look at me.

"Mimi," I give her a look of mock sympathy. "Or should I say 'big sister'?"

"And what do I get out of all this, humph? Nothing more than a gold-plated Monopoly piece?" She waves a dismissive hand as she scoffs. "Please."

I lean forward onto my knees, pinning her with a hard stare. "How about a seat at my side when humanity starts to fall, Michael's little plan to get Father to return fails, and *I* am the lone celestial left standing in the ashes, with the one and only person who's the key to opening the pearly gates begging at my feet?"

Mammon sets down the dice, leaning back in her chair as she looks at me. "All right, *now* I'm listening."

CHAPTER THIRTY-FOUR

Charlotte

After I'm done emptying the contents of my stomach into the drained pool, I manage to sneak into the penthouse undetected with a few drunken promises from Azmodeus that I'll hear from him about mine and Lucifer's engagement party in the coming days.

That night, I dream I'm back in the club again.

Yet instead of Azmodeus dancing with me, it's that handsome stranger.

The man from the edge of the dance floor, his lethal-looking body pressed against me, his hands sliding lower until . . .

I wake with my own hand down my pants, touching myself. I gasp, mortified by what I'm doing, and roll over, burying my face in my pillow with a groan.

What is *wrong* with me?

It isn't until my alarm clock goes off a few hours later and I get through my morning routine without interruption from Lucifer or one of his senior staff that I'm naive enough to think I might have actually gotten away with mine and Azmodeus's little stunt. But the moment I arrive at Apollyon headquarters, feeling like I'm on top of the world,

Jeanine informs me that Lucifer's summoned me to his office before I even have a chance to look at today's headlines, and my triumph is abruptly ripped out from under me.

"What in the bloody fuck were you thinking?"

I don't have time to settle into my seat across from his desk before he shoves one of this morning's tabloids at me. "Read it," he says, his voice surprisingly calm when I refuse to look toward the glossy magazine heading.

I hesitate.

"I said, fucking read it, Charlotte," he snarls, more animal than I've ever heard before. Like the red devil with the tail and horns you see in the movies.

Though now that I know about his current arrangement with Michael, the full truth of him is so much worse, so much more terrifying.

I follow the command without question, lowering my eyes so I'm forced to read the headline in front of me.

Lucifer Cuckolded! By His Own Brother? The Devil Is in the Details!

Followed by a full front-page spread of Azmodeus and me grinding together on the dance floor. Like I was with that stranger in my dream.

I snatch up the tabloid, staring at the photo of what I thought was a celestial-only space, some other dimension.

Apparently, the club was more human than I gave Az credit for. Or was it?

How the hell did they even get this picture?

I guess pretty much anybody can be a paparazzo these days, considering there's not a person I know who doesn't have twenty-four seven access to a high-quality digital camera in their pocket.

I throw the magazine back onto the desk, casting a pleading glance toward Lucifer. "It's not what you think."

The words are out before I can stop them, the tension thickening, and the worst part is they don't feel entirely truthful with how guilty I am about that dream. But it was just a dream.

There's no harm in fantasy, right?

Pain sparks in the back of my throat as I lower my head slightly.

My fault, that thing inside me hisses. *My fault, my fault, my fault.*

I shake my head.

No, not my fault.

This time I was only doing what I thought was right. What I could to save humanity.

And blowing off steam. The rest was the influence of Az's powers. Wasn't it?

"I will leave that cliched admission of guilt where it belongs inside your head, little dove," Lucifer says coolly, rounding the far side of his desk like he—

"You . . . you heard that?" I stammer. "Wh-what I was thinking?"

Lucifer has the audacity to look almost annoyed with me. "I can only hear what you direct at me, but I've been privy to your thoughts for some time now. Get with the program."

My stomach drops.

"But I . . . I thought . . ." My voice trails off.

My whole plan banked on the fact that he *couldn't* see inside my head. It was an advantage I had, one of the few things that helped make him fall in love with me, but that was back when I was human.

Now I'm something else.

Fully. Completely.

Despite all the ways I tried to resist it.

I press my lips together, my lack of emotion making my limbs feel heavy.

The way I mindlessly attacked that paparazzo should have been evidence enough.

Lucifer watches me for a long beat, his fingers steepled, his distant expression revealing nothing. But what *exactly* has he heard me think?

If it's about what I send to him, I can still pull this off, right?

I just need to tread carefully.

"The other night in the playroom?" I tilt my head toward him, watching him intently as I finally put two and two together. "Those were *your* thoughts I heard, weren't they?"

Lucifer doesn't answer me.

But his silence is answer enough.

This is a two-way street.

And until now, he had no intention of telling me I had access to it.

I have to bite the inside of my cheek to fight down my frustration.

"Open it." He nods toward the tabloid.

I shake my head. I don't want him to be able to see or hear what I've been planning, and I'm not exactly well-versed in how this mind-to-mind-connection thing works yet. "There's nothing in there that I want to—"

"I said, open it." He doesn't raise his voice, but the effect the order has is the same.

My blood runs cold, my mouth feeling drier than the Sahara.

Team Apocalypse: 1. Team Humanity: 0.

With shaking hands, I open the magazine to the corresponding page, trying my best not to send anything along the connection between us, but I have no idea if I'm even doing it correctly.

More stolen moments. More pictures of me and Az.

All put on display to sell a lie. A gossip story.

Each piece of fake news more and more damning than the last.

"It's not what you think," I repeat, suppressing the bitterness I feel at the fact he would *ever* dare question my loyalty. It doesn't matter that I'm working against him to stop the apocalypse now or that I enjoyed my stupid dream. I'm doing this for us *both*, even if he can't see it yet. "I would never betray you, Lucifer. You know I—"

"Spare me the excuses, Charlotte." He lifts a hand to silence me.

Is that all my love is to you? An excuse?

I try and send the thought down the line between us intentionally, and now that I'm aware of it, I can feel the exact moment it lands. His frustration with me flares.

I close my mouth, swallowing repeatedly.

But if he knows what I'm *actually* planning, how I'm attempting to undermine him and Michael, he doesn't let onto it.

It's not a betrayal. Or that's what I tell myself.

It's a desperate plea for his mercy, to save humanity.

Isn't it?

"I know you're not fucking my brother." He says it so artlessly, so confident and brazen that I cringe. "You're not *that* kind of whore."

I flush deep.

He *means* to humiliate me. To remind me of my place.

I deserve as much for the way I've behaved, honestly.

I draw a slow, fortifying breath in and out through my nose. "Then if you know none of its true, then why am I—"

"I told you to leave my family to me." He tosses a dossier he and his shadows materialize out of thin air onto the table in front of me. This time, he doesn't have to order me to open it. I flip back the cover readily.

The contents reveal several more photos of me and Az.

Me throwing the water bottle at the paparazzo.

Me kicking the man while he was down, his blood on the spike of my heel.

And the most damning yet . . .

Azmodeus holding me over his shoulder as we step into the ether, into what appears in the photo to be a black endless hole for all humanity to see.

I'd almost think it was photoshopped if I didn't know any better.

"I don't think I need to tell you what it would have meant for us, considering the ongoing investigation into your actress's death, if I hadn't paid to have *this* particular story killed in favor of this drivel." He swipes his hand across the desk, sending the dossier plummeting to the floor.

I tense.

"Olivia," I mumble, correcting him.

Her name comes out as barely a whisper.

"Pardon?" Lucifer quirks a brow.

"You called her my *actress*." I lift my gaze toward him, unchecked defiance rising in me. "Her name was Olivia."

Lucifer stiffens, his jaw tightening. "Be that as it may, if photos of this had gotten out, the information we've been keeping secret would have been leaked. Imagine the speculation. The public would finally have ascertained that you're an—?"

"An immortal?" I snap. "Some kind of half-human freak?"

Lucifer goes still at my sudden outburst, but I don't stop there. Every doubt, every insecurity I've been feeling spills out of me.

"Not a fallen angel. Not a demon. Not a human, but something *else* in between? An abomination of nature? Is that what you were going to say?"

"I've told you time and time again not to put words in my mouth. My patience with you runs thin and—"

"Your *patience* with me?" I nearly laugh, the idea is so ridiculous. "What about *my* patience with *you*, Lucifer? I'm tired of being told to sit on the sidelines." I slam my hand onto his desk, glaring at him. "You told me you were handling the apocalypse. You could have told me what you were planning, but instead all you've done is—"

"Enough, Charlotte," he growls, the blaze of hellfire in his eyes instantly silencing me. "I will *not* entertain this self-pitying human thinking any longer. Do I make myself clear?"

I clench my teeth, muttering from between them, "Crystal."

"As the head of this family and *your* future husband, it is my responsibility to ensure your safety, which means—"

"I was perfectly safe," I argue. "I'm immortal now, and Azmodeus was with me. If anything had happened, he would have—"

Lucifer stands, leaning over his desk, before he suddenly yanks me forward by my collar so that we're nose to nose. "If you think for even a second that my lust-crazed brother would have sacrificed himself for you, think again."

Abruptly, he releases me, and I shake my head, my gaze unfocused as I look away from him. "I'm immortal now. I don't see why it—"

"You are immortal, *not* invincible," Lucifer growls. "And starting today, so help me God, Charlotte, I will ensure that you learn the difference."

The shadows at the edges of the room shift at his will, the tension changing from tense to punishing. I know where this is headed. I know this feeling.

I remember it perfectly.

A sharp pain forms in my throat.

"What do you mean?"

He doesn't answer me.

"Lucifer, what do you—?"

He curses under his breath, the look he gives me one of furious resignation, like I've somehow forced him to do this for my own good, but he pushes through it, baring his teeth. "You want to test my boundaries? To be a brat? For me to *instruct* you? I'll give you instructions, darling." He laughs, though there's no amusement in it. "As of today, you will go *nowhere* without my permission. Your schedule will become my schedule, every aspect of your day, of your life within *my* control. Where you eat, when you sleep, where you go, who you fuck, and who you fuck with, *all* of it will be *mine*, until you start to behave like the immortal queen you have been chosen to be, do I make myself clear?"

Sudden panic rises in me. A feeling of vertigo.

All at once, his collar at my throat feels too tight.

This is more than what I bargained for. More than I—

"You can't do that. You can't—"

"I can and I will. Watch me."

Abruptly, he casts an all-too-familiar document onto the desk in front of me, and I know without looking what it is.

My employment contract.

The same one he used to trap me all those months ago.

Only this time, I walked right into it willingly.

My heart seizes.

The devastation inside me is immediate. The pressure building inside my chest from where I forget to breathe.

My life. My father. My choices.

And now . . .

My privacy. Both *inside* my head and out.

Every part of me—everything I am—stolen from me.

This is all I'll ever mean to him.

If I don't start fighting for something different.

"So, you'd let that be the crux of us?" The words come out as a statement, so low and injured and broken that if it weren't for his supernatural hearing, I'd be surprised if he could hear them. "The pretty little dove. The weak bird you keep in a cage. Not a true partner. Not someone worthy of your respect, your honesty. Just a toy made from one of your bones." I shake my head. "Well, I won't. Not anymore." I look at him then, meeting his gaze head-on. "It's *you* you've been trying to protect this whole time, not me. It always has been."

Lucifer's jaw clenches like I've just seen past all his defenses. He reaches out, and his thumb slowly traces over the diamonds at my throat. "I will not lose you to whatever foolhardy teenage-immortal rebellion it is you're waging, Charlotte." He stares at me, his dark eyes so full of worry that for a moment it stills me, until his gaze softens slightly, and he whispers, "I cannot bear to watch you die in my arms again."

The words cut through me, nearly causing me to falter.

He loves me. Of course he does.

He wants to protect me.

In his own cruel, twisted way.

But I'm done fighting him.

And for the first time since he remade me, I'm going to start fighting for *us*. I lift my chin as he drops back down into his chair. "I wouldn't have taken you for a coward."

A spark of fury lights in Lucifer's expression. Barely there, but present. "Excuse me?"

"You heard me."

But I don't stop there. I won't stop until I've forced out whatever fear, whatever vulnerabilities, have been holding him back.

The same way he did for me.

Who better to remind the devil of who he is than his vicious queen?

I turn up my nose like I'm disappointed in him. "First you allow your Mother to dictate our lives, our fate, and now this?" I scoff. "Why even bother calling yourself the devil?"

Lucifer remains unnaturally silent for a beat. "You are treading into very dangerous territory."

"Maybe I want dangerous." I thrust my chin forward, my expression full of defiance. "Maybe I want what only the devil can give me."

Lucifer comes up out of his chair, and I stand, meeting him at the edge of his desk.

"Be careful what you wish for."

"Do your worst." I eye him up and down, taunting him. "Lucy."

Abruptly, Lucifer clutches me by the throat, sending me staggering back onto his desk. The desk's contents crash to the floor as he drags me by my collar to the center of it, but he doesn't so much as blink.

His eyes never leave mine, his expression darkening. "Careful now, little dove. My hellfire doesn't know the meaning of mercy."

Then make me burn, I purr through our connection. *Light me up, Daddy.*

Without warning, Lucifer shoves me down onto the desk so hard, he knocks all the wind out of me, and the next thing I know, my hands are being roughly pinned above my head and my panties ripped from beneath my dress as he buries the full length of his cock in me.

But I won't let him pin me down that easily.

He thrusts into me, growling in approval at how wet and slick I already am for him, but I maneuver my leg up between us and use my high heel to nail him straight in the chest. He eats it, taking the blow without so much as a wince, as he's knocked a few feet back into the wall of his office. Apparently, I don't know my own celestial strength.

Lucifer throws back his head and laughs wickedly, the sound crazed, unhinged. But I don't stop there.

"What's wrong, Lucy?" I taunt, hopping down from his desk and rounding the far side, so that he'll have to chase me. "Don't like being bested at your own game?"

"Minx," he purrs. "Witch."

Before he dives for me.

I barely manage to skirt his grip, but just when I think I've gotten away, he snatches me out of midair, throwing us both up against the glass wall of his office so I'm pressed flat against the cold glass.

"I'm going to be punishing you for this for weeks," he snarls.

"Worth it," I sass back.

The sound of his belt buckle follows, and the next thing I know, the snap of the leather hits my ass painfully. I yelp, unprepared for the blow. But the subsequent ones come so quickly, I don't get any reprieve. Over and over until I'm keening.

"You're lucky I don't put you over my knee."

The sting of my ass heightens, my pussy growing infinitely hotter until I'm gasping, aching for it. Suddenly I hear his belt buckle hit the floor before Lucifer spits into his hand and—

He takes my ass in one hard thrust, causing me to cry out in a mixture of pleasure-pain. My hands press flat against the window, the heat of my breath fogging my view of the city as I whimper. Holy fuck, he feels twice as huge back there.

We've been slowly building up to this for weeks, but this is the first time he's—

I let out a choked sound, my collar feeling tight against my throat as he slides home, bottoming out. His balls slap against my ass cheeks as he pushes past the last of my resistance, while meanwhile my pussy continues to ache. Somehow, the throb at the apex becomes impossibly worse as he digs into me, wrapping his hand in my hair to use it as leverage.

I moan greedily. "Please, Daddy."

Put me out of my misery.

But Lucifer has no intention of showing me any mercy.

"Do you have any idea how furious I was when you first showed up in my boardroom? How fucking angry I was?" He pulls my head back, growling, each stroke of his cock harder than the last, until his pace is unrelenting. Until I can hardly see straight.

I shake my head. "No, no, sir."

He palms my breasts. "I couldn't eat. Couldn't sleep. You have no idea how much I hated it, how much resentment I felt for—"

"Me?" I gasp, whimpering.

"For fuck's sake, Charlotte, no. Don't you see? The vulnerability you created in me." He says it out loud, but I feel the weight of it inside my skull.

The full extent of what it cost him.

For the devil to admit he'd fallen in love with a human.

My heart stutters painfully.

"And there you were, no less weak and vulnerable than a trembling bird in my palm. And what was I to do? Turn my back on you? Forget the way my stomach pitched into my feet whenever you looked at me? How I would have given up everything I'd worked for, everything I'd built, just to know the feel of you in my arms? Or worse, tell you? If I'd have told you, you'd have fucking run."

My breath catches in my chest, my throat constricting from the tears that gather in my eyes.

"I will *never* forgive my Mother for the choice she took from you, but I will *not* apologize for wanting you. For claiming what's mine. Don't you understand? Nothing you could ever do, nothing you could ever say, *nothing* will ever change that. I'm a bloody lunatic when it comes to you, don't you see? I've been lost, obsessed from the very start. Fuck fate. Fuck free will. Fuck my family. Fuck everything. You are *mine*, and that's all that matters."

"Lucifer, I—"

"Quiet, Charlotte," he snarls, and I smile as a single tear slips free. "If you're going to behave like a filthy whore, then you will stay silent while you milk my cock like one."

The next thing I know, Lucifer's hand is on my throat, and I'm being hauled up against him until . . .

He bites me.

I feel the length of his fangs sink into my neck, like a viper's strike, and something comes apart inside me.

I shatter, Lucifer's hand that's now over my mouth the only thing that muffles my screams. I pulse and pulse, the warm gush of him finishing coupling with the heat, the pleasure of his venom coursing through me, until I can barely hold myself upright.

I don't think I've ever come harder in my life.

Lucifer releases me, his mouth and teeth coated in blood from where he drank from me, as he spins me to face him, and I collapse into his arms.

He holds me upright, pinning me between him and the cold window at my back, both of us panting as we share breath.

"You bit me," I whisper.

"Marked you." He gives me a roguish smile.

His eyes fall to my wrist, and I follow his gaze there as he lifts it, gasping at the sight of the angelic light that snakes its way over my skin. It pulses, then fades, revealing the image of a black serpent. Like a tattoo.

"To remind you that you will always be mine," Lucifer whispers as he cups my cheek. "Saying I love you is an understatement. You are my soulmate. Every part of my tattered existence bleeds for you." He kisses me, the harsh, punishing brush of his lips making me melt.

We stay like that for a long time, lost in one another, trading breath.

"I wouldn't have run," I whisper.

Lucifer eases back, staring down at me incredulously. "Even though you fear me?"

The hurt at what he thought I was going to say at dinner a few weeks back flashes through me, a brief glimpse into his mind through our connection.

"I don't fear you, Lucifer. I fear how much you *mean* to me." I place my hand on his chest, feeling his heartbeat. "Our love is the apple. One bite and I was gone."

He smiles, leaning in to lay a gentle kiss on my forehead, before he steps back, forcing us to separate. "That's enough of your spellcasting for now. Best run along now, little dove. I have a meeting."

I smirk, righting my clothes. I pick my torn panties up off the floor, and I press them into his waiting palm. He grins appreciatively.

No way would he ever allow me to leave here with them.

I brush my hand over the stubble on his face. "You can't shield me from every danger we're ever going to face, you know. Even though I know you wish you could. If we're going to do this, you have to be honest with me. About everything. You wanted me to embrace being immortal, and I have. Now you need to let me make my own choices, my own mistakes."

Lucifer grumbles, swearing under his breath like that idea doesn't exactly thrill him, but then finally he gives a reluctant nod. "Only *after* you've had the proper training."

A slow smile spreads across my lips.

A compromise. Our first.

I give a curt nod. "I can live with that." I rise onto my toes, kissing him on the cheek before I turn and head toward the elevator, calling over my shoulder, "But don't think I'm not still furious with you about this whole Michael business."

"I wouldn't expect anything less." He places his hands in his pockets as he leans against his desk.

I watch him as I go, smiling to myself as the elevator door inside his office closes, and I glance down at my new ink. Soulmates. With the devil.

It has a nice ring to it, if you ask me.

CHAPTER THIRTY-FIVE

Lucifer

I watch Charlotte walk out of my office, fully aware for the first time in my long existence that I might have made a grave error.

It isn't until I'm standing in the middle of that blasted church near Seventh again, striding up the length of the center aisle toward the small prayer group gathered in the first several pews, that I realize how thoroughly the revelation has disturbed me.

"Back so soon?" Father Brown opens his arms in a welcome gesture.

When the few parishioners that join him lay eyes on me, they scatter like flies.

I watch them go, mildly amused at how they flee, as he sighs and forms a cone with his hands, calling out, "We'll resume next week." He turns his attention back to me as I start to pace. "What brings you here, Lucifer?"

Abruptly, I round on him, raking a rough hand through my disheveled hair "What did you mean when you told me not to make her choose?" I demand.

Father Brown quirks his head at me. "It depends. What did you think it meant?"

I shake my head, wagging a furious finger at him as I advance on him, my words rapid fire. "Ah, ah, ah, Father, I have neither the time nor the patience for any of your cultish bullshit. I practically wrote the handbook on manipulation. You will *not* answer my question with another question. Answer me."

To my shock, Father Brown doesn't appear the least bit fazed by how manic I'm being as I continue to shake my head, pacing back and forth like a madman.

I'm coming out of my own skin like a bloody lunatic.

Perhaps I am.

Mad, that is.

Out of my mind in love with her.

This is what she does to me.

In my most private moments. The ones she never sees.

I'm unbalanced, distracted, unhinged, only for her. So ridiculously tormented, so deranged, that here I am standing in the middle of a bloody cathedral, for fuck's sake, talking to a goddamn human priest who dares call himself a member of my Father's clergy.

She makes me question myself in a way I never would have done previously.

As if she has become my moral compass.

My guiding light.

The best and worst parts of me.

I drop into one of the pews and bury my face in my hands. Just when I thought I had everything under control, thought I *knew* what was best for her, for us, for the sake of our shared futures, I was forced to stand there and watch as she walked away with my heart pulsing in her hand. Cut to the quick by my own choices. As if I no longer hold any true power here.

In the face of my love for her, I'm powerless . . .

Exactly as I feared.

I cannot stand it.

"I don't know," I say. "I don't fucking know, honestly. Just bloody answer me already."

Father Brown watches me curiously. "Whatever meaning I intended isn't as important as the meaning you gave it, especially if you—"

I sit bolt upright. "Do you think that perhaps she's doing this on purpose? To undermine me? Could Michael have put her up to this?"

"Lucifer, did something—?"

"No." I shake my head, instantly abandoning the idea. "No, she would never do that. I've just been trying so hard to protect her that I've failed to see what was right in front of me. Failed to take into account what *she* might want." I lift my gaze toward him unexpectedly. "But love requires sacrifice, does it not, Father?"

Father Brown gives a skeptical nod. "In theory."

"And sacrifice is a form of surrender? Giving up one's power in service of the greater good?"

Father Brown sighs heavily. "I'm not certain I understand what you're asking me, Lucifer."

I beckon him forward, lowering my voice conspiratorially as he draws near. "Suppose I said that I wanted to change course, turn over a new leaf, wipe the ol' slate clean as it were—only for her sake, mind you—how might a devilish chap like me go about doing that, humph?"

Father Brown gapes at me. "Are you . . . are you asking for me to absolve you?"

I cast him a chastising look. "Don't get cheeky now, Father. We both know you don't hold nearly that kind of power. No matter what the Catholic church may claim. But, yes, I'm asking that if I needed for my celestial slate to be wiped clean, to be forgiven, for my wife's sake, what might you have me do? Shall I say ten Hail Marys and then call it a day?"

Father Brown presses his lips together like he's not certain what to make of me. "Well, I don't know if this idea will hold much appeal for you, but you could always"—he glances pointedly toward the ceiling—"*ask* for forgiveness."

I scoff. "Right. That'll be the day."

Father Brown smiles.

As if he knows exactly how desperate Charlotte's made me.

"Honesty helps, too, of course," he says.

I hesitate before I tilt my head at him curiously. "And if I *did* want to give that little idea of yours a go, do you . . . do you think He would listen?"

Father Brown chuckles softly. "Only one way to find out." He nods toward the confessional booth, and for a long moment I stare at it like a cobra prepared to strike. Then I abruptly stand and stride toward it. I glance over my shoulder to ensure no one is watching as I climb into the parishioner's box. I seal the little wooden door shut.

Father Brown climbs in on the other side and sits down in the booth across from me as he begins to make the sign of the cross over himself.

I lean forward onto my knees. "We're going to be here for quite some time, I'm afraid."

CHAPTER THIRTY-SIX

Charlotte

That night, I'm still too frustrated and angry over how powerless I feel in the face of this whole apocalypse situation to drag myself up to our room, so instead I lock myself alone in one of the guest suites.

I collapse onto the bed, screaming my muffled rage into Egyptian cotton sheets until it feels like there's nothing left but a cavernous hole where my soul used to be.

Fuck this.

Fuck doing nothing.

I rise from the bed, my hands, arms, and feet seeming to move of their own accord—like I'm a puppet on strings—until I'm standing at the top of our building. The same spot where Lucifer cast the aurora borealis over the city.

It's the early hours of the morning, most of the city's residents still asleep.

Those who don't know what lies in store for them, anyway.

The autumn breeze rolls through my hair, the chill making me wrap my arms around myself as I steel my resolve, my rage.

I glance toward Heaven. To the sky above me.

It's an odd mixture of darkness and light that reminds me of the power that now lives inside Lucifer and me.

And if I'm going to start fighting for our future, why not start at the top?

"Why me?" I shout, staring up at the never-ending sky.

Only the sound of the rooftop wind answers.

"Why me?" I yell, raising my voice even louder and letting all the fury I've been holding in for so long get the better of me. "It wasn't enough that I had to suffer at the hands of my dad? That I kept faith and prayed to you every night even though you *never* fucking answered a single one of my prayers?"

A furious tear slides down my cheek.

"It wasn't enough when I begged, when I *pleaded* for your mercy every time Mark would put his filthy hands on me?"

I brush away several damp strands of hair that have blown into my face.

"And then . . ."—I let out a humorless laugh, shaking my head in disbelief—"and then just when I think you've saved me, when I think you've led me to *your* son, I find out it's your goddess for a wife that actually did all of the work?" I shriek into the whistling wind. "What's it going to take? What's it going to take for you to hear me?"

The silence that answers is deafening.

I glance down at the city below, an insane idea sparking.

"All right, Big Guy. You want to play chicken? Abandon us all to do your bidding? I'll play," I shout, stepping up and onto the ledge. "If you're listening . . ." I yell up to God, just before I take the final step over the ledge. "Catch me, Motherfucker."

CHAPTER THIRTY-SEVEN

Lucifer

"I thought you might not show."

"I'm a man of my word, brother, unlike Father."

As I step forth from the courtyard's shadows, Michael quirks a brow like he can't possibly begin to understand what I mean.

I shrug. "Oh, you know, the whole 'I'll always be with you' bit. Seems rather disappointing now, doesn't it?"

My brother's eyes harden. "Father *will* return, Lucy. Once we've accomplished the task He left for us. Once all seven seals are opened and we've scorched what's left of this earth."

I scoff. "Whatever helps you spread your wings each morning."

We're standing in the middle of the Met Cloisters in Washington Heights—in the Cuxa Garden located on the south side of the main building. My brother could have chosen any of the other hundreds of churches, mosques, cathedrals, temples, or synagogues within the city proper, but he always did have a flare for theatrics.

He comes by it naturally, I suppose.

I step further into the garden, taking in the scene before me. In the middle of the darkened parterre, a human woman hangs suspended in midair by her feet, her muffled cries silenced by the bit of my brother's power he's using to hold her there. I don't deign to acknowledge her existence as she rotates toward me, her desperate eyes pleading.

I've never been known for my mercy.

And I have no intention of starting now.

I'll play exactly the villain they expect of me.

I glance toward the courtyard's other occupants. Dozens upon dozens of my angelic siblings. My former army. The nearest are Raphael, Uriel, and Seraph respectively.

The other Archangels the world would recognize by name are no doubt waiting somewhere in the wings. My brother would never go head-to-head with me alone.

He's too fearful. Too weak.

They *all* are.

I incline my head in my former generals' direction, relishing the way Seraph hisses and Uriel flinches away in disgust. As if they didn't once throw themselves at my feet. Now they cannot fathom the idea of a creature more unholy, more un-Godly, than me. They see through my mask to my true face with ease.

They'll never lay eyes on my angelic features again.

One of the myriad ways our Father chose to fuck me.

"Father of lies." Raphael spits at my feet. "Filthy whore."

I smirk. "I always fancied the old nicknames." I turn my attention to Michael. "You're bound by His word. We had an agreement."

He nods to one of our other siblings, Jophiel, who steps forth and extends a small golden chest toward him. Michael opens it and removes one of the seven sealed scrolls inside. "First your penance. Only *then* will I call the Righteous off your precious bride."

My expression remains flat, detached, as I glimpse the human still circling overhead.

For once, I do not hold the upper hand here.

"And Mother?" I ask. "What's your plan for keeping her on her leash?"

Michael shrugs. "What Mother does no longer concerns you."

"You underestimate her." I shake my head. "You and Father both."

"Or perhaps you *over*estimate her devotion to you. You're infamous for that."

My siblings chuckle.

"I've never overestimated anything." I step closer, and Jophiel stiffens as if she's prepared to come to Michael's defense, but Michael lifts a hand, allowing me to invade his space. I flick my forked tongue. "When Father cast me out, He chose *me* as His only worthy adversary," I sneer, allowing my pupils to turn serpentine. "What can be said of you? That you were second fiddle?" I scoff, turning to face my other siblings. "When you all tire of Michael's floundering leadership, you know where to find me."

Michael growls through his teeth, causing several of his angelic watchdogs to stir, but I lift my hands in mock surrender, capitulating. To my siblings, our exchange was nothing more than a petty jab. Celestial foreplay, if you will. *Exactly* the kind of prideful posturing they expect of me. But already I've planted the seed in their minds, sown doubt.

In Michael's leadership. His abilities.

It's only a matter of time before they're loyal to me again.

After all, I was their first and favorite leader.

A few of my siblings look to one another uncertainly, murmuring in hushed tones as Barachiel passes Michael his infamous sword, the Flame of Death. I will *never* forgive Azrael for forging it for him. Michael unsheathes it, performing for the crowd as he lifts both it and the first scroll above his head in show.

A triumphant roar echoes from my angelic siblings.

I roll my eyes, giving a few sarcastic, slow claps. "Yes, yes, it's all very exciting, isn't it?"

The first seal will soon be open, signaling what they believe will be our Father's return, the reason they celebrate, but I pay them no mind. No heed.

If Charlotte knew what I was about to do, she would never forgive me.

But she need not know the finer details, the lengths to which I would go for her.

The level of depravity to which I would stoop.

I would commit *any* manner of unconscionable acts in her name.

I am the first true sinner. Not Eve.

And for that, they already fear me. But they will learn to fear me more.

The crowd falls quiet again.

"A virgin? Really?" I catch sight of where the woman continues to rotate.

"A joke, I suppose? The human gods of old always *did* have a thing for sacrificing them, or so the stories say." Michael snaps his fingers, and the woman topples to the dirt.

For the first time all evening, I gift her my full attention.

She means nothing to me, *is* nothing.

Not if Charlotte will finally be safe.

The woman remains bound, her arms restrained behind her back, but she squirms feverishly, her endless cries muffled by my brother's power that gags her.

I reach out, using a bit of my shadows like a hand to remove it. "Lucifer! Lucifer, please!"

She latches on to my familiar face. Like I am the one and only hope she has ever known.

Though I am not, nor will I ever be, anyone's savior but Charlotte's.

I am their tormentor. Their torturer.

It's the image I'm banking on, quite frankly.

"Please," she sobs. "Please, I helped her. I . . ."

I meet the young nun's gaze, a taunting smile across my lips. "And for that, there'll be a special place in Hell for you."

My siblings' amused laughter echoes through the parterre. They are no different, no better than me.

They loathe humanity as much as I do.

I was simply the only one among us who ever had the balls to act like it in front of Dad.

The shadows at the edges of the room start to move, vibrating as I gather my power, but Michael lifts a hand. "Ah, ah, ah, Lucy." He wags a finger at me. "Not so fast."

I scowl at the nickname.

He lunges forward, wielding his blade in a wide arc, but I'm prepared for it. I catch it in my fist, using a bit of my light as reinforcement to keep him from severing the limb completely. Pain sears through my palm, sharp and biting as blood runs down my arm, but I cannot counterattack. I am outnumbered. Severely.

But I knew that when I came here.

"Mmm," I taunt, purring as I make a spectacle of cracking my neck before I lick some of the dripping blood from my wrist. "Punish me like you mean it, brother."

Michael steps closer, putting the whole of his strength against the blade until I have to fight not to wince as it cuts deeper.

But I do not move. Do not yield.

An animalistic growl tears from his throat, his face red with hatred, until the hiss of his voice in my ear is a cheap mimic of my own. "You didn't think it was going to be that easy, did you?"

Abruptly, he slices the blade down, and I swear loudly as he cuts through my hand's tendons.

"Fucking hell, Michael!" I roar as I use my other hand to cradle my bloodied palm to my chest, chuffing like a dragon while hellish steam pours from my nostrils. "What the fuck was that for?"

Michael wields his sword in another swift arc, this time using it to point toward the ground in front of me. "On your knees."

For a moment, the whole of the courtyard seems to hold its collective breath. Not one among the crowd moving. In anticipation of what I will do next.

Michael never could stand how they look to me.

I throw back my head and laugh, the sound entirely psychotic and deranged. "You think this is victory? Humiliating me while you play the role of Father's obedient servant?" I scoff, my nose wrinkled with disdain. "You're only His pawn. While *I* remain a true architect of fate."

Michael shakes his head. "You're nothing more than an ancient serpent thrashing in the dirt."

Neither he nor I move.

"You want to protect your precious human bride?" He sneers like the mere idea is beneath him. "Then on your knees, brother."

My mouth twists into a sour expression as I look past Michael rather than at him, my gaze falling to my other siblings. "Fine. You win." I take slow and deliberate care to strip off my suit coat, fanning it out onto the ground, before I slowly lower to my knees. "Isn't this precious? Tell me, Michael, does it make you feel like a big angelic man to have the great and almighty Lucifer bow down before you as *I* use my power to open the very seals that you can't? You must be so proud to have me groveling at your feet, or are you too busy admiring yourself to enjoy this little victor—"

Michael arcs his sword at the last second, slicing through the back of my knees. I go down hard, face-first onto the pavement. Laughter erupts throughout the courtyard. But it's my pride that's injured more than anything.

At how Michael has chosen to humiliate me.

White-hot fury courses through me.

I lift my head, fangs bared.

To my surprise, Seraph steps forward, as if for a moment she's considering helping me. She was once my friend. My most cherished sister. But I snarl at her, my gaze brimming with hatred and hellfire as she falls back in line, resuming her place.

I will destroy them *all.*

Every. Last. One of them.

A murmur ripples through the crowd as I slowly lift myself onto my knees. Already my tendons are beginning to repair themselves, knit back together—one of the many pleasures of being divine—but the reaction among the crowd is mixed. Everything from hatred to disgust to trepidation to pleasure.

They are used to my Father meting out punishment.

But they're not accustomed to Michael's open display of cruelty.

Bloodthirsty as they may be.

"Ah, so this is what it comes to, eh? The almighty serpent knelt before Heaven's most obedient lapdog?" I give an exaggerated bow to my audience. "How quaint. You must think you've won something, right, brother? Look at you, playing the hero."

Michael's lips pull thin. "I seek no glory. Only Father's mercy."

"Don't we all?" The edge of my mouth curls viciously. "But no matter how many times you force me to kneel, it'll never erase the truth, will it, Mikey? You're the real prisoner here. Trapped in this endless cycle of Father's divine will." I flash a cold smile. "You'll die a slave while *I* will always be free."

A few uneasy murmurs whisper through the crowd, signaling my siblings' uncertainty. In the absence of our Father's leadership, they cannot begin to know how to think for themselves, how to choose freely. They are nothing more than the well-trained sheep He made them. Michael silences them with the lift of his hand as he finally holds out the first scroll, unceremoniously popping open the first seal like it's little more than a pesky soda-can tab. His eyes scan back and forth as he reads the glowing angelic inscription.

"So what'll it be, humph? What gladiator-style feat of bravery or bit of hocus-pocus does Father expect me to perform to unlock His first trial for humanity? Kill a firstborn son? Build an ark with my bare hands? Walk on water? You tell me."

Michael's smirk widens as his gaze falls to me like he couldn't be more pleased. "Oh, this is rich."

The crowd laughs nervously as Michael begins to circle.

"Do you see what he's become?"

I sit back on my knees, casting my arms out in a crazed pantomime of Christ as I allow Michael to have this one pathetic victory.

I'm losing blood fast, and while my wounds are healing, angelic weaponry does more damage than any human-forged blade. It may not be enough to kill me, but he's weakened me.

And I cannot fight, cannot defend myself without starting a war the likes of which I am unprepared for.

Yet, anyway.

"Look at what his pride has wrought," Michael calls to the crowd. "Once the shining star of Heaven, and now?" He glares down at me. "Bleeding in the dirt on his knees. And for the love of a human, no less."

My siblings laugh.

My skin tightens, my Adam's apple bobbing.

But I pay them no mind, don't dare to respond as I allow my thoughts to drift to another place. To the hunger in Charlotte's eyes when she first kissed me. To the unshed emotion, the longing in her gaze when I first cast my light over the city. The look of betrayal she gave me the other night when I chose to let her believe the worst of me.

Nothing they do to me could ever compare.

The worst has already been done.

Already I have been brought low, humbled completely.

My jaw clamps tight as I fixate on Michael. "Are you going to tell me what I need to do, or are you going to keep playing childish games?"

"Careful, Lucy. There's only one of us still in Father's good graces here, and it isn't you."

He jabs the Flame of Death at me unexpectedly, the tip of his blade stabbing shallow and fast through my middle, making it difficult to breathe.

I sputter, coughing up a bit of blood as I snarl at him through crimson-coated teeth.

"You were the Morning Star, the greatest of us all. Now look at you. Reduced to a beggar." He tsks. "And now I get the privilege of finishing what Father started when He cast you out." He grins. "Stripping you of your power."

My eyes widen. "What?"

This is more than even *I* bargained for.

I stagger to my feet. "You can't do that, brother. Not when you still need me to open the rest of your precious seals."

"You think I don't know that the other *Originals* are just as capable of opening them? You're not the only one who's three steps ahead, Lucy."

I sway slightly, my muscles tensing as a sudden feeling of cold grips me.

"Hold him."

Raphael and Uriel step forward.

But like fuck would I ever make it that easy.

I should have known better than to underestimate what kind of punishment I'd need to endure in order to open the first seal, what act of penance my Father might expect of me in exchange for His permission to burn the precious world He created.

He's the God of the Old Testament, after all.

Known for His cruelty.

And the divine monster who created me.

He's nearly as vicious as I am.

I unleash my wrath, summoning the whole of my shadows and absorbing all my light into my body as my siblings charge me. All hell breaks loose inside the courtyard seconds before it plunges into darkness, my power blacking out the night sky and the stars overhead, until the world around us is an infinite nothing, a lightless void.

Someone screams.

The courtyard erupts in chaos as I release my hellish fury upon my siblings, but Uriel manages to locate and tackle me, sending us sprawling to the ground. The starlight illuminating the courtyard rushes back, revealing where Jophiel and Barachiel, along with several others, now lie dead, their severed, bleeding heads rolling at Michael's feet.

From where I used my shadows like a blade to gut them.

I make a show of licking their blood from my hands as a manic, fiendish laugh escapes me. I will pull out their entrails and feast on them. Gladly.

But my other siblings, the more experienced among us, the Archangels, have far more practice guarding themselves against me.

And I'm not the only one who came prepared, it seems.

Raphael conjures his Golden Staff out of the ether, wielding it in a mighty arc above his head. A protective force field pulses outward, nearly knocking me off my feet. I stagger, unsteady and bleeding, as Uriel summons the licking flames of his Holy Fire into each of his hands.

The blast comes hot and quick.

I hit the ground hard, rolling to try and avoid it, but some of it catches on the edge of my dress shirt, singeing me. A furious snarl tears from my lips, the sound of an animal, not a man, as the smell of my own burning flesh causes me to falter.

Mulberry silk may be the height of luxury, but it is *not* the best choice when it comes to flammability, apparently.

But Uriel's pathetic char is nothing compared to my hellfire.

"You want to play with fire, Uriel?" I spit blood onto the pavement beside me, steam pouring from my nose. "I'll show you how infernal true fire can be."

My shadows swirl around me as they bend to my will and transform me. My limbs and bones instantly rearrange themselves as I grow ten times my human size and become the very serpent they expect of me. I unhinge my jaw, flashing poisonous fangs, my forked tongue hissing, and a stream of hellfire pours from my open maw. Uriel tries to fight fire with fire but fails as I whip him aside with my tail, sending him flying. A large crack forms where he lands at the center of the courtyard.

The nun screams in terror.

Flames ignite across the garden, forcing my siblings to either take to the skies or risk burning.

I shift into my usual form as I throw back my head and let out a deranged cackle. "Is that all you've got?" I call out, taunting them. "Why don't you—"

But it is at that *exact* moment I realize I have made a foolish error.

And taken my eyes off Michael.

He plunges his sword through my back as I sputter, the blade protruding from my middle, so that when I look down, I recognize the sight of my blood on its tip.

Blood rushes from my face as I sway slightly. "I should've expected such a cheap shot from you, brother," I rasp, "but then again, you learned your dirty tricks from the best, didn't you?"

Michael withdraws his sword, a furious war cry tearing from his lips as I crumple onto the stones before him.

It can't be helped, really.

I feel Azrael beside me in an instant, though I'm not conscious enough to know if he reveals himself to the others.

"Not yet, Lightbringer," he whispers to me. "He still has plans for you yet."

Abruptly, I feel myself hauled up and lifted.

Not by Azrael, but by Raphael.

As he uses his powers to heal me.

I thrash, crying out with the agony of it.

But to me and my siblings, this is nothing more than a bit of celestial horseplay.

I black out and come to seconds later, Michael once again standing over me. "The only thing worse than killing you, Lucy," he says, "is to make you into one of the humans you used to loathe so thoroughly."

The temperature inside my body drops, then rises on a swell of fury until my skin starts to steam, searing where my siblings grip me. A guttural rumbling growl that seems to echo from the depths of Hell bursts from my throat, vibrating with a sinister, demonic resonance. "I will make Heaven tremble when I break you, Michael. Your wings will be nothing but dust in my wrath. I will tear the light from your soul, so that you will know what it means to be nothing."

It takes Raphael's and Uriel's full strength, plus several others, to hold me as I fight and thrash, snarling and biting like a venomous viper unleashed from the pits of Hell, my shadows bolloxed due to the protective shield Raphael cast and Seraph is now reinforcing.

This was Michael's true purpose in threatening Charlotte, in manipulating the Righteous to carry out his means. To use my love for her against me.

I let out another inhuman roar, my Adam's apple writhing as Michael extends our Father's open scroll toward me. "'Those whom I love, I rebuke and discipline. So be earnest and repent.'" Michael grins. "Revelation 3:19. I would think you'd be familiar with it, Sammael, fallen son of Laodicea. For you there is no praise, no mercy."

"I will fuck you every day for the rest of eternity," I snarl, my voice thick with an ancient evil. "For I am legion, and you cannot fight what you cannot see. Take heed, brother. Every whisper in the dark is my voice. Every shadow my hand reaching for you. There will be no escape."

"Do you want your precious bride to live or not?" Michael roars, the tip of his blade nicking into my skin. "Your little rebellion isn't just yours anymore, Lucy. I'll make her feel the weight of your choices. If you will not bow to me, then *she* will."

But I am bound by my angelic word.

By my brother Gabriel's power to seal celestial promises. To my deal with Michael.

And it is for that reason alone that I lower my head in submission to him. Debase myself completely.

"I thought so," Michael sneers. "He preached rebellion," he calls out to the crowd of my siblings that remain. "He preached freedom, but he was wrong. Freedom is an illusion. Father's plan is perfect, and *his* desire"—he points to me—"was to see you bleed."

Michael crouches, using the tip of his sword to lift my face so that a trickle of blood runs from my chin to my now-bare chest. "You believed you were the light of Heaven, but you're nothing but a fool blinded by your own hubris. And now, you'll be *exactly* like the humans you believed so thoroughly beneath you." He stands. "Repeat after me."

I shake my head.

"Fucking say it, Lucifer!"

I spit straight into his smug face, a gelatinous glob of blood.

Slowly, Michael wipes it away, his hands shuddering in fury.

"One more thing." I grit my teeth, smirking. "'And there was war in Heaven. Michael and his angels fought against the dragon, and the dragon and his angels fought back.'" My deep voice reverberates as I start to shake.

Raphael may have healed me but only enough so I'd survive, not enough so I wouldn't suffer. "'But *he* wasn't strong enough, and they lost their place in Heaven.'" I lift my head toward him, allowing every bit of my hatred to bleed from me. "Which of the two of us do you think Father was referring to, Mikey? It never was quite clear to me."

I feel a bit of my hellfire singe through my gaze, what little I'm able to summon as I bleed. "If I'm going down, brother, then I swear on all that is righteous and holy that I will bring you down with me."

"I'd like to see you try." Michael grins, stepping forward as he drags his thumb through some of the blood from my neck, using it to paint an angelic sigil across my chest.

The symbol sears like acid against my skin, and I thrash once more, but it's little use. In my weakened state, fighting to break my siblings' hold is futile.

"Repeat after me," Michael orders.

I snarl.

"I, Lucifer Sammael Apollyon, Lightbringer, Morning Star, Prince of Darkness, fallen son of Laodicea."

I repeat the words, the string of sounds falling from my lips as if someone else were speaking them, but I feel nothing.

Nothing but hatred for what's being done to me.

If there was ever any chance I would forgive my Father for casting me out, for expecting nothing less than divine perfection and blind, unquestioning servitude, *this* would destroy it.

I will *never* forgive Him.

Never again seek His mercy.

And for the rest of my immortal life, I will do whatever it takes to undermine Him.

His little apocalypse be damned.

Agony courses through me, white hot and searing, at the sensation of my powers being slowly severed from me. In exactly the same way my wings were. I'm being torn apart from the inside out, desecrated completely. But my fury, my resistance, is no use as Michael continues to chant in Angelic over me.

A few of my siblings gasp in a mixture of terror and awe as the darkness in the courtyard seems to come alive, Michael's exorcism causing my shadows to swirl and shoot out like a chaotic deathly plague in search of the nearest vessel to contain them.

"Say it, Lucifer. Renounce your power, your worth. Submit to the will of our Father, the Lord Almighty, for you are nothing but the consequence of your own pride."

"No," I rasp, even as I start to tremble from the agony. "No. Not even for her, and she would never ask that of me," I rage through gritted teeth, more deranged, more unhinged and animal than I have ever been, "because it was *she* who taught me that I am so much more than the villain you and Father conspired to make me."

"How touchingly tragic." Michael places a mocking hand over his heart. "Good thing I don't need your permission to see it through."

My brother resumes his chanting, his voice growing louder with every word, and I feel my shadows, my light, my hellfire, my untethered power rising into the night sky like a furious tidal wave, the edges of the building crumbling to dust from where it brushes the top of the museum.

I cry out, searing, unrelenting agony tearing through me, shredding my very existence in two as my Father's proclamation, His command, spoken at my brother's behest, reaches an apex.

My power zeroes in, searching for the nearest available victim.

The innocent nun who has now cried herself hoarse at my brother's feet.

She wasn't part of the plan, unfortunately.

With Michael's final word, it crashes down like a tsunami toward her, the gnarled tendrils of fire and light and shadow converging at the last second to plunge down her throat. An abundance of radiant light bursts from her, and an inhuman sound tears from me, just as the nun releases an echoing, earsplitting scream. The pain of a thousand knives slashes through me, severing whatever twisted tatters are left of my wretched, blackened soul.

The agony is so intense it causes me to black out momentarily, my earthly power stripped from me. When I come to only seconds later, the nun's spine is still arched forward with the force of what hit her, her body levitating off the ground as a beam of my uncontrolled light billows toward Heaven.

She was the sacrificial lamb in all this.

Nothing more than the vessel meant to contain me.

A corresponding crack of lightning splits open the sky as the earth beneath us begins to shake. A thundering rumble echoes through the heavens, louder than trumpets, the sign of the first seal dissolving.

The sound of the White Rider unleashed.

Pestilence will now lay siege upon humanity.

And I'm powerless to fight against it.

Fucking inconvenient, that.

Abruptly, the nun falls limp onto the garden's bricks as I slump forward, blood pouring from her singed eye sockets, from where my holy light scorched her from the inside out. My siblings release me, casting my feeble and limp body onto the pavement.

I am as raw as the day our Father stripped my wings from me.

"Would you look at that." Michael smiles like the fox who just found the door to the henhouse wide open. "How does it feel to be truly defenseless, Lucy?"

My siblings laugh.

I grip my bleeding middle, barely capable of staggering to my feet. My breath and my pulse echo like a loud rush against the ringing in my ears as I rasp, "There are no lengths to which I wouldn't go to protect what is *mine*." Slowly, I glance about the destroyed garden, my eyes landing upon each and every one of my siblings as I bare my teeth. "Remember that when you soon beg for my mercy."

CHAPTER THIRTY-EIGHT

Charlotte

My alarm goes off at 4 a.m. the following morning, and I groan, immediately hitting the snooze button, prepared to go back to sleep, only for a newly installed digital clock on my bedside table to begin screeching. Someone flicks on the overhead light, the sudden brightness searing my retinas.

What fresh hell is this?

I growl, lifting my head just enough to find Mia standing at the foot of our bed, a tablet in hand.

What. The. Fuck.

I glance to my left only to find Lucifer's side of the bed looking pristine, which means he either didn't come to bed or is already up for the morning and didn't sleep. Again.

And me stepping off the edge of the building, asking for God to catch me, the cold arms that caught me somewhere halfway down, must have been—

All just a dream.

I flop back onto my sheets with a groan, using my bare arm to cover my eyes.

"Chop, chop." Mia claps her hands in tandem. "We've got a tight schedule this morning."

"*We?*"

When Lucifer told me he was going to be taking charge of my schedule yesterday, there was no mention of Mia and her freaking little tablet, not that there was much that could have made the moment worse, honestly. I remove my arm from my eyes, only to find she's now standing over me.

How is it I'm only *now* realizing exactly how good at torture my future husband can be? I throw back the sheets, and Mia's eyes go wide at the sight of my naked body as I tear out of the bed toward the en suite to retrieve my bathrobe. I'm still not exactly comfortable with my own nudity, or with others aside from Lucifer seeing me naked, for that matter, but I *know* for a fact becoming immortal has made me more polished around the edges than I was previously.

And I have every intention of shocking Mia as much as her being here has shocked me.

Along with that too-real dream.

"So, what are you doing here?" I ask.

She swallows, then shakes her head a bit, like the question somehow brings her back to herself. Her eyes return to my face. "Lucifer put me in charge of managing your schedule. Keeping you on track."

"Oh, has he?" I lift a brow, wishing I felt more surprised than I do. *Of course he has.*

He and I are going to have a little chat about that soon. We're going to have a little chat about a *lot* of things.

"I don't need a handler." I turn on my heel and shut the en suite door in Mia's face. Normally, I try to be as polite as possible to the staff, but Mia strikes some kind of annoying chord in me I can't seem to put my finger on.

Plus, the slim possibility that she had some kind of previous relationship with Lucifer still makes me jealous as all get out.

When I emerge from the bathroom nearly an hour later, my hair freshly washed and styled to my satisfaction and my collar on, all thoughts of that awful dream are gone, but Mia's still standing there, waiting for me.

"Apparently, you do," she says.

"Do what?" I brush past her, heading for the closet.

"Need a handler."

I sigh. "What are you talking about?"

"That's what I'm here for, and thanks to you, I'm already failing miserably, considering you're going to be late for training in"—she taps her tablet—"four minutes."

My eyes go wide. "Shit!"

Lucifer made it abundantly clear when he emailed me my new schedule details yesterday—yes, *emailed*, don't even get me started—that if I'm even *one second* late for anything he's outlined for me, he's going to punish me this evening. While normally the idea would hold a bit of appeal, I'm still so annoyed about him making me wait until after I'm trained to tell me everything, I don't want to give him the satisfaction.

Though a small part of me secretly loves what an overprotective bully he's being.

I break into a run down the hall, heading for the stairs that lead to my wardrobe room, and to my surprise, Mia keeps pace with me, shoving a pair of workout leggings, a sports bra, and some underwear into my arms.

"Here," she says.

Clearly, she came prepared.

I lift a brow, shocked that she did something almost . . . nice for me? "Thanks, I guess?"

I stop where I am right in the middle of the hall and change into them—what does it matter now?—leaving my bathrobe abandoned on the floor. One of the maids will take care of it.

"Are your tits real?" she asks.

"Of course they are." I glare at her as I wiggle on my leggings.

As soon as my clothes are on, I'm charging down the stairs, headed toward the first floor in hope of snagging a bite to eat, but Mia blocks me at the third-floor landing. "You don't have time," she shouts. "Get in there!"

The next thing I know I'm being half shoved, half tripped over Mia's foot into the penthouse's private training facility, the recessed lighting automatically flicking on overhead.

I stumble a few steps into the room, barely regaining my footing before I turn to face the empty space. I've only been in the training center a handful of times, but it's basically Lucifer's sanctuary when we're not in the playroom together.

Not that I'm complaining.

His body and the results speak for themselves.

The space is empty, save for a few pieces of gym equipment, some potted plants, and a treadmill that sits not far from one of the penthouse's several balconies. I blink, trying to push away the intrusive thoughts in my mind.

I have a distinct memory of racing past one of those balconies.

My body twisted against the wind in freefall.

But . . . no memory of anything after that.

I shake my head a little. *Weird.*

I don't think I've ever had a more vivid dream.

I ease closer to the balcony window, noticing that it looks like it's . . . snowing? I open the balcony door, stepping outside as I watch the steady downfall, but when I catch one of the flakes on my palm, I realize it isn't snow.

It's ash.

What the—?

A sudden chill rushes through me as the hairs on the back of my neck stand on end.

What could have—?

"You aren't going to jump again, are you?"

I jerk around to face the open training room just in time to see a swirl of gray smoke form into the man who's now standing there.

A man I've never met before, except . . .

"You." The word's out before I even mean to say it, but he doesn't respond.

Instead, he slowly prowls forward, his eyes raking over me.

The man from the club. The In-Between.

The one who's been haunting my dreams.

He's real?

I take a small step back.

"How did you—"

"I reversed time," he explains. "Put you to bed where you belonged."

I gape, glancing between him and where the sky's raining ash. I remember it all now, the memory returning like a rush of wind.

How he plucked my half-frozen body out of freefall.

How he held me in his arms as I fell apart.

Only to deposit me safely back into Lucifer's bed before he placed a hand to my cheek and . . .

The weight of the situation washes over me.

It wasn't a dream. It wasn't a dream after all, which means . . .

Neither was the shock of lightning that split the sky on my way down, or the awful sound that followed. Like the whole world rumbled and shook.

I glimpse at the falling ash.

Which must mean . . .

The first seal is open.

My stomach drops, my adrenaline spiking as I struggle to breathe.

With no real thought for what I'm doing, I pull my phone from the pocket of my leggings. The morning's headlines stare back at me.

> **The Day the Earth Shook: Global Quakes Leave Billions in Peril**

I swipe through the coverage, each headline more terrifying than the last.

Hundreds of buildings. Countless people.

Pestilence will be free to ravage the world now.

A fresh wave of panic shoots through me. But despite the horror I feel, my mind still can't fully comprehend it.

"Lucifer," I breathe, making a move to dart around this new guy.

But he steps into my path, blocking me. "He's fine," he says. "Nothing but a little roughhousing between siblings."

I sputter. "But he—"

I test the connection between us. At a distance it normally feels a bit thready, but now I can hardly feel it at all.

My jaw sets.

He did this. Lucifer and Michael.

But somehow that doesn't stop my feeling of concern for him.

I have to believe he can change course.

That together we can fix this. Do what's right.

"And what about the humans still stuck in the aftermath? Is he—"

"There's nothing you can do for them now. Trust me." My unknown savior's expression turns grim, and despite that I have no reason to believe him, I feel more than understand what he means. "Lucifer said to tell you not to worry," he says, like he can see right through me. "He'll see you tonight."

In the playroom.

Another chill rakes over me. I don't know this man or his power from Adam, other than from my—*ahem*—vivid dreams about him, but he seems to know me. His power wraps around me, but instead of feeling foreign, it feels . . .

Oddly familiar.

"Where have I—"

My words are cut short the moment his dark eyes meet mine. There's something terrifying and uncanny about him, and it's almost too much to take, though I can't place my finger on why that is. Maybe it's the current events.

The stench of humanity's collective terror in the air.

I swallow, taking the whole of my strange savior in.

Where Lucifer is all sharp lines and trim edges, *this* man is rugged to his core. Harsh angles, rough features, broad muscled shoulders, with long hair pulled back into a loose-hanging man-bun, which according to Jax either signals "self-obsessed narcissist" or "grade A douche," but in this case, it's seriously working for him. Coupled with that divine body that looks like it was built for war . . .

My tongue darts out, wetting my lips.

Every inch of this guy is built, lethal . . .

Except for his lips.

His lips are the only thing about him that appear soft.

Like they could destroy you slowly.

I don't think I've ever seen a more perfect pair of lips on a man before.

And then there was that freaky skeletal mask I could have sworn I saw him wearing at the club that made my instincts stand on alert like I was prey. Not to mention the array of black tattoos down his arm are . . .

My ovaries stand at attention.

I tear my gaze away, trying my best not to ogle him and feeling ashamed that I'm even capable of doing so, considering . . .

I glance to where the sky continues to rain ash.

Tattoos are just that. Body art. Nothing more, nothing less. Except for mine. I glance down at the new snake on my wrist. Lucifer has several. A few black angelic runes and sigils that creep over his chest and shoulders, sometimes peeking through his shirt collar when his tie hangs loose, though they're nothing like this.

Nothing that makes him look like he's unfit for polite society.

Though I know *exactly* how much of an animal Lucifer can be.

He's just light-years better at concealing it than this guy.

I glance down at the headlines still glaring on my phone.

"Who are—"

"I ask the questions here." My stranger starts to circle, like a tiger stalking its prey, and I think I see a flash of that skeletal face again.

But it can't be.

I jerk back. "Excuse me?"

"What were you doing on the roof yesterday?" he asks, his deep, graveled voice vibrating through me.

Like he actually expects me to answer.

I gape at him. "I don't think that's any of your business."

"I'd say it is, considering it was me you were flirting with."

"Flirting with?"

Who does this guy think he is?

"Death," he says, reading my expression easily. A flash of that skeletal face shows.

No nose. Hollowed eyes. Shadowed bones. Exposed teeth.

There and gone in a blink.

No, it couldn't be. I shake my head.

"Tell me that's some kind of biker name," I plead.

He's *built* like a biker, or those hot actors who play one on TV, anyway, if you put him in a leather cut.

He doesn't answer as he continues to circle me like he's taking in the full measure of my worth and he's unimpressed by what he sees.

"Looked your fill yet?" I cross my arms, the bit of fear and the remaining adrenaline at the sight of all that ash raining from the sky coursing through me.

He comes to a stop, his cold eyes still watching me. "No."

I blush, looking away quickly. I don't have time for this.

"I need to go make some calls. Use Apollyon's resources to try and help. I need to—"

"I already told you, it's too late for them," he says, like he feels nothing for the billions of people who are now displaced, in danger, or worse, dead. "If you want to help them, your time is best spent here."

I eye him skeptically. I don't know why I choose to believe him, but some base, primal part of me tells me he wouldn't lie to me.

I can't say the same for Lucifer.

"So, you're my new trainer then?" I ask weakly.

"More of a watchdog," he grumbles.

"And what's your *actual* name?"

"Azrael."

"Azrael?" I repeat.

Something in my mind clicks into place.

Azrael. Angel of—

Death.

My spine runs cold.

He really *is* Death.

I stagger a little, the ground beneath me suddenly unsteady. "Are you . . . one of Lucifer's siblings?"

He chuckles like I've just said something amusing. "Not even close." He stalks around me then, watching me the same way I'm watching him.

If looks could kill—and maybe his can?—I'd *definitely* be dead right now, based on how he's glaring at me, but then I remember how unexpectedly gentle he was when he cradled me in his arms, allowed me to fall apart against him before he used his powers to cloud my memory, and I can't help but wonder if . . .

No. No, of course not.

Though he's definitely as beautiful.

I swallow, sinking into the distraction his presence provides from the chaos around me.

Holy smokes.

A thin white scar cuts through his right eyebrow, severing it in two, and I'm almost ballsy enough to ask him how he got it, but then I open and close my mouth a few times, like my brain can't seem to find the right words, until finally . . .

"We already have an Az," I mutter lamely, my thoughts turning to the drunk party-girl antics he witnessed the other night.

My face flames with heat.

I don't like the idea of this guy seeing me that way. And that's twice now he's seen me at my worst.

Three if you count—

"You came to retrieve me, after Mark killed me." It's a statement, not a question.

He's who's been haunting my dreams.

Those cold, deathly arms wrapped around me were his.

And sometimes . . .

My blush deepens.

He huffs like he thinks it's pathetic that I'm just now putting two and two together.

So, Azrael has saved me more than once then.

Or held on to me when Lucifer couldn't, anyway.

I shake my head. "Wait. Hold up. So, if you've been there all those times, have you . . . have you been *stalking* me?" I gape at him.

He watches me for a long beat. "And if I was?"

I open my mouth only to snap it shut again.

I don't have any idea how to answer that.

"Why didn't you let me fall?"

I wish I could take the words back the moment they leave me. The way his eyes darken like he's daring me to ask anything further sends a delicious chill through me. "It wasn't your time."

"But it's theirs?" I ask, furiously gesturing out the window.

I feel my face heat at how weirdly intimate his answer seems. What is *wrong* with me? I haven't felt this out of control, this unable to stop myself since . . .

Since I first met Lucifer.

I blow out a low breath.

Death makes me feel things I shouldn't.

A bit of fear, and also . . .

I swallow.

How fucked up is that?

I tear my gaze away from him then, refusing to look at him for another second.

I'm loyal to Lucifer.

No matter how much of a villain he's been lately.

I may have sold my soul to the Devil, but I am *not* stupid enough to fuck around with Death.

Am I?

"You can call me Death. Or sir, take your pick," Azrael says as he pulls out one of the training mats.

Apparently, he's just as bossy as Lucifer is, but in a less demanding way. Like he doesn't feel the need to show any overt dominance to get me to listen.

He just *expects* me to be a good girl and behave.

"There's only one person I call *sir*." I step onto the mat, lifting my eyes to his in challenge.

"Did this work on him?" He huffs, that skeletal face flashing again. Am I imagining that? I can't be. He quirks his scarred brow at me. "The bratty submissive bit?"

An embarrassed flush fills my cheeks.

I shake my head. "I don't know what you're talking about."

He smirks, his eyes falling to my collar. "I think you do." He watches me, his irises such a piercing, almost white shade of blue it feels like he could see into my soul.

Maybe he can . . .

He is Death after all.

I feel his power like it's sucking up all the air inside the room. Where Lucifer's is more of a devious, fleeting caress—a controlled, licking, lapping, teasing—Azrael's is more . . . all consuming.

Like if I allowed myself to get lost in it, it would suffocate me.

I've never experienced its equal.

But if he's not an angel and not a demon, then . . .

What *is* he?

I'm almost impulsive enough to ask him, but before I can manage to get any of the words out, he says, "Eyes on me," and without warning, my feet are knocked out from under me.

I tense, prepared for my back to slam down onto the mat, but what feels like a large pair of cool invisible hands catches me, holding me suspended about a foot away from the floor.

Azrael stares down at me, shaking his head.

"Hey, celestial paws off, asshole!" I snap.

Azrael quirks a brow. "Suit yourself."

Abruptly, I drop to the thin mat and let out an annoyed groan. It smarts worse than I expected, considering I was only a few inches from the floor. The training room is hard wood over concrete. Azrael doesn't move from where he stands over me.

He definitely has the ego of a fallen angel. Or something *else* maybe.

"You're weak. No surprise there."

"Gee, thanks, asshole."

"It's Death or—"

"Sir," I finish for him. "I remember."

Those cold irises seem to bore into me.

He offers his hand, but I shove it aside, stumbling to my feet as I level a pissed-off glare at him, doubling over to catch my breath.

His eyes narrow in kind.

"Lucifer's little siren," he purrs, shaking his head as he advances.

I put out my hand to stop him from coming any closer, but abruptly, he uses it to yank me upright. I tumble forward so that the heat of his mouth brushes next to my ear.

The moment I level out, my other hand accidentally connects with his chest as I try to steady myself, and all my base instincts come alive.

Predator meet prey.

I gaze up at him.

My body knows this dance thoroughly.

But this is the first time I've ever experienced it with anyone *other* than Lucifer.

And this is Death we're talking about.

I swallow thickly.

"Careful," he grumbles.

"Or what?" I ask, pulling away quickly.

Azrael chuckles like he already has me all figured out, and the way it echoes low and deep in my belly, like there's nowhere to escape him, sends an accompanying shiver racing through me. "Do you have to ask?"

I sigh. "Look, Death, *sir*," I say, aiming for sarcastic and ending up closer to bratty. "I don't know what it is you think you know about me, but I'm here to train. Just like—"

"Daddy told you?" he finishes for me.

I turn crimson, and Azrael smirks like he won the lottery.

"Is that what you call him? Daddy?"

Goddamn him.

My whole body is on fire from head to toe.

Burning with fury.

Azrael chuckles long and low. "Oh, you and I are going to have some fun, Charlotte."

I cross my arms. "Oh yeah, and why's that?"

Azrael draws dangerously close.

So close my gaze falls to his stupid, gorgeous lips.

Death's kiss.

I shiver.

No wonder his mouth is so tempting.

His tongue darts out, his thumb and closed fist positioned just to the side of that smug, lethal grin as he looks at me.

My throat writhes as I swallow.

Why am I such a sucker for dangerous men?

"Let's get one thing clear, little siren," he growls, his deep voice humming through me, making me soft in places it shouldn't. I'm forced to take a step back as slowly his face starts to transition until nothing but that deathly skeleton stares back at me.

Holy fuck.

Fear and adrenaline make my heart race, my nipples hardening.

He's practically on top of me now. Our chests nearly touching.

Those bared teeth widen into a cruel smile like he already knows the effect he has on me, even like this. "The bratty submissive bit may have worked on him, Charlotte, but make no mistake," he says, his voice dropping low just as he sweeps my feet.

Motherfucker!

I snarl.

"It won't work on me."

CHAPTER THIRTY-NINE

Charlotte

By the time Azrael is finished pulverizing me into the mat nearly two hours later, and I've finally learned how to properly breakfall—he can't possibly be serious that I'm somehow *falling* the wrong way, can he?—I'm so furious and exhausted that I want nothing more than to shower and crawl back into bed for the foreseeable future.

And maybe use one of the playroom's vibrators to ease the throbbing ache between my legs. To distract myself from the global news this morning. I groan.

No. I will *not* allow myself to acknowledge how Death and his creepy stalkerish ways have been the star of my recent freakish fantasies.

I am *so* not going there.

I force my thoughts to turn to Lucifer.

It isn't until Mia meets me outside the training room, her shiny goddamn tablet in her hand with the Calendly schedule Lucifer created for me already pulled up, that I realize this torturous morning is only just the beginning. Day one of my punishment.

I scowl. "Where's Lucifer?"

He may have played a key role in causing all this, but it doesn't mean I'm not worried about him. I knew who he was when I chose to stay with him. I knew what I was signing up for.

Even if I never could have fathomed something like this.

I just need to be certain he's okay.

"He's busy." Mia brushes off my question. "You'll see him at seven. Your next appointment is with Greed."

"Greed?"

Mia passes me a scone, and I stare at it, slightly shocked. "Thanks?" I quirk a brow at her.

This is the second time today she's done something kind for me.

Maybe I was wrong about her?

I nibble a few bites, but after the full-body workout Azrael put me through, I'm basically dead on my feet.

Daddy Death takes no prisoners.

I cough, nearly choking on my scone at the unintentional nickname I've given him.

No. No, no, no, Charlotte. Why? I internally berate myself.

Just because loving Lucifer feels difficult right now doesn't mean . . .

I stuff another bit of scone inside my mouth to keep myself from groaning.

But the nickname is kind of perfect, actually.

And what does a bit of harmless fantasy hurt?

Lucifer would likely say the same thing.

And Azrael strikes me as a little too serious for his own damn good.

He's not nearly as playful as the Lucifer I fell in love with, though I haven't seen much of that side of Lucifer the past few weeks.

My thoughts turn to the dark circles I noted under his eyes the other day, the way the weight of the world seemed to hang on his shoulders.

Not that he's bothered to confide any of it in me.

And why would he? that awful doubt inside me whispers.

Especially considering I just spent half the morning ogling another man while simultaneously getting my ass handed to me.

And *not* in the fun kind of way.

Maybe I've been asking too much of him.

Team No Apocalypse is looking pretty grim at the moment.

"Are you sure Lucifer is okay?" I turn back to Mia, too tired to care that I've got a bit of powdered sugar on my lips.

I just can't shake the feeling there's something wrong. Like he's hurt in some way.

Horribly, terribly wrong.

"I told you. He's fine. You'll see him later tonight." She points to a red block on the Calendly schedule that reads "Playroom."

"So, you're like my personal assistant now? Is that what this is?"

She frowns at me. "I'm the house manager, and I'll remain the house manager. This is only a . . . temporary reassignment of my duties."

I snort. "Keep telling yourself that."

Just like my reassignment as Imani's assistant was temporary.

Or mine and Lucifer's initial engagement.

We didn't even get to talk wedding plans before everything went to hell. Literally.

My amusement turns sour as I trudge after Mia.

"And how do you feel about . . . you know?" I gesture around us. "About today's headlines."

She scrunches her nose. "About what? The world falling apart?"

I nod.

I'm curious to hear a regular human's perspective on all this.

"I'm pretty sure the whole world's been collectively holding their breath and waiting for something like this since the moment Lucifer and the other Originals came topside. Scary shit happens. Life churns on. We've all gotten so used to impending doom, we're just sort of numb to it now." Mia shrugs.

"Way to be a nihilist," I mutter.

Though I suppose she has a point.

She leads me down the stairs into the sitting room.

Greed is already there waiting for us, looking as impeccable and indulgent as ever in an elegant side-split shawl dress that matches the Balenciaga clutch she's holding. From the hang of the material and the sheen of the real-gold buttons, it's clearly a custom-made Oscar de la Renta that, on her generously curved figure, makes her look like the new age of haute couture.

"Charlotte." She comes to my side and makes a show of kissing me on both cheeks, without smearing any of her lipstick, before she glances toward Mia, who's not exactly gawking but is fairly close to it. "Why are you still here?"

Mia takes the hint and quickly collects herself. "Oh, a-apologies, Ms. Apollyon. I'm just a huge fan. That's all." She says the word "huge" at the exact moment her eyes land on Mimi's full chest. She blushes and mumbles something about needing to check on my dry cleaning before she disappears to some other part of the penthouse.

I nod in Mia's direction. "Feel free to be as much of a bitch to her as you'd like."

Though I'm not certain I really mean it anymore.

The idea of Mia with Lucifer in any capacity still makes my insides harden with rage, but even as annoying as it was to have her show up in our bedroom this morning, I'm legitimately grateful that she saved me from Lucifer's punishment tonight.

If he's even capable of it, considering the state he might be in.

No. I shake my head. Azrael said it was just celestial roughhousing between siblings.

But what does that even *mean*?

"Do you know if Lucifer's okay?"

Greed casts me a confused look. "Why wouldn't he be?"

Like she's blissfully unaware of how the world's burning.

"I don't know. I just . . ."

Have a bad feeling, I almost say.

I shrug it off. "It's nothing, I guess."

Azrael said he was fine, and so did Mia for that matter.

Mia wouldn't lie to me at least, would she?

Mimi sighs, like my obsession with her older brother disgusts her. "I'm not my brother's keeper, Charlotte."

"I know that."

"In a bitchy mood today, are we?" Mimi smiles knowingly.

We haven't had the chance to be alone much since I last met her at her office down on Bond Street, the headquarters of Zest, her lifestyle company, where she offered me a job with the stipulation that I ditch Lucifer along with Apollyon Incorporated.

It wasn't long after that when I learned she was responsible for killing Paris Starr, with Michael serving as the middleman, her hired muscle apparently.

All in an attempt to undermine Lucifer.

The knowledge that she's as vicious as any of her brothers has shifted my perception of her—just like my gallery visit with Azmodeus did of him—but I'm not sure if it's to a better one, honestly. Is it respect or disgust I feel when I look at her?

Maybe a little of both?

"I'm really tired from training with Azrael, that's all."

"Azrael?" she says, her eyes lighting up like I've just told her the most delicious gossip she's heard in a century. "Oh, that's an interesting choice now, isn't it?"

"What do you mean?"

"Don't worry your pretty little head over it." She pats the crown of my hair like I'm a dog being told to sit.

But I'm not about to let this go.

"Who is he, Mimi?"

Greed simply shrugs. "I suppose you could say he's Lucifer's most loyal guard dog." She smirks at me.

I have a distinct feeling she hasn't begun to tell me the half of it.

"If that's true, then why haven't I—"

"That's enough questions." She claps her hands. "Come along now. We don't have all day."

"All day for what?"

She isn't dressed for the gym or any kind of combat training.

"Haven't I already done enough training?"

"Azrael's job is to train your body"—she smiles like there's something painfully amusing about that—"but it's *my* job to train your mind. Make you a true celestial. Teach you how to embody your feminine divine power." She spreads her arms wide, and for a moment, she looks exactly like the self-love wellness guru all her followers believe her to be. "Come."

She takes my hand, and before I can stop her, the stars inside the ether are swirling around us, making me dizzy so I can't gather my bearings before we land hard. My stomach bottoms out at the sight before me.

Because my father is standing right there, furiously glaring at me.

CHAPTER FORTY

Charlotte

"What is this?" I snap, glancing to my right at Greed.

I've barely even processed what happened last night. Lucifer's lockdown. My unplanned jump. Azrael saving me. Lucifer opening the first seal. And now...

My father standing before me inside our old living room.

But this can't be real.

It *can't* be, because I...

I recognize this scene.

We're in the middle of our old house. The one we lived in *before* my mother's death. Before my father became so focused, so obsessed with the congregation, the church, so caught up in his own grief and zealotry that he...

"What is this, Mimi?" I repeat, panic making my breath shallow and quick.

"Lucifer tells me that your powers come out when you're angry." Greed glances down at her manicured nails and shrugs unhelpfully. "So, get angry, Charlotte."

I blanch, my panic reaching an apex. My heart thumps as my father prowls toward me, but then he steps right through me as if I'm made of mist, not even there, heading toward the little girl I now notice cowering underneath the couch behind me.

My stomach drops.

Me.

The little girl is me.

My father was never a kind man. I'd seen him hurt my mother plenty of times before, but never once had he . . .

I turn and drop to my knees, vomiting the scene I just ate onto the old shag carpet as the younger version of me starts to scream.

"Too much for your first time then?" Greed says, seemingly undisturbed by the little girl's—by *my* pain. "Perhaps something different."

She snaps her fingers.

Suddenly the carpet beneath me is concrete.

Greed stands near the fence beside me. The playground outside my old youth group building. I'd been barely a day older than eleven, not even a full preteen, but unlike most of the girls in our congregation, I'd developed early. Early enough that the older boys from our youth group had thought it would be funny to try and pull down my shirt.

My father had blamed me, of course. No surprise there.

For wearing something so "promiscuous."

Never mind that it hadn't been anything more than a standard V-neck "Jesus Loves Me" tee from the previous year's mission trip. This was the first moment I learned that there were boys, men, who believed they were entitled to my body.

No matter how many times I said no.

"Stop it," I say to Greed, staggering to my feet and refusing to look toward the crowd of boys now surrounding the younger version of me, heckling and grabbing at her until I wince at the all-too-real memory. I inspect Greed's face, and for the first time I know *exactly* how she came to be the woman I know her to be.

A bitch. A bully. The "selfish" greedy monster.

Because she was once a little girl just like me who craved her Father's love so desperately, she'd do *anything* to get it. Hoard any crumb she was given.

And a sister. A little sister whose softness was tortured from her by her more powerful angelic brothers, unempathetic to the sound of her screams, until she was no longer weak.

Until she became hard like them.

Exactly like she's doing to me.

"Mimi, please." I close my eyes and wince at the sound of my younger self's sobbing. "Whatever this is, please stop it."

"You want me to stop, Charlotte?" I open my eyes again, and she tilts her chin as she steps toward me, her heels clicking against the summer pavement. "Now that the apocalypse has begun, do you think any of my brothers or my angelic siblings will stop should they or the Righteous or any of Lucifer's enemies ever get their hands on you? Do you think *they* will stop?"

She shakes her head at me, her shoulders dropping, and in that moment I can tell that she doesn't take any pleasure in the task Lucifer has given her.

Torturing someone the way she's torturing me.

It's nothing personal, but that won't stop her from fulfilling her duty either.

To break me. Toughen me until I become hard like she is.

"I will show mercy today and today only." She snaps her fingers, and we're back in the penthouse's sitting room as if we never even left in the first place.

As if it was all an illusion or a dream.

A nightmare of my own creation.

I feel the cold wind from last night whip past me. Feel the burn of it on my face.

"Our enemies will do more to you than your father or any playground bullies ever could, Charlotte. Don't forget that." She looks me over from head to toe almost regretfully before she turns away. "That's the end of your lesson for today."

CHAPTER FORTY-ONE

Lucifer

The Dead Sea Scrolls and other various family memorabilia, on loan from the Rockefeller Museum along with several more of my many museum contacts, have now taken over the space inside my study. I'm poring over one of the desecrated scrolls in a desperate, fevered search when Azrael enters the room.

"How are you feeling?"

I scowl. "Like Death warmed over."

He frowns at the joke, his eyes tracking to where my hand nurses my rib cage. "I never envisioned you a scholar."

"Clearly, you don't remember any of my early obsessions between the fourth and twelfth centuries." I take a step toward another artifact and wince slightly.

Healing at a mortal pace is bloody inconvenient, it seems.

Azrael nods thoughtfully, looking pensive. "I'm still convinced Arius and Constantine were secretly fucking."

I smirk for the first time since last night. "Their chemistry *was* off the charts, wasn't it?" I set down the sliver of ancient scroll I was holding as I look toward him. "How did she do?"

Azrael grumbles something unintelligible, clearly a bit perturbed that I asked, before saying, "She's weak."

"Of course she is." I nod, turning back to my scrolls. "I'm learning that about humanity the hard way." I shake my head. "Physically, she has a long way to go, yes, but mentally, I'd say that with a bit of training, perhaps someday she could—"

"Don't insult me." Azrael scoffs.

I look toward him then. Any jealousy he might have felt toward Charlotte isn't particularly unexpected, considering our history, but I sense there's more to it than he's telling me. Not that Death is ever particularly forthcoming. The fact that he's grumbled more than his customary two syllables is already a small feat. Though I suppose when you haven't seen someone in a few centuries, there's quite a backlog.

I tilt my head to the side. "Is there something you'd like to share, Azrael?"

He remains quiet, contemplating, his gaze trained on the far side of the room. The perfect soldier at ease. "No."

I draw closer, my right leg dragging a bit. "No, sir, you mean."

Azrael's eyes lock with mine, his jaw tight as we both go still. "I no longer answer to you that way."

We glare at one another.

"No. No, I suppose you don't," I finally relent.

I abandon him as I return to my scrolls and the other loaned artifacts scattered about the room. The Book of Enoch. The Gospel of Judas. Even the Odes of Solomon and sections of the Gospel of Mary. Though I won't pretend it doesn't irk me that I must *borrow* my Father's things.

I will reclaim what Michael has stolen from me.

As soon as I find who last had that ruddy spear.

When Azrael speaks again sometime later, I'm surprised to find him still there, watching me, but voyeurism was always one of his favorite things. "What is it you seek?"

"A family record." I shrug. "Which of my angelic siblings last had control of the crucifixion blade."

Azrael's brows shoot up in an uncharacteristic show of surprise. "The Holy Lance?"

"One and the same."

He's quiet, neither of us saying anything. Then, almost reluctantly, he grumbles, "I . . . might be able to assist."

This time, he has my full attention.

"You're offering to help me?"

This wasn't part of our deal.

Death does favors for no one.

No one except for me.

Azrael glances away, his expression purposefully cold and distant. "Death follows wherever the blade goes."

I smirk appreciatively. "And you would do that? Follow the blade to protect her?"

"Not her." The piercing stare Azrael gives me is deliberate, one of cold fury. "If the blade is in play and you're stripped of your powers, hers isn't the only immortal life at risk."

"You think I don't know that?" I sigh, long and low. "You're more sentimental than humanity ever gave you credit for, Reaper."

"I could say the same, Deceiver," he says, using the old nickname deliberately.

Reaper. Deceiver.

Lightbringer. Endbringer.

We once were both foolish enough to believe we were two sides of the same celestial coin. Though my Mother had other plans, it seems.

Despite that I'm no fan of fate, I can't bring myself to regret those years.

I limp to the far side of my desk, casting the scroll aside and supporting my weight with my arms as I lean against the edge of its surface. "And my siblings?"

"Are you asking me to serve as your shield? For both Charlotte *and* you?"

"When I have my power back, which we both know that I will, I'll make it worth your while."

Azrael's expression darkens.

I lift a single brow. "You'd do it for free?"

"Are you going to tell her?" he asks, instead of answering me. "About what you sacrificed for her?"

My spine goes cold.

I do not relish the idea of alerting Charlotte about my current... predicament, the thought of her seeing me brought low.

"I'm not certain she would believe me," I offer.

Not after all the ways I have lied to her.

To protect her.

It was never about anything more than that.

Azrael gives a curt nod like he understands me.

I cast him a sidelong look, considering him. "One would think you'd be more inclined to my brother's bid for Armageddon, Azrael. You're the final Horseman, after all. The Pale Rider. The Harbinger. Bringer of Ends." I eye him up and down. "Wouldn't the apocalypse suit you?"

Azrael shakes his head. "The others may be eager to spell humanity's end when they awaken, but not me."

I squint slightly, still unable to get a read on Death's finer proclivities. "And why's that exactly?"

Azrael's eyes darken, more infinite and endless than mine will ever be. "Perhaps for the same reason you allow her to believe there is no bit of good in you, Radiant One."

With that, he turns and disappears, leaving me standing there, still wounded and healing amid my family's oldest heirlooms, lost in the past of more than one painful memory.

CHAPTER FORTY-TWO

Charlotte

It's 7 p.m., and I'm on my knees in the playroom, so thoroughly exhausted I can hardly think straight. Lucifer's new schedule for me didn't give me a moment to breathe. Training with Azrael; then whatever the hell that living nightmare was with Greed; followed by a jam-packed workday complete with several live interviews, including a full-fledged photo shoot with *Vogue*; followed by a fragrance consult with Maison Francis and an early work dinner with Imani and Cartier and one of Apollyon's subsidiaries. I'm just one hard blow of the winter winds that're now sweeping through the city from being knocked off my feet.

My muscles have never been this sore, my brain never this fried, and I feel like I can hardly string two words together, let alone think.

I'm pretty sure that's by design, of course.

I haven't once considered pulling another stunt like I did with Azmodeus. Or been able to dwell on the devastation the general population is experiencing. I haven't worried about my powers or my immortality, about being fated, or even the seemingly inevitable apocalypse that's pending. I haven't had a moment to think.

I'll never admit it to Lucifer, but it's been strangely nice getting to turn my brain off, today especially.

Not having to make my own decisions twenty-four seven.

These days I'm so used to girlbossing my way through everything that having someone *else* consider all the ways I need to take care of myself and then make all the plans for me feels indulgent, if I'm honest.

Even if I am barely able to keep myself upright.

When Lucifer enters the playroom, I know for a fact I'm in for more of this torture since the sight of me on my knees turns the look on his face from one that's oddly grim to supreme satisfaction.

He's *enjoying* this, the asshat.

Day one of my brat taming. Day one of the apocalypse.

I stiffen.

He must know about my ridiculous freefall experiment by now. He *has* to.

I've spent more than a few moments wondering if somehow my misguided attempt might have tempted God into letting this all happen, but no matter how I spin it, that seems a little self-obsessed, even by Lucifer's standards.

I watch as he approaches me, fully expecting that to be the first thing out of his mouth, but he catches me off guard. "I hear you were supremely well behaved today."

I blink at him, too stunned to speak.

Which means . . .

Azrael didn't tell him about my skydive incident last night.

He kept my secret for me.

I don't know exactly how I feel about that as I hold my head low, not looking toward Lucifer. I try to tell myself it's because I'm too tired or because I haven't been given permission to do so, but a small part of me feels . . . guilty for hiding something so pivotal from him.

I frown at the thought.

No.

No, I will *not* blame myself for treating him the same way he treats me. I won't give in so easily. No matter how stupid an error in judgment.

I don't know what possessed me to take such an over-the-top gamble with my safety. Maybe some naive need to test the boundaries of my own immortality? Challenge God to finally be there for me?

Hell if I know.

But in truth, now that I'm a bit more distanced from it, I feel ashamed of how I risked myself.

Ashamed for not being stronger.

For not being able to handle the impossible implications of my own eternal existence. The apocalypse, our fate, Lucifer's cruelty . . .

All of it.

Not to mention I'm still furious with him for even agreeing to open the freaking seals for Michael in the first place.

I thought things would be so much better if I had more understanding of what he was doing, but now . . .

Now I'm simply worried in a whole new way.

"You can look up now, little dove."

I lift my head, trying to infuse the look I give him with all my confusion for why he's keeping me at arm's length, but then my gaze falls to the way his left leg drags slightly, to how he keeps his elbow tucked too close—like he's trying to cradle a hidden wound in his ribs—and instead the emotion that lies *beneath* my uncertainty bubbles over, and my eyes begin to water unexpectedly.

The anxiety. The hurt. The worry. It's all there.

I blink, trying to push my feelings away, but that only sends several tears cascading down my cheeks. "Are you all right?"

He's hurt. I can feel it.

And our connection is weak, barely hanging on by a thread.

Lucifer goes still. He's standing near the rack a few feet from me, his suit coat hanging from one of the pegs. His tie is stripped off, and the first several buttons on his shirt are loosened, so that, even with his suspenders overtop, I can still see several of his tattoos peeking out from beneath. Somehow, the thought of them, of all those tempting thoughts inside my head as I trained this morning with Azrael, only makes the tears come harder.

"Charlotte," he breathes.

"Last night I saw the sky open. Azrael said you had—"

He curses under his breath. "I'm fine."

"You don't sound fine."

"It doesn't concern you," he says, his tone sharpening.

I flinch, my chin trembling like he's slapped me. "Right. I almost forgot. I'm just your paid whore."

Lucifer tenses, his whole body tight as a bowstring.

He hangs his head as he leans overtop the new bondage table, using his arms to support his weight.

"Give me a color," he says, before we've started the scene. Before I've even changed into my actual play collar.

"Red," I mumble.

My tears come hard and fast, though I stay silent, unmoving.

Lucifer crouches in front of me, tipping my chin up so that I'm forced to look at him. "Where do we go from here, darling?" he whispers.

There's so much more loaded in his words than what he's asking me, but I have no idea where to begin. It feels like there's been so many cosmic fractures between us, we might as well be shouting at each other from opposite sides of the universe. Each of us fighting desperately to be heard.

But we have to start somewhere, to try to heal this, heal us.

No matter how angry I am with him, how much I may hate what he's done, I still love him.

I will always love him.

That's why I jumped off that ledge, I think.

With the ridiculous hope that somehow, he'd be there to catch me.

In all the ways he's failed to catch me before.

Choose me over what he believes is his destiny.

My immortal body isn't the only thing that needs his protection.

And my heart is the one thing he can't keep under lock and key.

Due to all the ways he continues to try and guard himself from me.

The silent admission sends a fresh round of grief rolling through me, a sense of powerlessness that's so similar to freefall, it makes my ribs ache.

Regardless of what he does, I think that'll always be true, unfortunately.

That I love him.

I'm not sure there's anything he could ever do that would make me push him away.

To make me abandon him like both our fathers did to us.

I shrug weakly, uncertain where to begin. "Mia," I mumble, sniffling from where I'm now close to ugly crying.

God, why is *that* the first thing that pops out of my mouth?

It's so insignificant, childish really.

Maybe because his reassurance is all you need to rebuild, a small voice inside me says.

All my nerves seem to fire at once.

I need to know that, amid the chaos, he's the one rock that cannot be moved.

My mountain. My North Star. My constant.

Conquer me. Love me. Keep me safe. Even when I try to push you away, I need you to catch me, hold me. No matter how I'm falling apart, I send down the line between us.

But he doesn't seem to hear me.

"Mia?" he asks, lifting a brow like he doesn't have the slightest idea what I'm talking about.

I stammer. "You . . . her . . . she . . ." I can't string the words together, so instead I let out an embarrassing sniffle.

Ugh, why do I have to wear my emotions on my sleeve?

But Lucifer doesn't bat a lash at my ridiculous blubbering.

Instead, he scoops me into his arms—wincing a little in a way that makes me even more worried he's injured and keeping it from me—and carries me to his devil's chair. He unceremoniously flops down in it, settling me onto his lap like he's a king and I'm his consort.

I nuzzle my head into the crook of his neck eagerly as he strokes a hand through my hair like he does during aftercare.

"I'm worried about you. Last night. This morning."

"I'm fine, Charlotte." Though there's something incredibly tense about the way he says it that doesn't ease my worries.

"And you would tell me if you weren't?"

He doesn't answer. "I'm more concerned about you. Talk to me." His words are a whisper, less of an order and more of a plea.

Like he needs our connection almost as much as I do.

He's so much better at this than he could ever realize. When he wants to be.

"Mia said something that sort of implied or made me think that, before I was around, that maybe the two of you used to . . ." My voice trails off.

"You think she and I were together?" he asks, his tone both amused and shocked, like even the idea is one of the most ridiculous things he's ever heard.

"Yes?" I admit, sniffling. "Well, I did until you just responded like that, but it's not like we've ever actually talked about what your life was like before we—"

"Charlotte." Lucifer grips my chin again, silencing my nervous rambling with a single brush of his lips. "There is no one for me other than you. There will never *be* anyone other than you. You're my dove. My light in the dark. My past, my present, my future. I would give up *anything* for you. Do you understand?"

His words feel charged like there's a deeper meaning cloaked just beneath the surface, but I don't bother to ask him what it is. He likely wouldn't tell me anyway.

I nod before I snuggle into his chest, causing him to grimace slightly, like he's somehow in pain, but my relief is so thorough, I feel lighter without the weight of it.

Maybe *this* is all we need. To connect. To hear one another.

To trust each other completely.

He kisses me then, and as his lips meet mine, his tongue parting and exploring me, something unexpected comes alive inside me.

Effervescent. Like stardust.

Like hope.

When Lucifer finally releases me, my lips are swollen pink and my position in his lap has changed so that I'm now straddling him, rocking my hips against his growing erection greedily.

He grips my ass with both hands, guiding me. "Shall we resume our roles, my love?"

"Yes."

I open his fly, and we both let out a shared groan as he lifts me up and I slide down, fully seating myself on his length.

"Tonight, I want you to make me forget."

CHAPTER FORTY-THREE

Charlotte

I wake extra early for Azrael's training session the following morning, before Mia and her tablet can creep up on me. "Brat taming and apocalypse training day two," I mutter, rolling my eyes as I strap on my collar. "Let the fun begin."

When I enter the training room, Azrael is already there waiting for me.

Our eyes lock on one another knowingly.

"You didn't tell him," I whisper.

It comes out faster than I'd planned.

He shrugs. "I didn't see the need."

"Why?"

He quirks a brow at me. "Did you *want* me to tell him?"

I contemplate my answer for a long beat before finally I shake my head. "No."

Already, I feel ashamed, regretful even.

"Then why?" he asks in return.

I know almost instinctually what he means.

"I don't know," I admit. "Why does anybody?" I shrug. "I guess because I'm weak."

Azrael watches me curiously, like he's considering what he says next. "In my experience, it's more often because fate has forced someone to remain strong for too long."

I drop my head, my mouth dry, hesitating. Slowly I step toward him. "Isn't that your job? To teach me how to be strong?"

"No." He stares out the window, closing his eyes and inhaling, before he casts a wistful look at me. "My job is to teach you how to protect yourself so that you no longer have to be."

CHAPTER FORTY-FOUR

Charlotte

The rest of the day flies by. If Azrael's idea of a warm-up—a five-mile run on the treadmill that has me huffing and puffing until I'm beet red in the face—followed by a ridiculous amount of core and strength training wasn't enough to break me (Exactly *how* did he expect me to focus on my form after stripping his shirt off mid-workout?), then my session with Greed definitely would be. For every taunting jab from Azrael, Greed does me one better.

"Get angry, Charlotte."

"I'm trying!" I snap, though she's the only one I can *get* angry with, currently.

No matter what I do, I can't access the furious thing that'd been prowling around inside me until Azrael showed up. It's like my body wasn't the only thing that plummeted toward the city's concrete.

Thus far, all I've managed to do is conjure a bit of pulsing light into my palms. Not even enough for it to escape from inside me or do anything more than give me some stupid glowing ET fingers. It's not like I, or Greed, know what I'm supposed to be capable of anyway.

Greed seems to be taking the approach that whatever my powers happen to be, they'll reveal themselves if I just *try* hard enough.

Or if she bullies me to the point of fury.

At the end of the day when I collapse onto mine and Lucifer's bed, feeling the other side once again empty, I don't have the time or the energy left to scream.

But I swear I still feel Azrael's presence there, watching me.

Even when I can't see him.

Before I know it, two weeks of Lucifer's hellish schedule have passed, then three. Until I've fallen into a strange kind of rhythm.

Azrael. Greed. Work. Playroom. Repeat.

Until I'm certain I could do it all in my sleep.

Except for the playroom part, anyway.

Lucifer can clearly sense the distance between him and me, and he appears to have decided that he can somehow find a way to punish it out of me.

I've been pumped full of him so many times, I'm starting to get worried I'll be pregnant before year's end.

Not that I'm complaining.

Our sex life has never been better.

Each time he thrusts into me, it's like he's trying to prove something. A clash of wills.

Endless nights. A mix of devilish love and hate-fucking until we're both raw in a way that reminds me of the first few weeks we were together.

But he can't exorcise this particular demon from me.

This time, I somehow know it's *my* responsibility.

That evening, when he's finished with me in the playroom, he's once again kept his promise to fill me up. He has every night he's been home.

No matter how certain I feel that someday I want children with him, right now I'm not positive I could handle it mentally, so I'm still taking my birth control. And praying.

I've yet to rediscover the hope I felt in the playroom with him the first night of my training, my renewed spark, even though our tax bracket has kept me largely insulated from the chaos happening all around the world.

Team No Apocalypse is low-key struggling.

"I have a surprise for you, little dove," Lucifer says as he deposits me on our bed for the evening, cleaned and cared for but still dripping, I'm so full of him. His cum leaks down my leg, and he uses two fingers to swipe at it and shove it back up into me.

I lift a brow, turning toward him tentatively.

"Get dressed, and the security team will take you down to the car."

I nod and do as I'm told.

I haven't been giving him the slightest hint of resistance lately. I've been such a good girl, he honestly seems a little put off by it. Apparently, my good behavior doesn't thrill him as much as he thought it would. Like maybe he *enjoyed* what a brat I was being.

Though these days, I don't have the energy.

When the security team finally leads me to the car, I'm surprised to find that Lucifer isn't there waiting for me. Instead, without explanation, Dagon drives me to a restaurant in Tribeca I've never been to before, Belly of the Beast.

When I step inside, I can't help but feel confused about why I'm in the middle of a high-end sushi place with Lucifer nowhere in sight. He's not exactly the biggest fan of sushi. He says it "tastes like the salt and brine in the air" when God first created the seas.

I think it tastes delicious. Even if it doesn't smell great currently.

But my confusion subsides when, in Lucifer's place, I find Jax there, waiting for me.

"Jax," I breathe, rushing toward her and practically throwing myself into her arms.

I haven't seen her in weeks. With my and Lucifer's private engagement soiree planned for us this weekend—a masquerade play party at the penthouse, because *of course* any get-together Azmodeus throws would involve some element of a public orgy—plus the philanthropy work I've been doing to try and help people through all this, and the upcoming CFDA Awards, I wasn't sure I'd get to connect with her before then.

"I've missed you," I whisper, clinging to her like a lifetime has passed since we've last seen each other.

It sort of has for me.

"I've missed you too." She pulls back, smiling awkwardly.

Right.

I'm still in the doghouse for being a completely shitty friend, but even strained conversation with Jax is easy. She has a way of putting anyone around her at ease.

She launches into telling me about how Lucifer had Apollyon's secretary, Jeanine, reach out to her. Apparently, she seems to think he's worried about me, but as she's talking, out of the corner of my eye, I catch sight of an unexpected someone near the kitchen.

I hold up a finger. "Can you hold that thought?"

I'm beelining away from our table before I can think twice about what I'm doing, and then the next thing I know I'm through the kitchen door, Gluttony—or Beelzebub—staring down at me.

"Z." I lift a hand in greeting.

"If you're going to do it, at least do it properly," he growls.

I blink, thinking at first he's talking to me until the entire kitchen staff answers back with a resounding, "Yes, Chef."

Z turns away from me like he's too busy to be bothered by my presence.

"Z? Or, er, Mr. Beelzebub, sir?" I follow him as he heads toward the other side of the kitchen.

Gluttony and I have barely exchanged more than two words with each other. I'm not even sure I've been formerly introduced to him. Once you reach a certain level of celebrity, introductions sort of become, well, redundant. And technically, we're family, I guess.

Or we soon will be.

"Uh, Mr. Beelzebub, sir?" I say again, trying and failing to get his attention.

He's examining a piece of raw tuna like Lucifer examines my pussy when he's got me spread open on one of the bondage tables.

Like he can't wait to put his mouth on what he sees.

"Azmodeus tells me you only call Lucifer *sir*." He lifts a knowing brow at me, his eyes falling to my collar. It appears to be a diamond choker to anyone who doesn't know better.

My cheeks flush until I'm nearly as pink as his tuna. "Z, then?"

He grunts as if he doesn't give a damn what I call him and then moves on to examine the next station. A woman stirring some kind of pale-amber sauce. Gluttony plucks a nearby spoon from out of thin air, or maybe from his chef's apron—how the hell would I know?—and dips it into the sauce before giving it a taste. "Needs more acid."

"Yes, Chef," the whole kitchen calls out in unison.

"Um, Gluttony . . . er, Z, I wondered if you might be willing to . . ." My voice trails off. I'm not even certain what I'd planned to say.

Let me do PR for you. Give you what your brother can't so that you'll maybe help me stop the impending apocalypse that nobody else seems to be noticing.

Initially, the headlines over the past few weeks confused me.

I don't think any other seals have been opened yet, but after scouring every news source I could find, I've felt way too concerned about the uptick of the city's rat population. That, along with the destruction that leveled several buildings in Washington Heights, has been causing even more delays in the subway than usual, and I've also been obsessively worried about the world's rapidly declining population of bees.

Until finally it hit me.

Pestilence.

The first Horseman is Pestilence.

When Lucifer opened the first seal, it must have unleashed him. According to the Bible, that's how it works, and he's the first of the four. One for each of the first four seals.

Apparently, there's even a new virus brewing in Hong Kong.

Though everything else appears to be business as usual.

Humanity is blind, it seems.

Or just so terrified, they're numb to it all.

Except for the Righteous, of course.

They controlled my life for so long that it's not difficult for me to guess what they're up to. I'm pretty sure they're paying attention, too, but they're likely celebrating what they believe will be their inevitable rapture, whereas I'm losing my ever-loving shit that we're nearing the end of the world.

Though from a PR perspective, they've been unusually quiet lately.

Because Lucifer told Michael to keep them under control for you, remember?

No, not for me.

For whatever his strategy is.

I'm not allowing myself to fall into that trap anymore.

Gluttony turns to me abruptly, a spoonful of some kind of Asian soup in his hand. "Try this," he says before suddenly shoving the spoon into my mouth.

The flavors hit my tongue a moment later, sweet, salty, sour acid, bitterness, and umami in a perfect balance. I groan appreciatively.

This is freaking good.

The side of Z's lips quirk up, like he's taken a sudden interest in me.

Or like he's enjoying the unwilling offering I've just given him.

"Can I have another?"

"Always." He smiles appreciatively, producing another clean spoon and passing it to me. "Good, isn't it?"

I nod in agreement. "More than good."

A small spark flickers in me.

Maybe I *can* do this.

Maybe I let my feelings over Lucifer and all the chaos happening in the world around us cloud my way.

Maybe I *have* got what it takes to get Team No Apocalypse off the ground.

"Z, would you like to host a family brunch at the penthouse this weekend? The morning before Az's play party? Whatever you want to make. No budget is too big or small."

"Brunch?" Z quirks a suspicious brow. "Did my brother put you up to this?"

"Which one?" I ask, batting my lashes innocently.

He gives me a pointed look.

There's only *one* among the seven Originals who's ever been in charge.

Until now.

Things are going to change.

At least if I have anything to say about it.

"Lucifer will likely be in, well, you know." I nod toward the floor, expecting Z to understand. I've noticed there's a rhythm to the days and times Lucifer "pops downstairs," as he calls it. It's like a second work schedule, really.

Some days I'm not certain how he manages it all.

Though now that I'm thinking about it, I haven't caught him smelling like brimstone in a few weeks.

"And does he know?" Z asks, his eyes narrowing like he already senses I'm up to something.

I shrug. "Not unless you want him to."

Z smirks wickedly. "Tell Farouq to have the kitchen ready for me."

I grin victoriously. It doesn't surprise me in the least that he knows our personal chef by name.

CHAPTER FORTY-FIVE

Charlotte

When I return to our table a few minutes later, I'm panicked to see Jax gathering her purse, prepared to leave.

No.

"Jax!" I call out as she starts to walk away.

She rounds on me, her expression not only hurt, but like she's disappointed in me. "I'm done, Charlotte. I'm done trying to be your friend when all the effort's been one sided ever since you and Lucifer started dating. You never come home anymore. You don't answer any of my texts. You haven't even checked in to see how me, or Evie, is doing. We—"

"Would you just listen to me for a moment? Please?" I take hold of her hand, trying to edge her back toward the table.

She looks at me reluctantly, but finally she gives a tight-lipped nod.

We both collapse back into our seats.

"I know I've been a shitty friend lately."

She scoffs. "That's an understatement. Do you know all the shit the general populous has been going through? The subway keeps shutting down as they move all that rubble in Washington Heights to find more of the victims, and *everyone* I know has been calling in sick at work. Not to mention, you didn't tell me that you and Lucifer are *actually* getting married now. I had to find out from Ian, who overheard Az talking about some engagement-turned-play-party at the penthouse this weekend while he was at work, which I didn't even get an invite to."

I wince. "I know. I know I should have told you, but . . ."

But what?

I've been just as dishonest as Lucifer's been.

And that's when I finally decide to confess everything to her. The truth about the Met Gala. God's redemption. Being immortal and fated. The anthrax. The PR firm. Olivia. God's blade. The impending apocalypse. Lucifer opening the first seal. Pestilence. My stupid jump. Azrael.

Everything.

By the time I'm finished, Jax's mouth is hanging open slightly, and most of the color has drained from her face, the usual brown of her skin turning a pasty shade of tan.

"I'm . . . going to need a stronger drink," she says, signaling the waiter.

Two Long Island ice teas and half a cosmo later, she seems a bit steadier, or just buzzed enough to finally process everything I've been saying.

"This is all . . . That's . . . that's wild, Charlotte."

I nod weakly, stirring my piña colada. "You're telling me."

"No wonder you haven't been texting." She shakes her head, and in the next second our eyes meet, and we both burst out laughing.

We laugh until both of us have tears running down our faces, until we're practically crying over what remains of her sushi and my soup, and then we both start crying for real, and hugging, until I feel fully whole and like myself again for the first time in what feels like forever.

"God, I missed you." I pull her over to my side of the booth, giving her another too-tight squeeze.

Jax rests her head on my shoulder, squeezing right back. "You should've told me sooner."

"I didn't want to scare you, and then after I saw you and Evie at our apartment together, I—"

"Evie could *never* replace you," she whispers to me. "We're ride or die. Remember?"

"Even if that means we're both riding toward the apocalypse?"

"*Especially* when it means we're both riding toward the apocalypse. A bitch has gotta do something with her last days, you know? You only live once." She takes another hearty sip of her drink, then she sets it back onto the table, her eyes going distant and glossy. "So, what are you going to do?"

"I don't know," I admit.

"I think you should go through with it. The PR thing."

Convincing Lucifer's siblings to take my side, she means.

"If anyone can change their minds, motivate them to help, you can."

I snort. "You have *way* too much faith in me."

She shakes her head. "No, Charlotte. I don't. You don't have nearly enough faith in you. You're the woman who managed to get *the devil* wrapped around her little finger. Lucifer would do anything for you. That's its own kind of power, honey."

I nod, considering what she's saying.

Maybe she's right.

Maybe I *have* been going about this whole thing the wrong way.

Trying to use someone else's power instead of recognizing that my own has been sitting right in front of me this whole time. My interaction with Gluttony earlier is proof of that.

"About the last time I was at our apartment," I say, abruptly changing the subject.

She lifts a curious brow, like of all the insane directions she expected this conversation to go, this wasn't it.

"When you, you know, had that vision. What did you see?"

She swallows, her throat writhing. "I wasn't exactly sure what it was I saw at first, but now that you've given me some context." She nods to where my hand sits in my lap, and I extend it across the table toward her, my palm facing up. She uses her finger to trace a particularly deep *X* shape in one of the creases there. "This is the Mark of Lilith. A lot of women have them. It's pretty normal, but when your hand brushed against mine the other day, I . . . I saw her."

"Lilith?"

She nods. "She's angry, furious even, that God locked her babies away for so long. That He . . . took some of her power away."

All the breath rushes out of me. "And?"

"And she wants vengeance. Against God, I think."

"But I thought she—"

"Charlotte." Jax levels me a serious look. "I don't think Lilith is God's wife like you think she is."

I lift a brow.

Jax swallows. "I . . . think she's His *ex*."

My stomach bottoms out, sudden realization flooding through me. "I have to go. I'm sorry, but I have to go. I have to tell Lucifer that he—"

"Charlotte." She catches my hand and uses it to hold me in place. "There's something else I need to tell you too."

I pause, her grip on my wrist going slack. "Okay?"

"The day we first met in Times Square, when I gave you your first reading, do you remember that?"

I nod. "Of course I do."

She looks down toward the table, like whatever it is, she's ashamed to tell me. "There was a . . . fourth card that I didn't want to show you. One that came after the Devil inside your spread. I held it back at the time because I didn't want to scare you, and you already seemed like you were coming out of your own skin, considering all you'd been through, but I . . ."

"Jax, what are you trying to tell me?" My heart races.

She lets out a slow breath. "I'm trying to tell you that the other card that came after Lucifer's, it . . ." She grips my hand tightly. "It was Death."

CHAPTER FORTY-SIX

Lucifer

"You've been overdoing it."

I let out a sharp hiss as Azrael probes my side, the cool feeling of his touch like ice over the heat of my skin.

"I am not *over*doing anything," I grouse as Azrael works to remove one of my many stitches. "I'm simply *reminding* myself of how fragile humans can be."

He grumbles something incomprehensible before Kalimor enters. "It's been three days, my lord."

"Good. Let's get this over with." I'm sprawled across an armchair within the Library of Lost Souls, the ancient archives inside my hellish palace.

I've been popping downstairs, with a bit of Azrael's assistance, more than usual in hope of healing more quickly, and I do not relish the feeling of powerlessness I now experience whenever I'm topside.

Bookshelves tower over me, their dark wood stretching up and into the endless ceiling. In the rafters, some of the more restricted shelves seem to float, their iron bars suspended by an unseen force. The air is thick with the scent of old parchment mixed with a faint trace of blood, and the books themselves are alive, their leather covers calling out for an audience with me. They seep a faint, bleak glow as they whisper the damned's secrets.

The betrayal of a friend. A lover's sin.

The downfall of humanity.

Azrael removes one of the torn stitches from my side, causing me to curse as I stare up at the ceiling. Some of the more interesting specimens are locked away behind iron gates, their knowledge too dangerous, too vast, even for me. Those who venture here unaware of how to navigate its halls might find themselves lost in an endless maze, hearing the fevered, whispered echoes of the records of my most tortured souls from every shelf.

Tempting all those who dare to listen.

My library is the embodiment of my divine authority here. My twisted beauty. The eternal torment of those bound by my domain.

I look down, and the young nun stares back at me.

"Where . . . where am I?"

I sigh, my mounting frustration getting the better of me. "One would think that much would be obvious."

Azrael casts me a flat, agitated look.

He always had far more patience for this sort of thing than me.

"You're in Hell," he says. As if she couldn't have gathered as much from the sight of me.

The nun approaches us both slowly, like she's uncertain whether to be afraid. "You . . . kept your promise?"

I lift a brow.

"That there would be a special place for me."

"Caught that little play on words in the middle of my verbal sparring session with my siblings, did you?" I tilt my head, watching her curiously. "Does that surprise you?"

She doesn't answer. She glances down at her hands. "I . . . don't deserve to be here."

Azrael and I exchange a solemn glance.

"No," we both say.

Her eyes grow wide, like she's seemingly shocked we all agree on something, but she's too terrified to do anything but whisper. "Are you . . . are you going to send me home then? Where I belong?" Her gaze flits helplessly toward the ceiling.

I wave Azrael off, coming to sit fully upright in my chair. "Tell me, Ms.—"

"Santiago. Maria Santiago."

"Ms. Santiago," I say, using her God-given name as I smirk wickedly. "Tell me, are you familiar with the story of Lazarus?"

CHAPTER FORTY-SEVEN

Charlotte

I don't know what to make of Jax's reading—or her prophetic vision, I guess?—as I ask Dagon to speed back toward the penthouse, toward Lucifer.

I still love him, after all, and I barely know Azrael.

But I won't deny there's some kind of weird attraction between him and me.

An understanding that seems to run bone deep.

I find Lucifer alone in his home office, having recently returned from Hell, if the smell of brimstone on him is any indication, and poring over what appears to be—

"Are those—?"

"The Dead Sea Scrolls? Yes." He doesn't glance up from where he's reading.

"And why are you—?"

He clears his throat. "I'm *trying* to locate something."

"Locate something?"

He rubs his temple like he's quickly growing impatient with me. But I don't have time to be annoyed at how dismissive he's being.

"About your Mother," I say.

That gets his attention.

"She wants vengeance against God for locking you and your siblings away."

Lucifer sits back in his chair, steepling his fingers as he looks at me. "I'm aware."

"And you also said she's the one who told you that God's growing tired of humanity, correct?"

He inhales a deep breath, holding it. "I'm not certain I understand where you're heading with this."

"What if she lied?" I say, going all in on my play. *Let the chips fall where they may, I guess.* Who wants to accuse their Goddess of a future Mother-in-Law, God's furious ex-wife, of lying? "What if she lied to both you *and* Michael?"

Lucifer's brow pinches. "And why, pray tell, would she do that?"

"I don't know."

"And do you have any evidence of this?"

"No, nothing, but . . ."

Lucifer's eyes narrow before he stands, gathering his papers. "Now, you're talking nonsense, Charlotte. I don't have time to listen to any half-baked theories. They—"

"They're not half baked." I press my palms flat on top of his desk to support my weight. I tell him about Jax's vision then. About the dreams I had about his Mother even *before* he ever met me. "She's been manipulating us all from the start. Don't you see?"

Lucifer waves my accusation off, heading to the cabinet to pour himself a glass of whisky. "Even if that were true, little dove, even if you had any proof, what would it change? What purpose would it serve? Michael is hell-bent upon starting the apocalypse whether you, I, my Mother, or the whole blasted universe like it or not."

My mind reels, my eyes darting back and forth as I struggle to connect all the dots. "What if she's planning something worse?"

Lucifer leans against the edge of his desk beside me, raising his brows.

I glance toward the floor, my hands drifting up to my neck to touch my mother's crucifix. "I would have done *anything* to get back at Mark for what he did to me. *Anything.*" I lift my gaze toward him.

Lucifer nods once, like he understands, before he takes a sip of his whisky and sets it down on the desk. He stares past me for a moment, as if deep in thought. "That may be true. But to what end? To what point? For what purpose would she—?"

"To punish Him. To punish Him for what He took from her."

Lucifer goes still, our eyes locking. "You mean for the love she freely gifted Him?"

Neither of us is talking about his parents anymore.

I shake my head, placing my hand over his. "It's not freely given if He wasn't honest with her. If her love was wrapped up in His manipulation."

Lucifer swallows visibly, pushing off the desk. "Be that as it may, Charlotte, this is all conjecture, speculation. Unless you have—"

He staggers, clutching at his side.

"Lucifer?"

His face pales.

"Lucifer?"

I step toward him, but then he collapses onto the floor.

"Lucifer!" I run to his side, my hands flitting over where he now lies on his back, his eyelids flickering like he's struggling to remain conscious.

I don't know how or why I choose what to do next, but suddenly, I'm gripping his shoulders, shaking him as I shout, loud enough the whole penthouse has to hear me, "Azrael!"

Azrael appears from a cloud of smoke that swirls at my side, his eyes falling to Lucifer as he swears loudly. "I *told* him he was overdoing it," he growls.

Without saying anything further, he lifts Lucifer up underneath his arms, hauling him into a nearby chair.

I run to the door, meeting a frenzied, concerned-looking Ramesh there. "Call a doctor. *Now*."

Ramesh nods and rushes off.

I turn to find Azrael holding the half-drunk glass of whisky Lucifer abandoned on his desk. He splashes it into Lucifer's face, but Lucifer doesn't stir until Azrael hauls back and slaps him.

I sputter.

"Fucking hell, Reaper," Lucifer growls, finally rousing as he paws at his cheek. "Next time use something *bottom* shelf." He groans before he lurches to the side and spits out a glob of blood onto the office floor, from where he must have bitten his cheek.

Azrael ignores him. Abruptly, he grips Lucifer by his hair. Lucifer grumbles, attempting to swat him off as Azrael roughly pulls his head back, shining a penlight he snags from his back pocket into Lucifer's eyes.

Meanwhile, all I seem capable of doing is standing there, my throat constricted with worry as I watch the Angel of Death manhandle my future husband.

Now *might* be the time to say something.

"What the hell is going on?" I cross the room to Lucifer's side, shouldering Azrael out of the way with a chastising frown as I perch on the edge of the armchair so I can get a good view of Lucifer.

His face is pale, the dark circles under his eyes I've been so concerned about even darker than usual. Some of the color's returning to his cheeks, though his eyes are still hazy, and a clear sheen of sweat coats his skin.

I place my hand to his forehead, my eyes widening in shock as I realize . . .

Holy hell. He's burning up.

"What's happening?" I ask, glancing toward Azrael. "Why's he like this?"

Azrael looks toward me, a hint of confusion and then pity in his eyes, before he turns toward Lucifer. "You didn't tell her?" he growls.

"Didn't tell me what?" My eyes dart between them.

Azrael gives Lucifer a furious glare, like if he doesn't start talking fast, Azrael will give him a *real* reason to pass out.

And to my shock, Lucifer actually listens.

"I lost my power," he whispers softly, his eyes narrowing into thin slits as he casts daggers toward Azrael with them.

"You *what*?" My gaze flits over him, my hands moving in tandem in search of what injury could have caused this.

Lucifer mumbles something unintelligible in Azrael's direction as he pops open one of the buttons of his dress shirt before unceremoniously ripping it open the rest of the way. He lifts the undershirt he's been wearing lately to reveal—

I gasp, my hands flying to my mouth.

His torso is covered in stitches. Dozens and dozens of them. Someone used a blade to run him clean through. The skin around the stitches is red and inflamed, like it might be infected, and over his heart there's a new puckered scar from where Michael must have—

I gulp.

Where Michael branded him with his angelic sigil. Azrael's been giving me lessons in more than just celestial battle training. He's seen nine apocalypses now—yes, *nine*—and my coffee dates to go over the play-party details with Azmodeus have been, well, enlightening.

"He needs a doctor," I say to Azrael. "A *human* doctor. Now. This is infected."

"I've never needed a bloody doctor in—"

I shoot Lucifer a furious look, and he falls silent. Uncharacteristically prudent.

"I'm on it," Azrael says, before he disappears.

No wonder Lucifer nearly passed out. If he no longer has his powers, that likely means he doesn't heal the same way he usually does, and if he doesn't heal like usual, does that mean he's . . .

"Mortal," he finishes my thought. "Yes, though only when I'm topside."

My fingers shake as I trace over the raised lines of Michael's sigil. "Why? Why didn't you tell me?" Tears gather in my eyes as I think of all the agony he must have been in.

Without me.

And for what?

Because I was angry? Because I didn't like the choices he was making?

Or was it because he'd kept me at arm's length? Made me feel like he couldn't trust me?

All that seems so childish now.

"To open the first seal, I had to give up my earthly powers, Charlotte," he says softly. "That was the penance my Father expected me to pay."

"Your Father?" I breathe, my eyes sweeping over the extent of his wounds. "He did this to you?" If his injuries are this bad now, how bad were they when he . . .

"My brother actually," Lucifer answers. "At my Father's behest."

So still on God's orders.

My jaw tightens.

What parent, God or not, would ever do something like this to their child?

Suddenly, Lilith's anger feels justified.

Azrael reappears on the far side of the office, drawing our attention. "The doctor's on his way."

I give a curt nod in thanks before I look away.

The way he's watching Lucifer, the worry on his face. The way he touched him as if Lucifer and his body were incredibly familiar, it's almost like he . . .

"You were there, the night this happened?" I ask, shoving the train of thought aside.

"Unfortunately," Lucifer grumbles, wincing a little as he tries and fails to readjust his position in the chair.

Azrael gives him a reproachful glare. "I haven't seen him look that bad since they severed his wings."

"Severed?" Suddenly, the reality of that seems even more horrifying than it did previously. I glance between them.

There's a long and sordid history there that I can't even begin to comprehend.

Not fully.

"Why? Why would you give up your powers like that?"

Does he truly hate humanity that much?

Lucifer shakes his head, like he knows what I'm thinking, though I can't hear him on the other side of our connection. No wonder it's been so weak. "I thought the trial would be something more trivial. I did it to protect you."

I frown. My fear and worry for him quickly twist into frustration. "Don't you dare pretend that you did it for—"

"I *did* do it for you, Charlotte," Lucifer growls, grabbing me by my collar and hauling me into his lap ruthlessly. Even in a weakened state, he's stronger than I'll ever be. "Everything I am. Everything I've done *ever* since you first walked into my brother's club has been for you, don't you see?" He grips the sides of my face with both hands, pressing his forehead against mine, his eyes desperately searching mine. "I'm utterly and completely lost for you, darling."

My breath hitches.

"It's true." This from Azrael.

I tear my gaze from Lucifer's to where Azrael stands a few paces away, watching us. I don't know why, but I don't like him standing on the other side of the room. Like he's somehow separate from Lucifer and me.

He's ... supposed to be here right beside us.

I push the thought away.

"I've known your Lightbringer since longer than you are capable of perceiving time, little siren, and never *once* has he pleaded for me to not reap a soul the way he pleaded for you."

"I wouldn't exactly say *pleaded*." Lucifer loosens his tie like he's suddenly uncomfortable with this level of vulnerability.

"Would you prefer *begged* then?" Azrael shoots him an agitated look.

Lucifer's eyes narrow, his lip curling slightly, but if how he allowed Azrael to manhandle him is any indication, Azrael doesn't have anything to fear from him.

Especially not in his current state.

"And Michael? The apocalypse?" I ask, steering the conversation back on track.

Lucifer is the one to answer. "I intended to play both sides. Convince some of my angelic siblings to come to the aid of humanity. We're severely outnumbered, you see, and with Michael having the blade." He shakes his head. "I knew opening the first seal would require a sacrifice, a trial, but I . . . underestimated what my Father's punishment might ask of me. We're playing the long game. I fully intend to get my power back, but I needed everyone, you included, to believe I was the villain they expected, so I could—"

"Undermine him," I finish. Which means he didn't tell me for my own protection. For my own good. Because Michael, or anyone else for that matter, could have used me as a tool against him until I was properly trained and able to better defend myself. "You planned to save the whole of humanity, go against everything you've ever stood for, for me?"

"Of course, Charlotte." He cups my cheek. "Flawed as your kind may be, they gave me you." He lays a gentle kiss on my hand, cradling it against his cheek. "And I've never loved anything more."

I throw myself into his arms, only to realize my mistake when he lets out a sharp hiss. "My ribs are still a bit tender, darling," he groans.

"I'm sorry," I whisper, easing back. "I'm sorry I ever doubted you."

My eyes fall to his bare stomach, his stitches. No wonder he's been keeping most of his clothes on every time we play.

"I didn't want to worry you," he says.

Like he's been thinking of me. Considering me every step of the way.

Like I'm his equal.

Like he's finally ready to share all the parts of his life with me.

My resolve softens.

It's time to come clean.

"I could've died the other day."

"You *what?*" Lucifer's rapid blinking is the only sign I've shocked him.

I turn away from him, standing and walking toward the other side of the room. "I could've died, and you didn't know it."

Lucifer sputters. Legitimately sputters.

Before his eyes narrow. "Who do I have to—"

"The night after you used my employment contract against me, to put me on lockdown," I say, cutting him off before he launches headfirst into a full-blown murderous rampage. "I . . . stepped off the top of the building."

His furious snarl is his only response.

I have a feeling I'll be getting punished for that for the rest of my immortal days. "If it weren't for Azrael, I . . ."—I look toward him—"I would've hit the ground."

Lucifer casts a sideways glimpse at Azrael like he might *actually* murder him for not disclosing that all-important detail.

"I was trying to see if you or your Father, I'm not really sure which of you honestly, would catch me. I'm guessing I would have survived it, considering I'm immortal now, but I don't think that—"

"Matters?" he finishes for me. "Of course it matters. You matter. You have always mattered to me."

I shake my head. I don't know exactly why I feel more confident confronting him about everything that's been keeping us apart with Azrael standing right here, but it's like his presence acts as a shield for me.

A layer of celestial protection that I didn't realize I needed to stand on my own two feet until now. My hand flits to my collar.

Like a balance. A scale.

To level the playing field between Lucifer and me.

"Not enough for you to be open with me. Not enough for you to trust that I could handle all this. Would you even have told me you'd lost your powers if I hadn't been here to witness this?" I gesture to his wounds, the sweat coating him.

He'll need a full course of antibiotics and plenty of rest for sure.

Azrael stands with his arms crossed over his chest like he's not going anywhere.

Lucifer rubs the back of his neck. "You can imagine how emasculated I might have felt."

My features soften. "All of them?" I ask, wrapping my arms around myself. "You really lost all of them?"

"All the earthly ones, I'm afraid." He nods slowly, and I blanch.

"And Michael? He still doesn't know what your plan was?"

"No."

"And what's the new plan?"

Lucifer glances toward Azrael uncertainly, who gives a curt nod of encouragement.

"You are, Charlotte," Lucifer says, locking eyes with me.

"I'm sorry?" I can't have possibly heard him right.

Lucifer looks away from me, pinching the bridge of his nose and squeezing his eyes shut. "I meant to give you more time. To shield you from this for as long as I could while Azrael and Greed trained you."

My chest tightens. "What are you trying to say?"

He turns to me. "There is only one immortal capable of navigating between all three realms, between Heaven, Hell, and everywhere In-Between, the only person aside from Christ—"

"And Lazarus," Azrael grumbles.

"Who's ever been brought back from the dead. The only being who has both my Father's power and *mine* in one corporeal body."

I gape at him. "And who . . . ?"

"You, Charlotte," Lucifer says, watching me as if he's trying to gauge my reaction.

His emotions play out on his face. Pride mixed with fear.

A flare of adrenaline fires inside my brain.

Like he's incredibly proud of me, but also . . . tortured by the thought that he might have put my life in danger.

But what choice did he have? To let me die in his arms?

Suddenly, all the ways I blamed him for our shared fate feel incredibly selfish.

Lucifer speaks softly then, as if he fears the full knowledge of all this might shatter me. "I'm afraid when I gifted my Father's redemption to you, I unintentionally made you the only immortal capable of reopening the pearly gates. The only person capable of navigating all three realms. The only one who would ever be capable of searching for my Father, to find Him, to demand He put a stop to all this."

I exhale slowly, my breath shaky. "So, all this punishment, this training, was because you planned to . . ."

"Use you as a celestial weapon?" he asks.

I nod slightly, my stomach twisting at what the answer might be.

Another manipulation. Another choice made for me.

But this time, for the right reasons.

"The only intention I've had since the moment I first sent that press release, Charlotte, was to make you mine. It was never about anything other than that."

My knees buckle, the relief that fills me so complete I feel almost lightheaded from the shock of it. A shaky laugh tears from my lips as I turn away momentarily.

"*Thank you.*" I mouth the words silently, so neither Lucifer nor Azrael can hear. "*Thank you.*" I glance toward the ceiling.

For once, He answered my prayers.

He may be a shitty excuse for a Dad when it comes to Lucifer, but on this one rare occasion, He came through for me. That's all the reassurance I need.

"You should have told me sooner." I hold on to my mother's necklace like it might lend me strength as I turn back toward Lucifer.

"I tried to, but after your Father's funeral . . ." His voice trails off.

I try to see the situation from his perspective, to objectively consider how I reacted.

If I'd been in his shoes, would I have thought I'd be able to handle it? Would I have thought myself capable?

I sigh, already knowing the answer.

No. No, I wouldn't have.

Not when I was so busy resisting my fate rather than embracing it.

Fate may have led me here, forced my hand in some way, but now...

Now, I get to decide what I'm going to do with it.

"So, what happens now?" I glance between them.

Lucifer looks toward me, a knowing grin on his lips. "Your guess is as good as mine."

I stand taller as I turn toward Azrael, my head held high, not as Lucifer's fiancée, but...

As his queen.

For the first time ever.

Azrael seems to inherently know what to do. "Hell's legions, they grow restless, my lady. They're more likely to rebel every day."

I try not to let my shock at that thought show as I lift a brow. "Why?"

"Before you, they were promised that Hell would be brought to Earth," Azrael says.

The perfect soldier reporting for duty.

I cast an annoyed sidelong glance to Lucifer, but he only shrugs and says, "I won't apologize for my past, darling."

I nod. I'd never expect him to. Just like he's never expected that of me.

I knew what I was getting into when we were first locked inside that private room at Azmodeus's club.

I wanted a villain. Not a hero.

But I got a little of both.

"And Michael? Lilith?" I ask.

"Michael knows, or more likely suspects, that you're equally as capable of opening the seals as I am. Once Azrael trains you, if we can convince my brother that you want the apocalypse as much as I do, that you're acting on my orders, then—"

"Then he won't see either of us coming." I try to tamp down the fear that sparks in me. I can't fall apart every time he confides in me. Not if I want him to continue to treat me like an equal moving forward. The equal he's helped make me.

That was his plan all along, it seems.

To lift me up. Push me beyond my current limits until I . . .

Recognized my own power.

Just like he does every time we're alone in the playroom.

"One last thing before the doctor gets here." A feeling of certainty expands inside my chest, making my breathing easier, more confident. "I'm having brunch with your siblings soon. I'll explain why later, but if we're going to do this, we need to be fully honest with one another moving forward, to trust each other completely. I understand why you weren't, but I need to know that you'll always be honest with me, Lucifer." I meet his gaze head-on. "If you love me, if you truly love me, I need you to trust me, to believe in me."

"I trust you, Charlotte. I was just waiting for you to trust in you too."

I smile. "And you still want to be my husband? My king? Even if that requires full transparency?"

He smirks like he can already see where this is heading, wicked strategist and master manipulator that he is. "Of course, little dove."

"Good." I smile as I turn on my new Prada heels, my head held high, and stalk out of the room. "Then start acting like it, husband."

CHAPTER FORTY-EIGHT

Charlotte

I am the reason the devil's feeling nervous today. It's a meme of me someone left on my social media, and after the other night, it's become my new mantra.

I punch into one of Azrael's outstretched hands, the kickboxing glove he's wearing catching the brunt of my hit. "You're still weak," he grumbles. "But you're fired up today."

I'm surprised he's making conversation with me.

Azrael's more of a silent observer.

And I'm sure he's been following me everywhere I go lately. I'm about to tell him as much when the door to the training room opens and—

"May I join you?"

The unexpected voice comes from behind us. Like, somehow, I conjured him out of a dream. I turn to find Lucifer in a loose-fitting T-shirt and . . .

"Are you wearing *sweatpants*?" My jaw drops.

I've never seen him in anything *other* than a suit. Or naked, anyway. But he's been resting and recovering the past few days.

"They're Gucci," he says defensively, "and I have to work out in something." He smirks, but it's tentative, like he's testing the waters after all we shared the other night.

I glance over my shoulder to Azrael. "What do you say, Daddy Death?"

Azrael makes a feral grumbling sound just as Lucifer lets out an unabashed snort, failing to contain his laughter.

"Daddy Death, is it?" He cackles just as Azrael snarls, "The fuck you call me?"

I don't feel even a hint of embarrassment.

"It fits, doesn't it?" I quip to Lucifer as I place an appreciative hand on Azrael's biceps.

Lucifer's expression turns cold at the sight of me touching Death. That seems to knock him back down a peg.

Meanwhile, Azrael continues to glare at us both like he might *actually* be able to murder us with a single look, if he tries hard enough.

"Are you two finished?" he growls.

"No," Lucifer and I answer simultaneously.

When Azmodeus and I were planning the engagement party, we had to go over all the safety and consent waivers, and in the midst of all his usual lewd joking he told me that, in his expert opinion, a Dom is basically just the biggest brat in the room.

My eyes dart between them.

That suddenly makes a lot more sense.

I wonder if they've . . . ?

No. No, there's no way. Is there?

I shut the idea down fast. I already made that mistake with Mia, though if I'm honest, the idea of Azrael and Lucifer together doesn't seem nearly so . . .

Far-fetched.

I lick my lips, the thought inspiring an entirely different sensation than the jealousy I felt toward Mia. Now *that's* something I'd want to see.

Or be a part of, more specifically.

Lucifer's made it clear he's open to us taking on play partners, but at the time, the idea didn't hold much appeal for me. But now?

Now I'm reconsidering.

"So how long have you two—?"

"That's enough questions, Charlotte," Lucifer says, like he knows where I'm heading and he's not about to go down that road.

Azrael nods in agreement.

Oh yeah, there is *definitely* some history beyond what either of them are saying.

I can feel it.

Even with mine and Lucifer's mental connection now stripped, I can read him easily.

He's less guarded with me these days.

I've been trying really hard not to think about that too much, because the idea of Lucifer being something close to mortal, or, at the very least, unable to summon any of his powers while he's here in the city, fills me with so much terror and has so many far-reaching implications that I can't even begin to wrap my mind around it.

I have to trust that he's handling it.

The same way he knows how to handle me.

When Lucifer's power returns, Michael has no idea the punishment that's coming for him with Lucifer's vengeance unleashed.

The gloves will be off in a major way.

"So, what makes you want to join us?" I ask, looking toward Lucifer.

He paws at the back of his neck sheepishly. "It occurred to me that perhaps I may be a little out of practice in celestial war play, considering how Michael and my other siblings gained the upper hand."

I blink. "Did I . . . Did I just hear what I think I heard?" I ask Azrael.

Azrael grunts, crossing his arms over his chest, clearly unamused.

"Did I just hear you, Lucifer Apollyon, my future husband, devil and Prince of Darkness, actually admit you need *help* with something?"

Both my brows shoot up.

I have not been making Lucifer's journey into mortality easy for him. Not by a long shot.

But I have a feeling that will be coming back to me tenfold now that he's recovered enough we'll be back in the playroom soon.

"I think we've already established I'm not currently in my top form. No need to enjoy it so much, darling."

"Who says I'm enjoying it?" I say, trying and failing to suppress my grin.

"You're enjoying it a little too much," Lucifer says.

I cast a sly smirk toward Azrael. "Wouldn't you?"

The way his eyes go momentarily hot before he looks away tells me everything I need to know.

Oh, they have *most definitely* fucked before.

Though surprisingly, it doesn't bother me in the least.

Maybe because I'm feeling more certain of the full extent of Lucifer's love for me now.

He gave up everything for me. His Father's redemption. His power. Humbled himself totally.

I'm not sure how I ever doubted him.

I cast a wistful look at him. He showed me exactly who he was the first time he made love to me, and he's been showing me over and over again in the playroom every time since.

"So, what do you say, Daddy Death? Should we let him practice with us today?"

The scar over Azrael's brow twitches. "If you call me that one more time—"

"You'll what? Punish me?" I taunt as I slink behind Lucifer, like if Azrael isn't careful, he'll come to my defense.

Lucifer smirks. "Don't let him fool you, darling. He clearly loves it."

Azrael blushes. Legitimately blushes. And . . .

Oh God. I think I have a new favorite kink.

Making Azrael blush is my newest obsession.

"Fine," Azrael snarls, tossing down one of the mats like he doesn't have much of a choice in the matter with both of us ganging up on him.

Honestly, I know the feeling.

Azrael starts calling the shots after that. He is the trainer, after all, the three of us falling into a playful sync. We clearly all want to avoid what we know is inevitably coming, to pretend that the world isn't falling apart for a little longer, and I can't help but think that maybe it was always supposed to be like this.

With Death playing referee between Lucifer and me.

CHAPTER FORTY-NINE

Lucifer

"She's going to be a complete hellion now, you know."

I smirk appreciatively. "Why do you think I fell for her?"

I'm back in my office inside Apollyon headquarters, after a few days of rest at Charlotte and Azrael's insistence, catching up on the latest quarterly reports and starting to navigate some of our foreseeable closures now that Pestilence has made his topside appearance.

What my Mother was thinking when she created him in case my Father's little experiment with humanity turned sour, I'll never begin to know.

Plague and contagion were always more my Father's thing.

Azrael appears by the window, forming like smoke out of nothing as he stares down at the city, watching some of the passersby. "She's getting better. Stronger."

"Aren't we both?"

I fall quiet for a beat as I clench and unclench my fist, desperately wishing I could reach for a goddamn cigarette. Apparently, I have to stop smoking whenever I'm bloody topside or subject myself to the risk of lung cancer, according to both Charlotte and the private doctor we now keep on retainer.

One more awful fucking thing about being mortal.

How do *any* of them live like this?

My Father is a cruel, unkind deity.

"Thank you," I mutter into the quiet. "For saving her for me."

Azrael and I haven't been alone with one another since Charlotte revealed her jump to me. She's become more than a little curious about us. Our past history.

Another thing I'll have to disclose to her eventually, I'm afraid.

"I didn't do it for you," Azrael says.

I still haven't been able to get a read on what exactly is in all this for him.

Resuming his place at my side. Training and guarding Charlotte. Serving as my cover so my lack of power isn't yet known to the more sinful among my siblings.

"Well, you have my gratitude at any rate." I stand, buttoning my suit coat. I have a meeting with Imani and the other members of the executive board shortly.

"Did you mean what you said?" Azrael asks once I've nearly reached the door. "When you offered to share her?"

I freeze mid-step.

Don't make her choose, Sammael.

The priest's warning echoes through me.

I expected to share her body, but I didn't expect to share . . .

Her heart.

My spine runs cold, but my voice remains calm, collected. "Has she piqued your interest?"

Azrael doesn't answer, and when I turn back, trying to get a read on what Death's fascination with my future wife may be, he's gone.

Leaving me wondering if I may have made a foolish error in trusting them together so completely.

CHAPTER FIFTY

Charlotte

It's the morning of our family brunch, and my nerves couldn't be any higher. I flit around the table, fiddling with various aspects of the fall-themed centerpiece and straightening the napkins and silverware for what has to be the hundredth time within the past twenty minutes. My whole body feels like it's vibrating with energy, even though there's not much left to do.

Mia stands off to the side of the table, her tablet in hand. It didn't take much to convince her not to report the finer details of our family get-together to Lucifer, because I want to tell him myself when I'm ready.

All I had to promise was that I'd let her sit at the table with us next to Greed.

Now that she's serving as my personal assistant and I'm getting to know her, I'm starting to think the idea of her and Lucifer together wasn't just a projection of my own insecurity but categorically incorrect on several levels.

If her fangirlish obsession with Mimi is any indication, she might have no interest in men, actually.

The idea has warmed me to her considerably.

Which *may* be something I have to work out in therapy.

"Hey, Mia, do you remember when we first met in the foyer a few weeks back?"

Mia snorts. "Yeah, I remember."

I adjust one of the French porcelain plates from our Sèvres dinner set. "Well, when you said that you'd been handling Lucifer's household affairs long before I got here, what did you mean?"

Mia shrugs, glancing down at her tablet like she doesn't want to look at me. "I guess I was just taking a snipe at you, to imply that you and Lucifer weren't going to last long."

"Why's that?"

Mia rolls her eyes. "Because I was pissed you didn't remember me."

"Remember you?"

She sighs, shifting her stance. "We met on the first day you and Lucifer debuted. I was there to organize Xzander and Sophie's teams. I only said a few words to you, and I know you had to have been introduced to at least forty other people that day, but it . . . made me feel small, insignificant, and I . . ."

I rush forward, pulling her into a hug before she can finish.

"I'm sorry. I wish you'd have said something sooner."

I pull back and see she's blushing. "I was embarrassed."

I nod, understanding. "I know what it's like to be one of the staff. How it feels like you're background noise in the face of so much power and celebrity. I'm sorry I made you feel like that. I forgot where I came from for a moment."

Mia smiles softly. "Apology accepted."

"Though to be clear"—I pull back, still holding her shoulders—"you and Lucifer have never . . ."

"Ugh, no." She wrinkles her nose. "I'm into women exclusive—"

Her voice trails off as Greed enters the room, the first among our guests to arrive.

I press my lips together, stifling a grin as I mumble, "Yeah, I thought so," before I turn toward Greed. "Mimi, thanks for coming." I kiss both her cheeks before she can get a word in edgewise. "Have you met my new assistant, Mia? She's a big fan of yours, and I bet she'd *love* to hear about all the rare statues of Sappho you've collected to decorate your office." I give Mia an encouraging push in Greed's direction. Her eyes grow wide, and she flushes.

Lucifer's other siblings start to arrive after that, thanks to the celestial loophole in the penthouse's security that I still haven't spoken to Lucifer about. Not that there's anything either of us could really do about it now. He and Azrael are off on some mission this afternoon related to finding where his Father's blade, the Holy Lance, last resided before Michael managed to get his hands on it, in hopes that it might lead to getting the blade back, which I'm pretty sure Lucifer believes is step one of restoring his power. They won't return home until later tonight for our engagement-turned-play-party.

I was expressly ordered not to leave the penthouse for any reason while they were both out, but Lucifer said nothing about inviting others *in*.

Once the Originals who RSVP'd have arrived and everyone has our brunch's custom cocktail in hand—an apple-cider mimosa made from a blend of Champagne Brut Goût de Diamants and freshly pressed Honeycrisp apples from upstate (Gluttony really took my suggestion of doing something harvest/autumn themed to heart)—we all tuck in.

Bel—a.k.a. Sloth—is the one Original I didn't manage to get in attendance, though when I mention this to Wrath, who sits to my right, he snorts and says, "You honestly expected *him* to come to you? That's too much work for him."

I chuckle like I'm in on the joke, mentally trying to calm my nerves. A huge chunk of the world's monetary wealth is concentrated in this room, which is both a grim and incredibly depressing thought—capitalist hellscapes for the win—and that's not even considering the divine side of the power all the Originals hold.

Honestly, I'm counting myself lucky that I managed to get even this many of them to show up. Wrath and Envy are only here because Azmodeus called this in as part of a "small favor" they owed him, and apparently, he's willing to help me out now that he's my new "gay bestie." Or maybe he just really wants to fuck with Lucifer.

That's also a distinct possibility.

I spend most of brunch listening to Wrath complain at length about some supply chain issues one of his aerospace holdings is facing connected to the new virus in China. I'm pretty definite the virus is a result of Lucifer unleashing Pestilence from whatever—prison? cage? Hell if I know what—he was being held in. Meanwhile, as I'm trying not to spiral from thinking about that, I simultaneously try to nurse Envy's, well, envy, over the fact Wrath keeps dominating the conversation and speaking over both him *and* me.

I still haven't found a way for Lucifer to make amends to me for breaking open the first seal. Even if he was doing it for the right reasons all along, it still resulted in him being stripped of his powers, and more importantly, he *lied* to me about it. Or, at the very least, encouraged me to think the worst of him by omitting lots of details.

It's hard not to be angry about the fact that he fucked the world over so thoroughly and now has none of the power needed to fix it.

Now that he's powerless, it's not like he can continue with his plan to play Michael's game to show his other siblings what a monster Michael is and convince some of his old angelic lieutenants to come to his side of the celestial divide.

That part's going to be up to me now.

And Michael will no doubt find some *other* way to open the seals without him.

God had to have known what He was doing and built some sort of fail-safe, since Lucifer being stripped of his power was His proclamation, after all.

I just haven't figured out exactly what that is yet.

Which is why this brunch has become even more important to me.

If Lucifer can't regain his powers, the whole of Team No Apocalypse may come down to this. To me.

To my pitch to get all Lucifer's siblings on our side.

No pressure or anything.

We're nearing the end of the third course, and I've been absorbed in trying to keep Envy from throttling Wrath while simultaneously popping down to the far end of the table to be a good hostess. Azmodeus brought no less than *three* of his latest fuck buddies, which completely messed with my seating arrangement, making navigating between them all infinitely more difficult.

At the very least, Greed seems mildly amused by Mia in the same way a normal person would be with someone else's child or maybe a yapping puppy they're unable to escape, and Envy looks temporarily appeased. Meanwhile, I thank and praise Gluttony for his culinary skills on one of the few occasions he's popped into the room.

Together like this, they're all so *much*, I haven't been able to concentrate enough to truly enjoy anything.

I send up a silent prayer that Gluttony doesn't notice my less-than-wholehearted offerings. Thanks to my anxiety, my stomach hates me lately.

I'm headed back to my seat, dreading the moment we all know is coming—my pitch—as I overhear Azmodeus say something to one of his partners about an upcoming thing he has at Sloth's Hampton beach house.

Apparently, Bel's throwing a huge after-party following the CFDA Awards, and I make a mental note to do whatever the hell it takes to secure an invite for myself. I don't care if I have to suck Lucifer off every night for a week in order to make it happen, I *will* get that VIP invite.

Honestly, that doesn't sound like a half-bad outcome.

I can imagine having to do a lot worse to secure a spot.

Bel wouldn't want to snub me, after all, would he?

I *am* his future sister-in-law.

And one of the most sought-after celebrities in the city.

I inhale a sharp breath, steeling myself for what I'm about to do, as I lift my glass to make a toast, accidentally shattering it in my shaking hand.

Shit.

"Someone still doesn't know their own divine strength," Az quips, and the whole table laughs as he shoots a reproachful look toward Mimi.

"It's not *my* fault she's practically untrainable."

"I am not untrainable." I frown.

"Once a brat, always a brat." She grins.

"Enough about Charlotte," Levi says. He plays it off as if he's coming to my defense, but we *all* know it's because he's jealous I'm suddenly hogging all the attention.

"It's fine." I pat his hand like I appreciate the effort.

"No, it isn't, I can feel you wanting to throttle Mimi from here." Wrath cracks his neck, relaxing like he's just had his chiropractor adjust him or enjoyed a full-service massage. The off-the-book kind. "Lot of pent-up rage you got there, Charlotte. Care to let it out?"

"That's called sisterly love, right, Mimi?" I cast a fake affectionate grin in her direction but shut this line of conversation down before she can respond to me. "First, I want to thank all of you for being here, but especially Gluttony for all the delicious food he made." A few awkward claps come from the humans at the table—Mia, and Az's fuck buddies.

"Plus, a special thanks to Envy for sitting next to me," I mutter softly, trying and—from the annoyed look on his face—failing to keep him appeased. "I'm sure you're all curious why I invited you here."

Mimi scoffs. "That's the *only* reason any of us came."

I press my lips together into another fake smile.

Sisterly love. Sisterly love, I silently repeat.

"Of course. Thank you, Mimi," I say with only a *hint* of sarcasm just as Mia stands and announces, "Okay, humans, that's our cue. Everybody out."

She ushers out the remaining staff and Azmodeus's fuck buddies, each of whom he takes painfully long to make out with in lieu of a goodbye kiss, even though they're only headed up to the second floor for a few minutes. Assuming this all doesn't blow up in my face and end with several of the most powerful beings in the world brawling with one another on the penthouse floor. You know, like most human Thanksgivings.

As soon as everyone who isn't an immediate member of Lucifer's family exits, Azmodeus clears his throat. "So, are we going to get down to the naughty bits or what?"

The naughty bits?

Oh God. Here we go.

I lift a brow. "What do you mean, Az?"

"You know, the part where you tell us you're planning to fuck Lucifer and ask if we all want in." The other Originals nod in agreement.

"Fuck Lucifer?"

Az shrugs. "In a political sense, of course."

I forgot they still believe he's working with Michael, rather than against him. But maybe if they think . . .

No, I internally chastise myself.

Honesty is the best policy when it comes to family.

Even one this divinely messed up.

"I'm not doing this to fuck Lucifer."

"She already does that every night." This from Envy, who from the covetous way he's looking at me, might be more of a usurper than Az on that front.

"And most mornings," Az adds helpfully.

I shoot him a narrow-eyed look, and he throws up his hands in surrender. "What? I'm sure what the two of you have is supremely *special*, lovey, but I'm getting tired of feeling you getting reamed before I've even rolled out of bed." He takes a generous sip of his coffee, like it might shake whatever celestial hangover he's nursing. "Try to keep it to the evenings, would ya? You know, when the rest of divine civilization is awake."

"The bickering too," Wrath adds. "Could you believe that the other day they—?"

"Enough." I bang my fist down on the table as I stand, silencing them all.

Five devilish expressions turn toward me.

Apparently, they only like me when I'm allowing them to needle me.

I clear my throat, my nerves suddenly making my pulse race. All five of them watching me is infinitely worse than being pinned beneath Lucifer's gaze, or even Azrael's.

Why didn't I account for that?

But then I remember that the woman I was several months ago wouldn't have been able to handle any of this. That's one of the many things falling in love with Lucifer gifted me.

Confidence in myself.

Plus, a hint of a devil-may-care attitude, even in the face of my nervous doubt.

Or maybe I'm not doubtful, and it's because the stakes are considerably higher here.

It's just the potential end of the world that's at stake.

No pressure or anything.

Before I can stop myself, I blurt out, "I called you all here today to try and convince you to join Team No Apocalypse."

"Team No Apocalypse? What the fuck is Team No Apocalypse?" This from Az. "Is that some kind of band name or something?"

"The name is beside the point," I snap, causing Az to turn and scowl at me. Like he did when I told them there would absolutely *not* be any fireplay allowed during our engagement-turned-play-party tonight.

The last thing we need is the penthouse burning to the ground.

Even if at least seven of the guests are used to hellfire.

I let out an annoyed huff, already exasperated. How has Lucifer been dealing with all of them since the beginning of time? It's like herding cats. Or sins, in this case. "Clearly, I can see I was mistaken to assume any of you would ever take me seriously."

Mimi scoffs. "We're here, aren't we?" she says, subtly coming to my aid while simultaneously insulting me.

That is *so* Mimi.

The rest of them murmur in agreement.

I roll my eyes. Sisterly love indeed.

I give her a small nod as I inhale a deep breath, brushing myself off. "You all can't really be okay with the world ending. You can't possibly want that, for Michael to get his way, do you? Who would be feeding power to you if there was no more humanity?" I turn toward Greed. "Mimi, I know you don't want to subsist off what little crumbs your angelic siblings are going to throw you or give up the money you get from all your cultish self-love followers. Az, need I remind you you'd only have other celestials, Lucifer's demons, and whatever other weird creatures happen to be roaming around to fuck with? I know that probably sounds like a lot, but we all know it's not for you, and limiting your sex pool can't possibly be your idea of fun."

"There's also the Nephilim and the few primordials who are out and roaming about, like that fine piece, Death, you've been lusting after, but fair point," he cedes.

I flush and make another mental note to ensure I never allow our two Azs to be alone together in the same room. Not unless I want to die from embarrassment.

And what in God's name is a primordial?

I shake it off. That's a question for another time, another place.

And Az's half-hearted encouragement has bolstered me.

I turn to Wrath next. "Wrath, no more humans? No more war. No more killing or rage, and then you're all one big happy family again. Does *that* sound good to you? And, Envy, well, you'd be jealous of anything we all choose to do anyway, so why not be a part of the team? It's the same outcome for you either way. And, Gluttony," I say, the moment I see he's reentered the room, "I know you don't want to give up watching most of Western civilization regularly overconsume—"

"Enough, Charlotte," Azmodeus groans, rolling his eyes, like he's suddenly their unified spokesperson. "You didn't have to convince us."

I blink. "I . . . didn't?"

"None of us give two flying shits about our Father's apocalypse and certainly not about how Michael wants to have a little hissy fit fight with Lucifer and call it Armageddon until Dad finally decides to come home. Why do you think I offered to pop your celestial cherry?"

"O-kay," I breathe, drawing out both syllables. "What *do* you all want then?"

"For things to stay as they are, of course." Mimi wrinkles her nose as if the whole thing is obvious.

Az sits forward. "As you may have noticed, we kind of have a sweet deal going here now that Dad has let us out of Hell."

"But what about the redemption competition?"

Az shrugs. "Well, who wouldn't want to get back in Dad's good graces? But that doesn't mean we have to blow up the whole fucking planet."

Mimi gives him a pointed look from across the table. "She *would* think that, considering she's with Lucifer. You know how bombastic he is."

"Nearly as bad as Michael," Gluttony grumbles from the corner of the table he's now claimed.

"And you should probably know that humanity's offerings to us are more like divine bonus points. We still have all our powers without you," Az explains, admiring his reflection in one of our silver spoons, "even if my skin wouldn't have quite the same luscious sheen."

I lift both my hands. "Hold up. So let me get this straight. You mean to tell me that you all were just going to sit by and let Michael and Lucifer basically blow up the world, even though there's no benefit in it for you?"

The table goes quiet.

They're all more like Sloth than I realized.

"What's the point in trying to stop them?" Wrath asks. "Better to let them rip each other to shreds."

Of course he'd think that.

"And humanity? The fate of the world?" I ask.

Envy shrugs. "May the chips fall where they may."

"Oooh, that one pissed her off *real* bad." Wrath chuckles like he can feel the temperature rising in my face.

I pause and force myself to take a deep breath, inhaling through my nose. I can't allow my anger, or my powers, to get the better of me right now.

Can't allow myself to get any more out of control.

Or maybe that's the whole point?

Maybe I've been holding myself back too much? Not releasing all my righteous fury.

Maybe I should take a page out of Lilith's book?

"So, if you all don't give a crap about the apocalypse, why are you here then?"

"To see what you have to offer us," Mimi says.

Az rubs his hands together. "Your PR firm, lovey. Your little business proposal."

"Why should we trust handing our PR firms over to you? Why bother to consolidate?" Gluttony bites into a bit of scone he baked this morning. With his take-no-shit attitude, he's starting to become my new favorite.

I nod, a deeper understanding coming over me.

I've been going about this the wrong way. Trying to convince them to see the good in themselves when really what I needed to do was speak their language.

Show them how vicious you can be, Charlotte, Evie's advice comes back to me.

It didn't work out with Mia, but it just might be what I need with this crowd, I think.

I stand and place my hands on the table where I sit at its head, a reminder that I am now their wicked queen.

"Because I'm the only person in this city, in this whole goddamn universe, who has been both human *and* divine. If you think your current human teams are getting enough offerings for you without any true knowledge or understanding of what they're *actually* doing, imagine what *I* could do from where I stand straddling the celestial divide." I stand at my full height, snatching Envy's half-full mimosa glass and throwing back what remains of it before setting it down hard on the table *without* shattering it as I level a furious glare at all of them. "I take payment in celestial favors only."

CHAPTER FIFTY-ONE

Lucifer

"What in our Father's name are you wearing?" Seraph wrinkles her nose in distaste.

"When in Rome."

I'm standing in the junction of the four arms of the cruciform church in St. Peter's Basilica inside Vatican City, Bernini's statue of Longinus looming over our heads. The basilica and its surrounding city-state are so heavily warded with protective spells and other talismanic exorcist sigils that even *I* would never readily show my face here.

Not that anything they'd ever manage could keep me at bay.

Seraph glances down at my cheap "I ♥ Rome" T-shirt, purchased from a tourist stand in one of the human markets around the corner, and frowns. This is how low I've sunk. Coupled with the low black ballcap I'm wearing and the kitschy Italian flag fanny pack I forcibly strapped across Azrael, we could be any other pair of uncomfortably queer tourists.

Or some child's fathers, really.

A little girl darts past, squealing and nearly colliding with Seraph as she runs into her "Papa's" waiting arms.

My posture stiffens.

Despite the sordid fantasies Charlotte and I've been chasing in the playroom, I have mixed feelings about the idea of creation.

I am meant to corrupt. Not create.

No matter how the prospect might tug at the remains of my heartstrings.

Seraph follows my gaze knowingly, her angelic features softening. In her current form, she appears Indigenous, her skin russet and her cheekbones cutting. Her long dark hair falls in a sleek sheet down her back, serving to cover where she's hidden her many wings. Our Father created more than one set for her when she first became the guardian of His throne.

Not that she's ever offered to gift me one of the extra pairs.

"She would make a lovely mother, you know."

Charlotte, she means.

My chest constricts painfully. "Of course she would."

Attentive, kind, loving. She possesses every admirable quality a good mother should.

But I am no one's "daddy" but hers, I'm afraid.

And I likely never will be.

Seraph clears her throat, stepping closer as she whispers to me, "I wasn't certain I believed it when Michael first told me, but now I can see . . ." Her gaze drops to the floor with momentary pity. "You really do love her, don't you?"

My closest angelic sister was always a hopeless romantic.

I place my hands in my pockets, offering her a bitter grin. "Does it surprise you to find that I'm still capable of it?"

She holds steady as she offers me another pained look. "No, not really." She turns away, tilting her chin up at the statue of Longinus. The blind Roman soldier who speared Christ during the crucifixion. Seraph always did see the best in me.

Which is why she's here, I suppose.

I follow her view up to the loggia, one of several architectural structures that support the work of Michelangelo. A spear is clutched in the statue's hand, the Holy Lance, the celestial weapon that, thanks to the blood of my only human brother, will sway any battle in its possessor's favor. According to humanity, the spear is reportedly buried here deep within the Vatican's private vaults, save for the rare occasions and ceremonies where they bring it out to display. Or at several other locations, depending on who you ask.

But the real spear is not here.

Nor in any other human church or museum that allegedly possesses it.

It never was to begin with.

"The others cannot know I'm here," Seraph says, still peering up at Longinus.

The marble statue is over four meters high, towering over both her and me. Azrael has disappeared somewhere within the basilica's shadows, presumably to give Seraph and me some privacy.

"Your secrets have always been safe with me," I reassure her.

Her tone turns urgent. "We don't have much time, not before Michael grows suspicious."

"Is that why you're here? Now that you see how cruel he can be?"

"No." She shakes her head. "I . . . do not believe Father's absence was intended to lead to this." To Michael's little apocalyptic temper tantrum. "And I'm not the only one."

I shove my hands in my pockets, lifting a smug brow. I suspected as much. "And what information do you have for me that might help put a stop to all this bloody apocalypse nonsense?"

"That's truly your goal?" Her eyes widen.

I give a curt nod.

"The lance," she says, nodding toward Longinus's spear. "When I first heard the rumor it had resurfaced, I jumped to the most logical conclusion. I thought for certain Michael had been truthful when he said he had it, but when your wife's actress was killed by the true blade, the *real* blade, and I *knew* with complete certainty that Michael wasn't responsible, because he was with *me* that night and he'd never allow the lance to leave his sight, I knew something was amiss."

"What do you mean, sister?"

"I did some digging, turned over some old stones, and it turns out there are other versions of the blade in play, blessed copies that Father must have had Gabriel forge, but the real one is still out there. I'm certain of it."

My blood runs cold. "What are you saying, Seraph?"

She looks toward me, her expression grave. "I'm saying that the blade Michael has is a fake. He's been lying to us all, which means . . ."

"The real killer is still out there."

CHAPTER FIFTY-TWO

Charlotte

I'm headed back to the penthouse, to mine and Lucifer's engagement party, after my final fitting before the CFDA Awards, which is less than a week away, and the backseat of the Town Car smells like the amber-laced perfume I just sprayed.

I smile at my reflection in my phone's camera, admiring how on point my makeup looks. The girls are front and center tonight, since I've managed to squeeze my boobs into a new, sexy, scaled-up version of my too-tight purity dress.

Lucifer is going to love it.

"Eat shit, Dad," I mutter as I make a quick kiss face and take a selfie.

Tonight, I'm feeling bolder than I ever would have been a few months ago.

I caption the picture with something vague along with a few of my favorite hashtags and hit post before only the seat belt stops me from tumbling out of my seat.

The Town Car comes to a stop abruptly.

"Dagon?" I call out. "Dagon? Why are we stopping?"

From what I can see, there's no traffic jam on the road. I try to lower the window partition and ask, but the button seems to be jammed. I roll my eyes. What else is new? Sighing, I unbuckle my seat belt and move off the bench seat to knock on the glass.

Dagon doesn't respond to me.

What the hell?

My heart starts to race.

I fist my hand and pound the glass harder. It's bulletproof.

Nothing.

I shout, but when that doesn't do any good, I start to seriously panic. Adrenaline shoots through me. My iPhone and none of the car's electronics are working.

What's going on?

I test the handle, and thankfully it opens.

I stumble haphazardly from the car, inhaling deep breaths as I attempt not to hyperventilate at how the entire city suddenly appears frozen around me.

The Town Car is pulled to a stop mid-traffic, and it's not the only one. Passersby on the street stand frozen mid-step, and a woman near the crosswalk, holding her cellphone flat in her palm like she was talking on speaker, is paused midsentence.

What in God's name—?

The whole city is eerily still.

I take a few tentative steps, dropping my hands to my sides how Mammon taught me.

I can't do anything but make my palms glow enough to occasionally cause the curtains inside the penthouse to smoke, let alone blast anything, but right now even *that* feels better than nothing.

Slowly, I step forward, coming to stand in the middle of the intersection in front of the frozen Town Car where Dagon stares blankly out the window.

He's a demon, not a human, which must mean . . .

One of the streetlights at the end of the block goes out suddenly, and my muscles clench as I turn toward it.

Followed by another.

And another.

My stomach drops.

I watch in horror, my pulse racing, until finally the last remaining light snuffs out, and the whole block plunges into darkness.

Except for the eerie ethereal glow of my palms.

The wind blows, mussing my hair, and the nearest streetlight overhead flickers, illuminating where a naked woman steps forth from the shadows, covered only by her long hair. She's as nude as the day she was born.

Or the day *she* birthed everything.

I feel myself pale.

I know who she is instantly.

"Lilith," I breathe.

Lucifer looks just like her.

"Charlotte." She smirks, stepping toward me, her voice like a thousand furies.

My shoulders tense, and I have to lock my knees extra hard to keep from shaking. "Goddess." I lower my head slightly in deference.

It seems like the right thing to do.

She smiles. "Oh stop, it's Mother to you. We're family," she says, as if she can hear my thoughts. It sounds even more horrible coming from her than every time Mimi's said the same thing.

Lilith is darkness embodied.

Chaos in human form.

Somehow, I know that instinctually.

She steps near me, drawing so close I fight hard not to take a step back.

My Mother-in-Law is her own unique brand of terrifying.

And what do you even say in the presence of *the* divine Goddess? Of God's ex?

"I heard your cries," she murmurs to me, before she tucks a stray strand of hair behind my ear. The back of her hand grazes the side of my cheek, and I shiver from head to toe. "How you called out for my Husband." She tsks.

"He never answered," I whisper.

She casts me a pitying look. "He never does." She starts to circle, her fingers gently trailing across my exposed skin. Something about her touch feels vaguely threatening. Like with the tip of a finger, she could make me crumble into stardust.

Another tremor runs through me.

"You're . . . the Goddess of Scorned Women?" I ask.

Jax has been giving me a few lessons in the occult, in the blending of different cultures and religions. How one true figure might end up with many different variations, versions, and names. Circe. Medea. Tiamat.

Nyx. Kali. Hecate.

Lilith has had *many* names.

"But *I* heard you," she says, her voice simultaneously behind me and around me.

I twist, desperately searching to try and find where she went, only to turn back and find three different versions of her in front of me.

I jerk back, my knees locking so I'm unable to move from the terror that grips me. Thanks, Dad. My heartbeat thrashes inside my ears. I couldn't escape her if I tried.

She's everywhere.

The center version's eyes cloud with white, the autumn leaves around us swirling as a sudden gust of wind blows through the block. She lifts her arm like she's reaching for me, but I step back. Like hell am I going to let her get any closer. The wind whips at me in a growing maelstrom, and I'm forced to duck as a plastic bag and other city debris that are now flying around us nearly hit me, only for me to realize that the other two versions of her have surrounded me, blocking me in.

Maiden. Mother. Crone.

They speak to me in unison.

Their echoed voices screeching.

"The Daughter of Chaos approaches, born to deceive; in blood, she rises in the dragon's name. Birthed of the Holy Mother, against the will of the Father, she will strike where none dare tread. For within her she shall wield a power yet unseen by the heavens. For as it was written: 'She who was dead shall bring forth the living to the wrath of the Last Judgment.'"

Suddenly, the two new versions of Lilith are sucked back inside her, her body giving a distinct jerk. The clouds in her eyes disappear, and in the span of my next breath, the singular version of her stares back at me again.

She claps her hands together. "Oh good. It looks like you're going to help me fuck over my Husband, after all." She casts a wicked smile at me before she steps forward, patting my cheek. Her eyes fall to my still-flat middle, and she wrinkles her nose. "Get to work on those grandbabies, would you?"

And with that, she turns and is gone in a blink.

CHAPTER FIFTY-THREE

Charlotte

I'm still a bit shaken when I arrive at the play party, Lilith's prophecy playing in my head on repeat. I'm eager to tell Lucifer about it, though in the middle of our *actual* engagement party isn't the time nor the place. It isn't until Azmodeus meets me in the penthouse foyer, dressed to the nines in a costume that makes him look like the ringmaster of a seductive circus—or tonight's dungeon master—that I leave all thought of my Mother-in-Law behind.

"Welcome to Midnight Menagerie, Charlotte, where pleasure and pain are yours to command." Azmodeus sweeps out his arm, using some of his power or sleight of hand to open the penthouse door, and I draw in a quick breath at the sight before me.

The penthouse has been transformed.

Slowly, I step inside, taking in the dark, kinky decor. The first floor is unrecognizable, like I've stepped through a door into another world, into the most luxurious BDSM dungeon I've ever seen. The walls and floor-to-ceiling windows are draped in black, the purple and blue glow of the neon lights blending into sensuous shades of pink that alter the space to something luscious, to something dark and seductive.

Azmodeus wraps an arm around my shoulders as he explains that all five floors of the penthouse have different themes: power exchange, sensory play, bondage and restraint, fetishes and role play, and, of course, a designated space for aftercare.

A little kinky fun for everybody.

If the complimentary gift baskets are any indication, this floor's dedicated to aftercare, so newly arriving guests are eased into the experience before they decide which of the upper floors they want to explore. The contents of the aftercare baskets, lined on a table against the wall, are thoughtfully curated—gel packs, scented candles, essential oils, aloe vera, massage tools, soft blankets, snacks—anything our guests might want or need after their play.

Beside the interior elevator, a few of the performers and sex workers Azmodeus hired monitor the VIP guest list. They sit at a registration table filled with bowls of multicolored bracelets. There are color coded labels on each one, indicating that the wearer is open to the corresponding kind of play.

I reach for the one that says "impact" before Azmodeus swats my hand away.

"Not so fast, Charlotte. I have a special one for you."

He tips his chin at one of the workers, and they lean behind the table, removing a closed velvet box before passing it to me.

When I open it, a Tiffany diamond bracelet glitters up at me.

"Consider it an early wedding present." Az smiles as I thank him, plucking it out of the box and gently slipping it onto my wrist. "Everyone here knows that *this* means you belong to Lucifer. No one puts their hands on my brother's bride without his permission."

"Except you, of course?" I nod to where he cradles my wrist.

Az smirks, and a sudden burst of lust rushes through me.

Like he's helping me "get ready" in more ways than one.

I clench my thighs together, and his crooked grin widens. "I'm the exception that proves the rule, considering tonight your sins are mine." He releases my hand, circling me, then grips both my shoulders from behind and leans down to whisper into my ear. "My brother's waiting for you, Charlotte. Best run along to Daddy." He smacks my ass, and I yelp, but when I turn and glance back, he's gone.

I frown.

That little disappearing act of his is starting to get annoying.

Slowly, I make my way toward the staircase, allowing the party's atmosphere to wash over me. Dark ambient trip-hop plays in the background, the repetitive beat making the lights and atmosphere feel almost hypnotic, spellbinding.

I pass several couples in various stages of aftercare as I climb the first-floor staircase. There are a few well-known celebrities I've met at some of the galas and philanthropic events Lucifer and I frequently attend, and I think I spot a few of the city's politicians, who are—discreetly—on Apollyon's unofficial payroll, and who would probably prefer *not* to be seen. Hence, the masquerade masks.

Everybody who's anybody in this city is here.

Just as trapped under Lucifer and his siblings' spell as I am.

When I reach the second floor, my sense of direction inside the penthouse leaves me. The floor's been divided into new rooms with several roped-off sections and no indication of where our usual furniture should be. Like I'm lost within a tempting labyrinth.

A labyrinth of pleasure.

Azmodeus is a true artist when it comes to parties.

Play equipment I've never seen before, curated specifically for tonight, has been spread throughout to assist in each floor's theme.

I wander farther inside, and a masked woman to my right moans from where her play partner drips a bit of candle wax across her. I can't be one-hundred-percent certain, but something about the breathy tone of her moan seems . . .

My eyes widen.

Evie.

I flush and turn away quickly.

Watching her feels like a violation, even though she's out in the open and wearing one of Azmodeus's wristbands that says she's interested in voyeurism.

I head the other way. This floor's dedicated to sensory play based on the array of feather ticklers, impact play tools, and blindfolds lying about. Various hired sex workers prowl the corridors, ready to engage in pickup play with any willing guests.

They smile and watch me as I pass, their relaxed, half-lidded gazes making them look hungry for attention, but as soon as they see the diamond bracelet on my wrist, they step aside, allowing me to continue on freely.

Azmodeus was right.

Everyone here *does* know I belong to Lucifer.

And no one will dare touch what belongs to the devil without his permission.

Eventually, I find my way to the third floor, pausing on only a few short occasions to watch some of the masked performers engage in different kinds of bondage play. I stop and admire one of the hired demonstrators, a rigger who's strung up his playmate in such a beautiful shibari that it puts even Lucifer's more detailed ropework to shame.

I haven't laid eyes on my fiancé yet, but I have an idea of where he might be. I make my way through the rest of the third and fourth floors—bondage and restraint, and fetish and role play, respectively—until finally I find what feels like the labyrinth's center.

The fifth and final floor.

Lucifer's playroom.

Power play.

I step into the corridor that leads to his devil's chair, and I know I've guessed correctly, because already I can feel him there. The sense that he's something *other*.

Though how, when he's lost his power, is a question for another day.

The inside of the playroom is as transformed as the rest of the penthouse—I can't help but imagine this is the king of Hell's courtroom.

Brought topside to New York City.

Lucifer sits draped across his throne in the middle of it all, holding court like he's waiting for me. His attention locks on to mine the moment I enter the room, and the rush of power that sweeps over me has nothing to do with his missing divine abilities.

Lucifer's hold over me is primal, visceral.

So fundamental to who we both are, it transcends time and space.

And Michael's wicked games.

Lucifer's hands tighten over the chair's edges, that devilish smirk of his focused on me as I approach him. I'm not sure how he's managed to conceal his loss of power from his siblings tonight, but then my eyes fall to the corner, finding Azrael, who's serving as one of the dungeon monitors on this floor, and the answers fall into place.

Azrael's his shield.

He's using his powers in lieu of Lucifer's.

I feel his divine touch all over me, even in places I shouldn't.

My gaze darts back toward Lucifer. Even without his abilities, how anyone could perceive the vicious ruler of Hell before me as powerless is beyond me.

He's more god than mortal.

He's his Father's power embodied.

The height of His pride as He took stock in all He created.

Nothing Michael could ever do could change that.

I step forward as Lucifer summons me with the crook of two fingers until he stands before me. "I have something for you, little dove."

I lift a brow.

"An early wedding gift."

"First Azmodeus and now you? You're spoiling me."

Lucifer's twisted grin widens. "I think you'll find mine is far more practical." There's a gleam in his eyes that makes my breath hitch. He gestures to one of the performers, who steps forward, and immediately I recognize him as . . .

"Ramesh?" I breathe softly.

He gives a silent nod and passes a medium-size jewelry box toward Lucifer.

I gape at him. "Is . . . is everyone on the entire staff kinky?"

Neither of them answers as Lucifer turns his attention back to me.

His velvet-and-sin voice drops to the low register he reserves for when we're alone, and I feel it between my thighs. "On your knees."

I drop to the floor eagerly, the ivory white of my recreated purity gown circling me. The bodice pushes my breasts out like an offering, making me painfully aware of the weight of them, of how heavy they feel with anticipation. This version of my old dress is designer and a little more gownlike than my previous one, but for the moment, it's fitting.

I lower my head, waiting for my next instruction, but Lucifer's voice is surprisingly gentle as he whispers, "Please look at me, Charlotte."

I lift my gaze to him, and the whole room, the whole world seems to hinge on his next breath as he opens the box.

A new play collar.

One to match the diamond day collar at my throat.

My vision blurs with emotion, my heart nearly as open as when he proposed to me. I'm already his sub. But wearing his collar, being his, is an even deeper level of commitment.

A way to show the world that he owns me.

The room grows quiet and still, the universe stopping as Lucifer drops to one knee in front of me. He removes my day collar, only long enough to replace it with the new one he's given me.

The black leather Dior calfskin is lined with metal eyelets that can be used during our scenes, and smooth white pearls hang suspended from each of the individual circlets.

It's perfect.

Lucifer secures the collar around my throat, and from the fit, I have a suspicion it was designed for me. He gently grips it, using it to guide me to my feet. I rise and then he has me in his arms, smirking wickedly as he dips me so low, the ends of my hair nearly brush the floor. He claims my mouth in a hot and feverish kiss as I moan against him.

The watching crowd lets out a round of wolf whistles and applause as I grip the lapels of his suit coat, eager to strip it off him.

Oh God. I want him inside me *now*.

The way he makes me feel should be illegal, it's so unholy.

A few moments later we resurface from where we've lost ourselves in one another as he uses his fangs to tease and nip me. But I know it's only a hint of the pleasure-pain that's going to follow tonight.

"Go get undressed. I'll be waiting," he purrs.

I laugh as he uses my hand to spin me, twirling me once so that when I settle, I'm facing the entrance of the playroom, and Jax and Mia are there waiting for me.

My devilish bridesmaids.

They both usher me out excitedly like they've been waiting for this moment all night, leading me into a private corridor. The next thing I know, I'm being trussed up like some kind of kinky present, Mia helping take my hair down and darken my makeup as she openly marvels at my tits while Jax helps me apply a pair of glittering pasties.

When I reemerge, I'm practically naked, save for the buckled contraption—er, lingerie?—I'm wearing. Two white star-shaped pasties cover my nipples, and a white-lined garter belt—meant to signal that I'm the future bride—hold up a pair of thigh-high stockings. Other than the cover of the sheer lace thong and brocade ivory corset that cinches the sides of my waist in, I'm basically not wearing anything, but I've never felt so sexy.

So open and exposed.

I look in a nearby mirror, taking it all in.

Fuck you, Dad, I think.

He'd roll over in his grave if he were able to see me. But I won't let the shame he tried to instill in me ruin my night.

The idea of all the masquerade's guests watching me and Lucifer is tempting.

Azmodeus was sure to make the entire guest list present STD test results that were completed within the past twenty-four hours along with leaving several massive bowls full of condoms, finger cots, nitrile gloves, and dental dams in any available corner on every floor. He also sent me an extensive kink questionnaire he and Lucifer worked on together to be mindful of my limits during this whole thing.

Out of curiosity, I might have gone a bit wild and checked a lot of the boxes I wasn't completely certain about without really thinking.

Including one that read *threesomes and multipartner play.*

My thoughts turn to Azrael.

Is that who Lucifer had in mind when he—?

I shake my head.

No. No, I'm letting my fantasies get the better of me.

What I feel for Azrael is a schoolgirl crush.

It doesn't hold a candle to what I have with Lucifer.

I belong to Lucifer, plain and simple, and whoever he chooses to share me with.

All the guests are well-informed and signed hefty NDA agreements that require them to adhere to the stoplight system, and the dungeon monitors are here to enforce it if anyone gets out of line. I'm as safe as I possibly could be.

Jax taps me on the ass, the playful, unexpected sting causing me to laugh as we head back to the playroom. "Go get your man, Charlotte." She grins at me. "Or should I say *men?*"

"What?"

I turn to find Lucifer standing beside the exposure bench, shirtless and stripped down to only a pair of leather breaches that lace closed at the crotch. Azmodeus stands at his side, his outfit now changed so it's nearly identical to Lucifer's, except for the fact that his bare ass is completely exposed, because of course whatever pants he wore would be assless.

I blink, a little confused and weirdly disappointed, if I'm honest.

Azmodeus is not who I was expecting to see.

I glimpse to where Azrael stands with his arms crossed on the other side of the room, overseeing everything, but if he's thinking the same thing I am, he doesn't dare show it.

His cold blue eyes lock on to mine, and I blush, trying not to think about how exposed I am in these pasties, as I turn toward Lucifer.

Suddenly the collar around my throat feels incrementally tighter.

Can he see how looking at Death made my nipples hard? Would he care?

I'm not really sure of the answer.

I make my way toward Lucifer, and when I reach him, he takes my hand in his. "You're certain you're ready for this?" he asks, so low only I can hear him.

I nod feebly.

We've never done a scene in public before or with anyone else participating, so it's natural I would be nervous, but it's not the thought of everyone watching that has me uneasy. Or Azmodeus. My gaze flits to Azrael again.

Why does it feel so wrong that he's not here beside Lucifer and me?

"Yes, I'm ready," I say giving him the verbal confirmation he's waiting for.

"Good." Lucifer smirks at me. "I'll be gentle with you tonight. You know what to do."

He gives a quick tug on my play collar, a reminder that it's time to abandon all the polite pretenses we maintain in public. That familiar light feeling of subspace starts to bubble up inside me, and I sink into it.

I drop to my knees, and I think I hear someone in the crowd gasp—Jax maybe?—as I lower my head and gently kiss the tops of his steel-toed play boots.

"Is it time to play now, Daddy?"

"Yes, little dove." Lucifer straps on his fingerless leather gloves as I kneel before him, patiently waiting, before his voice deepens to a seductively low register. "On the exposure bench."

I do as I'm told, recognizing a few seconds later when I'm spread open and Azmodeus is cuffing my wrists over my head that a crowd started to gather while I changed. Slowly, the lights dim, spotlighting Lucifer, Azmodeus, and me, until it feels like the three of us are alone. The only face I can see directly across the crowd is . . .

Azrael's.

Oh fuck.

I pull against my restraints a little, the voyeuristic guests chuckling a bit as they mistake it for part of the scene.

Does Lucifer know who I'm going to be staring at the entire time he does this?

I glance toward him, and his eyes darken.

He knows. He *must* know.

This isn't the sort of detail that would ever escape him, which means . . .

Does he *want* me to watch Azrael?

Lucifer's expression doesn't give anything away, and with the crowd of guests present, he may as well have gagged me.

My arms are suspended above my head, my hands pressed together like I'm deep in prayer, and my high-heeled feet are positioned off to the bench's sides so that I'm open and spread wide for him. The sheer thong I'm wearing isn't doing much to cover my pussy, and I have no doubt Lucifer plans to rip the lingerie off me as soon as we get started anyway.

Lucifer steps back, his attention trailing over me like he's admiring his work. "What do you think, brother? Where should we start first?"

It's not until that exact moment I fully process that Azmodeus wasn't just teasing me earlier. He *is* allowed to touch me.

Lust and Lucifer and I are going to play.

As I stare down Daddy Death.

Oh fuck, I'm not sure I can handle this.

Azmodeus comes forward, giving a similarly hungry appraisal of me like he can see all my weak points, the inner workings of my nerve endings.

"For a schoolgirl like her, start with the pussy," Az says, licking his lips appreciatively. "Coy kittens need time to warm up before they come out to play."

Schoolgirl?

The way he says it is so dismissive and embarrassing, it's arousing, the sharp sting of his words whipping through me.

I'm nothing more than an object.

A nameless cunt for Lucifer and Azmodeus to take, to degrade.

And I love it.

Az looks to Lucifer, who gives a curt nod. With Lucifer's permission, Az pulls aside my thong to cup my pussy. I arch into his touch, straining against where my hands are cuffed to try and get more of it. It's the same one he used on me in the gallery the other day—or was that a few weeks ago?—I can't remember.

All at once, I can't think of anything other than how much I want someone, anyone who's willing to do the job, to fuck me, and considering it's Azmodeus who's currently stroking up and down the seam of my pussy, watching me in that mouthwatering way, he's the perfect first candidate.

But even though I can't see him at the moment, I can't help but think of Azrael.

I can feel his gaze on me, his power shielding Lucifer and me.

Waiting. Watching. Like he always does.

Above me, Azmodeus's eyes turn molten as his irises start to glow. Not like hellfire, but something similar.

Lust is ready to play.

He moves his fingers in just the right way so that parts of me wake up, parts I wasn't even aware of previously, and I realize I hadn't gotten the full blast of what Azmodeus's touch is capable of before this.

Until now that his hand's on my pussy, his deft fingers stroking me.

I'm so horny, I'm practically coming out of my skin.

I want him. I want all of them. One in every hole.

"Please. Please, Az," I suddenly hear myself begging.

Azmodeus chuckles, low and deep. "Please what, naughty girl?"

I can't bring myself to say it. To beg him to fuck me in the middle of mine and Lucifer's engagement party. He's *trying* to make me break protocol.

This is torture. Sweet fucking torture.

For my Dom's enjoyment.

I whimper, my eyes darting toward Lucifer for permission. "Please, Daddy?"

Can I have him? Can I have you?

Lucifer crosses his arms over his chest, shaking his head. "I'm sorry, Charlotte." He chuckles, the deep sound rushing straight to my pussy. He's being unusually soft with me tonight, easing me into this, like he's trying to get a gauge on what I need.

With a few quick steps to the right, Azmodeus's hand trails from my pussy up the line of my stomach. His eyes follow mine as he clocks who I'm watching on the other side of the room before he crouches to where my head's positioned, purring, "Who knew you were such a filthy little whore? I would've borrowed you from my brother a lot sooner."

The ache between my legs is throbbing so hard, it's torturing me.

"Please, Az?" I beg, turning toward him, my eyes saying it for me.

My lips are no more than a hairsbreadth from his.

Please. Please put me out of this misery.

Az purrs appreciatively, but he doesn't respond to me again, doesn't acknowledge that I've spoken to him. "Greedy little kitty, isn't she?" he says, talking about my pussy. He rolls one of my pasty-covered nipples in his hands like I'm not even here.

I arch up off the bench at the pleasure of it, my breasts growing tender and heavy.

"Suck them," I whisper, bowing my chest forward. "Please."

Az side-eyes Lucifer like he's checking in to make sure Lucifer's still enjoying this, but Lucifer simply tilts his chin, smirking as if he takes great pleasure in seeing me come undone as Azmodeus steps around to the front of the exposure bench and pushes two fingers up inside me.

My first orgasm comes hard and fast, an unexpected shout tearing from me.

Oh my God. Oh my God.

What would it be like to have Azmodeus's cock inside me right now? Or Lucifer's? Azrael's?

Fuck.

All three?

I shake and shiver, the walls of my pussy clenching and unclenching. I'm up on cloud nine, sailing into seventh heaven.

So out of my mind and wild with lust that I desperately want to know what it'd be like to . . .

I let out an uninhibited moan.

What would it be like to have Azrael *and* Lucifer inside me at the same time? One of them in each hole, fucking me so close, that they're nearly . . . fucking each other.

I cum again suddenly, even Azmodeus lifting a brow over how quick it came on. "What nasty little fantasy had you bucking like that, kitten?"

Azmodeus's glowing eyes meet mine, and I realize if Lucifer can see all our darkest sins, then Azmodeus can . . .

Azmodeus makes a beckoning nod at Lucifer, who steps forward for Azmodeus to whisper something into his ear.

Lucifer's eyes widen slightly, the difference so subtle it'd be almost imperceptible if I weren't completely fixated on his face. His gaze darts meaningfully across the room toward Azrael.

No. No, no, no, no.

He can't know that I . . .

Whatever look Lucifer and Azrael exchange, I'm unable to see it from where I'm leaned back on the exposure bench, but the next thing I know, Lucifer's striding across the playroom toward him, beckoning Death from where he was leaning, arms crossed, against the wall. Lucifer bends in close, whispering into the other man's ear. Azrael looks toward him, eyes narrowed and angry, before his chilling stare falls to me and softens.

A thousand unspoken truths seem to pass between us in a single moment.

Azrael glances uncertainly toward Lucifer and then strides toward me.

He's across the room and shouldering Azmodeus out of his way so fast, I can barely even process the relief of having Azmodeus's touch gone before Azrael's knelt beside me, one of his large hands stroking through my hair. "Eyes on me, baby girl."

His touch is so soft, so gentle, I can't help but lean into it.

"Your Lightbringer says you asked for me."

Lucifer now stands a few feet away from us, watching us both, his eyes narrowed in curiosity. I'm vaguely aware of Azmodeus making a signal to the crowd that we've temporarily paused the scene, but then Azrael's cupping my chin, his graveled voice rumbling through me.

"Don't look at him. Look at me. What do *you* want, little siren?"

I swallow, my throat writhing as I stare uncertainly into Death's infinite, knowing gaze.

"I . . . I don't know," I confess.

"Okay." He nods, a whole lifetime of understanding packed into one single look. He swipes away an errant tear from my cheek, still holding my gaze. "Then we wait, and you come see me after. Is that good for you, baby girl?"

I nod weakly.

When he calls me that, it's almost enough to wash all my insecurities away.

I belong to Lucifer, but . . .

Azrael feels like a true choice.

One not as wrapped up in fate.

And I don't even know how to begin to make heads or tails of that.

Azrael cradles my face, his nose nearly brushing against mine as his eyes fall to my lips, like whatever this strange ache is between us, he feels it too.

"Okay," he mumbles again, unexpectedly laying a gentle kiss on my forehead.

Abruptly, he releases me. He turns away, starting to stalk back toward his post, only to stop and whisper something I can't hear into Lucifer's ear.

Lucifer returns to me and Azmodeus then, who's just reappeared by my side. Lucifer gives a subtle shake of his head.

Daddy Death won't be joining us after all.

I look down toward the playroom floor, clearing my throat.

I think that might be for the best, honestly.

Until now I thought my attraction to Azrael was harmless. Nothing more than a silly, girlish crush. A fantasy.

But with how he just looked at me, the way it made all my heart's nerve endings fire until my limbs grew heavy, now I'm . . . not so certain.

I can't care for Azrael.

I'm in love with Lucifer, but would he—?

I think I know the answer to that the moment I look toward him. He crouches beside me.

"Look at me, little dove," he orders, gently gripping my face.

And I do.

I look to him with all the fear, uncertainty, and doubt I feel laid bare and open. I don't look anywhere else.

"Do you want him?" he asks, nodding over his shoulder.

We both know exactly who he means.

"I . . . I don't know," I whisper, giving him the same answer.

His eyes soften. "It's all right, darling. I've got you."

He'll always be here to catch me when I fall. Put the pieces back together when I break.

There's no sin I could ever commit that would push him away from me.

When he said he wanted all the darkest, messiest parts of me, he meant it.

He'll keep that promise.

Lucifer kisses me long and deep, until I feel a familiar spark come alive in me again—hope. He drops to his knees before me, kissing his way toward my pussy as he makes the signal to Azmodeus to resume the scene.

And I know in that moment, whatever lies in our future, it's going to be okay.

As long as he's with me.

My eyes lock on to Death's, where he now stands across the crowded room, and he nods to me, his infinite and knowing gaze heating until the icy hue looks almost like blue fire. As I throw back my head in pleasure at how Lucifer's tongue plunges inside me, as I stare into that open, endless abyss, I feel more than think that it might be okay if I died here.

If only the both of them would catch me.

CHAPTER FIFTY-FOUR

Azrael

I watch Lucifer and his brother work our little siren over until she's practically coming apart at the seams, my cock so hard I'm surprised I can even see straight from where all the blood in my body has begun to pool there.

She's orgasmed enough times while watching me with those big doe eyes that I've lost count of how many times she's cum, and from the asshole on my left who's been muttering under his breath about how insanely hot she is, I'm not the only one who enjoyed the sight. That bastard may be even closer to jerking off than I am.

But I don't miss the way her eyes continue to flit to mine and stay there.

Like she's begging for me.

Fuck, you would be so good for me, wouldn't you, baby girl?

Lucifer's little siren may not be much of a threat in the training room, but the way she's looking at me now . . .

Fuck, it undoes me.

I don't bother taking stock of who's noticed us making eyes at each other, not that I give a shit if anyone sees as I reach down and adjust the hefty bulge at the front of my jeans. Charlotte's eyes track the movement, her tongue darting out to wet her lips appreciatively.

Can she see how hard I am from where she's laid out for Lucifer like a present?

Fuck. What are you doing to me?

I've had to gnash and grind my teeth practically into dust to stop myself from walking back over there and demanding that little shit Azmodeus get the fuck out of my way. He may be lust itself, but I'm confident I could make her moan so much better.

Shit. This is a helluva lot more than I bargained for when Lucifer first offered her as part of his deal with me. Honestly, I hadn't put that much thought in it other than to feel sorry for her that he was willing to share her so readily. Now I can see why.

I'm the unexpected choice neither of them saw coming.

But whatever attraction I may feel for her now wasn't a consideration initially.

Despite what my pompous ex might think.

My eyes fall to where he's just finished inside her, his face and the five o'clock shadow on his chin still glistening from where he feasted on her cunt. I know what it's like to have his tongue on me, his cock inside me balls-deep, pushed to the hilt.

Even if we haven't fucked in over a century.

I still remember the feeling—what it's like to be the object of his desire, pinned beneath his fiery gaze. I'd be lying if I said I hadn't expected to feel jealous as all fucking get out when I chose to come here tonight and subject myself to playing dungeon monitor for this whole goddamn charade. But it's the revelation of exactly *who* I'm jealous of that surprises me most.

Azmodeus, that lustful fucker, is in my place.

How I know that it should be me who's pounding into Charlotte's ass right now, locking eyes with Lucifer, instead of trying to look the other way is a question for another day, but I'm as old and infinite as the universe.

And I've learned never to doubt myself.

I'm my own master.

Death yields to nobody.

Charlotte's eyes continue to hold mine, my hard cock giving a painful jerk.

Shit. The fact I'm even considering fucking with their dynamic when they're so clearly meant for one another shows just how far gone I am. Fucked in the head. Delusional. Mad as a goddamn hatter. I've spent the last century picking up the pieces of myself that Lucifer left scattered in his wake. Swore I would never allow anyone to hold that kind of power over me ever again. And what do I do the first time he summons me back?

Jump at the chance to be in his periphery.

He's the goddamn sun, and like all the other predictable little stars in the universe, I'm helplessly drawn into his orbit.

Except the reason he and I never worked is probably because he's been destined for someone else this whole goddamn time.

Fuck, fate hates me.

The desire in Charlotte's eyes softens this time as she looks at me, like even from where she's strung up on the other side of the room, she can see the rare glimpse of vulnerability that watching them creates in me, the mixture of pain and pleasure at seeing them together. I'd thought the ache of losing him was long gone, until I first held her in my arms.

Now, I realize I'd simply buried it, and every time I'm with her it's like she's excavating those parts of me. Laying me bare so those old wounds are given the air and space to heal. Those innocent doe eyes of hers disrupt any vague sense I had of my own gravity.

A little like someone else I know.

Lucifer's brows lift slightly as he watches Charlotte's face, like he's just now noticing that she isn't looking at *him*, but at me. My ex is the ultimate fucking narcissist, but everyone fucking loves him for it,

Charlotte and me included. His eyes track to where she's been staring into the crowd, following her gaze until it lands on me.

I turn my back before either of us have the chance to register how we feel about that, easily shouldering my way through the crowd.

Most humans fear me. If they can even bear the sight of me, that is.

But it isn't the potential for Lucifer's fist to land in my face for looking at his woman that I fear.

It's his pity. His understanding.

I turn tail, not bothering to glance back, even as I hear Charlotte call my name.

Fuck, baby girl. Don't do this to me.

I've got to get out of here. Now.

Right fucking now.

I can't give in and lose myself to either of them, or I'll be fucked in the head completely.

My own death can't start here.

CHAPTER FIFTY-FIVE

Lucifer

My gaze tracks to where Azrael now tears through the crowd, then to Charlotte's face falling. My heart seems to stop before it sputters and then my pulse is suddenly racing.

I should have expected this, and a small part of me did, but with someone *else*.

Not him.

And for once, I didn't see my own goddamn twist coming.

But now that I recognize it, now that I see what I've done, how I thrust the two of them together, it makes perfect sense to me. Some part of me knew *he* was the choice she needed to heal her.

I cannot unsee it.

This is the sacrifice she always needed from me. The opportunity to walk away. To choose someone *other* than me.

No matter how much I do not want her to.

Our scene has just finished, and Charlotte is still hanging from the suspension rack as we both watch Azrael tear through the crowd.

"You should go to him." My words are spoken so low that only Charlotte can hear them.

Already, the crowd has started to disperse and return to the party, and Charlotte's eyes go wide as I release her from her bindings. "I—"

I shake my head, cutting her off.

I can no longer stand the thought of her believing the worst of me, now that I realize I might lose her like this. I cannot allow her to believe for another bloody second I am as heartless as I can be brutal, to fear the vulnerability she creates in me. "Did you honestly expect I would be cruel enough to keep you for myself, Charlotte?"

She blinks up at me, trying and failing to understand. "Sir?"

My expression softens as I gently cup her cheek to reassure her. "I have lived a whole existence, a whole eternity, before fate brought me to you. Thousands of lives. Hundreds of centuries. Chosen lovers aplenty. Few that ever truly meant anything to me in the way that you do, but I would never ask you to . . ." My voice trails off.

Stop living for me.

Rob you of your choices, your freedom, your youthful mistakes.

All for my sake.

Her eyes widen, and I know from her expression that she was able to hear me as she stares up at me uncertainly.

"You are mine and you will always *be* mine." I cup my hand on the side of her neck, stroking my thumb over her skin, her collar, as she shivers. "But you are still so very young, so very innocent and green, and we have the whole of eternity, darling. I would never ask you to give up your choices, your freedom, for my sake, unless you want to." I swallow as I allow my hand to travel over her collar. "Go to him."

Charlotte glances to where the breadth of Azrael's large body cut a swath through the crowd and then back to me, hesitating, like now that she sees the path, the choice, her freedom laid out for her, she's too terrified to claim it.

I told my Father I thought the mix of free will and fate might be too much for them, might have been a mistake. His design is too bloody convoluted and celestial a concept for His precious creations to comprehend.

Though I think Charlotte may be coming to understand how they interplay.

Now that I've given her the choice to pursue her own fate.

Even when the whole of all our paths were created by His and my Mother's hands.

Don't make her choose, Sammael.

The priest's prophetic warning comes back to haunt me.

I failed to realize until it was too late that it wasn't my Father I had to watch out for. Azrael was the dark horse I never saw coming.

Placed in her path by my own hand.

"Go," I say again, giving her hand a reassuring squeeze. "I'll be waiting for you when you come back."

And she will. Come back to me.

In this I must trust, must believe.

Or risk forever losing all that she is to me.

CHAPTER FIFTY-SIX

Charlotte

The moment Lucifer tells me to go after Azrael, I hesitate.

I don't want to lose Lucifer, to risk him—risk *us*—but I know this is the right choice.

For both of us.

I reach up, hands shaking, and unlatch my collar. My heart thumps against my chest painfully as I pass it to him, but despite how much it pains me, how much I've longed to be his, I try not to let myself linger on the pride and hurt in his gaze.

Not pride for himself, but in me. At how far I've come. Thanks to him.

If I look too long, I might never allow myself to do this.

Risk everything.

Lucifer is my fate, my purpose. My very reason for existing, but Azrael is my . . .

My choice.

The first celestial decision Lucifer's gifted me.

We both need this. The freedom of certainty.

And while I don't know where any of this is headed or what any of this means for him, or for me—hell, for all three of us—we can figure the rest out later.

So, I kiss Lucifer on the cheek before I dart into the crowd to find Azrael.

I don't see him anywhere in the playroom, or on any of the other floors, and it isn't until I notice the glow of the city lights below, where one of the party drapes has started to fall away from the window, that I know exactly where to find him.

I stumble out onto the rooftop a few minutes later, nothing but a thin satin robe wrapped around myself, so I'm instantly shivering.

Azrael's perched on the roof's edge, his dark wings folding and unfolding, and my breath hitches. I rarely ever see them, and they're so beautiful, I wish he didn't have to hide them regularly.

The Angel of Death.

He may not be a *real* angel, but he's been that more than once for me.

Slowly, I walk to his side, and soon I'm sitting on the ledge right beside him, our knees brushing. "I'm—"

"Sorry," we both say at once.

The hurt in Azrael's eyes softens.

"You first," I whisper to him.

"I never meant for it to hurt you."

I lift a brow, not certain what he means, and I track how the muscled cords of his throat writhe.

"God's blade. The Holy Lance. The one Michael, and now Lucifer, have been searching for. The one Michael claims to have is a fake. But the *real* one, the one that killed your actress is still out there." He hesitates before he says, "And *I* was the one who put the real blade into play."

I suck in a harsh breath at the revelation, at what he's just confessed to me.

"Why?" I breathe.

"I did it to hurt him." His eyes dart back toward the rooftop's entrance as if I don't already know exactly who he means. "I never meant for it to—"

"You love him," I whisper.

It's not a question. I can see it right there in his cold blue gaze.

It's something we both have in common.

Death looks a little . . . lost as he stares back at me then, his expression an aching mixture of guilt, pain, regret, and longing. "I wish that I didn't, but I do. But also, I"—he swallows, and the cold fire in his gaze returns—"didn't expect to feel anything for you."

My heart starts to pound rapidly, so loud and forceful that the sound of it echoes inside my ears. "That's why you made whatever deal it is you made with him, isn't it? Because you love him, and also because you—"

"Didn't think I could bear the thought of seeing you hurt? No. Not after I'd held you."

An amused, self-deprecating huff tears from my lips as I shrug, turning to look back toward the glittering lights of the city. "I'm sure you've held *plenty* of other humans as they've died."

"None that were ever brave enough to look at me, to see me," he admits. "None that ever managed to escape."

I smile so wide I nearly laugh. "So that's what this is? It's the thrill of the chase for you?"

To Death I'll always be the one who got away.

The only former human who's managed to escape from him, even though it was my time. This strange fascination we have with one another, that we've been harboring since the very beginning . . .

It's as new and strange to him as it is to me.

Maybe that's why I've been dreaming of him, because some part of me knew that he'd played a role in gifting my freedom to me. Held me in his arms long enough to let Lucifer offer me God's redemption.

Even though he should have hated me from the start.

For falling in love with the fallen angel he's clearly been in love with for all eternity.

And to think I ever thought they were just fuck buddies.

Lucifer and Death's relationship is so obvious now.

It spans the whole of time, of human history.

God, I bet the two of them were freaking menaces when they were together.

"It was a bit of that initially," Azrael admits, his smile a little teasing. "And I like to watch."

"Of course, you do, you freaking stalker." I give his biceps a playful punch. "You think I haven't noticed how you've been following me? Total creeper energy for sure." I grin.

Azrael smiles back at me.

And I realize that's what I like about Death.

He sees down to the barest parts of me.

Like with him, I can just be an inexperienced twenty-three-year-old again.

Not the vicious queen of Hell I'm becoming.

I think some piece of me needs the reminder that I can be both.

"So, you like to watch, huh?" I bump my shoulder against his, and Azrael's eyes darken.

"Not *just* watch, little siren."

A shiver runs through me. One that doesn't have anything to do with the wind.

"I forgive you, you know." The words unexpectedly tumble from my lips.

Death looks slightly taken aback by that.

He lifts a brow. "You do?"

The Holy Lance nearly cost me my life, after all. Even if he wasn't the one to wield it, even if he only put the weapon into play, it was supposed to be me in Xzander's studio.

And Olivia's death still weighs on me.

But I have the feeling she's in a better place.

Azrael would have made sure of it.

"I know what it's like to love him"—I glance down at my clutched hands—"to be afraid he isn't capable of loving you in return."

"He didn't with me." Azrael shakes his head, though I can see how the truth in that hurts him. "Not like he does you." He meets my gaze. "He does love you, Charlotte. In all the ways he can. I don't want to get in the way of that."

"I know." I grin, my posture relaxing. "I know he does. But you won't. Lucifer and I could never be over. I love him, and I always will, but I have to be certain my choices are mine. That my life isn't just a product of God, or Lilith, or fate. I think that's all he and I need to be truly happy."

Azrael nods like he understands. "You need to be your own master first, before you can truly submit yourself to someone."

"Exactly." I give him a soft smile.

Death is sensitive in ways no one would ever expect him to be.

Maybe because, in the end, he's the one tasked with the job of putting us at peace, helping us move forward.

"What did you mean?" he asks unexpectedly. Azrael strikes me as a short-response kind of guy. Few humans are as okay with silence as he is. "When you said you were sorry?" he prompts.

"I'm sorry for not recognizing what Lucifer meant to you sooner. For dragging you into all this." My limbs grow heavy as I look at him, my heart on my sleeve.

The corner of his mouth turns up as he nods appreciatively. "You're not dragging me into anything, little siren. Lucifer offered to share you with me of his own accord as part of our deal."

My brows shoot up. "He did?"

I'm not certain how I feel about that.

Azrael reads my expression easily. "Your body. Not your heart. He asked, should something happen to you, for me to spare your life once more. Go against fate. He was desperate to protect you. I don't think he ever truly expected for me to take him up on it."

I shrug. "But still, he offered."

I'm not sure why that hurts me.

Yet another thing I have to unpack.

"Sometimes that strategic mind of his is two steps ahead of his heart."

"You think that he—?"

"Planned for this? No. At least not initially."

I squint, my expression turning pensive. "And what did *you* get out of it? The deal between you both?"

He smirks at me. "Who do you think asks the questions here?"

I flush, glancing down slightly. "So, we're really going to do this then? You, Lucifer, and me?"

Azrael shakes his head softly. "I . . . wouldn't say that, but if you want a choice, little siren, I'll be that choice for you."

My breath hitches. "I can't make any promises."

"Neither can I."

He moves closer, and I feign an interest in my hands. "And you should probably know that before Lucifer—"

"You've got a lot of darkness in your history. You and me both." He tucks a stray strand of hair behind my ear, leaning into me.

My eyes fall to his lips, and I nod.

But that's all the permission Azrael seems to need.

His mouth is on mine in an instant, a subtle onslaught that's as forceful and deliciously suffocating as he is. He comes forward, easing on top of me, nearly knocking us both off the ledge. I tug him closer, my hands fisted and tangled in the material of his shirt.

Death's kiss is a transformation.

The beginning and the end all in one.

Like life anew after the annihilation of everything I once was, everything I am, and everything I will be.

And maybe . . .

The choice that binds Lucifer and me together.

I'm not certain there was ever any other path for the two of us—no, the *three* of us—but this. Whatever and wherever it leads, we'll find a way forward. I'll make Lucifer see.

It was always supposed to be like this.

When Azrael pulls away, his lips hovering only a fraction above mine, we're both breathing heavy, the shock of what's just passed between us feeling like a revelation.

Its own kind of apocalypse.

Azrael glances down to where he's positioned overtop me. Like he knows as well as I do where this could go if we both allowed it.

"I should get back to him," I say, placing my hand on his chest.

We need to take this slow. For all our sakes.

"Mmph." He gives a low, grumbling purr, the noise rushing heat straight to my core as his eyes once again fall to my lips, like it physically pains him for us to separate, but then he moves off me, helping me sit up.

I twist so that my feet are now firmly planted on the safe side of the ledge, but then he's standing next to me, his large, wide shadow looming over me as his hand snakes to the back of my neck, cradling me there, and unlike Lucifer, he doesn't pull me to him. It's like he's guiding me. Like the choice to be with him *is* and always will be mine.

"I've waited an eternity for someone to see me the way you do—as a person, not just some terrifying concept." He stares down at me, his graveled voice thick and heavy with need. "I can wait one night longer. Go." He nods over his shoulder. "Go to him."

"And what about you?" I brush my hand over his cheek.

He shivers.

Death actually shivers in response to my touch, his eyes darkening.

"I am as endless and vast as this universe, Charlotte. More patient than even your immortal eternity." Death grins at me. "I'm not going anywhere, little siren."

CHAPTER FIFTY-SEVEN

Charlotte

"Back so soon?" Lucifer looks more than a little amused at the sight of me as he waves off Ramesh, who appears to have been bringing him a drink.

For safety, Azmodeus put a two-drink limit on all party guests, except the Originals.

Being immortal has perks, it seems.

Lucifer's eyes narrow as he notices the blush on my cheeks, my swollen lips.

Nothing about navigating this is going to be easy.

So, I just come out and say it. "I think it's only fair I give you an equal chance to court me. For us to start fresh. Now that we've agreed I'm allowed to . . . explore."

Lucifer quirks a brow in interest. "A competition between Azrael and me? Is that what you had in mind?"

I shrug, my face flaming. "Sort of. I guess?"

When he puts it like that, it sounds a lot more wicked than I ever expected it to be.

But the idea of the devil and Death competing for my attention, well it . . .

Makes that bit of power I now keep at the ready inside myself purr eagerly.

Lucifer reads the uncertainty in my expression easily. "Immortality can be fun, if you let it be, Charlotte."

Kinky and messy and fucked up, but what else would it be?

Lucifer snatches me toward him, so that I'm tucked against him, chest to stomach. He's a whole lot taller than me. "The only problem with that little arrangement is I fear the playing field may not exactly be level." Lucifer leans down so he can whisper into my ear, causing me to shiver from head to toe, like he did before, like he always has, *especially* before he gave his Father's redemption to me.

"Oh, and why's that?" I smile up at him playfully. "Because you were the one who made me immortal? Who first fucked the shame out of me?"

That devious grin of his widens, flashing fang. "No, no." He chuckles, the heat of his breath brushing against me. An intoxicating mixture of whisky and leather and smoke. "Who do you think taught Death all his best moves?"

Without warning, Lucifer casts his whisky glass onto a nearby table as he brutally kisses me, and all my breath, all my nerves, are sucked out of me like a force as I'm suddenly yanked forward and down into the ether.

Down into the fiery realm where he's king.

CHAPTER FIFTY-EIGHT

Charlotte

"What? How in God's name did you—?"

"Hell is and always has been my realm, darling. Not even my Father or my self-righteous sycophant for a brother could steal it from me." He steps back, taking hold of my hand to reveal the desolate wasteland around me. "I'm a man of my word and I made a promise to you that I would bring you here. I also promise to be honest with you starting now. Do you understand me?"

I nod. "I promise to do the same."

In truth, what I've been doing with his siblings weighs on me.

But I'll make it a point to tell him soon. When the time is right.

"I would never expect anything less." Lucifer extends his hand to me. "Do you trust me, Charlotte?"

I snort, smiling slightly. "Your brother asked me almost the exact same thing a few weeks back."

"My brother?" He lifts a brow as if to say which one.

"The one I ended up in the papers with."

The one you let have his way with me tonight. That part goes unspoken.

I have a feeling rumors of Lucifer and me being on the rocks will spread rapidly—even if it's not at all true. Everyone at the party signed a lengthy NDA and would never publicly utter so much as a word against us, but money talks.

And the money the press will pay for any hint of unsubstantiated, juicy gossip about Lucifer and me is substantial. More than most Americans make in a year, easily.

Especially since the first seal opening.

Humanity's more eager for celestial gossip than ever.

Lucifer frowns. "Azmodeus is a bloody prat who sticks his nose *and* his cock into everything, and I regret allowing him to touch you if it's going to be a while before we—"

"It won't," I say, smiling at how quickly the tables have turned, and for once, it's me who needs to reassure him. "Things with us are still as they were. I promise you. Our dynamic isn't over, and neither are we. The twenty-four seven D/s part is only . . . on pause for a minute. I just need some space to figure things out first. That's all."

"To figure out Azrael you mean?" Lucifer mouth quirks suggestively.

I flush, but Lucifer's crooked grin only widens. "Not *just* Azrael."

"I mean no judgment, Charlotte," he says, turning away from me. "Azrael is . . ." He lifts his brows once to imply that Azrael is, well, completely and totally fuckable.

A sudden burst of jealousy twists through me.

And interest.

How can he be so mature and okay about all this?

I can't say I'd be able to do the same if the roles were reversed.

And would they ever want to . . .

No. No, no, no.

I can't ask either of them that.

Oh God. I am definitely *going to have to unpack all of this in therapy.*

The poor woman will be working overtime with all I'll have to tell her about the three of us. Now that we're trying this open-relationship thing.

"Come, Charlotte," Lucifer beckons me. "There's something I'd like you to see."

He takes my hand, leading me from the dry, arid sand dune we're standing in. We wander through a gray and never-ending desert for what feels like ages—"The weight of all time stretched thin," he explains. No wonder he's sometimes gone for days when to him it seems like it's only been a few hours. All the times I've been frustrated and angry with him when he's been fulfilling his duties now feels incredibly selfish to me.

I didn't really know what I was signing up for before.

But this time, the choice will be mine completely.

"Is this all Hell is?" I ask once we've been walking for what feels like ages. "A gray and endless desert?" I hear an eerie, desolate sound in the distance, something animal, and my spine runs cold. I'm not sure I want to see whatever demonic creature that noise originated from.

"It was, originally," Lucifer answers. "Hell's landscape is more vast than the earth you call home, Charlotte, but it is most often . . ."—he hesitates for a moment, like he's trying to find the right description—"spaces that exist between defined states, the familiar made unfamiliar. I take inspiration from humanity's own horrors." He wrinkles his nose. "I find most human imaginations are sufficiently insufferable in their own right."

The dry heat in the air starts to lessen, then cools slightly, and I sigh in relief from where my lips were starting to crack.

If simply walking through certain parts of Hell is this bad, I can't begin to understand what other kinds of suffering it contains.

But I have a feeling, from the way Lucifer tugs at my hand eagerly, gently urging me onward, that he's got something new and completely unexpected up his sleeve. Just as I'm about to tell him I'm not going to take another step farther, we come to a stop, and suddenly his hands are overtop my eyelids from where he stands behind me.

"I wanted to be certain that *when* you choose to stay with me, to be mine forever and always, that I no longer have to leave you when I come here. That you would have a place here in Hell beside me, as my queen."

I lift a brow.

This isn't about to be some hellish BDSM torture chamber, is it?

Lucifer chuckles, hearing my thoughts loud and clear.

"What are you trying to say?" I ask.

"Open your eyes, darling."

He pulls back his hands, and I gasp, all the breath rushing out of me.

Because in front of me lies his real kingdom, his real court.

The one of his own making.

Made entirely out of stars.

The colors of the sweeping mountainous landscape before us are in the same palette as the northern lights he cast over the city.

And the starlight in Hell is actually twinkling.

"How? How did you—?"

"I had my suspicions that my brother might pull something of a coup, of course, so I've been pouring a fair amount of my power into this realm for years. It felt high time that I spruce the place up a bit." He snaps his fingers, and we're transported to the middle of an obsidian throne room, overlooking an outdoor balcony. Dozens of smaller dwellings pepper the hillside beneath, and I know without asking who they're for.

The souls.

The ones he doesn't believe deserve to be here.

Suddenly, my heart is in my throat, my chest tightening.

I should have known.

Like his Father, Lucifer is capable of mercy.

Mercy he was never given.

Because God couldn't bear to see His own flaws reflected in His son's face.

In all the Originals.

I shake my head. If what Azmodeus told me is true, then . . .

Man, God was a much bigger asshole to His own children than I ever would have expected He'd be.

Even if I do still plan to say my prayers in hopes that He and His followers become, well, self-reflective enough to help fix this whole apocalypse situation we're dealing with topside.

The amount of pride and ego it would take to not see themselves for the hateful monsters they've allowed themselves to become is, well . . .

Nearly as villainous as the fallen angel standing next to me.

Lucifer doesn't say anything for a few moments, like he recognizes I'm lost in my own thoughts, before finally he clears his throat. "Michael may have stripped me of my powers while I'm on Earth, but what he took is only a fraction of what lies here."

"You just need to figure out how to reclaim it."

He nods, taking my hand in his.

I honestly understand the feeling.

He draws me to the edge of the balcony then, and I watch a few of the souls move about below, one of them waving up at me.

"Is that—?"

"The nun who helped you from the church down on Seventh Avenue. Yes."

My brow furrows. "How did she—?"

"I'll explain later, darling, but what you should know is that since my Father abandoned us all, well, it seems you were the only one given the option to head upstairs, I'm afraid." He nods toward Hell's sky as if to indicate where Heaven waits somewhere above.

"So, everyone who's died in the decade that you and your siblings were released?"

Lucifer's jaw sets with a hint of bitterness. "All down here, I'm afraid. The growing population is becoming a bit of a problem actually."

"Overpopulation. In Hell," I exhale.

Exactly *why* did I want him to be honest with me again?

Sometimes I think staying ignorant might have been easier.

But then I wouldn't know if what he and I have is truly real.

Now we can choose one another without fate getting in the damned way.

"There's something about that I've been keeping from you for some time."

I nod. Whatever it is, I think I'm prepared for it.

"Tell me."

"When I gave you my Father's redemption, I also might have made you the only immortal capable of reopening the pearly gates."

All my breath rushes out of me.

"Oh yeah, sure. No big deal," I squeak, my tone going significantly higher at the end until I sound as mousy and timid as I used to be. "I'll just throw those ol' gates open and help fix your little overpopulation problem, while meanwhile your Mother expects me to be the champion of her freaky-as-hell prophecy *and* give her grandbabies."

"Her prophecy?" Lucifer's brows shoot up.

This is the first he's hearing of this.

"I . . . may or may not have met your Mom on the way to the play party. All *three* terrifying versions of her."

Lucifer sighs. "Sometimes her level of theatrics rivals my brother Gabriel's." He pinches the bridge of his nose like he's trying to find patience as I lean into him. "I apologize if she scared you." He pulls me to him and kisses the top of my head softly.

I wave a dismissive hand, trying to be far more nonchalant about all this than I feel. "Of course not. What could be scary about your future Mother-in-Law being a divine goddess?"

"She's a tad bit more than a goddess, little dove."

My gaze whips to his, my eyes widening.

"My Mother is the chaos from which the universe was created. The precursor to my Father's divine order."

I blink, taking a moment to process that. "Do you mean to tell me that God is a Dom, and He made Lilith, the embodiment of all divine chaos, his sub?"

Lucifer smirks wickedly. "Where do you think I get my more adventurous tendencies?"

CHAPTER FIFTY-NINE

Charlotte

Lucifer and I return topside after he's made thorough and slow love to me on the floor of his throne room. It's not as electric or as sinful as what he does to me when we're alone in his playroom, but still, it makes my heart feel almost whole and complete.

How will I ever be able to give a fair chance to trying things out with Azrael when Lucifer calls to the basest parts of who I am?

I don't know the answer to that yet, but I know I have to try and figure it out.

For all our sakes.

When Lucifer and I stumble our way back into the penthouse, it's early evening *again*, and the satin robe I'm wearing over my play clothes smells just as much of sulfur as he does when he returns from Hell, though I wasn't able to pick up on the scent at all when we were actually down there. But what truly confuses me is the sight of Xzander and Sophie, along with the rest of Lucifer's team, pacing the length of the first floor.

"What are all you—?"

"The CFDA Awards, diva!" Xzander practically shrieks. "The awards show starts in two hours."

"Two hours?" I blink.

Okay, now I *really* feel like an ass for all the times I've complained about Lucifer being gone. It felt like we were only down there for a handful of hours, not several *days*.

"I'll see you on the red carpet, my love," Lucifer says, laying a gentle kiss on my hand as he heads toward his team. He'll be ready long before I am, so even though we'll both be in the penthouse, we won't see each other again until we're already en route.

I don't know why, but the idea of that worries me.

Maybe I'm less prepared for some distance between us than I thought I was?

I feel uneasy.

Whatever it is, I can't put my finger on it.

I glance down at my phone as Sophie leads me toward her chair, expecting to see a full string of texts from Jax—does Hell even get cell service? Probably not, but I make a mental note to ask Lucifer—but instead, the long string of messages are from Evie.

Hey! Have you seen Jax?

She didn't come home after we left your party.
That one was from a few days ago.

Hey, Charlotte, Jax still isn't home, and I'm starting to get worried.

Let me know as soon as you get this.

Another that's days old.
And then finally:

She still isn't here. I can't call the cops.

Not without alerting my brother that I'm here. Charlotte, please answer me.

Followed by:

I don't have any choice. I'm calling the cops now. My brother's going to find me, but I can't keep doing nothing like this.

Charlotte, please answer.

And last but not least:
A photo text from a number I haven't seen that often lately.
Ian.
I open it only for my whole body to turn rigid, cold.
"What's wrong?" Azrael asks from where he suddenly forms beside me.
Ever since Lucifer assigned him as my "watchdog," he always just appears whenever I need him.
Slowly, I turn the screen of my phone toward him, my hand trembling.
Death's cold eyes take stock of the image of my closest friend, bound and gagged, the blue light of the photo now reflected in his knowing gaze. His jaw hardens when he sees the familiar blade in Ian's hand, and somehow, I know from the grim look on Azrael's face that *this* blade is the real one, the one he regrets putting into play. Though how did a human . . . ?
Then Death's sights fall toward Ian, a person I once thought was my friend. I may not have been on the best of terms with him currently, but I never would have thought he'd do something like *this*. He holds the Holy Lance ruthlessly against Jax's bleeding throat.
The last and only other text from him reads:

Come and get her, Mrs. Lucifer.

CHAPTER SIXTY

Charlotte

"We *have* to go after her!"

Lucifer shakes his head. Azrael's just summoned him and his style team from upstairs. "I shouldn't have to tell you all the reasons that is not a good idea right now, Charlotte."

Azrael steps between us, acting as a sort of immortal buffer between Lucifer and me. "That blade can kill you as much as it can her. Allow me to—"

"No," Lucifer and I say in unison.

At least he and I can agree on that.

If Azrael were to be killed, regardless of the fact *he* was the one who initially put the blade into play—something neither of us seem to have any plans of telling Lucifer yet—Lucifer's lack of power would no longer be shielded from the other Originals. And with me still having no idea how to use my powers or any of the other abilities Lucifer's finally disclosed that God's redemption gifted me, I'd basically be a sitting duck for Michael or another one of his siblings' taking, and then . . .

Chaos would ensue.

We all know it.

"I'll go." Lucifer brushes off the lapels of the Armani tux he's wearing. "I may no longer have my power, but I'm more than capable of offing a pathetic little human in other ways." He unbuttons the coat of his tux to reveal the loaded gun he's apparently now started carrying.

So, his suspenders really were a shoulder holster after all.

Why doesn't that surprise me?

An immortal with a loaded gun.

What could possibly go wrong?

I only started to realize over the past several days, when Lucifer began joining us in the training room, that he's just as much of a trained celestial warrior as Azrael is.

But that still doesn't make this a good idea.

"You don't know who he might be working with," Azrael counters. "He may not be acting as a free agent."

The Righteous. Or worse, Michael.

That seems to go without saying.

Lucifer's eyes narrow, like he's two seconds away from throttling Azrael.

"Then I'll go," I say.

Lucifer and Azrael turn in unison and snarl at me.

Clearly neither of them would ever allow me to consider it.

"You have to be on the red carpet in an hour, diva," Xzander chimes in as he passes by in a flurry. I don't have time to break his fashion-loving heart and tell him how absolutely insignificant that is compared to the celestial magnitude of what we're discussing.

I'm not sure he or any of the humans in the room have been able to follow any of this.

The humans in the room.

I've chosen a side, placed myself on the immortal end of the celestial divide.

There's no going back now.

"Even *if* that were important, there's no one better suited to this than me," I argue. "I know Ian, or at least I thought I did, and I also know Jax, and whatever *other* celestial might possibly be up to this . . ." I shoot a reprimanding glance toward Azrael. I may not be willing to out the role he played in all this—that reckoning is between him and Lucifer—but that doesn't mean I'm going to let him stop me from protecting my friend. "You've trained me. I—"

"You can barely hold a sword with two hands," he growls back.

My lips settle into a thin line, and I breathe through my nose as I try to find my patience. Is this our first fight?

And does that apply to only two or all three of us?

I don't have the time to consider it at the moment.

For all that I love him, Lucifer has the audacity to look nearly as bored with this as his siblings were with my PR proposal. "We're wasting valuable time entertaining this foolish line of thinking. Perhaps I can—"

"No," Azrael and I say.

For a moment, Lucifer looks like he's considering obeying it.

Mine and Azrael's combined command.

Oh, that is a whole other can of worms I cannot begin to get into right now.

Do I like the idea of Lucifer submitting to Azrael and me?

Of our dynamic going both ways?

Am I actually a *switch*?

Unpacking that will take a whole lot more therapy than even mine or Lucifer's bank account can handle.

I sigh, already exasperated. "Look, we all go together or none of us goes at all."

"*After* the CFDA Awards," Xzander shouts unhelpfully from across the room.

"We don't have time to—"

Lucifer gives me a pointed look. "He has a point, darling. If you and I don't show . . ."

The whole city will be on high alert, and our absence will be broadcast on live television, so any chance we have at stealth will be ruined.

"Fine. We'll all go together *after* the awards," I snap.

I'm not sure how I'm going to keep my cool in front of the paparazzi.

But if I plan to be leader of Team No Apocalypse, Lucifer's queen, and I'm giving whatever this little triad between Lucifer, Azrael, and I might be a chance, well . . .

I better start figuring out how to check my anxiety in the face of impending doom.

CHAPTER SIXTY-ONE

Azrael

I am *not* going to make it through this without killing somebody.

I slip undetected through the crowd of paparazzi, using my power to remain sight unseen. The press are falling all over themselves to get a glimpse of the "happy" couple. Charlotte's as beautiful as ever in a stunning mosaic stained glass gown, which makes her look so much like a moving art piece that practically every interviewer has asked about it. "It's a new in-house embroidery technique developed by Xzander Malone," she says for what must be the umpteenth time as Lucifer stands beside her in his usual Armani.

Timeless. Sophisticated. Authoritative.

He's been brand loyal ever since I brought him topside to a few of the city's fashion shows in the '70s and '80s.

When Gabriel threw open the gates of Hell and started God's little redemption competition over a decade ago, it wasn't the first time Lucifer and his siblings had managed to escape their cage. It was just the first occasion they'd all been given permission to come topside at once and stay here for any length of time.

Wrath's interference during WWII made my job particularly trying. I never did like that fucker.

Or any of my ex's divine family, for that matter.

I still remember the peace, the quiet, *before* his Dad got the crazy idea he should create "order" out of chaos.

I glance at Lucifer and Charlotte's screaming fans around me.

This is God's idea of order?

Lucifer's rebellion always made sense to me.

I pass through one of the paparazzi who's been absolutely relentless in his pursuit of Charlotte, feeling his heart sputter within my grip. He'll choke on a chicken wing later tonight alone in his apartment, and not a soul alive will be any wiser about it.

It's my job, after all.

And if this is order, well . . .

Then I say let chaos fucking reign.

I continue to slip through the crowd undetected, monitoring both Charlotte and my ex like a hawk as I keep my promise to play watchdog. One advantage of being Death is I don't need a corporeal body to contain me.

I am more infinite than this universe is vast. Both beginning and end.

But unlike my pompous ex, I've never allowed my celestial duties to go to my head.

Prideful motherfucker.

My gaze tracks to where Lucifer and Charlotte pose for yet another photo together on the red carpet. If it weren't for how fast her smile fades in between rounds of photos, you'd never be able to tell anything was wrong, that I fucked up—put the blade in play to punish Lucifer, and now her Seer of a best friend is in danger instead. But I've stalked the two of them long enough, even when they didn't know I was looking, that, though I may not have had Charlotte in all the ways Lucifer has, I know them both.

They're fucking perfect for one another.

It's almost disgusting, it's so obvious.

And they'll find a way to make it through any challenge.

Including this. And me.

Charlotte glances up at Lucifer, and there's such an intense, vulnerable adoration in her eyes that if I *had* a beating heart, I imagine it would ache at the sight of her love and devotion for him.

How could I ever consider coming between them when they're so clearly meant for each other?

But fuck, how I felt when she kissed me . . .

I haven't been able to get it out of my head ever since, and the answer to why I'm putting myself through this torture is simple.

My attention falls to Lucifer.

I know my ex. I know him well. I know him better than anyone, even Charlotte.

And while I may have *hated* her, loathed her very existence, the first time I laid eyes on her for how jealous I was of her, now that I know her, I . . .

Can't let him do to her what he did to me.

Break her heart. Destroy her because he's too fucked up to truly love anyone, Charlotte included. Not in the way they really need.

I still love him.

I don't fucking want to, but I do.

But I also hate him.

And in Charlotte, I've found a kindred spirit.

She understands me better than he ever could.

Because I once stood in her place.

He may have never looked at me with the playful affection in his eyes he has whenever he watches *her*, but I know for a fact that if left unchecked . . .

He'll destroy her. Even if he loves her.

Just like he nearly destroyed me.

Charlotte isn't ancient like I am.

She needs someone to protect her, be her buffer, so if and when the time comes, Lucifer's twisted obsession with her doesn't annihilate her completely.

And I guess I've decided there's no one better fit to protect her than me.

The former lover who's now going to be his enemy.

CHAPTER SIXTY-TWO

Charlotte

We're standing in what's essentially the backstage room at the CFDA Awards, held in the Beaux-Arts Court inside the Brooklyn Museum, and in less than five minutes Lucifer and I will be going out in front of the roughly five hundred and fifty celebrity attendees. I'm so full of nerves and unprocessed tension that my hands are practically shaking, but it's not the massive crowd of sitting dinner guests or even the thought of standing on stage in front of them all that has my anxiety skyrocketing.

Every minute passing on the clock feels like a mounting risk that something horrible will happen to Jax. If Lucifer hadn't gotten there just in the nick of time when Mark took *me* captive, if Azrael hadn't held on to my soul for a few moments longer out of sheer, devoted loyalty to the love he still holds for his ex, then I . . .

I can't even bring myself to think it.

My best friend is *not* going to die tonight.

Not if I have anything to say about it.

I need to find a way to get to her faster.

Waiting until the end of the awards show is definitely *not* okay with me.

My eyes dart to Lucifer. I understand where he and Azrael are coming from, where they might believe that my suggestion is the most logical, strategic, and fair agreement. They're trained celestial soldiers. For them, emotions aren't an important factor in decision-making.

But they are for me.

And I am not going to fail my best friend again.

Not for something as trivial, and honestly as out of touch, as these awards.

As I peek out toward the crowd from where I'm standing backstage, for the first time since debuting at Lucifer's side, I don't feel any admiration or kinship with them.

Instead, I feel disgust.

At the spectacle.

At what a monumental waste of money all this is.

There's no such thing as ethical consumption in a capitalist hellscape, I remind myself. Imani taught me that. She would think that, of course. But even to me, it's a flimsy excuse.

On the other side of the world, people are dying.

Hell, there are people dying here on these streets every day.

Yet we all conveniently ignore it and continue to prop up the system in the name of what? Capitalism? Corporate greed?

And like so many others, I fell into it headfirst.

Into the glitz and glamour. The seductive draw of the power it brought me. I'd spent so much of my life feeling small and powerless that at first it intoxicated me.

But what's the purpose of all this wealth if I'm not going to use it to create a better world? If I don't reach back my hand to help end others' suffering?

If not for that, then *what* is the goddamn point?

I nearly open my mouth to ask Lucifer that exact question, but he pulls me to him, and it's like whatever spell he casts that has me in an almost constant chokehold grips me by the throat again. Maybe Azmodeus is right.

Maybe I *don't* truly realize how dangerous Lucifer can be.

And now that I'm starting to, I'm . . .

Not certain I like what I see.

"Are you ready, darling?" he asks, that velvet-and-sin voice wrapping around me.

God, I want to lean into him, to melt into his arms like I always do, but something stops me.

A newfound sense of morality, I guess?

It's hard to justify this glamorous, glittering world he's made me a part of while I'm worried that my best friend could be out there dying because of me.

Because I didn't stop to consider that I needed to protect her. Her along with so many others. Team No Apocalypse? I almost scoff.

My mother would be ashamed of me.

I've become exactly like her.

A woman trapped by the will of a more powerful man.

The choice Lilith stole from me is about so much more than who my romantic partner is, about who I choose to fuck.

She robbed me of any chance or opportunity I might have had to self-actualize, to become self-reliant, my own person.

All my life I've been under the control of powerful men, and her son is no different.

Just as prideful. Just as wicked. Just as ruled by sin and greed.

The only difference is that Lucifer allowed me access to an extraordinary world. A more sinful, seductive side of myself that, at the time, empowered me.

I thought it was a stepping stone, and for a while, it was.

But really, now it's just the gilded cage I accused him of trying to keep me in.

And I'll stay forever trapped in that cage until I spend some time on my own, building my own life, making my own choices *without* his influence.

I'll never know if he's the one I'd choose.

If I don't start changing things.

For once, I need to rely on myself.

Something in my throat tightens.

This whole time it wasn't Lucifer who was taking my choices away. It was me.

It's always been up to me.

Despite how weak our connection's become, Lucifer must realize the depth of what I've discovered, because he steps back slightly, like he senses the space I need, and he doesn't just respect it, he yields to it.

"I can't do this, Lucifer. I can't."

His eyes narrow as he watches me. "Tell me you mean the awards show." Though we both know that's not what I mean.

"No." I shake my head. "No." I inhale a deep breath. "Please don't make me say it."

Lucifer's expression turns cold. "Ask me for what you want."

"I . . ."

Suddenly, I feel my heart in my throat.

This is what he's been training me for.

To be capable of standing by his side. Making my own decisions.

And now I see the true path before me.

Queen of my own life. Queen of my own goddamn choices.

"I've never lived this life for me or asked what I wanted, Lucifer. I can't go from being my father's captive to being yours. Not without learning who I am."

He looks at me curiously. "I thought we'd already been through this when we agreed about Azrael."

"We have, and I'm not talking about us romantically. What I said about giving both you and Azrael a fair chance still stands, but I . . . think I need to figure out who I am underneath all of that, without your"—I gesture toward him—"celestial presence looming over me."

"Before you willingly submit to being mine?"

I nod, almost shocked that he gets it.

Sometimes he's far more emotionally intelligent than I give him credit for.

He nods like this all makes sense to him, even though it's just now starting to make sense to me. "I understand. When my Father first cast me out, I had to rebuild. My identity, my sense of self, my kingdom. Once Lucifer, the Morning Star, the Lightbringer, leader of my Father's armies, His most faithful servant, and now—"

"The thief who stole my heart," I finish for him. "Prince of Darkness. Prince of wicked deeds."

He smirks at me. "Let me let you in on a sinful little secret." He leans in, whispering conspiratorially. "I thought I knew all the answers before you dropped into my life, but now I find I'm no longer so confident in what I thought was true."

I smile. I already knew without him having to tell me. "I can see that. The change in you." I take his hand in mine, giving it a gentle squeeze. "Now it's time for there to be some change in me. Maybe distance will be good for us both?"

He lifts my hand, brushing it with his lips. "Whatever you need, darling. For once, you tell me."

I grin at that.

"I need some time away from the penthouse. A chance to have my own place. Create a space of my own. Figure out what it is *I* want to do with my career, and this immortal existence you've given me, and then—"

"Then you'll come back to me?" he whispers hopefully.

"I will," I say honestly. "I always will. I know that probably sounds obvious considering that we're fated and all, but I'd like to think that if there's one thing I've learned from you, it's that I can be the architect of my own fate, the rebel of my own story, even if that makes me into someone else's villain. I want to shape my own destiny, make my own choices. For better or for worse. We're that much alike. I'll never be completely content with the idea of submitting to you, or anyone else for that matter, if I don't have this chance, this opportunity to make my own decisions, my own mistakes. Be my own person."

I take both his hands in mine. "Would you give me that? I know I'm already asking a lot of you, and I understand I don't need your permission anymore, but I guess I'm . . . asking for your support in this."

"Charlotte, my dove, are you asking for me to let you go so that, perhaps for the first time, you can fully be free?"

I nod, incredibly grateful that he seems to understand it, understand *me*.

He sighs long and low. "I don't like this. I don't fancy this at all, and if it were up to me alone, I would haul you back to *our* playroom right now and remind you of all the ways I know there are still parts of you that long to be within my control, but I will not make the mistake of holding you captive against your will again. Will not force you to choose us, choose me, even for my sake, because I love you. And so help me, I will do whatever it takes to prove to you that you have changed me, for the better this time. And *when* you are mine again—because let's both be honest, you *will* submit yourself to me, it's only a matter of time—you will do so of your own free will, and then your submission and the sinful promise of our eternity will be all the more sweet."

He leans down as if he means to lay a gentle kiss on my cheek, but before I can stop him, Lucifer hauls me into his arms, kissing me with everything he has, like he's pouring every bit of emotion he feels for us inside of me, so that when he releases me a few moments later, I'm needy. No longer so confident in my decision.

"Lucifer," I pant.

"If you think for a second I'm going to make this easy for you, or allow my little shit of an ex, Death, to steal you from me, you've both got another think coming," he whispers against my lips before he steals another quick kiss from me, catching my lower lip between his teeth and gently biting it until I moan as he tugs away. "Prepare for a seductive onslaught the likes of which you've never seen, because I am more stubborn and more strategic than even my Father, and if this competition between Azrael and me is to be a true war to win your heart, well, then best prepare yourself now. I never lose, and I'm not about to start. You'll be mine again before you know it."

CHAPTER SIXTY-THREE

Lucifer

As soon as Charlotte and I are offstage after finishing our quaint little intro speech to appease all the guests, I make a beeline to Azrael.

I don't need to see him to know he's there, lurking in the wings.

I make certain he and I are alone, and that Charlotte is out of sight—unable to see us both from where she's too busy with Sophie and the other members of our team fussing over her makeup as they prep her for our next onstage appearance in two minutes—before I reach out and grab Azrael by his invisible throat. The outline of his large body flickers a few times before he comes into full being.

I will fucking throttle him for getting inside Charlotte's head like this.

I slam him up against the nearest stage wall, baring my teeth, until he resumes his corporeal form. I slipped one of the museum's stagehands a few thousand dollars to ensure my microphone was turned off whenever I'm offstage.

A bloody good investment.

"If you think I'm going to allow you to steal her from me easily, think again, *lover*." I sneer the final word with all the derision I feel for him, a mocking gesture of what he used to be to me.

"That was never my intention," he growls back.

I release him quickly as one of the museum staff comes trudging by.

Even *I* cannot strangle out of him whatever semblance of life somehow animates the Angel of Death, though right now I wish to, quite frankly.

Whatever this bloody onslaught of temptation is that he's thrust upon *my* future wife, I will never forgive him for it.

Yet another reason he'll have to hate me.

It's hardly my fault I couldn't love him in the way he deserved.

We were both abundantly clear from the start what we could and couldn't be to one another. And though neither of us knew it at the time, I was bloody destined for someone else, obviously.

What I once felt for Azrael could never hold a candle to my devotion to Charlotte. Even if I do sometimes question what might have been different if my blasted Mother hadn't molded Charlotte with the sole purpose of her being my future queen.

"Then why?" I hold Azrael's cold, infinite gaze as if I can will the almighty Death to bow to my command. There once was a time I could, I'm afraid.

"I think you know," Azrael says.

My eyes darken. "Enlighten me."

And then he kisses me until I'm certain my lungs are no longer capable of consuming air.

Until I am reminded of all I was *before* Charlotte's love ruined me.

Her love has made me soft in ways that could be life-threatening for us both.

"What the fuck was that?" I snarl as his lips leave mine, my surprise sounding more like anger than what I actually feel.

The doubt he's created in me.

But neither of us are given a reprieve to answer that as Imani, Mia, and one of the stage managers come barreling up behind us.

"Where's Charlotte?" Mia demands, before Imani can get a word in edgewise, though if either of them saw what just happened between Azrael and me, they give no indication of it.

Imani lifts a brow, and I scowl at her. I have half a mind to fire Mia right then and there for using that kind of tone at me, along with whatever petty human jab caused her to sow a seed of doubt about my loyalty to Charlotte.

The same kind Death has just now sown inside me.

The insolent little fuck.

"I thought she was with you." I cast a surreptitious glance toward Azrael.

"She told us she was looking for *you*." Imani's eyes go wide. She exchanges worried looks with Mia and the museum's stage manager. The museum employee mutters a few words into her headset, and chaos erupts in the gallery room that's currently serving as backstage.

I know where Charlotte's gone off to before we've even fully begun to search for her.

I close my eyes, sighing long and low. Her friend.

That's what her quaint internal speech was all about.

She intends for her first true act of independence to be a heroic one.

I snarl. *Bloody fuck.*

I round upon Azrael. "Find her. Bring her back to me," I growl as if he is still *mine* to command. For the first time since my brother stripped my abilities from me, I feel what it means to be well and truly powerless.

And I hate it. I hate that I must ask this of him.

I fucking hate it so bloody much that as soon as I have a hold of that insignificant Holy Lance, the *real* one, I will use it to torture Michael for the rest of eternity.

As soon as this whole charade is over, regaining what my brother has stolen from me will be my first and highest priority. Along with reclaiming Charlotte's heart, of course.

My Father's Armageddon can wait until I'm well and goddamn ready.

Azrael's eyes go wide at the dominant tone of my command, but he doesn't try to resist it. "I can't, Lightbringer. If I were to leave your side . . ."

My siblings and everyone present would know exactly how vulnerable Michael has made me.

If it weren't for the trick, the distraction I have up my sleeve.

I attempt to snag Azrael by the throat again, but this time he's ready for me, using my weight against me so that suddenly our positions are flipped.

I chuckle and lean into where he clutches me like I am still the one with the upper hand. "If you truly mean what I think you do with that little kiss, Azrael, then allow me to make one thing abundantly clear." I draw as close to him as I'm possibly able. "You *will* choose her over me. Always. Starting now and for the rest of time. For infinity. She is *all* that matters, that is my one and only ask of you. Do I make myself clear?"

Azrael releases my throat as he swallows. "Yes, sir," he whispers.

A feeling of satisfaction courses through me.

Death is under my command once again.

At least when it comes to this.

"Good," I growl. "Then go find our girl, Reaper. Consequences be damned."

CHAPTER SIXTY-FOUR

Charlotte

I've locked myself in the ladies' room on the other side of the closed museum as I try to figure out what my next move is. It's not like I can make it out through the regular exits without anyone noticing me, and with the amount of paparazzi prowling around, that'd be asking for a whole different kind of trouble than I'm already going to be in.

Lucifer and Azrael are going to lose their shit over this.

But honestly, I don't really care.

I'm in charge of my life.

Me.

And making my first act of independence saving my bestie from some radicalized asshat who betrayed us both seems like the perfect decision to me.

That's my best guess as to why Ian's doing this. He was so salty because I refused to date him, he turned into some kind of freaking incel or something. Or maybe he was one from the start? He *had* to be the one who drugged Jax at Az's club. Just like I originally thought.

Ugh.

"Big Guy, when am I going to catch a break from all these unhinged men you keep throwing at me?" I grumble up at the ceiling as I pace the length of the bathroom.

Someone tries the handle a second later, and a loud shout follows.

Fuck. They've already found me.

It's not like I made it that hard.

Even in a museum of this size, there are only so many places with a locking door that isn't someone's office.

I have a matter of minutes or seconds to get the hell out of here before one of the security guards comes along with the key, or Lucifer—or Azrael, considering Lucifer's current celestial-dysfunction situation—manages to kick the door in.

"Think, Charlotte. Think," I mutter, gripping both sides of the bathroom sink.

I can't call Azmodeus for help, even though I'm sure he'd answer, because stripped of his powers or not, Lucifer would absolutely *end* Azmodeus if he and I were to get into trouble together again any time soon. I may not be his full-time sub currently, but Lucifer is the head of our immortal family, and we're likely still getting married for the sake of the press if not because we both clearly love each other. And I haven't mastered my own powers enough in mine and Greed's training sessions in order to—

That's it!

"Greed!" I practically shout, as if yelling her name into the empty marble bathroom of the Brooklyn Museum might somehow summon her. I left my iPhone with Mia while I was onstage, so it's not like I can pick up the damn thing and call Greed, where she's sitting in the audience. She likely doesn't have her phone unmuted anyway.

An idea sparks, fast and furious.

I sigh. "Please, God, let this work."

I draw Greed's sigil on the bathroom mirror using my lipstick—another witchy trick Jax taught me—before I pull out what spare cash I have inside my clutch. I have a few hundred-dollar bills along with the spare lighter I keep in there for when Lucifer's run empty. I hold up one of the bills and light it like it's sacred sage or one of my fiancé's cigarettes.

I fumble with the lighter, nearly burning myself.

Damn it, if this doesn't work, I'm going to look ridiculous the moment Lucifer and whoever else is outside the door manages to burst in here.

"Greed. Greed," I hiss under my breath.

It's like I'm back in Sunday school or church, trying to get the attention of one of my friends from the other side of the aisle in the middle of my father's preaching.

The fire on the edge of the bill sparks out.

Money doesn't burn as easily as you'd expect it to.

Even with the supposedly trace amounts of cocaine.

I relight it just as another hefty round of fist-pounding starts outside the door, feverishly muttering to myself as if somehow Greed can hear me.

If Lucifer can summon an archangel like Michael by killing a whole megachurch full of evangelical assholes, then surely, I can summon my beloved future-sister-in-law, Greed, by illegally burning a few bank notes in her honor.

Right? Right?

The logic seems a bit sus, even to me.

The bill sparks out again, and now the lighter's flint is also fucking with me, so I'm about to give up on that technique and desperately try another. Would making it rain with this small of a bill stack work? Maybe I need to *celebrate* Greed's love of money rather than burning some like an offering to her—but then Greed pops into existence right beside me.

She lifts a brow at the sight of her sigil drawn in lipstick on the bathroom mirror. "You tried to *summon* me?"

I gape a little at the sight of her. "It actually worked?"

She makes an expression that's full of pity. "No. Call it a big sister's intuition." She shrugs.

Another round of shouts come from outside the door as my eyes narrow on her.

"Oh all right, you and my brother were supposed to be onstage two minutes ago, and it's clear to the *entire* guest list and half the country who's watching the livestream that the real fun is happening backstage, so I thought I'd come looking for you. To help stir up a bit of sisterly trouble."

"How much trouble are you hoping to get into?"

Greed's red-painted lips twist wickedly.

Just as I hear someone fumbling with what sounds like a large ring of keys outside the bathroom door.

My heart races. "I'll pay you everything in my current bank account to get me out of here."

"Not enough." Greed eyes me up and down. "Though I like a woman who knows how to negotiate."

"I promise you'll like me even better if you get us both out *now*."

Greed bats her long, perfect lashes at me. "Money is my favorite, but offer me something *else* that interests me, little sister."

"An exclusive first look at my powers."

A crease forms between Greed's brows.

"You wanted to see me angry? I'll show you angry. I'm about to unleash all the power I've been holding in on some asshole who's gotten hold of my friend. And I'll let you livestream it."

That piques her interest. "Tempting, but no. My followers would love it, but I'm your trainer. I'll find out eventually, anyway."

"Fine. Then I'll come and work for you exclusively," I say. "Three months."

"You'll quit Apollyon?"

"I think I was already planning to."

Her brow furrows.

"Lucifer and I are . . . It's complicated. Though that may not be an option anymore if you don't hurry the hell up and get me out of here."

"Interesting," Mimi purrs, smirking at me just as the door to the bathroom bursts open.

I turn, thinking we've run out of options, that I won't be able to save Jax after all, or by the time I get to her it'll be too late. Not to mention Lucifer and Azrael might both murder me.

But then I feel the soft, buttery grip of Greed's plump hand wrap around my wrist, and suddenly I'm being sucked inside the ether, and everything fades to black.

CHAPTER SIXTY-FIVE

Lucifer

The moment it becomes apparent to me that Charlotte is no longer locked inside the ladies' room—having clearly absconded with my blasted bitch of a sister, if the sight of her sigil written upon the bathroom mirror in lipstick is any indication—I abandon that plan in favor of another.

Azrael *will* find her and bring her back to me safely.

I can't allow myself to entertain any alternative prospects.

And for now, I have a human audience to amuse, it seems.

I make a beeline away from the Beaux-Arts Court, where the awards show is currently paused, and head nearby to the museum's Egyptian gallery.

A large gold sarcophagus stands upright in a glass box in the middle of one of the rooms, and I make my way toward it. "I suppose I'm going to have to do this the old-fashioned way."

I strip off the coat of my tux, casting it overtop the display as I feverishly begin searching the other cases. It takes me a few moments, but then I find what I need.

An ancient ceremonial dagger.

The sizable donation I'll make to the museum for this will be well worth the trouble, as far as their curatorial staff are concerned.

Not bothering to wrap my jacket around my hand, I promptly punch straight through the glass of the dagger's case.

Which in hindsight is some questionable judgment on my part.

"Bloody fuck," I roar, cradling my now-bleeding hand. "How do any of them ever *live* like this?" Pain is considerably worse without my abilities.

I cast a wayward look at the dagger, realizing I no longer require it, as I'm vaguely aware of an alarm bell going off like a siren and flashing over my head.

What good do they think that god-awful sound or their security guards are going to do? Scare me off? Put me in jail?

I may be down on my luck as of late, but even without my powers, there's little any of them could do to stop me.

Already having what I need, I drop to my knees and manically paint several of my satanic symbols across the floor. I'm no Michelangelo, but for now they'll do as I chant in ancient Latin. "Procedite, legiones meae. Venite ad me."

Proceed, my legions. Come to me.

I continue my chant, feeling a bit of my hellish power called forth, though I'm not able to access it currently, but I can sense it there, lurking in the shadows.

Biding its time until the world is ready.

Abaddon appears at my side a moment later, still wearing the Canadian lumberjack he was previously. This time, he drops his gaze in deference. "You summoned me, my lord."

I nod, staggering to my feet. "Tell the legions it's time. Bring them forth." I let out an arrogant laugh. "Let all of Heaven and Earth tremble."

CHAPTER SIXTY-SIX

Charlotte

Inside the ether, the swirling mass of a map made of stars glitters in front of me.

In the few moments it takes for me to explain to Greed who I'm trying to locate and where I suspect Ian and Jax might be, I manage to convince myself this isn't a half-bad idea.

Until Greed announces she plans to abandon me.

"All right, well, now you're on your own. Ta ta for now, dear sister."

"Wait!" I make a grab for her, but she yanks her hands away. "Aren't you going to—?"

"I promised to get you out of there, nothing more. Nothing less." She stares down the bridge of her nose at me and shrugs. "Consider this a lesson in celestial dealmaking."

She moves to snap her fingers, and I have to practically dive on top of her to stop her from leaving. I thought we would be doing this *together*.

Greed's my trainer, after all. And that's what I'd hoped she was going to do.

Give me a little on-the-job training. Teach me how to rip Ian limb from limb.

Not abandon me at the first opportunity.

She is *absolutely* just like a big sister. And like every older sister before her, she plans to teach me about her world the hard way.

"Let me go," she growls, trying to shake me off.

"At least show me where I'm supposed to go," I say, clasping my hands over hers before I bring them together in front of me. Like I'm praying to her.

I'm not above getting on my knees and begging if it will get me to Jax faster.

Greed rolls her eyes. "Fine."

It takes only a second of her searching the glittering pinpricks on the celestial map before she announces, "See. There. Seers shine brighter than regular humans."

How she can tell the difference between *that* specific speck of stardust and the millions of others swirling inside the tiny starlit map of the city, let alone the surrounding world, is beyond me. But that isn't something I have time to figure out or consider.

I guess that speck *does* sort of shine a teeny bit brighter? If Jax were here, she would absolutely crack a joke about how I'm just too used to dimming my own light to recognize her true brilliance.

Now that I think about it, there may be something deeper to that, honestly.

Greed isolates the destination from the swirling stardust menu like she's annoyed she has to do it, but she still cues it up for me. "There. You're on your own now. Happy?"

And with that, she's gone.

Leaving me standing there alone inside the ether.

I almost start hyperventilating, but then I take a few slow, deliberate breaths, visualizing the calm, collected woman I want to be.

"You got this, Charlotte," I mutter as I touch the glittering bit of stardust Mimi selected for me.

A sudden force pulls me forward by a sharp tug at my navel until I feel like I'm being torn apart and then sewn back together again. A few pieces of the mosaic stained glass of my dress cut into me.

Note to self: Do not wear glass statement pieces during divine travel.

This is so much worse when I'm the one in charge of it.

But before I realize that my celestial roller coaster ride is basically over, my feet abruptly slam into the ground, and one of my heels cracks beneath me.

Jesus, I better learn to teleport in heels or next time wear tennis shoes, I think as I take in the scene before me.

Oh shit.

I so have *not* got this.

CHAPTER SIXTY-SEVEN

Charlotte

Like the celestial rookie I am, I expected to find Ian and Jax alone, since there was no indication he was acting as anything *other* than a free agent. But I know I've made a major mistake the moment I see Ian standing there, intimidated and shaking, terrified by the sight of my Mother-in-Law.

Honestly, I know the feeling.

Lilith advances on him like she couldn't care less about the blade in his hand, one of her turning into three as she surrounds him.

Even if it's the real Holy Lance, it probably won't work on her anyway.

I hunker down where I stand in the top row of the pews. We're inside my father's old megachurch, Victory in His Name, and thankfully, the stadium seating is completely empty, but I'm still far enough away that neither of them is likely to see me.

And I know this place like the back of my hand.

I practically grew up here.

Before my father transformed it into the Righteous stronghold it is now.

Not that it was any better *before* its Christian nationalism days.

A cult is still a cult by any other name.

Ian's head swivels back and forth between the three Liliths, and Jax starts to scream, the sound muffled by the gag Ian's shoved into her mouth.

I stay low, trying to get a read on what's happening without alerting Jax or anyone else that I'm here. My Mother-in-Law wants grandbabies, so even if I got between her and Ian, she wouldn't hurt me, right?

But then Michael steps forth from the shadows, and any chance I might have had of getting both Jax and me out of this safely is gone.

What the hell is *he* doing here?

Michael's eyes immediately fall to the blade in Ian's hand, his gaze narrowing like he's insanely pissed that Ian has a hold of it, and I finally put two and two together.

Whoever possesses it is said to win any battle, Lucifer's voice echoes inside my head.

That's why Michael is approaching so slowly.

Why he hasn't just lunged at Ian and taken it.

Which means . . .

I read Azrael's expression earlier correctly.

This blade *isn't* a fake. Even if the one Michael had previously was.

My blood runs cold.

"Mother, we had an agreement," Michael says. "Your Seer for my blade."

"What?" Ian says, rounding on Michael, a desperate look in his eye as the blade he holds against Jax's throat cuts into her skin and she starts to bleed.

She lets out a muffled cry, and I flinch.

Focus, Charlotte. Focus.

How am I supposed to get us both out of here?

"That wasn't what *we* agreed on," Ian continues.

An idea strikes as I make my way toward the church's sound and recording booth. *Please, God. Please let this work. Please.*

There are very few things I've prayed for harder.

The audio booth is exactly as I remember it, which makes it so I'm able to work quickly. It was only a few months ago I was regularly in here.

God, it seems like a whole lifetime has passed since then.

I focus my attention back on Michael as I move through the motions, trying to parse out the implications of what I'm overhearing. I could practically do this in my sleep.

If Michael used Ian and the Righteous to abduct Jax in exchange for the blade, the *real* one, that means . . .

Lilith had the true blade all along.

The anthrax. Olivia . . .

It was all her.

But did she *actually* want me dead?

Or was she playing Lucifer and Michael off one another?

She's the one who destined me for Lucifer, after all.

I finish setting up the recording equipment, breathing deep to calm myself from where my hands are starting to shake.

But I've got this. How many times did I have to help the boomers in the congregation with the PR equipment? Too many times, if you ask me.

It's *not* that hard to learn.

You can look basically anything up on your phone these days.

Including a random Kansas megachurch's livestream.

Michael may have his angelic army, but he won't have the loyalty of the Righteous anymore. Not for long.

Not if it's up to me.

"You honestly didn't expect me to keep my word, did you?" he says to Ian. "You humans were always too trusting of anyone with wings. You might remember that Eve made the same mistake."

"You promised *us* the blade. Rapture. That we'd enter God's kingdom as the ones who made the Serpent fall, if only we did what you asked." Ian looks a bit panicked as Lilith in all three of her forms circles him, and for a moment, I almost feel a little sorry for him.

If he wasn't still holding a knife to Jax's throat, I might even consider trying to save his sorry ass.

"And you shall." Michael's lips twist into a cruel, mirthless smile. "Enter my Father's kingdom, that is. Now that my siblings and I are through with you."

Suddenly Azrael appears at my side, covering my mouth with one of his large hands to stifle my scream. "Shhh, it's only me, baby girl," he grumbles next to my ear, causing a shiver to run through me. "Don't tell me you didn't anticipate that I'd find you?"

"I did actually, which is part of why I was willing to risk my own neck and come here. I *knew* you'd follow me, you freaking stalker."

"Always." Azrael grins at me, the skeletal side of his features flashing.

"Do you know how to work a camera?"

"Why wouldn't I—?"

"Lucifer doesn't even like to text, so I thought maybe you—"

"Celestial beings are not a monolith," he hisses at me, quickly growing impatient. Daddy Death may be the stoic, silent type, but he has a furiously cold temper when I push him. Needling him during our training sessions has taught me that much.

"Okay, okay." I throw up my hands in surrender. "Point taken. Just press this button when I'm down near Michael"—I point to it—"and then help me get Jax out of here, would you?"

Azrael's nostrils flare. "You expect me to let you face Michael and Lilith? *Without* me?" His eyes take on a fiery blue look, like there's no way in hell he'd consider ever doing such a thing.

"It's not your choice," I snap. "You don't own me."

He goes still, understanding exactly what that means.

I'm a free agent now.

And I won't let this go.

"You can come right after me. Please, Azrael."

"If Lucifer finds out about this—"

"Then don't let him find out," I whisper as I slip out of the sound booth.

CHAPTER SIXTY-EIGHT

Azrael

The last time I had to save Charlotte from herself, I understood that, despite all appearances to the contrary, she didn't actually have a death wish.

This time, I'm not so certain.

She strips off her heels and barrels down the aisle with all the grace of a bull in a china shop. I never have figured out how humanity came up with that particular saying—what idiot fucked around and found out? Though, in truth, I've seen stupider deaths—but in this instance, the description is fitting.

Lucifer likes his women gutsy, I'll give him that much.

All eyes turn toward Charlotte as she rushes down the stairs, her friend thrashing and struggling at the sight of her.

I take that as my cue and hit the recording booth button, fading into the Nothing so that I'm no longer visible. When I reform, I'll be right where Charlotte'll need me.

Michael and Lilith might feel me, but they sure as fuck can't find me.

I'm a ghost, plain and simple.

That feeling you get when you think someone's watching you, only to turn around and find there's no one there.

The hairs on the back of Charlotte's friend's neck rise. Like she can feel me too.

She's a powerful Seer. No wonder Lilith wants a piece of her.

Lucifer's Mother loves her fucking prophecies.

Michael, that predictable fucker—who I *so* regret gifting my old sword to—looks furious at Charlotte's sudden appearance. "I thought I told you to stay out of my way." His voice is full of self-righteous fury.

Fuck, I regret ever dating him.

Lucifer never would let me live that particular rebound down.

But when you're as old and ancient as we are, well, everybody ends up fucking everybody sooner or later. There's no such thing as a choosy immortal.

Or a heterosexual one, for that matter.

Charlotte smiles, giving a devil-may-care shrug. "Why don't you ask Lucifer how good I am at listening?"

I chuckle. Lucifer's little siren is ballsy.

A she-devil in her own right.

Clearly, she's been taking a page out of her "Daddy's" playbook.

Though it won't be long before Lucifer's not the only one she calls Daddy.

Come hell or high water, I'll make her mine.

She turns her attention to the guy with the knife on her friend. "I'd say I'm sorry that Michael fucked you and the other members of the Righteous over, but I'm not, so . . . Sorry, not sorry?" She shrugs like she couldn't care less about this whole thing.

Though I know that couldn't be further from the truth.

She's a freaking Chaos Muppet.

How did I not see it sooner?

She and Lucifer are starting to make a whole lot more fucking sense. Even without Lucifer's malicious bitch of a Mother having a hand in it.

"There's only one way to expose a false prophet for what he is, did you know that, Ian?" Charlotte turns her attention back to Lucifer's brother. "You let him speak his truth for the masses. Say hi to the world, Michael." She points up toward the high-end cameras mounted on the ceiling and gives a cheeky wave.

The church's livestream is broadcasting this whole thing.

But Michael's truly in this for the blade.

He withdraws the sword I gave him so long ago, and Charlotte's eyes go wide.

Like hell will I let him use it on mine and Lucifer's woman.

Because until she makes her choice, she's exactly that.

Ours.

I can't speak for Lucifer, but I won't ever make her choose.

I seize the moment to reform as I tackle Michael, just as Lilith lunges forward like the venomous snake of a son she gave birth to and tears into the guy with the spear who's got a hold of her precious Seer. She's been a total man-eater since God majorly fucked her over.

Not to say that I blame her.

The asshole with the lance gets what was coming to him.

Within a few seconds he's nothing but blood, a few wayward limbs, and viscera. Charlotte's friend is screaming for her ever-loving life behind the gag before I'm pretty sure she passes out from shock. Charlotte pales like she's all of two moments away from doing the same, but then her eyes narrow on where the Holy Lance has now clattered to the floor, and she darts toward it.

Just as Michael manages to land an uppercut on my jaw and wriggles himself out from under me. He moves to blast some of his blinding light toward Charlotte.

Lucifer isn't the only one of his angelic siblings who has light-wielding abilities. He was just the first who was smart enough to figure out how to wield *other* kinds of light. Hence, Lightbringer. Plus, the whole spreading knowledge to Eve and humanity is its own kind of enlightenment. No more shadows-on-the-walls-of-Plato's-cave sort of thing.

Even if I will *never* admit to him that I thought the whole thing was fucking brilliant.

"Charlotte!" I shout, drawing her attention just in time for her to dive out of the way and roll.

I growl in approval.

Clever girl.

I fucking told her those practice falls would come in handy.

Lilith breaks out of her feeding frenzy then as she lets out a furious shriek. "Absolutely *not*, Michael! You will not ruin my one chance of your brother finally giving me grandbabies." She rounds upon Michael, stepping in between him and Charlotte with the furious look only a mother can give, and Michael shrinks back like the celestial child he's always been.

"Mom, be reasonable." Michael lifts his hands in surrender, backing away as Lilith advances on him. "I just want the blade, that's all."

I take that as my cue and evaporate as I make my way toward Charlotte's friend.

Charlotte's now covered in blood, mostly from the guy whose soul I still need to reap.

Though some of the blood may actually be hers thanks to the shards of that fucking glass dress she's wearing.

As her trainer, we're going to have a long discussion about choosing fashion over function. Glass clothing is *not* practical for battle.

Charlotte picks up the Holy Lance, clutching it tight with the correct grip just like I taught her.

Good girl.

Something dormant inside me stirs.

Lucifer isn't the only one of us who has dominant tendencies.

Another reason why he and I didn't exactly work out.

"He aimed to kill me," Charlotte says, egging Lilith on. Despite how she just witnessed Lilith completely eviscerate the guy who was about to hurt her friend, for some reason she trusts her future Mother-in-Law not to turn on her.

What *is* it with this goddamn family?

I can't begin to make heads or tails of it.

"Did you?" Lilith's head snakes back toward Michael, and the edges of her naked body flicker like static on an old television screen. The Goddess of Creation is considering becoming three again, instead of one.

Michael shakes his head. "It wasn't like that, Ma. I wasn't trying to kill her, just stop her. I want to *convert* her."

"To help in your effort to get your Father to return?" Lilith sneers. Now Michael has *majorly* pissed her off.

Nothing like divorce drama between the two creators of everything.

Michael looks to Charlotte. "Come to my side, and there doesn't have to be any more fighting. Mother's just going to borrow your little Seer here, and then—"

"Oh, shut up, Michael," Lilith snarls. She snaps her fingers, and Michael suddenly doesn't have any lips, his mouth no longer even there. He paws at his face, desperately trying to shout but sounding like Charlotte's friend did before she passed out.

Lilith turns her attention to Charlotte.

I take that as my cue.

"What do you want with her?" Charlotte asks, inching slightly closer toward her friend.

Lilith's eyes track the movement, but she seems stymied over what to do.

She *really* wants grandchildren.

One of the many reasons she was never thrilled about the prospect of Lucifer and me.

Death isn't exactly known for creating life, even if I'd chosen to take a female form.

And Lucifer is Lilith's oldest and favorite child.

The apple didn't fall very far from the tree.

Lilith watches Charlotte curiously, as if she's trying to divine what the new little immortal she created is going to do next. I'm not sure what God expected when He shaped the divine chaos that created Him into the form of a woman and then made her into His wife and sub, but I don't think it was this.

Lilith is a true monster.

And that is why we do *not* fuck with raw celestial materials.

"I just need to borrow her for one teensy-weensy little prophecy." Lilith smiles, and the look is so similar to Lucifer's, Charlotte stiffens slightly.

Almost there, baby girl.

I circle the matter that will soon be my hand around her friend's wrist.

"I thought you could make your own prophecies?" Charlotte says.

If I had eyebrows right now, they'd definitely be lifted.

Okay, clearly Charlotte and Lilith have met before.

I nearly swear and give my exact location away. I *knew* I shouldn't have left her alone before the play party the other day. I've kept my eye on her every other minute. Save for when Lucifer has her in his playroom.

I'm not *that* much of a creeper.

"That was *my* prophecy." Lilith smiles like a human mother who's patiently teaching her daughter how to cook. "Your Seer is one of my Husband's prophets, and I'd love to know what He's doing."

Just keep her talking, baby girl. I've almost got you.

I snake what will soon be my other hand around Charlotte.

This would be a helluva lot easier if I knew Lilith couldn't sense me, but she's taking her sweet old time because she's trying to discern how to find me, sniff me out.

She hated when I refused to be locked up along with the other boy toy Horsemen.

I am no goddess's concubine.

Except maybe for the budding little goddess right in front of me.

Charlotte's going to give Lilith a run for her money by the time Greed and I are done training her. If Lucifer doesn't fuck it up in the meantime.

"And what do you need His prophecy for?"

Lilith remains uncharacteristically patient. "I gave up some of my power to support my Husband's creation. The fail-safe to His little humanity experiment, which we locked away as—"

"The Four Horsemen," Charlotte finishes.

She's a quick study.

Lilith nods. "Well, three of them were locked away. Their power belongs to me, and when Michael and Lucifer release them, I intend to reclaim it as mine."

"To do what?" Charlotte asks. "Punish God?"

"Yes." Lilith grins like she's ridiculously pleased that Charlotte understands her.

Charlotte's gaze darts toward Michael. "Then why not just let Michael start the apocalypse? Why play him and Lucifer off one another?"

"Caught on to that, did you?" Lilith's smile widens.

The only reason I haven't dragged Charlotte and her friend right the fuck out of here is because whatever Lilith's up to, I'm pretty certain Lucifer and Charlotte need to hear it. I'm poised to go at any second.

Until one of Lilith's heads tilts toward me, and I know that she's found me.

Motherfucker.

"Why don't you tell her yourself what ending my Husband would mean for the souls He created, Azrael?"

All at once, Lilith turns into three, the nearest snatching a clawlike hand out toward me, but then a blast of dark shadow sends her tumbling backward, and I realize that Charlotte has just dropped the Holy Lance and used some of her powers on purpose. For the first time.

To pick a fight with her future Mother-in-Law over me.

Shit. We are so fucked.

An echoing bang sounds from the church's stadium doors, drawing all attention.

I become corporeal and lift my gaze just in time to see that the one immortal who could manage to talk Lilith out of destroying both Charlotte and me has just arrived.

"Lucifer," Charlotte gasps.

"Fashionably late as always, I'm afraid." He grins.

How the hell did he—?

He steps into the megachurch, Lilith and his brother's eyes going wide at the sight of what—no, *who*—he's brought with him.

Demons.

Hundreds. Thousands of them.

His legions brought topside.

Their possessed, blackened eyes train upon his Mother.

Holy shit.

My ex has finally unleashed full Hell upon Earth.

Dread twists in my gut as I realize how majorly fucked we're all about to be.

God help us.

CHAPTER SIXTY-NINE

Charlotte

I glance at my hands, only vaguely aware I just used them to nearly blast my soon-to-be Mother-in-Law in two, all the anger building up inside me over the last several weeks coming out in one enormous rush. But I can't even consider that right now.

My heart races at the sight of my fiancé.

"Lucifer," I breathe, an odd mixture of fear and warmth expanding inside my chest.

My devilish savior.

Lucifer descends the center aisle of the stadium seats, his footsteps echoing despite the thousands of black-eyed people that silently trail him, at the ready.

His legions. Thousands of them.

All brought topside to protect me.

I can hardly comprehend what I'm seeing.

"I believe you and I have a few scores to settle, Mother."

"Lucifer." Lilith's voice takes on a nervous edge, like she's desperate to placate him.

My devil of a fiancé certainly knows how to command a room.

My heart flutters, the heat in my body rising in admiration as his gaze flicks toward me.

Go, he sends down the line of what's left of our connection. *Get out* now.

I give the barest shake of my head.

The choice is mine.

And I'm not leaving here without Jax.

The hellfire in Lucifer's eyes turns molten, and I know that the next time he has me alone in the playroom, he'll punish me for risking myself like this.

I press my lips together, suppressing my coy grin.

I look forward to it.

Slowly, I inch toward Jax, trying not to draw Lilith's attention. Michael is still too busy trying to undo whatever bind Lilith's placed on him, which appears to have stymied him in more ways than one and Azrael is working hard not to draw any further attention to himself.

"I only ever had your best intentions in mind, sweetheart," Lilith says, placing her hands over her chest as she makes her plea. "You know better than anyone what your Father's like. It's high time He get a taste of His own medicine. Locking my babies away, siphoning my power, and now abandoning us all? Well, you might see where I thought having *you* take His place would be a better—"

"Enough, Mother," Lucifer growls.

And to my shock, Lilith falls silent in deference to him.

I can see the way she might have once catered to her cherished baby boy, spoiling and doting upon his every need.

I roll my eyes. No wonder he always expects to get what he wants.

"If you so much as lay a hand upon Charlotte, I'll throw you back into the Abyss and lock you in the cage Father put you in, and you will never lay eyes on a single one of your grandchildren."

Lilith's lip quivers. "You wouldn't."

Lucifer's nostrils flare, the expression he gives her loud and clear.

Try me.

Lilith begins to tremble, her hands clenched into fists as the ground gives a sudden lurch, nearly knocking me and everyone else in the room off our feet.

The blade falls from my hand, clattering to the floor, but I can't even consider how I'm going to try and reach it as time and space start to warp around us unpredictably.

My eyes fall to the Goddess's face, and I realize, it's . . .

Lilith's tears.

Fuck my life.

One streams down her face, its descent distorting reality until we're all being molded and crushed at the edges. Pressure erupts inside my skull, the pain causing an earsplitting ringing.

"Lucifer."

I'm uncertain how to put a stop to this, how to end this hell, but somehow amid the chaos of it all, I know if that tear falls, reality will rip. Like a black hole. A fissure.

A tear in the fabric of the universe itself.

"I won't let him do that."

Abruptly, reality rights itself, and I realize only as I bring my hand to my head, still in a haze, that the tender words came from me.

Lilith looks to me, a terrifying bit of hope in her eyes.

"Charlotte," Lucifer growls, as if to say *Let me handle this.*

But I'm not about to let him make her cry once more.

"I won't agree to him keeping you from your grandchildren."

I meet Lilith's eyes, and for the first time, I see what connects her to me.

Her subjugation. The abuse.

I know what it's like to feel as if your power has been stolen from you completely.

"I understand why you did it. Played Michael and Lucifer. Why you want vengeance against God. Truly I do." I nod as she slowly faces me. "You want what's best for your son, for your children, and He took that from you. Made you feel powerless."

"Yes," she whispers, her eyes clouding with white, a bit of her divine form unleashed. Though her expression is full of adoration, like she couldn't be prouder of what she created, and it . . .

Terrifies me.

My pulse thrashes in my ears.

But I am no one's celestial plaything.

Not even Lilith's.

"But I can't allow you to end humanity like this."

"We can restart," she says, reaching out as if to take my hands in hers. "You, me, Lucifer. Build anew."

And, for a moment, the offer is . . . strangely tempting.

I've spent so much of my life seeing the brokenness of this world. The worst humanity has to offer.

But I have to believe there's beauty to be found in it all too.

Beneath the rubble.

"I can't let you do that."

She smiles softly. "My prophecy says otherwise."

"About that," Lucifer interrupts as if he intends to tell his mother *exactly* how he feels about her "quaint little prophecy."

But I won't risk him upsetting her again.

"Later," I say, shooting a tense look at him.

He and several of his demonic army have drawn so close to Lilith now, they could reach out and touch.

And I can feel Azrael's chilling presence looming behind me.

"Time to get out of here, little siren," he whispers into my ear.

But Lilith and I are both an equal distance away from Jax, and the Holy Lance still lies at my feet.

I shake my head.

I can't leave without her.

"Your prophecy was wrong," I say to Lilith. "I won't allow you or anyone else to control me."

Lilith's lips quirk. The smirk she gives me is so reminiscent of Lucifer, I can't seem to breathe.

What have I gotten myself into?

But then Lucifer appears just behind Lilith's shoulder. "*Now*, Charlotte."

Chaos erupts inside the sanctuary.

I lunge for the blade, intending to use it against Lilith, just as Lilith throws herself at Jax, narrowly escaping Lucifer's grip.

Lilith and Jax vanish in a flash, the chair Jax was still tied to taken with them.

There and gone in a blink.

A sudden incapacitating fear takes over me. Like there's not enough oxygen in the room.

"No. No, no, no, no, no."

I can't lose another friend.

Can't allow anyone else to *die* because of me.

Lucifer is crouched at my side seconds later. "Take her," he orders, and I realize from where he's looking overtop my head that he isn't speaking to me.

Azrael.

The cold brush of Death's grip circles my wrist, just as I realize—

The blade.

I missed it, my hand knocking it askew by several feet.

It lies on the floor on the other side of the stage, where Michael now stands unbound, at the ready. He bends down and picks it up, chuckling.

"Go!" Lucifer shouts, and this time, I know better than to disobey him.

I'm wrenched backward, my body being sucked or dragged in a way that's a thousand times worse than traveling through the ether. The next thing I know, I'm lying on the floor in Lucifer's office, someone else's blood—Ian's, my brain identifies—completely coating me.

Once again, the dress I'm wearing is ruined, and considering this one was on loan from Xzander's latest contribution to the Fashion Institute, this seriously can't become a habit.

I sit up, swaying slightly as the full gravity of what just happened settles into me.

"Jax."

I scramble to my feet, desperately searching around myself like I might find some way to get to her.

But there's nothing.

Azrael's at my side a moment later, gripping the sides of my face with both hands as he kisses me. The feel of his lips on mine calms me. Helps me find my center.

"You're okay. You're okay. You're safe now," he whispers against me.

And it's only then I realize I'm trembling.

"Jax. Ian. He—"

"I know," he says, holding me tight, refusing to let me go. "I know, baby girl."

And the Holy Lance. Michael.

"Lucifer."

A fresh round of panic shoots through me.

Azrael pulls me into his chest, cradling my head to keep me from trembling. "He'll be fine. He always is," he whispers feverishly.

My thoughts take a dark turn as I survey Lucifer's office. It's completely unchanged. Though my entire world has just been knocked on its side.

"We'll find her," Azrael says, knowing exactly what I need to hear. "You have my word."

I nod weakly, still in shock. I'm uncertain if there's anything else I can do at this point.

I can't face Lilith on my own. Even if I knew how to find her.

I was a fool to think I could.

"You saved *me* this time." Azrael tips my chin toward him, the intensity in his eyes softening. Like he can see I need the reassurance that I didn't totally fuck this whole thing up.

"Can you even die?" I ask, my voice hoarse and thready.

He tilts his head from side to side as if to say more or less. "In a matter of speaking. But it takes a lot to destroy me."

"A lot meaning someone like Lilith?"

"Mm-hmm."

The image of her furious tears comes to mind, making my knees feel weak.

No wonder Lucifer asked Azrael to protect me.

He's basically the celestial version of bulletproof.

"Do you think Lucifer will manage to—?"

"Get the blade?" Azrael finishes.

I nod meekly.

"I don't know."

Slowly, I ease away from Azrael, turning to look out the window as I consider Jax's fate. I have to believe Lucifer will help me save her, that he'll do whatever it takes. "What was Lilith talking about when she said I should ask you what the end of God would mean?" I whisper, despite my hands still shaking.

Azrael scowls, like the idea of sharing that makes him uncomfortable, but still, he answers me. More readily than Lucifer ever would. "God put a little of Himself into all of you. Human souls are contingent upon His existence, which means if He's destroyed, then . . ."

"No more God, no more souls?" I ask.

His shrug isn't nearly as uncaring as he wants it to be.

"So, Heaven and Hell would be . . ."

"Empty," he says.

My stomach roils.

At least in Michael's apocalyptic nightmare, we'd all get a decent shot at an afterlife.

But in Lilith's?

Nothing.

Just endless nothing.

I shake my head. I can't allow that to happen. I can't just stand here and allow myself to break.

I have to *do* something.

"What time is it?" I glance to the clock on the wall. It's nearly 10:30 p.m., which means . . .

I'm already late for Sloth's after-party.

True celebrities never hurry, Charlotte.

Lucifer's advice from when we attended the Met Gala comes back to me.

Arriving fashionably late tonight is for the best, obviously.

It'll take a long, hot shower to get all this blood off. Thank goodness it isn't mine. Though the sight of Lilith feasting on Ian . . .

A shiver runs through me.

And Jax . . .

I shake it off.

I have to stay focused. I have to do anything that might help me gain a better chance at saving her. Starting with returning to my original plan.

More celestial favors in my pocket, more of the Originals indebted to me.

I'm getting used to this whole staring-down-impending-doom thing.

"Azrael, I need you to take me to the penthouse and then drop me off at Sloth's after-party."

"In the Hamptons?" He quirks a brow.

I give a quick nod. "When Lucifer returns, tell him I'm safe and I'll be back at the penthouse sometime in the morning."

Azrael's brow furrows. "He won't like that."

"He doesn't have to." I shrug, rising to my feet. "I'm in charge of my life now. Remember?"

I'm going to do whatever it takes to stop the apocalypse *and* save my friend.

Come hell or high water.

Azrael shakes his head. "I'm starting to understand why he wanted to keep you under lock and key for as long as humanly possible."

"Well"—I smile up at him, holding my arm out like he's my date and he's escorting me—"good thing for you and Lucifer that I'm no longer human, then."

EPILOGUE

Charlotte

Something hard and pointy is nudging against my side, and from the sharpness of it, I don't think it's anyone's dick.

I come to in a foggy haze, vaguely aware that I'm sprawled across the floor of someone's beach house. Lucifer's? No, he's not a fan of the beach. Maybe . . .

I sit bolt upright as the memory of everything that happened at Sloth's party comes rushing back to me. The celebrities. The music. The alcohol.

So much fucking alcohol.

I sway slightly, my vision a bit fuzzy as I squint up at the figure who stands backlit against where the early afternoon sun is trying its best to blind me.

What in God's name did I do to myself?

My stomach roils as I blink several times, until I'm finally able to determine from the thick hourglass shape that it's Greed.

"Oh, you," I mumble as she once again nudges me with the pointy tip of her high heel.

"My brother sent me to fetch you, unfortunately." She scowls like it's somehow my fault she chose to help me and is now likely in the celestial doghouse with Lucifer.

My stomach churns again, and I honestly try to aim in the other direction before I . . .

Vomit all over her shoes.

Alcohol and shellfish are clearly *not* intended to mix.

Greed snarls at me.

"Ugh, you're lucky these aren't new. Get up." She grabs me under my arm and hauls me to my feet. I blink, taking in the various partygoers who are now passed out in every imaginable position, as she frog-marches me out of Sloth's beach house and into the waiting Town Car.

By the time we reach the Upper East Side, where Apollyon headquarters is located, I've managed to sober up enough to actually feel proud of the previous evening's accomplishments.

I got Sloth on board with the rest of the Originals.

He was the last one holding out on me.

And he even reluctantly agreed to help me retrieve Jax, too, if I need it.

Team No Apocalypse: 2. Team Apocalypse: 1.

Things are definitely looking up.

When the Town Car pulls to a stop, Greed directs one of her security team to lead me into the building, still furious and fussing over how I ruined her shoes, as she forces me to take the literal walk of shame up to Lucifer's office rather than having the team escort me up the back service stairs.

It's not like she doesn't have enough money to buy herself, and half the western hemisphere, another pair of Stuart Weizmans.

When I enter Lucifer's office, a small part of me is aware that Azrael is likely there, waiting in the wings, but it's not him I'm eager to see right now.

It's my devil of a fiancé.

I stride toward Lucifer's desk, trying not to feel embarrassed at what a hot mess I must look like. I showered and changed clothes before the after-party, but I look like someone who's just stumbled out of a celebrity bash down in the Hamptons.

I think I even have a bit of sand where it shouldn't be.

I'm not really sure how it got there.

Lucifer's brow lifts at the sight of me. "I give you free rein to run wild for one bloody fucking night," he says, shaking his head at me. As if he *hasn't* seen me messier than this when he's finished with me inside the playroom.

But I guess that's not usually in broad daylight.

"Jax?" I ask hopefully, still praying that somehow, Lucifer was able to . . .

Lucifer's expression falls. "Still with my Mother, I'm afraid."

My spine runs cold. "You don't think she'll—"

"No," he says quickly. "She loves her prophets, and as one of my Father's, your friend is a rare breed. Too valuable to lose."

Which means one of my first true acts as an immortal, other than stopping the apocalypse and whatever Lilith's planning, will be doing anything it takes to save my friend.

I can't think of a better celestial path to take.

I glance toward Lucifer, shaking my head at the thought of how far we've both come.

It all started with a leaked press release.

But now it's going to end with my PR proposal.

Between all six of the other Originals and Lucifer's demonic army, we *have* to be able to save her and stop the apocalypse. Don't we?

I take my proposal, that I retrieved from my office on the way up here, and toss it down onto the desk in front of him. "Read it," I say in the exact tone he used when the tabloids caught Az and me.

Lucifer frowns before he does what I asked. He picks up the folder and quickly thumbs through it. "What is this, Charlotte?"

"My PR proposal. You said no outside angel investors, so I got *in-house* ones."

Lucifer's brow lifts as he reopens the folder and looks again.

"All six of them signed on." I stand taller. The pride expanding inside my chest isn't meant to be an offering to him, but I know he'll appreciate it all the same.

Lucifer watches me for a long beat, leaning back in his executive chair as he drums a few of his fingers over his desk like he's trying to figure out what to do with me.

"Aren't you going to say congratulations? Or that you're proud of me? I've accomplished something you've never been able to do. I got *all* of them to agree to something. Your siblings are going to help us fight Michael, *and* they can help us get Jax back."

Lucifer lets out a long sigh through his nose. He places both hands on his desk, hanging his head slightly, before he lifts his fiery gaze toward me.

My stomach does another flip at the furious look he gives me.

"Do you know what happened the last time all my siblings worked together?"

I tilt my head to the side, suddenly fearful. "No?" I say slowly.

The blaze of hellfire coupled with the weary look in Lucifer's eyes is the same one he had when that mysterious package was delivered to the penthouse, the same one from when he realized it was *anthrax* I was holding.

Like the danger we now face could be catastrophic.

"Did it ever occur to you, Charlotte, that there might be a compelling *reason* I chose to keep my siblings separate?" he says through clenched teeth. "The fall of humanity? The great flood? The plagues of Egypt? Ever heard of them?"

My heart starts to pound as I realize the full gravity of what that might mean.

For me, for the apocalypse, for Lucifer.

Oh fuck.

AUTHOR'S NOTE

Thank you for reading!

If you enjoyed *Wicked Believer*, you're just one click away from FREE bonus content and deleted scenes featuring Charlotte, Lucifer, and Azrael plus . . .

- Exclusive giveaways and NSFW character art
- Being the first to hear about new releases
- Sneak peeks at Kait's newest titles

Sign up for Kait's newsletter and receive your free *Wicked Believer* bonus content now! www.kaitballenger.com

ABOUT CONSENSUAL KINK

The depictions of BDSM in this book are for fantasy entertainment purposes only and are not intended as an accurate representation of the BDSM/kink community. For many, BDSM and its queer history is sacred, hallowed ground, but I hope readers feel I've used it to appropriately and thematically fuck with the power structures that be.

For those interested in learning more, please seek out resources on risk-aware, consensual kink.

ACKNOWLEDGMENTS

So many people had a hand in the production of this book, and I could not imagine doing this without them. I am forever grateful.

To my agents, Nicole Resciniti and Lesley Sabga, for the lightning-fast turnaround read and for believing in this idea from the start. I'm so grateful for your support.

To my editor, Maria Gomez, for always trusting and believing in my vision, and Sasha Knight, for finding all the ways to make this story better.

To Christian Bentulan for the amazing covers, and to the whole Montlake team for championing this series, and to Lauren Boyle for the fantastic character illustrations.

To Abigail Owen for all the brainstorming sessions and listening to me go on about this book endlessly, and to Kim Rust for the early read.

To my husband, for holding together both our house and our family, even when the writing days are long and our evenings together short, and to my boys for always cheering me on. I love your enthusiasm. Even if I still hope you don't read this until I'm dead.

To God, the Universe, or whatever amazing twist of fate resulted in this book having *exactly* sixty-nine chapters, because, well, you all know why.

And to my readers most of all, loyal and new, for following Charlotte and Lucifer, and now Azrael, for another book and beyond. Thank you for going on this journey with me.

ABOUT THE AUTHOR

Photo © 2025 Yuliya Panchenko

Kait Ballenger is an award-winning author of dark romantasy and paranormal romance. She is obsessed with tales of morally gray, sometimes villainous heroes and can't resist a spicy redemption arc. When Kait's not busy writing kinky paranormal fantasy, she can usually be found with her nose buried in someone *else's* naughty books. She lives, unfortunately, in Florida's Bible Belt with her husband and two adorable sons—and will gladly use that belt to whip you.

You can find her on TikTok @kaitballenger and Instagram @kait.ballenger or sign up for her newsletter at www.kaitballenger.com.